Ken
Lussey

THE
DANGER
OF LIFE

The Danger of Life
Ken Lussey

Published by Fledgling Press, 2019
Cover Design: Graeme Clarke
graeme@graemeclarke.co.uk

ISBN 9781912280223

www.fledglingpress.co.uk

Printed and bound by:
Ashford Colour Press

For my grandson Alistair

PROLOGUE

'Just as courage is the danger of life, so is fear its safeguard.'
Leonardo da Vinci

*

Stan had expected it to be easy. There had been no problems during practice on the ground in Norway. First you pulled the lever to open the hatch, then you dropped head first into the blackness below while facing towards the rear of the Junkers Ju 88 bomber. That way you avoided being hit in the face by the blast of the slipstream. Then it was simply a nice tranquil ride beneath your parachute down to an arrival in Scotland.

Stan had spent the flight from Norway lying on his stomach with the weight of his parachute, his radio and his other supplies pressing down on his back. The aircraft's gunner was positioned just above him, while equipment and aircraft systems hemmed him in on both sides. This was no place for anyone suffering from claustrophobia. Stan was thankful that was not something that caused him a problem. Especially not right now, when there were more important things to worry about.

The main concern was the news over the radio that

the diversionary air raid on Aberdeen, just to the south of them, had failed to find its target in the heavy cloud that had materialised in place of the forecast clear skies. The aircraft assigned to the raid were still looking for the city but were unlikely to continue doing so for much longer. If they turned back it would leave a single bomber flying steadily south west at 3,000m and looking very obvious to the British radar operators. The thought made Stan feel extremely vulnerable.

It was no real surprise when the intercom suddenly came alive with shouted warnings of a night fighter. A member of the crew had reported he'd seen a silhouette of an aircraft hunting them through a hole in the cloud. The pilot took violent evasive action and Stan found it was all he could do to avoid vomiting up the brandy he'd consumed before takeoff.

A little later they emerged from cloud for long enough to catch a glimpse of the coast, which confirmed they were over Scotland. But it was obvious to Stan that no-one on board the aircraft was certain which bit of coast they had crossed, or where they were in relation to his intended landing point. It was equally obvious that the crew was much more interested in evading the real or imaginary night fighter than they were in precision navigation. Stan had some sympathy for them.

'Time for me to go, I think, oberleutenant,' said Stan over the intercom to the pilot.

The gunner tapped him hard on the shoulder and gesticulated frantically. 'No, wait, we need to connect the static line first!'

Stan realised that he'd been on the point of dropping

through the hatch without the line that automatically opened his parachute being attached. As the instructor had said, gleefully, on the parachute course, 'It's not the fall that kills you, it's the sudden stop at the bottom.'

Once the static line had been properly attached, Stan took a deep breath, and before he had time for second thoughts he operated the hatch release lever, as he'd been shown in Norway. A bad night suddenly got much worse. Somehow, he tumbled rather than dropped, and found himself wedged in the hatch in the floor of the aircraft, upside down.

Then Stan felt a Luftwaffe flying boot pressing down very firmly on his rear end, and suddenly he was falling free. The parachute opened while he was in cloud. Once clear of the cloud, he could still see nothing in the darkness below him. He was beginning to consider the frightening possibility that they had been wrong about the coast and he had been dropped over the North Sea by mistake when he caught a glimpse of what might have been a tree off to his right. He had barely braced when he landed heavily in a field, winding himself in the process.

So far, so good, he thought, after recovering his breath and gathering his parachute. Now he just needed to find a telephone, and a strong drink, though not necessarily in that order.

They said it always rained in Scotland. Private Hannes Lambrechts had seen pictures that proved that wasn't true. But, in the short time since he'd arrived in this godforsaken corner of the country, the heavens had done little to prove the cynics wrong.

If it had been quiet in the big hut you'd have been able

to hear the rain now, beating down on its outer skin. But it wasn't quiet. The largest available space at Achnacarry was crammed with khaki-clad men, talking, cheering and shouting. The building was perhaps three or four times as long as it was wide, and in its centre was a boxing ring. The early arrivals and the officers had been able to take advantage of the folding chairs set in rows up the sides of the ring and at either end of it. But much larger numbers were standing behind the chairs, some trying to see around the heads of the men in front of them, others making surreptitious wagers on the outcomes of the contests taking place in the ring.

Hannes was standing at one end of the hut, where he could only catch glimpses of the action. He knew that he was witnessing 'milling'. It was the sort of recreational activity that could only have been dreamt up in a place whose whole purpose was to prepare men to kill other men as effectively as possible and avoid being killed themselves in the process.

The contests were a highlight of every course. Each troop picked their best ten men and they were matched weight for weight against representatives from another randomly selected troop. One team of ten wore black shorts and shirts, while the other team wore white. At the blow of a whistle, the first pugilist from each team entered the ring, wearing boxing gloves, and tried to defeat the other team's first representative. At the end of a minute the whistle was blown again and the first man from each team was immediately replaced by the second, who carried on the contest without a pause. At the end of ten minutes all members of both teams had fought, and points were totted up on the basis of two for an individual win, one for a loss and none for a disqualification. The overall result for each troop versus troop contest was then announced, not always to the approval of the audience. It was boxing stripped back to its barest essentials, and it varied from the comical to the savage. As soon as one ten versus ten contest had finished, another was lined up to begin.

Hannes wondered if the experience he was about to endure at Achnacarry would turn him into the sort of man who could flail away with boxing gloves at another man simply because he represented a different troop. But that wasn't his primary concern right now. Hannes was looking for someone. He scanned the backs of heads and profiles of the men around him. He'd already tried the other end of the hut without success. Wartime training and diets, military haircuts and khaki uniforms gave a certain sameness to everyone present, but Hannes was sure he hadn't been mistaken. He had only seen the man for a moment in passing that morning, and it was only the odd look on the other man's face that allowed Hannes to believe that his first instinct had been right. But he needed to be certain.

Then, to his right, he saw a pair of eyes turn swiftly away from his sweeping gaze. The man was off to one side of the throng. Hannes began to ease his way through the tightly-packed and highly excited crowd. If the man knew Hannes was approaching, he showed no sign of it. Then, when Hannes came within a couple of metres the man turned to look directly at him, and Hannes knew immediately that he had been right. Something was different, but this was the man he had been looking for. He paused, wondering what to do next, then realised that the man's gaze had shifted, looking over Hannes' shoulder at someone behind him. The man nodded and looked away. Hannes felt a sudden sharp pressure on his back, like a punch.

The knife was swiftly withdrawn. As the life ebbed out of him, Hannes remained standing, supported by the surrounding crowd for just long enough to allow his assailants to move away unnoticed. Even after he had collapsed onto the floor and the medical officer had been summoned from the ringside, it took a little while for the blood seeping from the small wound in his back to reveal that his collapse was due to anything other than natural causes.

CHAPTER ONE

Group Captain Robert Sutherland kept to a height of two thousand feet as he flew his Airspeed Oxford training aircraft along the southern coast of Fife. After taking off from RAF Turnhouse he'd flown north east to pass over Cramond Island before crossing over the Firth of Forth and picking up the coast near Kinghorn. It was raining, and they were being buffeted by gusts and turbulence, but the base of the cloud was well above the aircraft, and visibility was good enough for Bob to keep clear of the barrage balloons. A little later he watched the naval air station at Crail slip below his left wing before he turned left at Fife Ness and headed north west, beginning his descent as he did so. At this time of the morning, even in the latter half of October, Bob had expected a little more brightness, but wherever he looked there was nothing but grey gloom.

'A lovely day for a flight, isn't it?' Bob glanced to his right, where Flight Lieutenant George Buchan was beginning to look distinctly uncomfortable in the seat usually used by the navigator or instructor on these aircraft. A little behind them the occupant of the third seat in the aircraft, Sergeant Peter Bennett, seemed to be dozing, although since he was facing backwards it was hard for Bob to tell.

Buchan smiled. 'If I'm honest, sir, I'm just grateful that all those anti-aircraft gunners back around the approaches to the bridge and the dockyards realised we weren't a threat.'

Bob didn't admit that the same thought had crossed his mind. The aircraft he'd borrowed belonged to 289 Squadron, based at RAF Turnhouse, whose job was to help test and train anti-aircraft gunners across Scotland. At least that meant that the various types of aircraft flown by the squadron were very well known to the men on the ground in this part of the country. He glanced again at the flight lieutenant. 'I take it that you'd have preferred to travel up by car?'

'No offence, sir, but we'd have had priority in any queue for the ferry, and from North Queensferry it's only 35 miles or so to Leuchars.'

'Remind me who we are meeting,' said Bob.

'Flight Lieutenant Charles Rutherford, sir. He commands the RAF Police flight at Leuchars.'

'You'd consider him your normal contact on the ground here?'

'Yes, sir. As you know, the job is a bit of a mix. Our role is partly to advise on security measures, and partly to keep the military police on the ground on their toes with spot checks and exercises. But we also collect intelligence with a view to identifying any patterns or emerging threats. For all those things our first point of contact, in my case at each RAF unit in Scotland and northern England, is the officer, or in some cases the senior non-commissioned officer, in charge of the RAF Police flight. The important thing to remember sir, is that none of these people report to us. Flight Lieutenant Rutherford reports partly through the admin structure at RAF Leuchars to the station commander, and partly through a separate command structure to the RAF Provost Marshal.'

'You are suggesting I should adopt a diplomatic approach?'

Buchan glanced across the width of the cockpit at his new boss. 'I'd not have phrased it quite like that, sir, but we tend to achieve a lot more by working with the men on the ground than we would by being heavy-handed. As far as most of them are concerned, MI11 is a bit of an oddity. A fifth wheel on the wagon, if you like. It makes their life much easier if we write favourable reports about the security at their establishments after we've made an inspection, and many of them recognise that our broader view, especially across different services, means we can offer advice they'd not get anywhere else. But they come in all shapes and sizes, and some are much more open and receptive to us than others.'

'What about Flight Lieutenant Rutherford?' asked Bob. 'How does he feel about MI11?'

'He's one of the good guys, sir. It's been a while since I've seen him. But our visit today was his idea. It seems he felt the circumstances made this something we should look at rather than the RAF Police's own Special Investigation Branch, and that was why he telephoned me first thing this morning.'

Bob had cleared their approach on the radio with the control tower at Leuchars and after catching his first glimpse of the runway he lowered the undercarriage and flaps in preparation for their landing. 'And the circumstances are that in the early hours of this morning one of his men shot and killed an intruder trying to access a parked aircraft at Leuchars?'

'Yes, sir, apparently the intruder fired first when challenged, but missed. The RAF Police corporal didn't miss when he fired back. The thing that made Rutherford decide to call me was that the intruder turned out to be a Polish Army sergeant, normally based at their camp at Tents Muir, just over there.' As the aircraft swept in to land from the sea, Flight Lieutenant Buchan gestured towards the swathe of dark green forest visible behind the broad beach to their right. 'The potential diplomatic and security complications mean that he wants the incident investigated by someone completely independent of the RAF Police, and I understand that the station commander at RAF Leuchars agrees with him.'

Bob was directed to park the aircraft at the end of a line of Handley Page Hampden torpedo bombers, in front of one of the large hangars that clustered together on the north side of the airfield. It was still raining and Bob was thankful that a car had been provided to take them to the station headquarters.

Flight Lieutenant Rutherford turned out to be a man in his forties who greeted them at the front entrance to the building before showing them to an office on the ground floor. Flight Lieutenant Buchan effected the introductions and the three visitors sat down around a wooden meeting table to an obligatory cup of tea.

Bob could see that Rutherford was a little unsure of his own involvement in the meeting and tried to put him at his ease. 'Don't mind me, Flight Lieutenant. I took over MI11's northern operations at the beginning of the week and am here mainly to get a feel for the work we do. George will take the lead, assisted by Sergeant Bennett.'

Flight Lieutenant Buchan took this as his cue. 'You told me what happened on the telephone, Charles. We'll obviously want to talk to the corporal who killed the intruder.'

'Corporal Fred Taylor,' said Rutherford. 'He's a good man, and quite upset by what happened. He's waiting to talk to you.'

'We'll also need to talk to the Poles in Tents Muir,' said Buchan. 'Do they know what's happened?'

'Yes,' said Rutherford. 'They've been good neighbours over the past couple of years, and part of their role has been defending the coastline here, including our own coastal margin. But there's a major reorganisation going on and the unit that's been stationed there is moving out, with others moving in, though on a much smaller scale. The invasion threat's no longer present in the same way of course, but one of the changes we've made has been to increase our own RAF Regiment presence to make sure our coastal boundary to the east and along the River Eden to the south is secured now the Poles are moving out.'

Bob asked, 'Do we know how the intruder got into the base?'

'Yes, we do, sir,' said Rutherford. 'As they've been running down their presence in this part of Fife, we've been helping the Poles with some of the services that have been withdrawn. It seems that the gentleman concerned, Sierzant or Sergeant Jacek Winograd, had been on camp several times over the past couple of days to sort out mechanical problems they had been having with a lorry. Our motor transport flight was happy to help. As far as I can find out, Winograd came onto the base late yesterday afternoon and never left. He presumably hid somewhere and in the early hours of this morning made his way around the airfield to the 540 Squadron dispersal.'

'540 Squadron?' said Bob. 'That's not a unit I've come across before.'

'Not many people have, sir. They were formed at the beginning of the week from two of the flights of what used to be No. 1 Photographic Reconnaissance Unit. They fly photo reconnaissance Spitfires and Mosquitoes. It was one of their Mosquitoes that Sergeant Winograd was showing a close interest in when he was spotted by Corporal Taylor.'

'Sorry,' said Bob, 'I've sidetracked you. You were talking about the Poles.'

'Yes, sir, the outgoing senior officer up at the Polish camp is Major Bartek Kaminski. Group Captain More, the station commander here at Leuchars, spoke to the major first thing this morning, and he is expecting a visit from us. I don't know if the major still has field security police on his staff, or whether they have already moved out, but my betting is that he will have been doing his own check on Sergeant Winograd's background.'

Buchan put his teacup down and looked across the table at Bob. 'Do you think we ought to talk to Corporal Taylor, sir?'

Bob remembered he was supposed to be letting Buchan take the lead. 'Of course.'

Flight Lieutenant Rutherford stood up. 'It might be most convenient if I brought him in here. As I said before, he's a good lad and he's had a shock,' he said, looking at Bob. 'Go easy on him will you, sir?'

Corporal Fred Taylor looked like he hadn't yet seen his twentieth birthday and wore his uniform and white-topped service cap as if it belonged to someone else. He was obviously extremely nervous.

'Hello, Corporal,' said Bob. 'Take a seat. I'm Group Captain Sutherland and I'm here mainly as an observer. This is Flight Lieutenant Buchan, from Military Intelligence Section 11, based in Edinburgh, and this is Sergeant Bennett, also of MI11.'

'Am I in trouble, sir?' asked the corporal.

'We are here mainly to find out what the intruder you discovered last night was trying to achieve and why he was here. Could you start by telling us what happened?'

'I was on routine foot patrol, sir, over at the dispersal used by the photo reconnaissance squadron. It was about 1.30 a.m. and I thought I heard a noise coming from one of the parked aircraft. It was dark, of course, but the moon's not far off full, so there was some light coming through gaps in the cloud. Then I caught a brief flash of torchlight and another sound, which I thought was the aircraft access hatch being opened.'

'What did you do then?' asked Flight Lieutenant Buchan. Bob was pleased that Buchan was keen to take over the interview.

'I walked over towards the aircraft and then saw a movement underneath it. I shouted out a challenge and switched on my torch. I was about twenty yards from the aircraft and, in the light of the torch, saw a man in army uniform raising a pistol towards me. I threw down the torch to avoid giving him too much of a target and raised my Sten gun. He fired his pistol, and then I fired a short burst at the muzzle flash. Then I picked up my torch again and went over to him. It seems I had hit him twice, and the access hatch of the aircraft once.'

'What happened then?' asked Buchan.

'The sound of the gunfire brought others to the scene very quickly. The Polish sergeant, as I'm told he was, was taken to the medical centre in an ambulance, but it seems he was already dead.'

'Was there any indication as to what the intruder was trying to do?' asked Bob. 'Any sign of explosives or that sort of thing?'

'No sir, though I'm told that a copy of the local one-inch to the mile Ordnance Survey map was found on him.'

Buchan asked, 'Did anyone else witness what happened?'

'Not as far as I know, sir, but quite a few people heard the shots. I know why you are asking, of course. But you have to believe that I'd never have fired first. If I'm honest, I'd never have thought that I could shoot a man. Training on the range is one thing, but knowing that you are firing at a real living person is something totally different. In the heat of the moment, though, and after he'd fired at me, it was somehow easier than I expected.'

Bob found he believed the young man. As a pilot Bob had been no stranger to death, or to killing, but it was only recently that he had been forced to confront the need to pull the trigger of a gun pointing at a man standing a few feet away from him. The corporal's account brought back unpleasant memories, but the truth of what he said was compelling.

Sergeant Bennett drove the borrowed staff car out of RAF Leuchars and through the neighbouring village. Bob sat in the back with Flight Lieutenant Buchan.

In the village they turned right to pass the eastern end of a spectacularly decorated church. 'You don't see many like that,' said Bob.

'No, sir,' said Sergeant Bennett. 'That's St Athernase Church. The blind arcading around the chancel and apse at this end dates back to before 1200. It's said to be one of the two or three finest pieces of Norman stonework anywhere in Great Britain. It's nice to see something that reminds us that the world wasn't always at war.'

Buchan saw the look of surprise on Bob's face. 'Peter was studying to be an architect before the war, sir. Travelling around the country with him is a real education.'

Bennett said, 'There's not much call for architects in wartime, sir, as it seems possible to produce anything you want in concrete or corrugated iron. And I suppose that after the war the priority will be on minimising cost and maximising speed when we rebuild what's been destroyed.'

'I'm not sure I entirely agree, sergeant,' said Bob. 'I get the feeling that after years of austerity, people will want something different and better.'

'I hope you are right, sir,' said Bennett.

'What did you make of Corporal Taylor's account of

what happened this morning, sir?' asked Flight Lieutenant Buchan.

'I believed him,' said Bob. 'It ought to be possible to confirm his story about who fired first by talking to those who heard the shots.'

'Yes sir, that's something Sergeant Bennett and I will look at when we get back to Leuchars. Anyone within earshot should have a clear idea of whether the burst from the Sten gun was before or after the shot from the pistol. Though, like you, I think we will find he was telling the truth.'

Sergeant Bennett turned the car off the narrow road they had followed from the village onto a gravel track that led towards the edge of a forest. A few hundred yards into the forest they were flagged down by two men in khaki uniforms at a barrier across the road. Beyond was a large clearing which seemed to be full of corrugated iron-clad Nissen huts.

'Your favourite sort of architecture, sergeant,' said Bob as he wound down his window to talk to the nearest soldier, who looked miserable in the rain. 'Hello, Group Captain Sutherland and colleagues to see Major Kaminski. We are expected.'

Bob was vividly reminded of the last time he had been confronted by a man in a Polish army uniform carrying a rifle and found himself wondering what Lady Alice Gough was doing now. At least these men were actually Polish and not German.

'Yes, sir. You need to take the first left, over there, and follow the track for a couple of hundred metres until you see a brick-built building on your left. The wooden hut next to it is the camp H.Q. You will find Major Kaminski there. There's a parking area on the right, opposite.' The Polish soldier stepped back and waved to his colleague to raise the barrier.

'Major Bartek Kaminski of the 2nd Polish Rifle Battalion at your service, sir.' The major was a wiry man in his late thirties who gave the impression of having considerable pent-up energy.

Bob returned the major's salute, then introduced himself and his colleagues. 'I'm sorry our meeting couldn't have been under slightly better circumstances, Major. I understand you know what happened at Leuchars earlier this morning?'

'Yes, indeed, Group Captain More telephoned me this morning. Very regrettable. Look, we don't get many visitors here, could I offer you some real coffee?' The major left the three of them in the small meeting room into which they'd been shown while he went out to organise refreshments.

Once they were all sitting round the table, there was a slight pause while Major Kaminski passed round cigarettes. 'No thanks, Major, I'm a pipe man myself.' Bob rarely smoked his pipe, but it was a convenient deflection on occasions like this.

'Do you mind if I ask a question, Group Captain?' said the major.

'Not at all.'

'Are you quite certain that Sierzant Winograd was, as you might call it, up to no good?'

'It does very much look that way, Major. Flight Lieutenant Buchan and Sergeant Bennett will be talking to anyone they can find who heard the shots, but it does seem very likely that Sergeant Winograd fired at the RAF Police corporal first, before being shot by him.'

'Then it is a matter of great sadness to me that we should end our time in this part of Fife under a cloud. We have been on very good terms with our RAF neighbours since we established the camp here.'

'I understand you are on the move, Major?' asked Bob.

'Yes, indeed. My unit has been based here at Tents Muir for some time now. But times change and the Polish army in Scotland is reorganising as our equipment improves and as we change away from a defensive stance and towards preparation for the liberation of our homeland. Like most of my men I am a refugee twice over. You may be aware that in early 1940 the governments of Poland and France agreed to form a Polish army in France. There were over 80,000 of us in France when the Germans arrived there. Those of us who could, escaped from Dunkirk in May and June 1940 with men of your own army and French troops. For most of the last two years we have been stationed in Scotland, mainly helping defend the east coast.'

'What will become of your camp here?' asked Bob.

'In the short term, part of the camp is being used to accommodate men from the Polish parachute battalions that are training up to operational readiness in Fife, but that's only a temporary measure. I expect the last of my men to have left by the end of next month, and I can't see the paratroops staying far into next year. I imagine the camp here will then begin to return to nature, unless some other use can be found for it. But I don't know what that might be. It's much too close to the coast, and to RAF Leuchars, to be used as a prisoner of war camp.'

'What are you able to tell us about Sergeant Winograd, sir?' asked Buchan.

'Ah, yes, down to business. I am sorry to have to tell you that I have been able to find out very little so far. He was a new arrival here, being a member of the 4th Polish Parachute Battalion who are based on the south coast of Fife at Elie. I've spoken to his porucznik, or lieutenant, and it seems that Winograd was quite a new member of the battalion who no-one seems to have known very well. The lieutenant has gone to their battalion headquarters to see what records they hold about him. And I have alerted the security people at our divisional headquarters about what has happened, with a request that they, too, see what can be found out about Sierzant Winograd.'

Bob said, 'One thing it would be helpful to know is whether he had ever had any pilot training. It's too early to say, but it's possible that he was trying to steal an aircraft rather than damage or examine one.'

'Most of our men with pilot training found their way into the Polish squadrons of the RAF, sir,' said the major. Then he gestured at the medals and wings on Bob's uniform jacket. 'But I'm sure you knew that already.'

Flight Lieutenant Buchan stood up. 'We're really grateful for your time, sir' he said to Major Kaminski. 'I think that Sergeant Bennett and I will be at Leuchars until tomorrow. If you come up with anything about Sergeant Winograd's background, would it be possible to let me know? I will be contactable via Flight Lieutenant Rutherford's office there. After that, you can reach me on this telephone number.' He handed over a card. 'In the meantime, is there someone here who at least knew the sergeant well enough to come

13

down to Leuchars this afternoon and identify his body? It will be a step in the right direction if we can establish that the man carrying Sergeant Winograd's papers was actually Sergeant Winograd.'

'Yes, of course,' said the major.

As the car approached the village of Leuchars, Bob turned to Buchan. 'I get the sense that you'd prefer to take this on from here, Flight Lieutenant?'

'If I'm honest, sir, I'm not sure how much more there is for us to do. The Polish security people might or might not come up with something on Winograd that explains what he was doing and why, but we are very much in their hands for that. We have some checking to do on Corporal Taylor's account of events, but that's really a case of tying up loose ends rather than looking for any great revelations. We will also pay a visit to 540 Squadron to see if it's physically possible for someone to start up and take off in a Mosquito without external assistance. Do you by any chance know, sir?'

'No, I'm afraid not, though it's a good question. How will you get back to Craigiehall when you are done?'

'I'll get one of the drivers to come up in a car and collect us, sir. I'm assuming you'll be flying back to Turnhouse this afternoon?'

'That's the plan, Flight Lieutenant.'

CHAPTER TWO

As it turned out, things didn't quite go to plan. On returning to the station headquarters, Flight Lieutenant Rutherford passed on an invitation from the station commander for Bob to lunch with him. Bob was directed up to Group Captain More's office on the first floor.

'A belated welcome to Leuchars, Sutherland,' said More. 'I'm sorry I was elsewhere when you arrived.' The well-built man in his forties pulled on his service raincoat in his outer office. He then turned to his secretary, sitting behind her desk. 'Marjorie, if anyone wants me, I am showing an important visitor around the station and will get back to them later. I take it you fancy a bite to eat, Sutherland?'

'Yes, of course, Group Captain.'

'Call me Andrew, please. Do I call you Robert?'

'Bob would be better.'

Group Captain More led the way out of the main entrance. 'It's only a short walk to the mess and the rain's eased off. I've asked Wing Commander Eric Gill to meet us there. Since the beginning of the week he's been the officer commanding 540 Squadron, though before that he was in charge of the two flights we had based here that became his squadron, so it's business as usual really.'

Wing Commander Gill turned out to be a lightly-built man of above average height in his early thirties. Bob had a slightly unsettling sense of having met him before but couldn't quite remember where.

As the mess steward showed them to their table, the wing commander said, 'I wondered if it was you, Group Captain. You commanded 605 Squadron at Croydon during the Battle of Britain, didn't you?'

Bob found himself trying to place the face. 'Yes, I did, but I'm sorry: though you look familiar, I can't quite remember why.'

'They were busy times, sir, and I flew for the competition, so you'd probably not have noticed me.'

At last it clicked. Bob said, 'You were a flight commander on 111 Squadron at Croydon Aerodrome at the same time, weren't you? Call me Bob, by the way. I was a wing commander myself until the beginning of the week and I'm still getting used to the idea I'm being addressed if someone says, "group captain".'

Group Captain More laughed. 'You had the Luftwaffe turning up in large numbers to bomb the hell out of out of London all day and every day, and 605 and 111 Squadrons still regarded one another as "the competition"?'

'We did,' said Bob. 'Though come to think of it, not nearly as much as we both tried to get one-up on 72 Squadron, who were also at Croydon for the first couple of weeks of September 1940. They flew Spitfires, you see, and the Hurricane squadrons always felt the Spitfires got more than their fair share of the glory.'

'I can see that's an argument that must have been had in many messes,' said More. 'I've spent the last few years in Coastal Command so can't really comment with any authority. But as I've got the benefit of the company of two ex-fighter men, which do you both think is better, the Spitfire or the Hurricane?'

Lunch had been served. Bob's ham, egg and chips looked as if it should see him through until evening with little difficulty. Bob looked across the table at Gill. 'Have you any thoughts on that, Eric?'

'I think I'm probably biased as, of the two, I only flew the Hurricane in air-to-air combat. The photo reconnaissance Spitfires are wonderful aircraft but not comparable. But didn't you fly Spitfires as well, Bob, or have I got that wrong?'

'Yes, I did, with 602 Squadron at Grangemouth and Drem, before I was posted onto Hurricanes with 605 Squadron. I'm not sure that the early Spitfires were representative of what has followed since, but both types of aircraft have their plus points in combat. Overall the Spitfire seems likely to outlast the Hurricane, which has already been moved in large numbers to training or ground attack roles. I'd imagine that the photo reconnaissance version of the Spitfire is a pretty special aircraft?'

'They can fly high and fast, certainly,' said Gill, 'but there's something about the idea of being in a single seat fighter that doesn't have guns that is a little disconcerting.'

'I know what you mean,' said Bob. 'I find that even if I'm only flying a Hurricane down to RAF Northolt for a meeting in London, I want it fully armed. You never know who you might meet.'

Group Captain More said, 'I heard you put that into practice on a Junkers Ju 88 up at Wick a few weeks ago, Bob. That must have been unexpected.'

Bob thought back to his encounter with the German bomber over the sea off Wick. 'That's true, and it also upset a Spitfire pilot from RAF Castletown who thought the kill was going to be his. A successful day all round.'

'But now you've moved on to very different pastures,' said Group Captain More. 'Or is that something you can't talk about?'

'No, I see no problem with that. I've taken up the offer of a job as deputy head of MI11, or Military Intelligence Section 11, in Edinburgh. I started on Monday and spent Tuesday and part of yesterday in London, so I'm very much the new boy. I'm here with one of my teams to get a feel for the sort of work we do.'

'Is it what you expected?' asked Gill.

'I'm not certain what I expected, if I'm honest, but I can see there's a fair amount of work to be done to establish a distinct role for ourselves. At present we sit in a slightly grey area with large overlaps with a number of other agencies.' Bob was going to go on to describe the extent to which that seemed to have caused a lack of focus within MI11 but decided that might be a revelation too far.

'Are you based at Turnhouse?' asked More.

'No, I'm living in the officers' mess there, having fought off invitations from my parents to move back in with them. They live in Cramond, only a couple of miles up the road, but I take the view that 30 is just a little old to be returning to live under the parental roof. MI11 has offices at Craigiehall, an old country house quite close to Turnhouse. It's home to several army units, so security isn't a problem. The proximity to RAF Turnhouse has one real bonus as far as I'm concerned. MI11 has set up an arrangement with the officer commanding 289 Squadron that allows me to borrow one of his aircraft when the need arises. That means I can keep my hand in on the Hurricane or use an Airspeed Oxford if I need more seats. The Oxford isn't my favourite aeroplane, I must admit.'

They were enjoying a cup of tea to round off the meal and the other two men were smoking. Gill sat back in his chair and said, 'Did you have any plans for this afternoon, Bob?'

'I need to get back to the office at some point, though I suspect they will be able to survive without me. Why do you ask?'

'Our discussion about the Spitfire and Hurricane led me to wonder whether you would like to fly in a twin-engined aircraft that I think is better than either of them, or any other single-engined fighter on either side.'

Group Captain More laughed again. 'I suppose I should have seen this coming. Eric here is a huge enthusiast for the Mosquito. I have to admit I like my aeroplanes to have a little more substance to them, and a little more room in them, but I can't deny that the de Havilland Mosquito is an outstanding aircraft.'

Bob grinned. 'I'd love to.' He'd only ever glimpsed the Mosquito at a distance on the ground and thought it one of the most beautiful aeroplanes he'd ever seen. He'd have mortgaged his parent's substantial house for the chance to fly in one, but it seemed that no-one was asking him to.

*

It had stopped raining as Bob looked out of the squadron's office window towards the aircraft he was due to fly in. Gill had driven him around the north side of the airfield to an area that was contained in the angle of the two main runways. Several Mosquitoes and Spitfires were visible, apparently placed at random. He knew that in reality this was a carefully planned pattern of parking intended to minimise the impact of any sudden attack by a German aircraft coming in from the sea.

Gill came into the office, which occupied part of a wooden hut. 'I'm told that the weather's clearing from the west. We'll head that way to give you a chance to see the view from high altitude and appreciate the performance. Sorry about the fleecy boots and overalls.' He gestured at the clothing Bob had pulled on. 'They're hardly elegant. We tend to get togged up to look like the Michelin man when we fly. It can get very cold at altitude, even with the cockpit heater on full blast.'

'Is the aircraft the Polish sergeant was trying to get into last night out there now?' asked Bob.

'No, it was towed off to the squadron hangar for repair. The RAF policeman only put one hole in it, in the access hatch, so it should be easy enough to fix. Anyway, are you ready?'

'Yes, I took a comfort break before I put these on.'

'Just as well, it's not great to get caught short in a Mosquito.'

The two men made their way out of the hut and over to an aircraft parked fifty yards away, on a square concrete area protected by blast walls. 'I'll do the external pre-flight checks while you get aboard, Bob,' said Gill. Bob paused briefly to look at the aircraft. The beauty of the Mosquito that he had admired from afar was even more striking when he was this close to one. This example was painted an overall mid blue colour and looked extremely purposeful, as if it were as keen as he was to leave the ground behind.

Bob followed the instructions of an airman and clambered awkwardly up a short ladder into a hatch on the underside of the aircraft. With his Mae West life-preserver and a parachute harness on over his thick overalls there was very little room to manoeuvre. Once inside the aircraft he was directed by the same airman, who now had his head and shoulders inside the bottom of the cockpit, to strap himself into the right of two seats, positioned a few inches further back than the left one.

While he waited for Gill, Bob looked around the inside of the cockpit. He'd flown a number of different aircraft and was very used to those with Merlin engines, though not as a pair. He put himself in the position of Sergeant Winograd and wondered if he'd have been able to work out without instruction how to start and take off in a Mosquito. Having decided the chances of missing some vital stage in the process were simply too high, he reminded himself that Sergeant Winograd had also been trying to access the aircraft in the dead of night and would have been concerned to use his torch as little as possible for fear of discovery.

Gill's arrival proved that the cockpit was even snugger than Bob had imagined. With Gill in the pilot's seat and Bob in the navigator's, the two men were pressed against one another, the front of Bob's left shoulder making contact with the rear of Gill's right shoulder. 'Cosy, isn't it?' said Bob, over the intercom fitted in the leather helmet he had donned.

'It's certainly not a fat man's aeroplane, and that's all the more obvious because of the cold weather gear we have to wear for the altitude.'

The airman had closed the access hatch in the floor of the aircraft. Bob looked around again. 'Given the struggle I had getting into the aircraft, I now understand why you were at such pains to talk me through the procedure for getting out in a hurry.'

'Do you remember it all?'

'I think so.'

'So long as you don't forget to attach your parachute pack to your harness you'll not go far wrong. As I said, if you get stuck in the hatch, it's up to me as the pilot to help with a good push of my foot. You can rest assured it will be a very good push!'

'A couple more things you really need to know before we set off,' said Gill. 'If we crash-land, then there's an escape hatch in the roof of the cockpit, which can be opened by these levers here. And while it's not such an issue for the navigator, if you find yourself in the pilot's seat of one of these and you crash-land, then remember to pull your feet right back on impact.'

'Because of the lack of strength of the lower fuselage?'

'No, because your feet are otherwise directly in line with the arc of the propellers. Experience has shown that when the propellers strike the ground there's a reasonable chance of them disintegrating and blades coming through the side walls of the cockpit at speed. There have already been cases of serious injury caused in accidents the crews should have been able to walk away from.'

'Thinking about last night's shooting,' said Bob, 'would one man on his own be able to start a Mosquito without outside assistance?'

'In theory, yes. Some models of the Mosquito need an external power source, but we are self-contained. Though you'd need to know a lot about the aircraft to be able to start it up in the dark and then taxi and take off without taxi or runway lights, which I believe were switched off at the time.'

Bob looked around again. 'Maybe he was hoping to hide in the aircraft until first light this morning, though that would have been getting on for 7.30 a.m.'

'That seems high risk. The place would have been coming to life by then.'

'You are probably right. Let's see what my team turns up.'

As they were talking, Bob had been watching Gill going through his pre-flight checks.

'Right, we're ready to start.' Gill took a last look outside to ensure none of the ground crew were standing near the propellers before starting up the engines, one after the other. The pilot waved to indicate to the men outside that the wheel chocks should be removed, and Bob watched as the aircraft eased forward, gathering speed as it taxied away from the parking area.

'I'll talk you through the process in more detail on the way back, Bob, but for the moment it's simply worth you knowing that once you've taken off and got the wheels up, half the battle's won. Sensitive throttle management is essential to avoid swinging to the left as the power builds up. The key point to bear in mind is that the aircraft will become airborne at not much more than 100 knots, but the minimum safe speed for single engine flight is over 180 knots, even when you've raised the undercarriage and flaps. There's always an uncomfortable few moments after you lift off as you wait for the speed to build up.'

'What happens if there's an engine failure during that time?'

'You crash, it's as simple as that. If you've got any sense you fly straight ahead and aim for the flattest piece of ground you can see. Trying to turn will just mean you crash more badly. It's not helped by the fact that the undercarriage takes 25 seconds to retract and only then will she really begin to accelerate. And if one engine did fail, the hydraulic pressure would be lower, and the undercarriage would take twice as long to come up.'

'Thanks, Eric, that makes me feel even better,' said Bob with a laugh.

Gill lined the Mosquito up at the end of the runway and Bob felt himself holding his breath. He was always happier when flying as pilot and was a poor passenger in an aircraft. And the knowledge that the failure of either of the two Rolls-Royce Merlin engines when they were working hardest just after takeoff would have such serious consequences certainly focussed his mind.

He needn't have worried and they were soon flying into the base of the cloud over Guardbridge, to the west of Leuchars.

'We're going for a maximum rate climb, Bob,' said Gill. 'I want to give you a feel for the high altitude performance. Make sure your oxygen is switched on, will you? It will be essential for this flight. The regulator's on your side, near the entry through to the nose section.'

'We talked over lunch about the unarmed Spitfires. How do you feel about flying unarmed Mosquitoes over enemy territory?' asked Bob.

'Oddly enough, I have no problem with the idea. For me the Mosquito simply feels right for the job. It's also a relatively safe way to fight the war. It's early days yet because the aircraft's not been flying in this role for much more than a year, but I've seen some figures that suggested our losses haven't been much more than one aircraft for every 500 hours of operational flying.'

'That is pretty exceptional,' said Bob. 'I'd hate to think what the comparable figures were for the Croydon-based Hurricane squadrons in September and October 1940.'

'I doubt if it was a tenth as good as that,' said Gill, 'or perhaps even worse.'

'Wow,' said Bob as they broke through the top of the thick layer of cloud over Fife and into sunshine under blue skies. 'That's a sight that never fails to thrill me.'

'We're only at 12,000ft, not even nearly there yet. The aircraft ceiling's well over 30,000ft, and we often use everything we have. We'll go up to something like that, then descend. I had in mind a quick turn-around at the naval air station at Machrihanish near Campbeltown on the Kintyre peninsula, and then thought you might like to fly her back to Leuchars. How does that sound?'

It sounded great to Bob. He spent part of the outward flight transfixed by views that seemed to take in a large part of western Scotland and, later, through the haze, Northern Ireland.

At Machrihanish, Gill taxied the Mosquito around the quieter southern side of the airfield. 'Right, Bob, this is where we get really cosy, though it can be done. I'd prefer to avoid stopping the engines, which I'd need to do if one of us got out of the aircraft to allow us to change seats. So, what I want to do is squeeze in front of you and get myself down into the nose compartment. You can then move across into this seat, and I will climb back up into the navigator's seat.'

The process was made more awkward by the thick clothing they wore, but the two men were able to change seats.

'Right,' said Gill, 'let's taxi round to the eastern end again, and get clearance for takeoff.'

Bob did so, finding the view forward was even better from the pilot's seat than it had been from the adjacent navigator's seat. At Gill's instruction, he moved out onto the runway and lined up along the centre line.

'As I said earlier, this is the tricky part, Bob. Well, this and the landing. Can you remove your left outer glove while we take off? The throttles need a really gentle touch and I don't want your glove deadening the feel. I talked earlier about the problem of the gap between takeoff speed and safe minimum single engine speed, and all you need to remember about that is to clean up the aircraft as quickly as possible once you are certain we are airborne. The flap control is here, in the centre of the console, with the "F" on it. Next to it is the undercarriage control. Are you ready?'

'Yes,' said Bob, keen not to spend too long sitting on the end of the runway.

'Right, grip both throttles in your left hand and twist your wrist a little so the left throttle advances ahead of the right throttle. Ever so gently, now. There's not much movement between idle and full throttle. And watch out for the pull to the left. That's the tail up, and we're airborne. Wait long enough to make sure we're not going to sink back down onto the runway, then raise the flaps and the undercarriage. That's it. Well done.'

Bob found he was sweating. 'Will you navigate, Eric?'

They kept low and fast on the flight back, dipping back beneath the tail of the cloud as they crossed East Lothian. They remained under it as they turned north towards Fife and landed at Leuchars.

'Hello,' said Gill, 'it looks like we've got a welcoming committee.'

As the propellers came to a halt and relative silence replaced the roar of two Merlin engines, Bob looked over to where Gill had indicated, to see Flight Lieutenant Buchan and Sergeant Bennett standing beside a RAF staff car. 'It does look like that's for me,' he said. 'Thanks, Eric, that's been a real revelation. I'm very grateful.'

'Not at all, Bob. Group Captain More has suggested more than once that I'm on a mission to sell the Mosquito to anyone who'll listen to me, and I'm grateful for the opportunity to add another convert to my list.'

'It's an impressive aircraft, I have to admit. For the first time I can understand why there are so many enthusiasts for the Mosquito as a weapon of war.'

'That's all I can ask for. Remember that in the fighter versions you get four cannons in the front of the belly and four machine guns in the nose as well. They really do pack a punch. Anyway, that's the end of the sales pitch. Have a good trip back to Turnhouse.'

An airman had brought over Bob's service shoes, raincoat and peaked cap and he stripped off his overalls and boots on the tarmac before walking over to the car.

'Hello sir,' said Flight Lieutenant Buchan. 'Sorry to be dogging your heels, but Major Miller has been trying to reach you. I understand that the Security Service have some sort of emergency on, and insist they talk to you personally. There's a secure phone you can use back at station headquarters.'

CHAPTER THREE

Bob had only met his second in command, Major Miller, briefly at the beginning of the week and knew he was going to have to work hard to overcome an instinctive dislike of the man. There was something about him that Bob simply didn't trust. It may have been the sense that he had been quite close to Bob's predecessor, who had been sidelined as part of a far-reaching shake up of Britain's intelligence agencies that had, in part at least, been Bob's doing.

Mostly, though, it was simply the sense that Major Miller gave of wanting everything to be done in the way it had always been done. Bob knew he was going to have to make changes to his northern outpost of MI11 and felt that Miller was going to be one of the problems he needed to tackle, rather than an ally. It didn't help that Bob had walked into an office at Craigiehall on Monday just as Petty Officer Andrew MacDonald, the junior member of his Royal Navy team, stopped himself in the middle of a sentence whose final spoken words were 'Major Mother Hen'. Bob had pretended not to hear but wondered whether MacDonald's lack of regard for the major was widely shared.

Bob used the phone in Flight Lieutenant Rutherford's office. Bob's secretary, Joyce Stuart, put him through to Miller. 'Hello sir,' said the major. 'I'm glad I've been able to reach you. Flight Lieutenant Buchan told me you were testing out a theory about what the intruder was trying to do with the aircraft, and that meant actually flying one.'

Bob made a mental note that if it came to picking sides, then Flight Lieutenant Buchan seemed to be on the side of the angels. Bob was Miller's boss and had been given free rein to run the place pretty much as he saw fit. But if the two of them were going to have a parting of the ways, he needed to avoid giving the major more ammunition than was strictly necessary. And something that could be presented as a joyride in a Mosquito with an old chum could clearly be used as ammunition. Anyway, that was for the future. Right now, he needed to know what was going on. 'Hello, Walter. I'm told that something's come up to do with the Security Service?'

'Yes sir, there's a lady there who seems desperate to talk to you. I've confirmed she is who she says she is, but she won't tell me what the problem is. Could you telephone her?'

'Of course, Walter. Can you give me her name and telephone number?' Bob wrote down the Whitehall number. 'And the name?'

'She said you would know her as Madame Dubois.' Bob was glad there was no-one else in the room to see what must have been a look of complete surprise on his face. 'Are you still there, sir?'

'Yes, no problem, Walter. Thank you. I'll telephone her.'

'Hello Monique, it's Bob. How are you?'

'Hello Bob. I'm well. I hear congratulations are in order on the promotion and the new job.'

'Thank you.'

'It seems you have decided to come over to my world, dealing with unpleasant and dangerous people. I did tell you that teaching young men to fly was a more worthy and worthwhile calling.'

'Yes, you did, but other people thought differently, and after a while I came around to their way of thinking. But I'm sure that's not why you've been trying to get hold of me.'

'No, that's true. You can't imagine how much I'd like to avoid doing this, Bob, but I need to ask you a very large favour.'

'What is it?'

'Is this a secure line?'

'Well there's no public switchboard involved at this end, if that's what you mean.'

'Fair enough. We've got a critically important operation that is in grave danger of collapse, with consequences that could be very far-reaching. I need your help in stopping the damage getting any worse. It means asking you to go over to Glasgow immediately, Bob, to sort out a mess that some of my people have got themselves into.'

'I'm intrigued. Of course I'll help. What do you want me to do?'

'One of the members of my section, a man called Arthur Thompson, is part of a team in Glasgow minding a man called Geoffrey Smith. The two of them were arrested by the police early this afternoon at Hillington, west of Glasgow, because they were behaving suspiciously near the Rolls-Royce factory there.'

'The one that manufactures Merlin aircraft engines?'

'That's the one. Look, Bob, I am sure that the police will have material that looks very incriminating, but we badly need this whole problem simply to disappear. The men are being held at the main police station in Renfrew and, with your background in the Glasgow police and your new role in Scotland, we thought you might be able to persuade the police to release the men into your custody without any fuss. I've spoken to the senior officer on duty there, a Lieutenant Callaghan, and as well as having a military rather than a police rank, he's a by-the-book man. I'm a woman telephoning from London, and a foreigner to boot, and there's no way he's going to take action at my request.'

'"Lieutenant" is a police rank in Scotland, Monique, it's below superintendent. You know that you could just get the head of MI5, the Security Service if you prefer, to telephone the Chief Constable of Renfrewshire Constabulary and shake the tree from the top down. Incidentally, that's the force you are dealing with. I was with the City of Glasgow Police, though I grant you we had pretty good contacts across boundaries with our neighbours.'

'I know we could take this to the top Bob, but we are really keen not to. It's imperative we keep all this quiet. Ideally the police who have been involved so far need to be sworn to silence. If anything gets into the newspapers about the arrests, or the factory, or still worse about links between them, then an important operation will be wrecked.'

'I'll see what I can do. What do you want me to do with the two men if I can get them out?'

'They've got a safe house in the Glasgow area and there are another two members of my section there, but there's always a chance that taking them there could simply broaden the police interest if they realise what's happened. If you could find somewhere out of the way to keep them for a couple of days that would be ideal, until we can work out how to clear up the mess properly. Can you let me know how you get on?'

'Can I reach you on this number later tonight?' asked Bob.

'Yes, I'm not going anywhere until things are resolved. There's one other thing. Geoffrey Smith is a man with a past that is nearly as complicated as my own. It's important that he doesn't know the name I use in the Security Service in London. If you need to refer to me within his hearing, please stick with "Monique Dubois". That's also the name I used when talking to the policeman in Renfrew, who I believe will still be on duty this evening.'

Bob ended the call and leaned back in his chair, tapping his fingers on the desk. He thought it intriguing that Monique was so keen not to be referred to as "Vera Duval". He'd only ever thought of her as Monique anyway.

He looked at the clock on the office wall. It was 4.40 p.m. Sunset would be at a little before 6 p.m. and it would be completely dark perhaps forty minutes later.

This mattered to Bob because of his vision. He'd already worked out that the simplest way to get to Renfrew would be to fly there. Renfrew Airport was right next to the Rolls-

Royce factory and only a few minutes drive from the town of Renfrew itself. A plan, of sorts, was coming together in his mind, but he had no idea how long it would take to persuade the police in Renfrew to release the two men they had arrested. The problem was that he couldn't fly at night. His partial blindness had initially caused severe problems with depth perception and three-dimensional vision. Over what had seemed to him to be a very long time he had learned to adapt and cope, to the point where flying in daylight really wasn't a problem. But flying at night was an altogether different proposition, with many of the visual cues he used to circumvent the effects of his injury no longer available to him.

His initial idea had simply been to fly the Airspeed Oxford directly from RAF Leuchars to Renfrew, then fly back to RAF Turnhouse with the two men on board. But that seemed impossible to achieve before nightfall.

His next thought had been to fly back to Turnhouse and have a car and driver take him over to Renfrew. Again, though, the problem of darkness intervened, this time because of the difficulty in covering what couldn't be much more than 50 miles across central Scotland in the blackout. Shielded headlights and the absence of street lights made driving at night extremely difficult and dangerous. That left no option but to put in place a rather more complicated third-choice plan. He leaned forward to pick up the phone again, hoping that those he needed to talk to hadn't already abandoned their offices for the afternoon.

Flight Lieutenant Buchan sat in the back of the car with Bob, as Sergeant Bennett drove them to where the Airspeed

Oxford was parked. Bob looked across at Buchan. 'Have the Poles come up with anything about Sergeant Winograd yet, George?'

'No, sir. I was going to have another word with Major Kaminski in the morning, before deciding whether to return to the office.'

'You may have found out yourself' said Bob, 'but it seems that Winograd could in theory have started up the Mosquito without external assistance, though it would have been extremely difficult in the dark. The thought crossed my mind that he might have been intending to hide in the cockpit until first light this morning, and then steal the aircraft. That's why we need to know if there was any chance he had the skills to fly the thing.'

'You know better than I do, sir,' said Buchan, 'but I can't imagine that it's a straightforward process to steal an aircraft, even if it's theoretically possible.'

'No, you are right. Do you know if there's been an inventory taken of what Winograd had on him at the time he was killed? Corporal Taylor talked about a local Ordnance Survey map, but could you take a close look at anything else he had with him? I'm particularly interested in anything that might have been a checklist or instructions for starting a Mosquito.'

Sergeant Bennett spoke from the front of the car. 'Sir, I took a look through what the RAF Police had collected while I was waiting for the body to be identified this afternoon, and there wasn't anything entitled "How to fly a Mosquito" in either Polish or English. But maybe we should be looking for something less obvious. I can take another look at his stuff if you like, just to double-check.'

'Thanks, Peter,' said Buchan, 'that would be very helpful.'

After an uneventful flight directly into the setting sun, Bob was back on the ground at RAF Turnhouse by 5.45 p.m.

As he got out of the aircraft Bob was met by Lieutenant Michael Dixon, the naval officer who headed up his naval team, and the only team leader who had been in the office at Craigiehall when Bob had telephoned. Bob knew that Dixon was in his mid-twenties, and that he was highly regarded by MI11.

Lieutenant Dixon saluted. 'You owe Wing Commander Spencer a few favours, sir, but he seemed pretty amenable'.

'What were you able to organise?' asked Bob.

'We've got the use of the station flight Avro Anson, sir, and a pilot. That gives the room you need.'

'And the overnight accommodation?'

'That's also arranged sir,' said Lieutenant Dixon.

Wing Commander Bernard Spencer was the station commander at RAF Turnhouse, and Bob reflected that if this worked out as he hoped, then he would indeed owe the man a few favours. It crossed his mind, not for the first time, that it must be a little awkward for a wing commander running a RAF station to have a more senior officer living on the base and borrowing station and squadron assets. But, so far at least, Spencer had seemed relaxed about the arrangement.

'What about when we get to Renfrew Airport?' asked Bob.

'A staff car will be waiting for us, sir, but no driver. I will drive us into the town and back. What do you want me to do when we are at the police station, sir?'

'Just follow my lead, and don't look surprised by anything that happens. I'm not sure what the police have on the two men we want to release. Hopefully we can find out tonight.'

Bob was very familiar with Renfrew Airport and the area around it. His love of flying had first blossomed after attending the Scottish Flying Club Pageant held there in 1933. Most of his disposable income as a young policeman with the City of Glasgow Police had been spent on learning to fly at Renfrew, in the days when flying cost £2 per hour if you flew with an instructor or 35 shillings per hour once you could fly solo. Bob seemed to recall that there was also a special rate of 21 shillings, or a guinea, per hour that was charged on the first Sunday in every month, an offer he used to the full while building up his hours.

Three years later in 1936, still aged only 24, Bob's enthusiasm for aviation led to his being invited to join 602 (City of Glasgow) Squadron of the Auxiliary Air Force, which was based at Abbotsinch, only two miles west of Renfrew Airport. As a member of what some referred to as the best flying club in the world, Bob's flying was now free of charge, and he trained on the Hawker Hind biplane light bombers operated by the squadron, while continuing to pursue his career as a policeman. Then, in May 1939, he had started to learn to fly the Spitfire at Abbotsinch. This was an area that held very many, mainly happy, memories for him.

This all crossed his mind as the Avro Anson made its approach to Renfrew Airport from the east. Just to the south of the airport Bob could see in the last of the daylight the grid pattern formed by the roads leading through the vast Rolls-Royce factory at Hillington, apparently the reason for his visit. Bob had watched from the air as the factory had been built during 1938 and early 1939, and he knew the vital role it played in the war effort. The Merlin engines it produced were used in Spitfires, Hurricanes, Lancasters and Mosquitoes, and while Rolls-Royce did operate other factories in England, this remained one of the most important, and sensitive, industrial sites in Scotland.

'I learned to fly here,' he said to the flight sergeant pilot as they taxied to a parking area by the hangars.

'You were lucky to be so close to home, sir,' said the flight sergeant. 'I learned to fly in Canada, in winter. That may be why I never complain about the climate in Scotland.'

Bob laughed. 'Thanks for the flight. I'm not sure how long we are going to be, but I doubt if it will be much less than an hour, and it might be rather longer.'

'Don't worry, sir, I'll be waiting.'

Renfrew Police Station stood close to the centre of Renfrew, a town on the south side of the River Clyde some five miles west of the centre of Glasgow. It was a large and imposing sandstone building whose design echoed that of a Scottish castle.

Bob led the way in. The lobby beyond the front door was dominated by a reception desk, occupied by a sergeant who looked as if he enjoyed a pie and a pint, who stood up as he saw the gold braid on Bob's peaked cap.

'Hello, Sergeant. I'm Group Captain Sutherland and

this is Lieutenant Dixon. I'm here to see your Lieutenant Callaghan.'

'Yes sir. Is he expecting you?'

'No, he's not,' said Bob, 'but he will want to hear what I have to tell him. Is it possible to let him know I'm here, please?'

'He's not actually in the building, sir. He's out on patrol in the town centre with two new constables. Just showing them the area, you understand.'

'Are there any other senior officers in the building?' asked Bob.

'No, sir, Lieutenant Callaghan is the shift commander. I don't expect him to be very long, though. Do you want to wait for him? Can I offer you both a cup of tea?'

Bob and Lieutenant Dixon had barely sat down in an interview room with their cups of tea when the door burst open. Bob looked up to see a tall man in police uniform standing in the doorway.

'Well, damn me! Look what the cat's dragged in!'

'Hello, Jack,' said Bob, smiling at the sudden realisation he knew the man, 'how are you? Perhaps I should do the introductions? This is Lieutenant Michael Dixon, who works with me. Michael, this is Lieutenant Jack Callaghan.'

'I'm guessing that you know one another?' asked Dixon.

'You could say that, Lieutenant,' said Callaghan. 'You've done well for yourself, Bob. When the front desk said there was a group captain waiting for me it never crossed my mind that it might be you. Do you know that the Herald did an article about you a couple of years back, during the Battle of Britain? You'd just shot down five German fighters in a single day and been awarded another medal. They did a "local boy makes good" story, though they neglected to mention that the local boy in question actually came from Edinburgh.' Callaghan grinned. 'Then I heard you'd been shot down and wounded, and nothing since.'

Bob's mother had sent him the cutting from the Herald at the time, to his acute embarrassment. But there was something more pressing he needed to say before he could turn to the reason he was there. 'I was very sorry to hear about Mary and the children, Jack.'

'Yes, thanks for saying so. That was a real tragedy. I've sometimes thought that if you and she...' He paused.

'If I'm honest, the same thought has occurred to me,' said Bob. 'But I try to tell myself that you can't live on "what-ifs" and "might-have-beens".'

Callaghan looked across the table at Lieutenant Dixon. 'You're looking a little lost, lieutenant. Do you want me to explain, Bob?'

Bob nodded. Callaghan continued. 'Before the war, your boss and I were detective sergeants together in the City of Glasgow Police. We live in strange times, and it seems that in four years in wartime it's possible to move up the slippery pole from detective sergeant to lieutenant in the police, or to group captain in the RAF.'

Bob felt there was a need to fill in a little more of the background. 'A few years earlier, Jack and I nearly became brothers-in-law. His sister Mary and I were very close. But that was about the time I started to learn to fly. Police work is never easy on relationships, and Mary began to feel that she was my third priority, after the police and aeroplanes. She was probably right, I regret to say. We simply drifted apart. A couple of years later she married a foreman at John Brown shipbuilders and they had two children. Mary and the children were amongst those killed during the German bombing raids on Clydebank in March last year.'

'I'm sorry,' said Lieutenant Dixon, who was beginning to look as if he wished he hadn't been in the office when Bob had telephoned earlier.

'Well, you're right, Bob, we can't change what's done,' said Callaghan. 'And I'm guessing that you've not turned up on my doorstep on a Thursday evening to pass the time of day and reminisce?'

'That's true,' said Bob. 'I'm here because at the beginning of the week I took up a new job in Edinburgh as deputy head of Military Intelligence Section 11, or MI11.'

'Ah,' said Callaghan. 'Am I right in thinking your visit relates to a telephone call I received earlier from a French lady in MI5 in London?'

'Yes, it does. She's someone I know well and trust, and although I still have to uncover the background, I am convinced that it is important to national security that you release the two men you are holding into my custody.'

'I'm surprised to see you here, Bob, but if I'm honest I was half-expecting someone like you to arrive. Madame Dubois did sound very anxious and was fairly convincing. On the other hand, what we've found does look pretty serious.'

'Could you tell me what happened today?'

'Yes. My people here took a telephone call early this afternoon from the security office at the Rolls-Royce engine factory at Hillington. They'd seen two men in a car acting suspiciously. It seems they'd been driving around the site using the public roads that skirt its edges. There's not much else out there on three sides of the site, so they stood out as odd. From time to time, they'd been stopping and getting out as if to look at parts of the factory through the fence. We sent out a patrol car which pulled the men over. When asked what they were doing, they came out with some rubbish about writing an article for an architectural magazine in the United States. When we searched them we found documents identifying the men as two British citizens, Geoffrey Smith and Arthur Thompson, with addresses in London. We also found a notebook with pencil drawings of parts of the factory as seen from outside the fence. Given the strategic importance of the Hillington factory we immediately detained both men.'

'What's happened since then?' asked Bob.

'When they arrived here, one of them, Thompson, asked if he could ring the Security Service in London. He did so. Not long afterwards I was telephoned by Madame Dubois. I've tried to interview the two men, individually, but neither is saying anything at all.'

'What's your view about what's going on, Jack?' asked Bob.

'I don't know, Bob, but I'm not very happy about the idea of the Security Service, or MI5, mounting some sort of operation on my patch without my knowing anything about it.'

'I am pretty sure you are right, Jack, and if it's any consolation we had no idea in MI11 that anything was going on until I talked to Madame Dubois not long after she spoke to you. Do many of your officers know what's happened?'

'No. I've instructed the two constables involved in the arrest to keep quiet. And only my desk sergeant and I know of the involvement of MI5, or MI11 for that matter.'

'Does that mean you are happy to hand the two men you arrested over to me?' asked Bob.

'Come on, Bob. You should know as well as I do that it's not as simple as that. Telling the officers involved to keep quiet is one thing. By then they'd already filled in some of the paperwork they must complete when bringing suspects in. I'd have been on their backs if they hadn't. I can't simply tell them the whole thing's gone away and I've released the men.'

'I'm not well placed to argue this one with you, Jack, because I know no more than you about what's really going on. But I do get the feeling that while MI5 would prefer not to make ripples, they'd also be prepared, if necessary, to have their director ring your chief constable.'

'In other words, although you're making it sound like you're saying "please", what you're really saying is that I've got no choice?'

'I'm sorry, Jack. As I read things, that's exactly right.'

'Alright then,' said Callaghan. 'But I am attaching three conditions to this, and I want your personal agreement to them all.'

'What are they?' asked Bob.

'The first is that you get to the bottom of what is going on and pass on my concern about these people wandering around my patch to MI5. The second is that you take personal responsibility for these two men until you can hand them over to someone senior in MI5. And the third is that at some time soon you come over to stay with Flora and I and, over a glass or two of whisky, you tell me what's behind all this.'

'I accept,' said Bob. 'Now where do I find Smith and Thompson?'

CHAPTER FOUR

The man looked up from the bed as the cell door swung open.

'Are you Arthur Thompson?' asked Bob. The man nodded. 'Good. I'm Group Captain Sutherland and I'm here at the request of Monique Dubois. I'm the deputy head of MI11. You and Geoffrey Smith are being released by the police into my custody. For the benefit of the lieutenant here, can you confirm that you are happy to accept that?'

'Yes, of course, sir.' The man stood up. 'I'm short of things like shoelaces and my belt and tie.'

'Those will be returned at the custody desk,' said Callaghan.

'Madame Dubois was guarded on the telephone,' said Bob, 'but is there anything I need to know about Geoffrey Smith before we release him? He's not going to try to do a runner on me, is he?'

'No, sir. He's a bit wild when women or champagne are involved, but he's otherwise fairly well house-trained.'

'Just so long as you know that the rest of your career in the Security Service depends on it,' said Bob.

Geoffrey Smith's cell was several removed from Arthur Thompson's. The door swung open to reveal a tall and extremely thin man with a pencil moustache who looked in his early thirties. He stood up, almost to attention, when Bob asked him to confirm his name, and seemed content to follow the lead taken by Arthur Thompson as their few belongings were returned to them.

Very little was said in the car as they made their way cautiously through darkened streets while avoiding poorly lit traffic.

The pilot held open the door as the four men climbed into the cabin of the Avro Anson utility aircraft. Bob again took the seat next to the pilot's, in the cockpit, after telling Smith and Thompson they were taking a short flight to Turnhouse.

As the aircraft climbed away from the runway, Lieutenant Dixon came to the front of the passenger cabin. 'I'm not sure how you are going to take this, sir, but there's a request from the gentlemen in the back to fly over the Hillington factory when we turn to head east, so they can see what it looks like from the air at night.'

'Can you pass back a simple refusal, Michael? You can push your luck too far, and I think that would be doing so. Flight sergeant, would you mind turning to the right and following the line of the River Clyde when we head east? I want to stay well clear of the factory to the south of the airfield.'

'Thanks, Bob, I'm very grateful.'

Bob had telephoned Monique from the duty officer's room at RAF Turnhouse. 'That's no problem. There are a few strings attached, however.'

'What do you mean?'

'Perhaps I should have made the connection when you mentioned the name, but it turned out that Lieutenant Callaghan and I were close colleagues before the war, and ten years or so ago it looked for a while like we might even become brothers-in-law.'

'He was the brother of the lady who died in Clydebank?'

Bob had guessed that Monique would remember the story he had reluctantly told over dinner in Caithness the previous month. 'Yes. He attached a number of conditions to his release of your two men into my custody.'

'He can't do that!'

'Well he did, and more to the point, I accepted them. The most significant was that I took personal responsibility for Smith and Thompson until I could hand them over to someone I trust in MI5.'

There was a silence on the other end of the line. Then Monique said, in a very neutral tone, 'I see.'

'The problem I have is that the only person I know well enough in MI5 to pass on this responsibility to is you, Monique.'

'Bob, this sounds a little as if you are proposing to hold my people hostage against my coming to Scotland.'

'Not at all, Monique, I'd be equally happy to fly down to London with them and hand them over there.'

'Maybe I was wrong,' said Monique. 'Maybe you are Machiavellian enough to fit right in to this unpleasant little world of ours.'

'Is that a "yes"?'

Monique sighed, slightly theatrically, on the other end of the line. 'I'll make my way up to Edinburgh tomorrow. I'll contact you when I've arrived, and we can take things from there. Where are you keeping Thompson and Smith?'

'They are out of harm's way in the officers' mess accommodation at RAF Turnhouse. Thompson has assured me that Smith won't make a break for it, but I've got them in a twin room just in case.'

'That sounds reasonable,' said Monique.

'There is something else you can help me with.'

'What's that, Bob?'

'Lieutenant Callaghan was not happy that your people were mounting some sort of operation on his patch without telling him. I have some sympathy. I want you to talk to Arthur Thompson and tell him that he can brief me on why he and Geoffrey Smith were taking such a close interest in one of the most strategically important factories in Scotland. I also want you to tell him that he can brief me on Geoffrey Smith, who I get the feeling is rather more than he appears.'

'That's a very big request, Bob.'

'I know it is. But on Monday I became deputy head of the branch of military intelligence that's responsible for military security. Given what is manufactured in that factory, I think I can legitimately claim that military security has an interest, don't you?'

There was a long pause, possibly while Monique consulted someone else present at her end of the conversation as she held her hand over the mouthpiece. 'Very well, Bob, we agree. But you'll have to wait until tomorrow. I'll fill you in on the background myself.'

'Excellent. See you tomorrow, Monique.'

'How do you feel about getting drunk for your country, Michael?'

Lieutenant Dixon shrugged. 'I can think of worse things to have to do for my country, sir. What did you have in mind?'

They were standing at the bar in the officers' mess at RAF Turnhouse. Smith and Thompson had been settled into a twin room on the upper floor of the building and, as added security, Lieutenant Dixon had taken the room next to theirs. Bob also had a room in the building, though not in the same wing. 'Madame Dubois from MI5 is travelling to Edinburgh tomorrow to take our two friends off our hands. She has promised me a full account of what has been, and presumably still is, going on. She has also agreed to tell me more about Geoffrey Smith, who I find rather intriguing.'

'So where does the alcohol come in, sir?'

'Smith and Thompson know we are with MI11 and so are, up to a point at least, on the same side as them. Being locked up in a police cell this afternoon couldn't have been a very pleasant experience, and I'm wondering if Smith might be the sort of man to feel the need to celebrate being released. It seems to me that we have what's left of the evening to see if we can persuade him to divulge anything that might be of value which I can use to cross-check with what Madame Dubois tells me.'

'Don't you trust her, sir?' asked Dixon. 'I seem to recall you telling Lieutenant Callaghan that you did.'

'She works for the Security Service, Michael, so I can't

49

afford to trust her unquestioningly at a professional level. Look, you know the area better than I do. Can you think of anywhere with a bit of atmosphere nearby that we can go? Ideally somewhere that doesn't close too early and where we can get a bite to eat as well as a drink.' He looked around the bar. 'Here would be ideal, geographically, but it's got no atmosphere, and I get the feeling that everyone's a bit reluctant to let their guard down in the presence of a group captain.'

'I stay in the officers' accommodation at HMS *Lochinvar*, sir. It's on the river, west of the Forth Bridge at a place called Port Edgar, and very convenient for Craigiehall. It's used as a training depot for the Royal Naval Patrol Service and the officers' wardroom has developed a bit of a reputation for enthusiastic celebration. I normally steer clear, but it might be just what you are looking for. And I've got an account, so there's no question of needing to find the cash. And, with all due respect, sir, nobody there is going to care how senior you are when you are wearing that colour uniform.'

Bob smiled. 'That sounds ideal. Let's get a car and duty driver from Craigiehall to take us to Port Edgar. Could you arrange that and round up the jailbirds?'

The contrast between the mess bar at RAF Turnhouse and the officers' wardroom at HMS *Lochinvar* was as marked as Lieutenant Dixon had forecast. The night was far from young, and Bob had the impression that some of those present had been drinking for quite some time. Noise levels were high, and games of darts and snooker were in full swing. The noisiest area was a corner occupied by a group of Women's Royal Naval Service officers, who seemed particularly adept at repelling advances by male colleagues.

Lieutenant Dixon managed to stake a claim to another corner alcove and the four settled in. Once they'd eaten it became clear that Geoffrey Smith was a champagne and cigar man who saw it as his duty to take the lead in ensuring his table's consumption did not lag behind the rest of the wardroom. Bob had seldom seen anyone put away expensive drink, however cheap it was as champagne went, quite so quickly.

Arthur Thompson, on the other hand, had perfected the art of appearing to drink without really doing so and seemed content to chain-smoke cigarettes. Bob drank modestly and saw that Lieutenant Dixon was doing the same. As the conversation flowed across pre-war English football, the contrast between Scotland and London and, with Geoffrey Smith taking a strong lead, the relative merits of women in uniform and civilians, Bob realised that a clear pattern was emerging. While Smith was uninhibited, Thompson saw himself as the protector, and an important part of his role tonight was to ensure that Smith said nothing that might be of use to Bob.

They were on their fourth bottle of champagne and Bob was thinking of calling it a night when a chance comment by Lieutenant Dixon brought an unexpected breakthrough. 'I suppose that getting out of those cells must feel like a good reason for a celebration,' he said to Smith.

'Not really,' said Smith. 'If you'd been in as many prisons as I have, you'd realise that a few hours in Renfrew Police Station is something of a rest cure.'

'Geoffrey, I'm really not sure this is the time or place for this,' said Arthur Thompson.

'Oh, do be quiet, Arthur. I'm sure the group captain is a man of the world.'

'What do you mean, Geoffrey?' asked Bob.

'Well, if after the war there's a market for a book on the prisons of Europe, then I'm your man to write it. I've seen a good few of them.'

'How did you manage that?' asked Bob. 'Michael, can you get us another bottle of champagne if they're still serving?'

Thompson turned to Bob. 'Sir, I must protest. You are taking advantage of the amount Geoffrey has drunk.'

'Are you suggesting I can't hold my drink, Arthur?' said Smith, as Lieutenant Dixon went to the bar. 'One of the things the Abwehr used to do was get me drunk to see if I told them a consistent story. I'm not going to tell the group captain here anything I don't want him to know. You see, Group Captain, before the war I was a bit of a lad.'

'That's an interesting way of putting it,' said Bob. He watched Thompson resign himself to Smith's boasting.

'In 1931 I joined the army, the Coldstream Guards, but got bored polishing buttons and boots and guarding Buckingham Palace. I ran off with a girl I met in Soho, but the army caught up with me and locked me up in the glasshouse in Aldershot.'

'So that was your first time in prison?' asked Bob.

'Yes. After I got out I earned a reputation as a safe cracker. Learning a little about explosives in the army had its benefits, you see. I got caught a few times, and spent a few more spells in jail, but life was pretty good when I wasn't in jail. Plenty of money and a never-ending queue of beautiful women. After a while things got a bit too hot. It came to a head after I was arrested here in Edinburgh and was charged with blowing up the safe in the Edinburgh Co-operative Society headquarters. For some daft reason they let me out on bail and I headed for Jersey.'

'What happened there?'

'By this time my photo had been on the front page of just too many newspapers. I was having dinner in a hotel with a girlfriend when I spotted the police coming for me through the two doors into the dining room. I smashed the front window with a chair and escaped. The problem was that I had no money with me, so that night I went and had a good time at a night club, then robbed the safe in the office. The police turned up and caught me in the act.'

'That was unlucky,' said Bob.

'Not really,' said Smith. 'Given the list of jobs I was wanted for in England and Scotland, I'd have been lucky to get away with 15 years in prison if I'd been taken back to the mainland. But because I got caught doing a job on Jersey, they insisted on trying me there, and I was given a two-year stretch.'

Bob had been working out the chronology in his head. 'What happened when Jersey was invaded?'

'The Germans took over the running of the prison, though not much really changed, not until food began to be a wider problem for the island, anyway.'

'How did you get out?' asked Bob.

'I wrote a letter in German offering my services to the Abwehr as a spy.'

'And they simply said how nice that would be, and let you out?'

'Far from it, Group Captain. They took an awful lot of convincing that I was genuine.'

'And were you?'

'Ah, the trick question, Group Captain, and very well played. No, obviously I wasn't genuine, or I wouldn't be sitting here talking to you now. But after a while the Germans came to believe I was. Not before I spent rather longer than I care to recall in Fort de Romainville, a sort of half-way house to the concentration camps, on the edge of Paris. The place was a mixed sex prison so had its compensations, but if ever I do write that book I was talking about, Fort de Romainville will feature as the very worst prison I've been locked up in.'

'But they let you out of there, too?'

'They did. Then they trained me up on Morse code and on the use of larger quantities of explosives than would ever have been needed to blow a safe. And then, at the end of last month, they flew me in a Junkers bomber from Norway to Scotland and I landed by parachute in a field. I immediately contacted the police and MI5 and offered them my services as a double agent.'

'I remember the Edinburgh Co-operative Society robbery,' said Bob. 'I was in the police in Glasgow at the time. Your real name is Stanley Harrison, isn't it?'

Arthur Thompson raised his hands, as if in surrender. 'Sir, would you mind leaving things there? From what you told me earlier, Madame Dubois will be here tomorrow, and I am sure she will fill in the gaps for you.'

'That's fair enough, Arthur, but I would like to know what the interest is in Hillington.'

'I'm usually just called Stan Harrison, Group Captain.

I'm pleased my fame reached as far as Glasgow, though it's perhaps as well the police in Renfrew didn't make the connection earlier today. We might as well tell him the rest, Arthur, it won't take long.'

'Alright, but can we all stick with the name "Geoffrey Smith", please?'

'You see, Group Captain,' continued Geoffrey Smith, 'the main reason I was sent to Scotland by the Abwehr was to sabotage the Merlin engine factory at Hillington. When I return to Germany, which is the plan at present, I will need to have a faultless and extremely detailed cover story worked out, and that was why we were at the factory today.'

It fell to Lieutenant Dixon to ask the obvious question. 'But you're not actually going to sabotage the factory?'

It was Arthur Thompson who answered. 'No, though I believe steps are going to be taken to make the Germans think that it has been sabotaged. Then Geoffrey will return to Germany as a hero.' Thompson looked at Bob. 'Before you ask, sir, neither Geoffrey nor I have any idea how the deception will take place. We just need to make sure that Geoffrey's story matches what the Germans think they know, to the minutest detail.'

Geoffrey Smith staggered slightly as he stood up and headed for the toilets. 'I was beginning to think that the man would never get drunk,' said Bob.

'I've never met anyone with his capacity for alcohol, sir,' said Thompson. 'And frankly, I don't think you did get him drunk. He's naturally boastful and simply saw an opportunity to talk about himself for a while to an attentive and non-judgemental audience.'

'I don't know about you chaps, but I think I might have had enough for one night,' said Bob.

'Yes, sir,' said Thompson, stubbing out a cigarette. 'Perhaps it is time we made tracks. Has your driver been waiting all this time?'

It was Lieutenant Dixon who pointed out that Smith's toilet break was taking rather a long time. The three of them tried not to look hurried as they headed for the corridor leading to the toilets. They found Geoffrey Smith kissing a young Women's Royal Naval Service officer against a wall at the far end of the corridor.

Thompson's voice was quite gentle. 'Sorry, Geoffrey, but we need to go. Sorry, miss.'

The couple parted with obvious reluctance, the WRNS officer looking embarrassed when she realised they had been interrupted by a senior officer and a naval lieutenant.

As they walked out to the car, Thompson said to Bob, out of Smith's hearing, 'I've never met anyone with his capacity for women either, sir. The odd thing is that they all seem to chase him rather than vice versa, and it always seems to be the really attractive ones.'

'Are you jealous, Arthur?' asked Bob.

'No sir, but I'm hoping to pick up a few pointers during my time with him. I can't say it's worked so far, though.'

CHAPTER FIVE

Despite the late finish, Bob was up early the following morning, nursing just the slightest hint of a hangover. After he had eaten breakfast in the officers' mess he went up to talk to Smith and Thompson in their room. Now he had a clearer idea what they were doing in Scotland, his main concern, other than physically securing the two men, was to ensure that Thompson couldn't speak to Monique Dubois on the telephone before Bob did so in person. That meant holding them in a degree of isolation, and he had been able to borrow two members of the RAF Police detachment at RAF Turnhouse to keep the men under what amounted to house arrest in their room. Food, reading matter and a radio would be provided, but a telephone certainly wouldn't. That freed Lieutenant Dixon to return to the office.

Bob then went to see Wing Commander Bernard Spencer, the officer commanding RAF Turnhouse, to thank him for the loan of the station flight Avro Anson the previous evening and for his wider support. It proved a fruitful meeting with a man who really did seem genuinely relaxed about Bob's decision to live on the base. They agreed to have dinner together early the following week and parted as friends.

The next appointment in his diary, still at RAF Turnhouse, was one Bob approached with more mixed feelings. He was scheduled to meet a weapons instructor on the station range for training in the use of the small Walther PPK semi-automatic pistol he'd been issued with in London. This had been a cause of some dissent on his part, but his new boss, the head of MI11, Commodore Maurice Cunningham, had ordered him to ensure he was never without the weapon. So, late on Tuesday afternoon, he had gone down to the bowels of a building in Whitehall to be issued what felt like a tiny pistol, plus a shoulder holster that held it perfectly.

When Bob had pointed out that this prevented his uniform jacket fitting properly, he had been sent that same evening to visit a tailor in Savile Row who was retained by MI11, apparently for that purpose. Bob had been measured up for a new uniform while wearing his pistol in its shoulder holster, and on his return next morning found that two complete uniforms had been made for him overnight, even down to rank insignia, pilot's wings and the correct medal ribbons. Service with a smile, and all at no cost to himself. He had changed into one of the uniforms immediately and arranged for the other to be sent on to him in Scotland, with his old uniform.

The weapons instructor at RAF Turnhouse was a sergeant who whistled when Bob withdrew the Walther from his unbuttoned jacket, as if it were a fabulous piece of jewellery. 'Now that's a real beauty. May I take a look, sir?'

'Of course.' Bob handed over the pistol. 'It's loaded. Sorry, I don't know your name.'

'It's Michael James, sir.'

After removing the magazine and checking there wasn't a round in the breech, Sergeant James turned the pistol over in his hands, looking at it from every angle. 'I'm sure you know already, sir, but it's a Walther PPK. Think what you like of the Germans, they certainly know how to engineer something like this. The name PPK is an abbreviation of the German term "Polizeipistole Kriminalmodell", or "Police Pistol Detective Model". It's an ideal concealed weapon as it's physically small and relatively light. This one, like most PPKs, is designed to use the standard .32 automatic cartridge, also known as the 7.65 mm Browning cartridge, so you'll never have any difficulty getting hold of ammunition for it. The magazine will take seven rounds, plus one in the chamber, though you should never use that option in normal operation. Far more people have been accidentally shot through forgetting there's a round in the chamber than have ever been shot by an enemy as a result of the moment it takes to pull back and release the slide to chamber the first round. At the back of the weapon there is an indicator to show that the chamber is loaded, but it's fairly subtle.'

The sergeant demonstrated how to load and unload the magazine, and how to use the slide to place a cartridge in the chamber, ready to fire. 'When you've got more time, sir, we can run through how to strip the pistol down and reassemble it, but I understand that for today you mainly want a chance to get a feel for how it performs when you fire it?'

'That's right,' said Bob.

By the end of the session Bob had proved himself to be a reasonable shot, once he'd got the hang of holding the pistol in two hands and bracing himself against it. He still didn't think he'd ever get to share Sergeant James' sheer enthusiasm for the Walther PPK.

Craigiehall was a fine country house built for the Earl of Annandale in the closing years of the 1600s. It was later extended several times, most significantly in the 1820s. The house stood close to the north bank of the River Almond not far from the western edge of Edinburgh.

This placed it very close to Cramond, where Bob's parents had moved from another part of the city when he was ten. At that time the grand house had been empty and abandoned, and Bob, like many local children, had enjoyed exploring the extensive grounds. When Bob was about fourteen the house was renovated and reoccupied, and forays into the grounds had to be undertaken with much more discretion. His parents had told him when Craigiehall was converted into a hotel in 1933, and a year or two before the war he'd stayed there once with a young lady he'd met through the Auxiliary Air Force. He'd chosen the location mainly because he'd wanted to know what the interior of the house was like, but found the two night stay extremely uncomfortable, worrying that a fellow guest or member of staff might recognise him and tell his parents that he'd been in the area without calling in on them.

Bob smiled wryly at the memory as he stopped the staff car and showed his pass to the guard at the main gate, who stood back and saluted. Craigiehall had been requisitioned by the army at the start of the war, and the main house had been joined by assorted Nissen huts and wooden buildings. Bob drove himself around to the grand entrance to the house itself. Much of the main house was used as a headquarters by Royal Artillery and anti-aircraft artillery units whose operational elements were scattered along both banks of the Firth of Forth and on islands in the river. Bob's predecessor had been an army colonel and had negotiated the use by MI11 of a series of first floor rooms in the extension added to the original house in the 1820s. It was early days yet, but Bob's initial impression had been that the accommodation worked reasonably well, and as he'd told Group Captain More at Leuchars, the location suited him perfectly.

Bob had discovered the extent of his empire on Monday. As well as his secretary, Mrs Joyce Stuart, who he shared with his deputy, Major Walter Miller, he had inherited three teams, each comprising an officer and a senior non-commissioned officer. Each team was staffed from one of the three armed services. The teams spent part of their time making visits to military establishments around Scotland and northern England to test and report on security. They also had a role undertaking investigative work into incidents such as the one that had occurred at RAF Leuchars. Anything that might compromise military security was fair game, but it was already obvious to Bob that he didn't have the resources to mount thorough or large-scale investigations, and equally clear to him that there were conflicting demands on his teams' time that he suspected meant that neither of their main roles could be carried out as well as was desirable.

There was also a general office with two typists who doubled as filing clerks, and two drivers who doubled as field security police. The office had two cars, one of which Bob had used to commute to work in that morning, in addition to the car allocated to each team. Bob had yet to find out how the structure really worked in practice. He had introduced himself to most of the team on Monday and felt he could put names to faces for all those he'd met. But in terms of really getting to know what people did and what their hopes and ambitions were, he had achieved next to nothing.

'Good morning, sir,' said Mrs Stuart as Bob entered her office, which lay between his and Major Miller's. 'As you know, you are due for lunch at Edinburgh Castle at 1 p.m., and Major Miller would like a word if possible. Something about champagne on an expenses claim from Lieutenant Dixon.'

Mrs Stuart was a stereotypically Edinburgh lady in her fifties and seemed to be a model of efficiency. Bob wondered how he would shape up in her eyes as a new boss. By all accounts his predecessor had been something of an old school infantry officer, who had done very well in the Great War but was not renowned for his imagination or flexibility. 'Thank you, Mrs Stuart,' replied Bob. 'Is the major in his office?' It occurred to Bob that his predecessor and Major Miller must have got on like a house on fire, albeit a genteel and tightly controlled house on fire. He reminded himself that it couldn't be easy for Miller to have someone so different in background and outlook running the place, and that he should avoid forming judgements about the man too quickly.

'He is around, sir, but there's something else you should be aware of. I had MI5 on the phone a little earlier. A lady called Madame Dubois is due to arrive at RAF Turnhouse in just under half an hour from now. I understand you are expecting her? And by the way, sir, I am happy to answer to "Joyce".'

'Thank you, Joyce,' said Bob. 'I rather assumed that Madame Dubois would be arriving by train sometime later this afternoon. No matter. I should be able to meet her at Turnhouse and still get to the castle in plenty of time.' Bob wondered if he should offer up his own first name in the interests of informality but decided that might be a step too far for Mrs Stuart in Bob's first week in the office.

'Yes, Group Captain. You need to remember that Lieutenant General Gordon is a stickler for punctuality.'

Bob smiled. 'Don't worry, Joyce, I'll not let the side down. Could you offer my apologies to Major Miller and tell him that so long as Lieutenant Dixon isn't claiming for more than five, or perhaps it was six, bottles of champagne and four meals, then it's a legitimate expense. We were trying to loosen the tongues of a couple of our friends from MI5 at Port Edgar last night.'

Mrs Stuart returned the smile, 'I'll do that, Group Captain.'

'Where is everyone else?'

'Flight Lieutenant Buchan and Sergeant Bennett are on their way back from RAF Leuchars. Lieutenant Dixon and Petty Officer MacDonald are undertaking a routine security check on the naval dockyard at Rosyth. And Captain Bell and Sergeant Potter drove up yesterday to Lochaber to investigate a suspicious death at the Commando Basic Training Centre at Achnacarry Castle north of Fort William. They cleared their involvement with Major Miller. I believe it's of interest to us because the dead man is Belgian and there's a possibility of other nationalities being involved, including some Germans who are being trained there at the moment.'

'We train Germans at the Commando Basic Training Centre?'

'Apparently so, sir.'

'Well you learn something every day. Thanks Joyce. I'd better be going.'

Bob had collected Smith and Thompson from the officers' mess at RAF Turnhouse before being driven to where he had been told the Avro Anson due in from RAF Northolt near London would park.

He instructed the two men to stay in the car with the driver as he watched the aircraft come to a halt. It was raining again. When the two engines fell silent, Bob walked over to the side of the aircraft and opened the cabin door.

Monique Dubois was a dark-haired woman who was, Bob knew, 30 years old. In fact, she was just seven months younger than he was himself. She was classically beautiful in an attractively flawed sort of way. But there were times when, especially if she was caught unawares, her eyes could take on a slightly haunted look. Bob knew enough of her story to understand why that was.

The two greeted in the Gallic fashion.

'I got the impression you were coming up by train,' said Bob.

'I decided to take a leaf out of your book, Bob. You are right, you know, this is the only way to travel. Besides, I wanted to get things back on track here as quickly as possible.'

'Look, should we take a walk?' said Bob. 'This umbrella should keep the rain off.'

They strolled slowly over towards the nearest hangar.

'The gold braid suits you Bob,' said Monique, indicating his peaked cap.

'I get the sense that you've been promoted, too?' asked Bob.

'Yes, I'm perhaps not quite as small a cog in the wheel as I was last month. Do I take it that we are standing out here in the rain because you've got Arthur Thompson and Geoffrey Smith in the car?'

'Yes,' said Bob. 'There's something you should know about that. I took them out for a few drinks last night with one of my colleagues and gained a reasonable idea of Geoffrey Smith's life story, and who he really is. I also have some idea of what they were doing at Hillington yesterday.'

Bob had expected an angry response, but Monique smiled. 'Of course you did, Bob. In your shoes I'd have done the same. Though, and please don't take this unkindly, I think I might have found easier ways of getting him to tell his story than by feeding him alcohol.'

'Tell that to the WRNS officer who had him locked in an amorous clinch at HMS *Lochinvar* late last night,' said Bob with a grin. 'Mr Smith does seem to be a man with some very well-defined appetites.'

'I take it that Arthur Thompson was not happy about Geoffrey Smith revealing all to you?'

'No. Thompson did a pretty good job at deflecting us, but in the end, Smith simply wanted to boast about himself.'

'Yes, he's quite a character. Look, Bob, can you release them to me? There are things I need to do over in Glasgow this afternoon, and the sooner we set off the better.'

'Hang on a minute. We've got an agreement,' said Bob. 'I hand your two men over to you, and in return you bring me up to speed on what's going on.'

'I could argue that you already know all you need to know, Bob,' said Monique. 'And I could argue that you broke the terms of our agreement when you decided to open up Geoffrey Smith yourself. But don't worry, a deal is a deal. I need to be in Scotland for the next couple of days, and tonight I'm staying at the North British Hotel on Princes Street, next to Waverley Station. I've booked a private dining room for this evening and would be grateful if you could join me for dinner. How does seven-thirty for eight sound?'

Bob watched the Avro Anson taxi out towards the runway. He looked at his watch, remembering his promise to Joyce Stuart, and turned to walk swiftly through the rain towards the car.

'Hello, driver. I could do with getting to Edinburgh Castle as quickly as you can.'

'No problem, sir.'

'I'm sorry,' said Bob, 'I don't recall you being in the office when I was introduced to people on Monday. I'm afraid I don't know your name.'

'I'm Private Jenkins, sir, sometimes called Owen, but usually just known as "Taffy".' The man's accent was a pretty good indication of why he had been given that nickname.

'It was you we kept up to an ungodly hour last night, wasn't it?'

'Yes, sir. But the car's a comfortable enough place to wait, so long as you remember your greatcoat. And the entertainment value of what was going on outside the officers' wardroom was high. It was enough to make me think I was in the wrong service and should have joined the navy. I dread to think what your predecessor, Colonel Duncan, would have made of it.'

Bob thought it might have been a Frenchman who had originally observed that 'no man is a hero to his valet' some centuries earlier. He couldn't help thinking the modern equivalent would refer to the man's driver rather than his valet, and silently vowed to bear that in mind.

Edinburgh Castle had been a fixture in the visual backdrop to Bob's childhood and youth. Standing on the summit of an ancient plug of volcanic rock towering 260ft above the city it dominated, it was visible for tens of miles in every direction. No fairy-tale castle, this was the real thing, an uncompromisingly defensive structure that seemed to grow organically out of the living rock beneath it.

Continuously adapted to meet the military needs of the day, the castle had changed significantly over the centuries. Bob knew from school history lessons that over those same centuries its strength had been tested many times, successfully or unsuccessfully, by siege or by stealth.

And yet, though the castle was utterly familiar to everyone living in Edinburgh, it was also somewhere outside the experience of most of them. As the headquarters of the army's Scottish Command, large parts of it were inaccessible to most people.

As a teenager, Bob had visited on one occasion. Some of the boys from his school had been brought to the castle to be shown around. They'd visited the then very new Scottish National War Memorial at the top of the castle and gone to look at the display of the Honours of Scotland, the nation's crown jewels. They'd also toured the barracks, probably with the intention of interesting them in a career in the army. But to boys brought up in the years following the Great War, however protected they had been from the detail of the horrors faced by their fathers and uncles, the army had not seemed a very attractive idea.

Bob showed his pass to the armed guards at the foot of the Castle Esplanade, and to another outside the castle gate. He wasn't sure that the car would fit through the gateway, but it did. 'Do you know where we are going, Taffy?' asked Bob.

'Yes sir. Colonel Duncan used to be a regular visitor. I'll drop you outside the headquarters building, which is in part of what they call the New Barracks, even though they were built centuries ago. I suppose they are "new" relative to everything else here.'

Bob's credentials were checked for a third time at the entrance to the castle's headquarters building.

CHAPTER SIX

Lieutenant General Sir Charles Gordon was a larger than life man whose physical presence dominated the very fine office he occupied. With the formalities over, the general waved back towards the door that Bob had just entered by. 'We might as well go straight through to lunch. I've asked my deputy to join us.'

The dining room into which Lieutenant General Gordon led them was little short of magnificent. A large and obviously antique dining table was set in an even larger room whose walls were painted in dark green, the effect being offset by a deeply piled carpet. The walls were hung with individually-lit oil paintings depicting scenes of battles and portraits of senior officers in dress uniform. A sideboard groaned under the weight of a formidable display of regimental silver, while more was on display in an illuminated cabinet standing against the wall opposite the door. A fire was burning brightly in a highly decorated marble fireplace, while the final wall was home to three large windows, which Bob could see offered extensive views south west over an extremely smoky and very damp city.

An officer, also wearing a general's uniform, had been standing by one of the windows, and now walked over to greet Bob, with his hand outstretched. Lieutenant General Gordon did the introductions. 'Group Captain Robert Sutherland, can I present Brigadier General Sir Richard Blackett?'

'Pleased to meet you, sir,' said Bob. 'I think we almost met last month. You were on your way to Fort George as I left it to head north.'

'Ah, yes,' said Blackett. 'I must tell you, Sutherland, how impressed we were with the way you resolved things.'

'Most of the hard work was done by your Colonel Urquhart, sir, the commander of the Seaforth Highlanders at Fort George.'

'Perhaps, but it was your personal intervention that brought matters to such a satisfactory conclusion, with the loss of just one life in the final confrontation and the safeguarding of the king.'

'Can I ask, sir, what became of the German soldiers we captured? The men of the Brandenburg Regiment?'

Blackett said, 'The German commandos? Well, they were all wearing Polish uniforms, or British uniforms with Polish insignia if you want to be pedantic. We could have taken the view that that made their position tricky under the Geneva Conventions. On the other hand, they did surrender when you called upon them to do so. The decision was taken at the highest level that they should be treated as ordinary prisoners of war.'

'I'm pleased about that,' said Bob.

'Mind you,' said Lieutenant General Gordon, 'if it happened today, we might take a different view. You won't know this, Sutherland, but last Sunday, Hitler issued an order called the "Kommandobefehl" or "Commando Order". Under the terms of this, any British or Allied commandos captured on small scale raids into Europe will be executed, even if wearing British uniform. The Germans don't know we know this yet, and we are still working out a response.'

'Good God, sir, that raises the stakes!'

'It does,' said Gordon. 'It follows the Dieppe Raid back in August, and a small raid by the commandos on the island of Sark in the Channel Islands at the beginning of this month. The Germans believe that some of their men on Sark were killed after being taken prisoner and while bound. Look, should we sit down for lunch? We're only having something fairly light.'

Bob remembered the dinner invitation from Monique and found himself pleased at the idea of a light lunch. Lieutenant General Gordon sat at the end of the large table, with Bob sitting at the nearest end of one long side, looking across the table at Brigadier General Blackett. As the onion soup was served he turned to Gordon and asked, 'Do all army units in Scotland report to you, sir? Talk of the commandos reminds me that I have a team up at Achnacarry Castle in the Highlands.'

'Most do, but the Commando Basic Training Centre is rather different. The commanding officer is Lieutenant Colonel Edward White. Whenever my people here at Scottish Command or in the North West Highlands District try to exert influence over how Achnacarry is run, White tells them in no uncertain terms that he is responsible to Commando Group H.Q. and Combined Operations H.Q. I strongly suspect, though, that he plays the same game in reverse when those units also try to exert more control than he wants.'

Bob spent a moment trying to find a diplomatic way of asking the question on his mind. 'Is that something you're happy about, sir?'

Gordon laughed. 'The thing is that everyone agrees White is doing an outstanding job. Achnacarry only opened for business in March this year and he has already raised standards and increased the throughput of men available for posting to the commandos very significantly. I could wish that he wasn't the largest single user of live ammunition in Scotland, but I've enough sense to let him get on with what he's doing.'

'They train with live ammunition?' asked Bob.

'Yes, and large amounts of it. But the results are there for all to see. The commandos had a patchy first couple of years of existence, but although the Dieppe Raid in August was a fiasco, the commandos involved on the flank of the main raid performed superbly well. Much of that improvement in performance is attributed to Colonel White.'

As the main course was served, Bob wondered whether most residents of wartime Britain would regard grilled Dover sole and potatoes as a 'light lunch'.

'So, the answer to your earlier question, Sutherland, is that not all army units in Scotland report to the general officer commanding Scottish Command. It's a job with some nice touches, though. Since 1936 the officers who've held my position have also been appointed governor of Edinburgh Castle. It's not often you get to command anything quite so tangible or historically important.'

Brigadier General Blackett asked, 'I understand you know Edinburgh well, Sutherland?'

'Yes sir, I was born and brought up here.'

'What decided you to join the Glasgow police?' asked Blackett. 'I always get the sense the two cities have very different outlooks on life and on the world.'

'You are right, sir,' said Bob. 'But my father was a senior policeman here in Edinburgh, and still is for that matter. He thought, and I am sure he was right, that if I really wanted to join the police rather than go to university, then it needed to be a police force in which I could make my own way.'

'But the war intervened?'

'Yes, it did, sir. I'd started to learn to fly in 1933 and joined the Auxiliary Air Force a few years later. When war came around it seemed natural to mobilise with my squadron rather than stay in the police.'

'And during the Battle of Britain you shot down over twenty enemy aircraft and were commanding a fighter squadron when you yourself were shot down and wounded? And you shot down another enemy aircraft last month?'

'Yes, sir.' Bob wondered where this was going before deciding that perhaps it was just the brigadier general's way of making polite conversation.

'How are you finding the move from command of a training unit to MI11, Sutherland?' asked Lieutenant General Gordon.

'It's very early days yet, sir,' said Bob, 'but it's throwing up some interesting challenges.'

'How do you feel about the overlaps between MI11's

work and the work of people like the Intelligence Corps and the three armed services' Special Investigations Branches?'

'I understand that was discussed in detail fairly recently in Whitehall, sir. My own perspective is that there is a role for MI11 that allows us to make a distinct contribution to the war effort and doesn't conflict with the organisations you have referred to, or with others such as the Security Service for that matter.'

'I suspect you will find some on the military side of the War Office who would question that, Sutherland,' said Gordon. 'But the important thing for those of us out here at the sharp end, so to speak, is to make sure that we keep one another closely informed of issues of mutual interest. I'd be grateful if you would use Brigadier General Blackett here as your day to day point of contact in Scottish Command. We will of course endeavour to keep you informed of anything likely to be of interest to you that comes up.'

'Of course, sir, thank you.' Bob wondered as he looked around the dining room whether the men manning anti-aircraft guns out on the islands in the Firth of Forth would agree that this was the 'sharp end' of the war effort and smiled to himself as he imagined the likely response.

Having moved past what Lieutenant General Gordon clearly saw as the central point of the meeting, the discussion drifted on to an analysis of the pros and cons of Edinburgh as a city, and Bob found himself wondering how soon he could decently leave.

On his return to Craigiehall, Bob found Flight Lieutenant Buchan wanted to speak to him. 'I thought you'd like to know where we got to with Sergeant Winograd, sir.'

'Yes please, George,' said Bob as they sat either side of his desk. Bob realised that he was nearly a working week into the job and wondered if he'd spent more than an hour at his desk during that time.

'You were right, sir. When Sergeant Bennett went through Winograd's effects more closely, he came up with a page that looked like it had been torn out of a school exercise book. It was folded up tightly in a jacket pocket. I had a photograph taken of the document, which I've got here.'

Bob took the offered photograph. 'It's a series of initials, short words and arrows.'

'We wondered whether it was the checklist you wanted to find, sir.'

'You know, I rather think it might be,' said Bob. 'If you assume that the order on the page is a sequence, then the initials could refer to actions needed in starting up a Mosquito. On that basis, "FC" would be fuel cocks, "Th" the throttle levers, "RPM" the RPM levers; "SC" the supercharger controls, "Rad" the radiator shutters, and so on.'

'What about the arrows, sir?'

'Well the arrow next to the "Th" points to about eight o'clock, and "Mag", which I assume means magneto switches points to about two o'clock. I'd need to sit in a Mosquito again to be sure, but I think it's highly likely that this is a basic guide to starting up the aircraft, with the arrows pointing to where the relevant switches or controls are in the cockpit. It's as if someone has been shown how to start up a Mosquito while sitting in the cockpit or from photographs and made notes to help them remember when they came to do it on their own.' Bob stopped as he saw Flight Lieutenant Buchan's grin. 'What's so funny?'

'That was exactly what Wing Commander Gill said when we showed him the photograph first thing this morning, sir,' said the flight lieutenant. 'It was he who suggested I show it to you, to see how much you'd remembered from your flight yesterday.'

Bob could see the joke and smiled. 'Well I'm pleased I passed the test. Have the Poles come up with anything more on Winograd?'

'Not a lot sir. It seems he volunteered for the 4th Polish Parachute Battalion a couple of months ago while serving in a Polish tank brigade stationed down in the Scottish Borders. He came highly recommended, but the very nature of the arrival of most of the Poles in Britain means that there isn't much of a paper trail. I saw Major Kaminski this morning and he was at pains to emphasise how much trouble the Poles take to screen anyone whose loyalties are suspect. It seems they have a vetting and detention centre on the island of Bute, but there was nothing about Winograd that raised suspicions in anyone who knew him.'

Bob sat back. 'But despite that, we are now fairly sure that Winograd was a pilot, and that somebody was able to train him on the cockpit layout of a new and, until fairly recently, supposedly secret aircraft? Is there anything more we can do?'

'I've talked to a contact in MI11 in London, sir, and it seems that it's the norm for the Polish Army in Britain to look after its own security. Unless we think it's important enough to make a case to the Polish Government in Exile in London, then we must stay at arm's-length. The Poles will continue to see what they can find out about him, but I'm not sure how much more there would be, even if we had the resources to pursue it ourselves. I know that Major Kaminski is deeply unhappy about what has happened, which he feels reflects badly on him personally, so he's certainly not going to allow it to be dropped without a thorough job being done.'

'Fair enough,' said Bob. 'What's next on your agenda?'

'Sergeant Bennett and I have some reports to catch up on this afternoon, sir. Then over the weekend we are going to make ourselves unpopular with unannounced visits at RAF Drem, RAF East Fortune, RAF Lennoxlove and RAF Macmerry, all in East Lothian. Sometimes people let their guard down a little over the weekend, which makes it a good time to visit.'

Bob had been trying not to think about the large and growing pile of paperwork on his own desk, but after the flight lieutenant departed in the direction of the office he shared with Sergeant Bennett, Bob settled down to the part of the job he was least looking forward to.

Other than a few minutes spent in surprisingly cordial discussion with Major Miller, who put his head around Bob's office door in the middle of the afternoon, Bob worked solidly on his paperwork until he realised he needed to head back to his accommodation at RAF Turnhouse to smarten himself up for dinner.

CHAPTER SEVEN

As they drove along Princes Street, Bob tried to see the time on the clock on top of the North British Hotel, but it had got far too dark and in the blackout the clock wasn't illuminated. Not that it would have been the best guide anyway, he remembered, as the hotel clock was traditionally set three minutes fast to allow passengers a better chance of catching their trains in nearby Waverley Station. 'Are you going to want picking up and running back to Turnhouse later, sir?' Private Jenkins had stopped the car in front of the hotel's grand Princes Street entrance.

'No thanks, Taffy. I'll make my own way back. You have a Friday night off. It's the least I can do after last night.'

'Thank you, sir.'

Monique was sipping a drink in the hotel bar when Bob was shown through to join her. 'The effect is better now you're out of the rain, Bob, and aren't carrying that umbrella. You do look very smart.'

'And you look ravishing, as ever, Monique. I take it you still want me to call you "Monique"?'

'Flattery will get you anywhere, Bob. And yes, for reasons I will explain to you, I would prefer it if you referred to me as Monique Dubois.'

Monique looked around the busy bar. 'It might be best if we go through to the dining room I've booked, Bob. It's a bit crowded in here for a private discussion. Can you get yourself a drink, and a gin and tonic for me?'

The room turned out to have a comfortable seating area at one end, and a small dining table set for two at the other. The window was heavily curtained to comply with the blackout regulations, and lighting was subdued.

'This is all very romantic,' said Bob.

'More importantly,' said Monique, 'it's also very private. I hope you're not too hungry yet. I've arranged for dinner to be served a little later. That should give us more than enough time to get business out of the way before we eat. It also ensures we don't have waiting staff coming in while we are trying to talk.'

'That's fine by me,' said Bob.

They sat down, each taking one of the sofas that had been arranged either side of a low table.

Monique took a sip from her drink and smiled as she looked across at Bob. 'Jack Callaghan asked me to remind you that you agreed to visit him and Flora. I take it that Flora is his wife?'

'You visited Jack Callaghan this afternoon? Yes, Flora is his wife. I attended their wedding back in the days when it was the norm to form an honour guard of policemen holding truncheons outside the church after a policeman's wedding. It was the first time some of my colleagues had ever been in a Catholic church, and you could almost see them checking one another to make sure they'd not grown horns and a tail because of it. Jack was popular enough, and thick-skinned enough, to overcome the bigotry, but it wasn't nice to see it so near the surface.'

'Yes, I thought I should thank him for releasing Thompson and Smith to you yesterday. I also asked for his help in putting what we are trying to achieve in Hillington on a slightly more open-and-above-board basis, while still keeping it completely secure. That led to a meeting later this afternoon with the head of security at the Rolls-Royce factory in Hillington.'

'As I understand it,' said Bob, 'the aim is to lead the Germans to believe that Geoffrey Smith, assuming you still want me to use that name for him, has sabotaged the factory. Given the size of the place, I can't see how that's possible.'

'German intelligence, or the Abwehr, briefed Smith using out-of-date aerial photographs. According to them, the best way to sabotage the factory is to attack the power house, which forms part of the most north eastern block of the factory, the one nearest Renfrew and the River Clyde. What they failed to consider was that as well as generating its own, the factory can also draw electricity from, or feed it into, the municipal supply. That means there are a series of transformers in the same area. We are going to try to make it look like Smith has successfully destroyed part of that block.'

'But even if he did, surely it would only disrupt production for a very short time? I'd have thought nothing short of a large and very well targeted air raid, of the sort the Luftwaffe are incapable of mounting these days, could damage a factory of that size sufficiently to make much real difference?'

'You'd have thought so, wouldn't you?' said Monique. 'But that's what the Abwehr sent Smith here to do, and far be it from us to argue with their reasoning. I've got some very good deception and camouflage people coming up to Glasgow tomorrow, some of the same people who built dummy airfields to divert the Luftwaffe during the Battle of Britain. The security people at Hillington will show them round, and we will try to come up with a plan to simulate sabotage. I know German overflights are rare these days, but we think the Abwehr will get the Luftwaffe to try to photograph the factory after Geoffrey Smith radios to say he has damaged it. They've recently moved a few examples of a very high altitude reconnaissance aircraft, the Junkers Ju 86P, to one of their bases in Norway. We think that if they have a go with one of these, we can get the RAF to leave it alone without raising German suspicions that it was too easy. We're also considering how to get press reports about the sabotage out in a way that doesn't raise alarm at home but gives the Abwehr more reason to believe that Geoffrey is telling the truth.'

'Surely there are other Abwehr agents over here who can report independently on whether Smith has actually sabotaged the factory?'

'No, there aren't, and we know that with absolute certainty. Every single German spy they have tried to establish in Britain has either been imprisoned, executed, or in many cases has been turned to work for MI5, the Security Service, against the Abwehr.'

'But you can't know that for certain,' said Bob. 'You

can't prove a negative. You can't know that one hasn't been slipped in without anyone noticing.'

'Actually, we can, Bob. The reason for that is also the reason why I was allowed to book this private room for our discussion. I was quite busy before heading out to Northolt for the flight up here. Only a very small number of people are ever told what I am about to tell you. There was a meeting in London early this morning between your boss at MI11, Commodore Cunningham and my boss several times removed, the head of MI5. Also present were the head of MI6 or the Secret Intelligence Service, and the man who all three of them report to, Major General Sir Peter Maitland, the Director of Military Intelligence at the War Office.'

'I've met him,' said Bob. 'He tried to force me to take this job when all that was needed was something a little nearer to "please".'

'Well, this morning they agreed to let you into a very select little club. It's a club I only joined myself a couple of weeks ago. It seems they decided after our little escapade with King George that I could be trusted with the crown jewels, despite my chequered history.'

'You make this sound very melodramatic,' said Bob.

'Oh, it gets better,' said Monique. 'One of the conditions attached to membership is that you must in future avoid doing anything that causes the slightest possibility of your falling into enemy hands. In your case that means no familiarisation flights in bombers bound for Germany, or that sort of thing.'

Bob laughed. 'Come on, Monique, you are making this sound like something out of a John Buchan novel.'

'I'm being deadly serious, and I chose those words carefully.'

'You are, aren't you?' said Bob. 'Well, go on, I'd die of curiosity if we didn't finish this conversation.'

'You can't say I didn't warn you. First, though, could you go and get our drinks topped up? How about a bottle of Champagne as it's on MI5? Then we can pour our own.'

'I do hope it's better champagne than they serve in the officers' wardroom at HMS *Lochinvar*, where we took Geoffrey Smith last night.'

'I very much think it will be,' said Monique.

Bob returned with two glasses, while a waiter brought in an ice bucket, a cloth and a bottle of, according to the price list, very fine champagne.

Monique got up to check the waiter had closed the door behind him on departing. 'And before you ask, Bob, I have checked the room for any signs of hidden microphones. The trailing wires would be a bit of a giveaway, so I'm sure we are secure.'

'I wasn't going to ask.'

'What I am about to tell you is classified as Ultra Secret, Bob. I hope you've never heard that term before, because "Ultra" is a code word that applies to a particular type of intelligence whose existence we can't reveal to the Germans. The story starts in the 1920s when the German armed services started to rely on a type of electro-mechanical cipher machine to encode and decode their messages. In theory this was extremely secure. Over time a family of what became known as Enigma machines evolved, with the German Navy using a differently configured machine to the Army and Luftwaffe, and the secret service or Abwehr using a different type of machine to do the same job.'

'I'm guessing it didn't turn out to be as secure as they thought?'

'That's right. The breakthrough was made by the Polish Cipher Bureau in the early 1930s. In 1939 the Poles briefed the British and French on what they had discovered and passed over the results of work they had done to reverse-engineer some of the Enigma machines. On the outbreak of war, the Germans launched a new and much more complex, and as a result much more secure, version of the Enigma machine, but thanks to the head start given to us by the Poles, the Germans' coded messages were soon being decrypted in England. Within the last year, other German communications systems have been compromised in the same way. The result is that although it takes some effort at our end, a large proportion of what the Germans are saying to one another, believing it to be completely secure, can be read and understood by us.'

Bob took a sip of his champagne. 'And the security we attach to Ultra is because we don't want the Germans to know we are looking over their shoulders all the time?'

'That's right, Bob. They could easily change their systems and MI6, who have the lead responsibility for all this within the intelligence community, would have to start again from scratch. This sensitivity means we must be exceptionally careful about how we react to information gathered by Ultra. For example, we knew the Abwehr was planning to land an agent in Aberdeenshire at the end of last month from radio traffic between their Oslo office and Berlin. We knew his codename, "Adler" or "Eagle", and a little of his background, and we knew that he had been trained in the use of explosives. We had even been able to read his training and test transmissions as he was taught Morse code.'

'Was that how you caught him?' asked Bob.

'No, that's the point,' said Monique. 'We couldn't do anything to reveal we knew he was coming, so we simply stepped up security in the area in a "routine" way. If we'd been obviously waiting for him, it might have alerted the Abwehr to a breach in their security. In the event, he landed miles from where he had intended and it didn't matter anyway. The first thing he did when he landed was knock on a farmer's door and ask him to phone the police. The second thing he did was ask the police to contact MI5.'

'And that's why you are so confident there are no active German agents in Britain?' asked Bob.

'Correct,' said Monique. 'We know when each one is being trained, we see them coming, and we know when they have arrived. Enough have agreed to work for MI5 to allow us to paint whatever picture we want for their handlers in the Abwehr. The Germans are getting a huge amount of intelligence from their agents in Britain, but it is intelligence that we have very carefully prepared to lead them to believe a particular version of events.'

'That is a pretty powerful weapon. Hang on, though. You and I both know that up until last month the Abwehr had three active spies in Britain. Major Sinclair was in regular radio contact with them, and they had also placed someone in King George VI's household to pass on information about the king's movements and plans. We also had your old friend Ferdi busily killing people in Oban until the Soviets got to him.'

'I can only tell you what I was told when I raised the same point, Bob. It seems that the group within MI6 who were trying to promote a peace deal with Admiral Canaris were sufficiently influential to be able to cover up evidence of Sinclair's activities, and the existence of the other two. Apparently, Sinclair went far beyond what they were expecting when he arranged the German commando raid, but it would seem that two senior members of MI6 were so committed to the peace process that they didn't take action when they realised what Sinclair was doing, and Ferdi's activities were also seen by them as being justified by the end they were seeking. Thankfully Sinclair had never been admitted to the Ultra club, so he couldn't tell the Germans anything about it.'

'But the two senior officers were privy to Ultra?'

'They were, and they were ideally placed to suppress intelligence arriving by that means that was relevant to the operation. I believe that when everything unravelled a few people had sleepless nights fearing that Ultra itself might have been compromised, but it seems to be business as usual as far as the Germans are concerned. Apparently the two men involved set limits on their treasonous actions but they could never be trusted again. I don't think it is a coincidence that two senior members of MI6, presumably the same two, died in unfortunate accidents quite soon afterwards. One fell under a tube train and another appears to have fallen from a 5th floor window of a London hotel. That should tell you all you need to know about the importance with which security around Ultra is treated.'

'My God. I was told that some of those involved had suffered serious consequences, but it never crossed my mind just how serious.'

'Let's not dwell on it, Bob. While I think about it, do you want to accompany me on the visit to Hillington tomorrow? Another outcome of the meeting this morning was an agreement that MI5 and MI11 would work closely together on the deception plan.'

'I'd love to,' said Bob. 'What's the eventual aim of all of this? Geoffrey Smith told me last night that he would be returning to Germany. Is that what lies behind the pretence of sabotaging the factory?'

'Yes, it is. The Abwehr are poor employers and have done next to nothing for the agents they've sent over. In the early days, when I was sent over by them myself in September 1940, for example, they simply told their agents that once the invasion had taken place they would be able to return to Germany. When that was no longer credible, they promised submarine extractions to the people they sent over, but never lifted a finger to put them in place. They've promised the same to Geoffrey Smith and they've also promised him a large amount of money when he gets back. He does have a fallback arrangement, however, which would see him join a merchant vessel bound for Lisbon, then jump ship there.'

'And that's why you are keen to ensure he doesn't know the name you normally use within the Security Service in London?'

'That's right. We believe he's genuinely on our side, but don't want him to have any information that would cause damage if he revealed it, willingly or unwillingly, to the

Abwehr once he gets back to Germany.' Monique looked at her watch. 'Perhaps it's time we had some dinner? Is there any champagne left?'

'Can I just raise something with you, first, Monique?'

'What's that?'

Bob told her about Sergeant Winograd's apparent attempt to steal a Mosquito from RAF Leuchars. 'I rather assumed that if he was working for anyone, he was working for the Germans. I have no idea how he was instructed in the start-up procedures for a Mosquito, but at the very least it would have needed someone with a good set of photographs of the interior of the cockpit. From what you tell me, however, there are no German agents in the country who could have done that.'

'That's right.'

'Which raises the question of who he was working for and where he was going to fly the aircraft to. All he had with him was a local Ordnance Survey map, which frankly seems a little odd.'

Monique placed her empty champagne glass on the table between them. 'What's the range of the aircraft you think he was trying to steal?'

'I'm not sure. Far enough to get to Berlin and back, at least.'

'Here's a thought,' said Monique, 'I'd need to check on a map, but it can't be much more than twice as far to Moscow as it is to Berlin. I've heard the Mosquito is something of a wonder weapon. Perhaps the Soviets have heard the same thing and want a better look at one?'

'You think the Soviet secret service, the NKVD, might have tried to steal one?'

'It has to be a possibility, doesn't it? They are our allies, but you and I both know they interpret that flexibly. And before you ask, Bob, as far as I know, we don't have the same window onto NKVD operations as we have onto Abwehr operations. Now, it's about time we had some dinner. I took the liberty of ordering for both of us earlier.'

CHAPTER EIGHT

Dinner had been thoroughly enjoyable. Over coffee, Monique asked how Bob was finding MI11.

He sat back on the sofa they were sharing. 'With the great insight afforded by five days in post, most of which were spent away from the office, my first impression is that it's remarkably varied. I suppose with hindsight that running a training unit did have an element of repetition about it, especially as I wasn't meant to be doing any of the flying or training myself.

'It's very early days yet, but I've not yet had cause to think I made a wrong decision in taking the post. The skill I'm going to have to develop is trusting my team leaders to get on and do their jobs. I went with my RAF team up to Leuchars yesterday. It's right that I get sufficiently involved to develop an understanding of what the work entails. But I did get the sense that the team leader would have preferred it if I'd been somewhere else. I tried to avoid heading off at any tangents, but I think he was relieved when I disappeared for a flight in a Mosquito with the squadron commander, who I flew with in 1940. By the time I was back you were trying to get hold of me on the phone, so he was rid of me entirely.

'My problem is wanting to get stuck in and sort things out myself. I heard this morning that my deputy, in my absence yesterday, had agreed that my army team should head up to the Commando Basic Training Centre at Achnacarry Castle, north of Fort William, to investigate a suspicious death. Entirely right, but my first reaction was to think that I should have been involved in the investigation. It sounds intriguing. The dead man is a Belgian and there's an added complication because some of those currently being trained there are Germans. It was news to me that we train Germans to be commandos and my first instinct was to abandon my in-tray and get a driver to take me up there. I think perhaps I've still got some growing up to do.'

Monique laughed.

'How about you?' asked Bob. 'How does being "not quite as small a cog in the wheel" feel?'

'It's early days for me too. This thing in Glasgow is my first real opportunity to show I've got what it takes to operate at a more senior level. However barmy the whole thing sounds, what we are trying to do does have the potential to disrupt the Abwehr even more than we've managed thus far. Smith and Thompson getting locked up was the absolute last thing I needed. I really am grateful, Bob.' Monique smiled and placed her hand on his.

'How grateful?' he asked.

'Grateful enough to suggest we abandon what's left of the coffee and head up to my room. I don't think there's any champagne left, but I can live without any more.'

If dinner had been enjoyable, what followed was even better. Afterwards they lay together in Monique's bed in the darkened room.

Bob could tell Monique was still awake. 'I thought about telephoning you, you know. A couple of times when I was coming down to London.'

'You should have done.'

'I was afraid you'd tell me to get lost.'

'Why would I do that?'

'Things were a bit strained that last night in Dunrobin Castle. I understand that it sounded like I was saying I thought that you'd betrayed me, and that really wasn't what I meant. But it was too late to unsay what I'd said. You came out with something about a couple of enjoyable nights together not being a basis for announcing our engagement in The Times, and if I'm honest I felt pretty rejected.'

'I'm sorry, Bob. I thought you'd go back to training pilots and I really didn't think our paths would cross again. For what it's worth, I'm glad they have and I'm glad you twisted my arm into coming up to Scotland, though I'd probably have had to come anyway.'

'If Smith and Thompson hadn't been picked up by the police and you had come up to Scotland, would you have called me?'

'An honest answer? I don't know. Your believing I would go behind your back within MI5 was hurtful. I've been hurt enough times in the past not to want to go back for seconds.'

'We're both sorry then. How are we going to make it up to one another?'

'Have you anything in mind?'

Bob reached out in the darkness and felt her arm. She was lying on her back. He gently trailed his fingertips up to her shoulder, before moving them down her body. 'Perhaps.'

Monique rolled over and embraced him.

Bob's watch told him it was still early. He lay back, thinking that there could be few better places to find himself at this time on a Saturday morning. He could hear from Monique's breathing that she was still soundly asleep in the darkness beside him.

That changed instantly when there was a loud double knock on the door. Bob walked over to the door, switching on the room light as he got there and putting on a dressing gown that had been hanging on the back of the door. He glanced round to see Monique sitting up in bed with the bedding modestly pulled up around her and a gun in her hand. He made a mental note to ask how she managed the trick of having a gun quite so readily available in bed, a trick he'd seen her perform at least twice before. Now he had a gun of his own, it was perhaps something he should learn. He also tried to remember whether, during the few nights they had spent together, there had ever been an occasion when they hadn't been awakened by a knock on the door.

The knock was repeated.

Bob opened the door a little, standing so as to obscure the view of the interior from the visitor. 'Oh, hello Lieutenant Dixon. This had better be really good.'

'I'm sorry, sir,' said the lieutenant. 'It's not good at all. I took a call from Sergeant Potter a little while ago. It seems that Captain Bell has been found dead at Achnacarry. Sergeant Potter rang me because my telephone number at HMS *Lochinvar* is on his emergency contact list. He asked me to let you know.'

Bob made a mental note to ensure his teams knew his out-of-hours contact number, then remembered that it wouldn't have been of much use on this occasion.

'Dead? What do you mean?'

'Apparently the sergeant last saw the captain early yesterday evening. Then his body was found in the early hours of this morning. It seems someone had bashed his head in with something hard and heavy.'

'Look, wait for me in the lobby, will you, I'll be down in a couple of minutes.'

Bob walked back over to the bed.

'Let me guess,' said Monique, 'something's come up?'

'The leader of my army team has been attacked and killed at Achnacarry.'

'I'm sorry, Bob.'

'It means I'm going to have to go up there myself. Please don't take it as showing any lack of interest if I don't come with you to Hillington today. And I've no idea how long I'll be gone. Can I contact you here at the hotel?'

'No, I'm moving over to Glasgow today. If you need to get in touch, try one of these numbers.' Monique passed him a card on which she had written a Glasgow number and a Whitehall number.

'Thanks,' said Bob, moving to kiss her.

Monique held up a hand to prevent him. 'Don't you have someone waiting for you in the lobby?' she asked.

'How did you find me?' asked Bob. He was in the back of the staff car with Lieutenant Dixon. It was 7.30 a.m. and just beginning to get light despite the rain that was still falling.

Dixon waved towards the driver. 'Private Jenkins here told me where he had dropped you yesterday evening, sir. When I couldn't find you at the officers' mess at Turnhouse this morning, the hotel seemed the obvious place to look. The drivers are billeted at Craigiehall, so it was easy enough to raise Jenkins once I'd spoken to Sergeant Potter.'

Bob sat back and watched a dismal Saturday morning Edinburgh slide damply past the window of the car. 'Michael, have we ever lost anyone before?'

'Not that I'm aware of, sir, not anyone based in Edinburgh at least.'

Joyce Stuart had locked all Bob's papers in his secure cabinet after he had left the previous afternoon, and as a result his office was the tidiest he had yet seen it. He was able to reach Sergeant Gilbert Potter on the telephone at Achnacarry Castle without too much delay. 'Hello Sergeant, it's Group Captain Sutherland here. I understand Captain Bell has been killed?'

'Yes, sir. You probably know that we drove up on Thursday, sir. We didn't arrive until late afternoon and set to work talking to men who might have known something about the murder that took place the previous evening. We carried on with interviews yesterday. At around 5 p.m. Captain Bell said he was going to take a walk to get a better feel for the area before it got dark, which gave him over an hour as the weather was good. He's a keen ornithologist and took his binoculars with him. I worked through notes and statements for a while, then went for a drink in the sergeant's mess. I expected to find Captain Bell back in the office we are using when I returned but didn't. I suppose I wasn't too surprised, it had been a long day and I thought he might have headed off to the officers' mess.'

'Did you see him at all last night?' asked Bob.

'No, sir. Then in the early hours of this morning they found his body in the river here, during a night exercise. He was caught up in a net they hang for safety reasons downstream from a rope bridge used for training. His body appears to have been bashed about by the river a bit, sir. We initially thought he'd died because of an obvious head injury, but the medical officer now says that was caused after death. Apparently, he died because he was stabbed, like the first victim.'

'How are you doing, Sergeant?' asked Bob.

'It's a bit of a shock, of course, sir. I've lost friends before, in France and at Dunkirk. But there you expected it. I didn't expect anything like this here, even though there had already been a murder.'

'I expect Major Miller to be in the office shortly, Sergeant, and will leave a message to ask him to contact you about arrangements for Captain Bell's body, and to inform his next of kin. I will be leaving shortly with Lieutenant Dixon, Petty Officer MacDonald and Private Jenkins to come up and join you at Achnacarry. Which way did you drive up?'

'We came up via Stirling and Crianlarich, sir. It's a bloody long way on not very good roads, and it was worse because there was a problem with the Ballachulish Ferry and we had to take a twenty-mile detour. It may be a little shorter and more straightforward to come up through Perth and cut across from Dalwhinnie, though that means taking the ferry over the Queensferry Passage.'

'Sergeant, could you do some asking around today to see if you can find anyone who saw Captain Bell after you did? Don't take any chances, though. I'd prefer it if you kept to public places.'

The sergeant laughed. 'Thank you, sir, but right now there's nothing I'd like more than the chance to grapple with whoever killed Captain Bell!'

Bob had only met Sergeant Potter briefly on Monday and remembered a formidably large man. 'Seriously, Sergeant, I don't want to lose two members of my unit in my first week here. It sounds to me as if whoever we are dealing with isn't going to think twice about killing again. Take care, and that's a direct order. On a separate note, could you let the commanding officer there know we are coming, please, and find suitable accommodation? And can you make whatever arrangements are necessary to ensure we have access to anywhere we might want to go?'

'Yes, sir,' said Potter.

The next call was one that Bob had never imagined having to make. It took MI11's duty officer in Whitehall what seemed an age to put him through to his boss's home telephone.

Commodore Maurice Cunningham picked up the phone himself. Bob realised he had no idea if the commodore had a wife or children at home.

'I'm sorry to disturb you at home over the weekend, sir.'

'I'm sure this isn't a social call, Bob. What's happened?'

Bob quickly told Cunningham about Captain Bell's death and outlined the circumstance as far as he knew them.

'What do you intend to do?'

'I'm going up to Achnacarry this morning. Once I'm there I'm going to find out who killed Cecil Bell. I have to admit I barely knew the man, but I owe it to him to do everything possible to bring his killer to justice.'

'Are you sure you feel up to this, Bob? You've not been in post a week yet and this is a big ask. I can fly some of my team up from London to conduct the investigation, if that helps. Given the circumstances, I can come up myself if you prefer.'

'Thank you for the offer, sir, but I most certainly feel up to it. Unless you're about to relieve me of my duties then I will be leading the search for Captain Bell's killer.'

'Take it easy, Bob. I wasn't trying to question your ability, simply to offer any support you think you might need.'

'Sorry, sir. You'll have gathered that I take the captain's loss very personally. Look, I need to get moving.'

'Make sure you take a good team with you and be careful. Keep me in touch, will you, Bob?'

'Yes, sir, of course.'

Bob's predecessor had shared the compulsion that army officers seemed to have for very large wall maps, and Bob walked over and ran his finger along the route Sergeant Potter had just suggested. Bob had considered alternatives to the long drive, but none had anything to commend them. The office had a current edition of Bradshaw's Guide, which revealed that a train from Glasgow to Spean Bridge was a theoretical option, but not an attractive one. Bob had even wondered whether he might be able to fly from Turnhouse to RAF Connel, north of Oban, before deciding that was also highly impractical. He looked at his watch.

Lieutenant Dixon had taken one of the cars to collect his kit and Petty Officer Macdonald from HMS *Lochinvar*. Bob had sent Private Jenkins to his quarters in one of the hutted areas at Craigiehall to pack a bag and get the car they'd take with them fuelled up. As soon as he was back, Bob would get Jenkins to run him for a quick shower and shave in the officers' mess at RAF Turnhouse, where he could also pack a bag.

With the four men and their belongings, plus the rifle and two Sten submachine guns and ammunition that Bob had instructed should be issued, the car looked as if it might be a little crowded.

Before leaving, Bob remembered to leave a note for Flight Lieutenant Buchan, suggesting that he ask RAF Leuchars whether a Mosquito could fly to the Soviet Union, and check with Major Kaminski whether the Polish security people had found any Soviet links in Sergeant Winograd's background.

CHAPTER NINE

As a child, Bob had always loved it when his parents took him and his younger sister, Pearl, to Fife on the old ferry that plied its trade across the Queensferry Passage. The ferry Bob remembered was a ship called the *Dundee*, a paddle steamer which to his boyhood eyes offered the promise of romance and adventure in equal measure. In 1934, after Bob had moved to Glasgow to join the police, the service across the Queensferry Passage had been transformed with the arrival on the route of two large new vehicle ferries, *Robert the Bruce* and *Queen Margaret*.

This was Bob's first crossing on one of the now eight-year-old 'new' ferries. The *Robert the Bruce* was a fine vessel capable of carrying cars and other vehicles on the main deck, plus large numbers of passengers. It was operated from a high-level bridge, set as if on stilts above the main deck. After they had boarded, Bob found himself thinking that progress was all very well, but while the newer vessels certainly seemed to operate a more effective service, he still felt a faint tinge of regret that he wasn't standing on the deck of the *Dundee*, now kept as a standby vessel for the crossing.

Private Jenkins had driven straight to the head of the short queue of vehicles on the slipway in Queensferry, claiming military priority, and they had been the first to drive over the ramp onto the side of the ferry. This had allowed them to position in a way that ensured they would also be first ashore on the other side.

The weather was so miserable it was barely possible to see from one side of the river to the other, and the top of the Forth Bridge, just to the east, disappeared into the cloud. Bob shivered and went back to sit in the car. When they reached the slipway on the far side, Private Jenkins headed north along the A90, guided by the map reading of Petty Officer MacDonald, who was sitting in the front passenger seat.

It was Lieutenant Dixon who voiced the thought in Bob's head. 'Removing all the road signs must have seemed a good idea when there was a real chance of a German invasion back in 1940. But it must cause huge problems for our own people.'

'That's true, sir,' said Petty Officer MacDonald. 'I know the area a little but think how confusing this is to the Polish Army in Scotland, although by now they will know the place pretty well too. And if the US Army start turning up in large numbers, it will be total chaos.'

'Speaking as a foreigner in Scotland myself, sir,' said Private Jenkins, 'a few road signs wouldn't go amiss. Though this place looks very much like home, apart from not being in a valley. Where are we?'

They were travelling through an area that Bob thought

probably looked grim on a nice day, and today was a long way from being a nice day. Rows of smoking chimneys darkened the skies even further, while in the background, just about visible through the smoke, was the unmistakable sight of colliery winding gear.

'We're skirting the edge of Cowdenbeath,' said Petty Officer MacDonald. 'We're in the Fife coalfield, so, yes, I suppose it must look like a lot of places in south Wales.'

After passing through the equally dark and smoky village of Kelty, the scenery improved even if the weather didn't. Bob must have dozed, sitting in the back of the car, because the next place he recognised was the town of Perth.

Lieutenant Dixon saw he was awake. 'Sir, what do you want to do when we arrive?'

'That's a good question,' said Bob. 'I understand that Captain Bell's body was found in the river. I think the most pressing priority is for us to try to work out where he was killed, which was presumably either where he was found or upstream of it.' Bob pulled out the Ordnance Survey one-inch map of the Ben Nevis & Fort William area he had picked up in the office. 'According to the map, the River Arkaig is only a mile and a half long, flowing from Loch Arkaig in the west to Loch Lochy in the east. While any evidence is still likely to be reasonably fresh, I would like us to start by walking up the banks of the river from where his body was found towards Loch Arkaig, to see what turns up.'

'Can I see, sir?' asked Lieutenant Dixon, reaching for the map. He braced himself in the corner of the back seat against the movement of the car. 'Typical. I once heard an army officer define a battle as "an event that invariably takes place at a point on the ground at which four map sheets meet". I was wondering how extensive Loch Arkaig is, but I see it falls off the northern edge of the map. It's pretty big, though.'

Bob pulled another map out of his overnight bag. 'You get more of a feel from the sheet to the north. The loch seems to be about a dozen miles long, with not much more than a pier and a school at the western end. But let's remember that Captain Bell was out for an evening walk, so he couldn't have gone very far.'

'That's true, sir.'

Bob continued, 'Once we've done that, to my mind the highest priority will be for you and me to talk to Sergeant Potter, in as much detail as possible, about what he and Captain Bell had done and who they had spoken to since their arrival. There are two reasons for that. The first is to ensure we know what ground they covered, and what they didn't cover, in their investigation of the first murder. That will allow us to pick up the threads and pursue that investigation with as little delay as possible. Perhaps more importantly, it seems reasonable to consider the possibility that the two murders were committed by the same person, and equally reasonable to consider the possibility that Captain Bell was murdered because the killer thought that Bell had discovered something of value about the first murder. I know nothing about the first murder yet, and precious little about the second, so can't really speculate beyond that. Assumptions can be dangerous, of course, so despite everything I've just said, I would like to try to keep an open mind.'

'It would be quite a coincidence if the murders were unrelated, sir,' said Dixon.

'That's very true, Lieutenant. While you and I are talking to Sergeant Potter, I'd be grateful if you two gentlemen in the front could try to find out whether anyone saw Captain Bell after he told Sergeant Gordon he was going for a walk at about 5 p.m. yesterday evening. I asked Sergeant Gordon to ask around carefully, but take no chances and stay in public areas. The two of you will be able to watch one-another's backs so will have a better chance of doing a thorough job.'

'Yes, sir,' said Petty Officer MacDonald.

'While we are talking about personal security, I told Sergeant Potter that I didn't want to lose any more members of my unit in my first week in the job, and it's something I'd like to repeat here and now. I have no doubt that whoever killed Captain Bell and, perhaps, the earlier victim, will be prepared to kill again. Once we arrive, the four of us and Sergeant Potter are likely to be right at the top of the killer's list of potential targets. That's why I wanted the Sten guns and the rifle with us. I see the three of you are also wearing your service pistols, which is good, and I've got a concealed pistol. But from what I was told at lunch yesterday, the Commando Basic Training Centre goes through more live ammunition than any other army unit in Scotland, so we really do need to be careful.'

North of Perth they followed the Inverness road thorough a series of villages including Dunkeld and then Pitlochry, where they were able to find a cafe that was open for a late breakfast and a cup of tea. Further on, the landscape became wilder and, once off the A9 and onto the narrow road that headed west towards Spean Bridge, progress became even slower.

Bob must have dozed again. It was Petty Officer MacDonald who woke him. 'Hello, I think we must be getting close.'

'Where are we?' said Bob.

'We've passed Spean Bridge, sir, and are just approaching a place marked on the map as Lochy. The road crosses the Caledonian Canal here, and everything beyond it is what they call the Protected Area, where you need a special pass even if you live there. I think that explains the checkpoint. The good news is that the rain's stopped and it looks like the sun might be trying to break through.'

The car was waved down by one of two military policemen standing at a barrier across the road. Bob wound down his window and showed his pass. 'Hello, I'm Group Captain Sutherland from Military Intelligence Section 11 in Edinburgh, and these are my colleagues. We are expected at the Commando Basic Training Centre at Achnacarry.'

The corporal who had stopped them looked at the pass Bob had offered and consulted a list on a clipboard. 'Yes, sir. Carry on.' He saluted as the car passed under the now raised barrier.

They followed a road that wound its way north above the western shore of what Bob's map revealed was Loch Lochy. Where the road descended towards a few houses clustered around the end of a bay that seemed to be full of boats, they came to metal gates on their left, guarded by more military policemen.

As they drove along the access road to Achnacarry, Bob caught a glimpse of a church in the woods to his right.

'Good God, look at that!' Petty Officer MacDonald

pointed above them and to their left, where Bob could see strings of men in khaki swarming up a rock face.

After they had topped one last rise, Bob could see Achnacarry laid out in front of them. In the background was a fine-looking mansion that seemed to his eyes to be Victorian or earlier, while a little distance away some cottages and ancillary buildings lay either side of the road they were following. But most of what must have once been the parkland in front of Achnacarry Castle itself was now packed with numerous Nissen huts, set around a parade ground. Not for the first time Bob found himself wondering how much of Scotland's beautiful countryside was being overrun by temporary wartime structures, erected in haste with little room for aesthetics. 'I'm not sure Sergeant Bennett would approve of the additions the commandos have made to the castle,' he said.

Petty Officer MacDonald laughed. 'No, sir. I think if he had his way whoever invented Nissen huts would be taken out and strung up from the nearest tree.'

They had reached a pair of gates that led to a tree-lined drive, now also lined on one side with the semi-cylindrical Nissen huts. This turned right off the road they had been following to approach the castle itself. Again, they were stopped by military policemen before being allowed to pass under yet another barrier.

'You know, with all this security, someone must have seen where Captain Bell went last night,' said Bob.

'Bloody hell!' said Private Jenkins. 'It looks like you might have a few more deaths to investigate, sir.' Jenkins brought the car to a halt in the drive. To one side, opposite some of the Nissen huts, was a row of graves. Each was formed by an apparently freshly dug strip of earth, surrounded by a rectangle of rocks, and each had a wooden cross at the end furthest from the drive.

'Those crosses have all got signs on,' said Petty Officer MacDonald. 'That nearest one says, "This man showed himself on the skyline". Then there's, "This man fired a 2-inch mortar under trees" and "This man advanced over the top of cover".'

'They're not real, are they, sir?' asked Private Jenkins. 'That one says, "This man thought his camouflage perfect".'

Despite the circumstances, Bob found it hard to suppress a smile. 'I think you're right, Taffy. I suspect they may be designed to make new trainees arriving at Achnacarry realise that it's a pretty serious business here.'

CHAPTER TEN

Lieutenant Colonel White must have been warned of their approach, because he stood waiting for his visitors outside the front door of Achnacarry Castle with another officer and Sergeant Potter. The lieutenant colonel was a slightly portly man with an impressive row of medal ribbons, which Bob noted included a number from the Great War. 'Good afternoon, Group Captain Sutherland, and welcome to Achnacarry. I see you were admiring the graves.'

'They do have good shock value,' said Bob, before introducing his men.

The second officer was introduced as the camp adjutant, Captain Sanderson.

'We are bursting at the seams right now, Group Captain,' said White. 'Do you mind sharing a room with your lieutenant in the castle? We've also allocated a room for your two men and Sergeant Potter in the other ranks' staff accommodation. I'd be happy to give you a tour of the centre if you like. Do you want a chance to settle in first?'

'Would it be possible for us to meet later, Colonel?' asked Bob. 'I'd like to start immediately by looking at where Captain Bell's body was found, and then dividing into two groups to walk back up both sides of the river to see if there's any chance of finding where he was killed. The longer we leave it, the less chance there is of finding any worthwhile evidence that might still exist.'

If the colonel was affronted that his invitation had been rebuffed, he showed no sign of it. 'Of course, sir. I can show you round whenever you like. I would be pleased, however, if you and the lieutenant would agree to be my guests later tonight for the best show that Achnacarry has to offer.'

Bob's doubts must have shown on his face. Lieutenant Colonel White laughed. 'Sorry, I could have phrased that better. We've got a night assault landing planned for tonight, down on Loch Lochy. It's the highlight of what we do here and offers the most realistic training available anywhere in the world. I'd be pleased if the two of you could join me as observers.'

'Yes, of course, we'd be delighted,' said Bob.

It was agreed that Bob and his men would take their overnight bags to the accommodation assigned to them, then reassemble outside the castle's front door.

Captain Sanderson led them through the busy camp. 'How many men have you got here?' asked Bob.

'As far as trainees are concerned, sir, we're at something over eight hundred other ranks and thirty officers at the moment, in four groups, though two of those groups are working closely together. We've also got a training centre staff of rather more than a hundred. It varies from month to month. At the moment two courses are overlapping for a few days, so until Monday we've got some of our latest arrivals in tents that we use as overspill accommodation, but that's hardly ideal given what the men here go through. Things will ease up on Monday when two of the groups complete their courses and leave.'

As Bob looked around he got a sense of relentless activity. Wherever he looked there were men training. One group he could see was doing physical exercises that seemed to entail six men lifting logs between them. More men were clambering over an assault course on ropes and nets set high in the canopy of the trees above them. A little more distantly, he could hear the sound of gunfire coming from the south and the west. 'They don't come here for a rest cure, do they?' he asked.

Captain Sanderson chuckled. 'Don't let anyone ever hear you asking that, sir,' he said. 'As well as what you can see we've got troops of men out rock climbing, on speed marches of up to 15 miles, and in the mountains fending for themselves for up to 36 hours at a time. We also train the men in weapons skills, using both allied and enemy weapons, in fieldcraft skills and living off the land, in unarmed combat, in small boat skills, in beach landings, and so on.'

'Do you have a high drop-out rate?' asked Bob.

'Yes, we do,' said Captain Sanderson. 'Every man who comes here is a volunteer, is recommended by his unit, and has passed an interview. But this is the toughest training we can devise, and quite a number find that it's not for them, or we find they are not for us.'

'What happens to them?' asked Bob.

'They are marked as "RTU", sir. It means they are returned to their home unit, with no shame involved. They pack their bag and get on the next train south from Spean Bridge.'

'Is that a walled garden?' asked Bob, pointing to a structure they were approaching to the right of the path.

'It is, sir,' said Sanderson. 'It's not much used for its original purpose now. We don't find much time to "dig for victory", I'm afraid.'

Bob looked round to find Sergeant Potter behind them. 'Where was Captain Bell's body found, sergeant?'

'Just down here, sir. There's a footbridge across the River Arkaig about a quarter of a mile down from the castle. This is the place.'

'That's right,' said Captain Sanderson. 'Just upstream from here, we missed it in the trees, is what we call the toggle bridge. It's a rope bridge made from the toggle-ropes that each man carries. We've got a few rites of passage here at Achnacarry and crossing the toggle bridge while explosives are being detonated in the water below is one of them. It's even more challenging at night. A few months ago, we had an incident when five men fell from the bridge into the river. Two of them drowned and their bodies were later found in Loch Lochy. After that we hung a grapple net from the footbridge, which is anchored to the bed of the river. Anyone going into the water from the toggle bridge, or who drops in from the death slide for that matter, now stands a much better chance of getting themselves out, even when the river's in spate.'

'How was the captain's body found?' asked Bob.

Captain Sanderson said, 'Most of what we do, we also

do at night, because that's when the men really need to be able to use their skills. In the early hours of this morning we had a group of men crossing the toggle bridge when one fell into the river. He was swept down to the grapple net, and climbed out, but then reported that he'd bumped into someone in the net. When we got the torches out, we found Captain Bell's body.'

Bob turned to Sergeant Potter. 'You told me that the medical officer had looked at Captain Bell's body. What did he find?'

'Yes, he did, sir,' said Sergeant Potter. 'He said that the cause of death was his being stabbed twice, once in an upwards direction into the stomach and once in the chest. The chest wound was deep enough to penetrate his heart, so was undoubtedly fatal. The medical officer also said that it looked like the captain had been bashed around by the river, and there were many other injuries on his body that seemed to have been caused after his death. That's why we initially thought he'd died from a severe head wound.'

'There are some rapids upstream, sir,' said Captain Sanderson, 'and the river's running quite fast following a lot of recent rain.'

Bob chose to walk back along the southern bank of the river with Captain Sanderson and Petty Officer MacDonald, and asked Lieutenant Dixon, Sergeant Potter and Private Jenkins to cross the footbridge and take the far bank of the river. 'Remember that we are looking for patches of beaten grass, blood, the captain's uniform cap or binoculars, or anything else that might be significant. And let's try to keep within sight of one-another.' Sergeant Potter and Petty Officer MacDonald were each carrying a

112

Sten gun, so Bob's division of his forces ensured each team had one available, just in case.

Bob reflected that in other circumstances the riverside walk back to Achnacarry Castle might have been considered idyllic. He'd not asked what the 'death slide' referred to by Captain Sanderson was, and now found there was no need, as he could watch for himself as men climbed high up a tree on his side of the river. Each in turn looped a short length of rope over a much longer rope tightly strung between the top of the tree and the foot of another on the far side of the river. Holding the two ends of the short loop of rope, each man then launched himself into nothingness and slid down to the far side.

'Do you fancy a try, sir?' asked Captain Sanderson.

'Even if we weren't here for a more serious purpose, Captain, there is no way you would ever get me up on that,' said Bob.

Just beyond the castle itself was the tail of a significant island.

Captain Sanderson said, 'The main stream is on this side of the island, sir. The river on the other side of it is rather narrower. A little further up there's a smaller island that's close to this bank, with the main stream flowing around the far side of it. As the water funnels past between the tail of one island and the head of the other there are some quite turbulent rapids. That's certainly the roughest stretch of water on the river. Given what was said about the injuries to Captain Bell's body, I would guess that he entered the river upstream of that point, and then went through the rapids.'

'Yes, that sounds likely,' said Bob. They made their way

past the smaller of the islands and reached a point at which the river turned sharply to the left. 'Hello, what's that?'

Captain Sanderson said, 'It's a weir, sir. I believe it was originally built in that dog-leg shape to give a head of water to power a sawmill that used to stand on this bank.'

They carried on until they were upstream of the weir and stood looking down at it. Bob could see Dixon and the others on the far bank. 'Found anything yet?' he shouted, above the sound of the water tumbling over the weir.

Bob couldn't hear Dixon's shouted reply and cupped his ear in a theatrical way. Bob could see Dixon shake his head in response.

'This gives us a bit of a problem,' said Bob. 'If Captain Bell was killed or was put into the water downstream of here but above where he was found, then we've not been able to find any evidence of it on either bank. But if his body went into the water upstream from here, would it have made it over the weir or would it have been trapped there?'

'I'm sorry, sir,' said Captain Sanderson, 'that's well outside my areas of expertise.'

Bob saw a log of about a foot in girth and perhaps two feet in length caught up in tree roots on the river bank. He turned to Petty Officer MacDonald. 'Andrew, as the naval man here, would you mind doing the honours? I'd like to see what happens when that log down there floats down to the weir.

The petty officer clambered down the bank and retrieved the log. Once back up the bank he held it by a branch that projected from one side and threw it, spinning end around end, out towards the centre of the river. They then watched as the floating log hit the top of the weir, and, after a brief pause, was pushed by the force of water behind it over the structure and into the flow heading downstream towards the island.

'Well, it's hardly scientific,' said Bob, 'and I suspect a floating log might behave differently to a floating body. But to my mind that suggests that Captain Bell could have been killed further upstream and we should carry on looking.' Bob looked across the river, intending to wave to the others to continue the search. It was obvious that Lieutenant Dixon had understood the purpose of the floating log and that he had drawn the same conclusion as Bob when it went over the weir. He and the two men with him were moving further up the river bank.

Bob's team reached the end of the river first, without finding anything of interest. At the point where the waters of Loch Arkaig flowed into the River Arkaig, the river was crossed by a long wooden road bridge, standing on four substantial stone supports sunk into the river bed between stone abutments. 'That's an impressive piece of engineering,' said Bob.

'Yes, it is, sir,' said Captain Sanderson. 'It's called the White Bridge. It occurs to me that those on the other bank might need some help. They are now on the wrong side of a tributary of the River Arkaig called the Abhainn Chia-aig, which flows down into the glen over the Eas Chia-aig waterfalls and joins the main river just over there, close to the far end of the White Bridge. There's a footbridge across the minor river only a few hundred yards north of the confluence, but it's heavily wooded over there and they might not realise that. If they cross the footbridge they can then follow the track that crosses the White Bridge. You can actually wade across the River Arkaig here, but I'm not sure I'd recommend it.'

'We need to look at the bridge anyway,' said Bob, 'for the same reason we've been looking at the river banks. That will put us a lot closer to where they should emerge from the trees, and we can shout over to tell them about the footbridge.'

'It looks like there's a boat moored on the far side of that pier over there, sir,' said Petty Officer MacDonald, pointing to a stone construction a couple of hundred yards along the south shore of Loch Arkaig.

'You've got better eyesight than I have,' said Bob, before realising how true that was.

'There are ropes attached to the mooring rings on the top of the pier,' said MacDonald, 'They have to be from a boat. I could come under the White Bridge in it and pick Lieutenant Dixon and the others up from the far bank of the tributary.'

'There shouldn't be a need for that,' said Bob, 'but there's no harm in you looking, just in case we need a backup plan.'

Bob walked across the White Bridge with Captain Sanderson, watching for the point on the shore where Lieutenant Dixon and the two men with him ought to emerge from the trees. They had still not done so by the time he reached the far end, and he paused for a moment, feeling for the first time a slight tinge of anxiety. He heard a shout from behind him and turned to see Petty Officer MacDonald standing on the stone jetty, gesturing urgently.

'It looks like he's found something,' Bob said to Captain Sanderson. 'Can you wait here and guide the others round?

I'll go and see what he's found.'

As Bob walked onto the stone jetty, Petty Officer MacDonald called out, 'I think we've found where Captain Bell was killed, sir.'

'What is it?'

'Look, sir.' MacDonald gestured towards a wooden boat of perhaps 20 to 25 feet in length. 'It's been covered by a tarpaulin to keep the rain out, which I pulled back at the stern to give access to the engine controls and tiller. As I was getting back out of the boat, I saw this, under that seat running across the boat.' He held up an army officer's cap.

'And if you look down there, you can see what might be a patch of blood on the jetty itself, staining the cement between the stones.' The petty officer pointed to a spot close to where they were standing.

Bob took the cap, then turned around as he heard the others approach. 'Sergeant Potter, what cap badge did Captain Bell wear?'

'The Hampshire Regiment, sir. That was his home regiment.'

'Well this seems to confirm that Captain Bell was here last night.' He held the cap for the others to see. 'It is of course possible that another officer from the Hampshire Regiment lost his uniform cap in the boat recently, but I very much doubt it. Did it rain last night?' Both Sergeant Potter and Captain Sanderson nodded.

'That would explain why what appears to be a patch of blood can only be traced in the cement between the stones and in the sunken areas of the stones themselves. The rest has been washed away. It does look as if Petty Officer

MacDonald has found the place where Captain Bell was killed. Well done, Andrew.'

Bob looked around. He suspected that he may not have been the only person present whose neck prickled at the thought. 'That seems to be the "where" settled. Now we need to start looking at the "why", in the hope that leads us to the "who".'

'Someone's coming, sir,' said Petty Officer MacDonald.

They had returned to the point at which the river flowed out of the loch, by the end of the White Bridge. Bob could see a car approaching along the track from the direction of Achnacarry Castle.

'This track is used to get to a back gate which gives access to the road that heads off west along the north shore of Loch Arkaig,' said Captain Sanderson. 'I'm not sure who'd be heading that way today. We'll need to stand back to give them room to pass.'

The car stopped just short of them and Bob saw the back door on the far side of the vehicle open. Monique Dubois got out. She stood to one side as the car turned then headed off back the way it had come, towards the castle.

'Hello Bob,' said Monique.

Bob could scarcely believe his eyes – eye, he corrected himself.

She smiled, warily. 'Are you going to introduce me?'

'Gentlemen, can I present Madame Monique Dubois, who is with the Security Service, MI5 if you prefer.' Bob went on to introduce his team, and Captain Sanderson. Before he could stop himself, he went on, 'You nearly met Lieutenant Dixon earlier today.'

Bob could see that Monique was very unsure of herself, in a way that seemed totally out of character. He desperately wanted to know what she was doing at Achnacarry, but was equally concerned not to lose face in front of his men and the captain.

'We think we've found where Cecil Bell was killed,' he said. 'Over on the stone pier in the loch. I'll take you to look, if you like. The others can walk back to the castle. We'll catch up.'

'Do you want one of the Sten guns, sir?' asked Lieutenant Dixon.

'No, thanks, Michael. I've got my pistol, and I'm sure Madame Dubois is also armed.'

'I'll take it, if you like, lieutenant,' said Monique.

'It would mean both groups had one, ma'am.' He passed the weapon over.

It was obvious to everyone from the way she held the submachine gun that Monique needed no guidance on how to use it.

They paused at the landward end of the pier and Bob watched as the others disappeared out of sight along the track.

'What the hell are you doing here, Monique?'

'Helping you, apparently. And before you say anything else, please believe me that this wasn't my idea. I had things to do in Hillington today, as you know. Coming here was the very last thing I wanted.'

'So how come you *are* here?'

'After you left this morning I checked out of the hotel and drove to the safe house we've got near Glasgow. I then telephoned my department head, Matthew Sloan, to discuss arrangements for today. In passing, and only in passing, I told him that MI11 had lost one of your officers up here. He asked what I knew, and I mentioned what you'd said about the victim being Belgian and there being German trainees here.'

Bob could see where this was going. 'But Monique, that was something I told you between friends.'

'I'm sorry, Bob, it was just a bit of gossip, really, before we got on to the real subject of the discussion. I didn't expect the response I got.'

'What response did you get?'

'I knew I'd made a mistake as soon as he started asking more questions, which I couldn't answer. Then he said he'd get back to me. We hadn't started to discuss Hillington at this point. Half an hour later he rang back. He said he'd talked to Commodore Cunningham in MI11, and they'd agreed that I should come and join your investigation here. I need this like an extra hole in the head, Bob, and when I protested I was needed in Glasgow, he made it clear that he was giving me an order. It seems the two of them felt that my knowledge of German might be of help. That's a pretext, obviously. Sloan just wanted to find a way of infiltrating me into your investigation, and for reasons that escape me, your Commodore Cunningham let him. I'm left as an unwanted appendage here, while trying to keep on top of my own operation at a distance, using dodgy phone connections.'

'Well, Cunningham's reasons don't escape me,' said Bob. 'Before I left, he tried to talk me into having the investigation taken over by a team he offered to fly up from London. He even offered to come up himself. Your

Mr Sloan's efforts to get you involved obviously struck a chord, and he decided it was too good an opportunity to refuse. If this all goes wrong, he can now share the blame with MI5. My new boss seems to have a shortage of confidence in his deputy, me, and you've allowed him to demonstrate that to anyone who might be interested.'

'Look, I said I'm sorry, Bob. It wasn't deliberate. Now I'm here, can you tell me what you've found? If I'm to help, then you need to keep me involved.'

Bob showed Monique the boat and told her the conclusions they'd drawn.

As they walked back to the castle Bob found himself cursing Monique, and Cunningham.

He tried to keep his feelings concealed behind the most civil front he could manage. 'How did you actually get here? It seemed to me that the train services aren't wonderful on a Saturday.'

'One of my people drove me up. We came via Glen Coe, which may be about the only good thing to have happened today. Lieutenant Colonel White was surprised by my arrival, but after he'd checked who I was, he found me a room in the castle and a car to drive me up to where I met you.'

'You must have covered ground more quickly than us, to have arrived when you did.'

'I don't know, Bob. I just sat in the back of the car, kicking myself for my stupidity and cursing you for giving my boss an excuse to divert me from my real job.'

CHAPTER ELEVEN

When Bob and Monique returned to Achnacarry Castle, Bob sought out and thanked Captain Sanderson for his help and promised to call in on Lieutenant Colonel White as soon as he could. They then joined the others in the tiny room in which Sergeant Potter and the late Captain Bell had based their investigation. This was in the complex of wooden huts a short distance to the south east of the castle itself, beyond the parade ground, which housed the camp administration and headquarters.

'I know it's a bit cramped,' said Bob, 'but I hope we won't be spending much of our time in here.' He turned to Petty Officer MacDonald. 'Andrew, can you and Taffy go and find the medical officer and pass on my request he accompanies you immediately to the pier on Loch Arkaig, to confirm whether what we found is blood, and if so whether it is the same blood type as Captain Bell's?'

'Yes, sir,' said MacDonald.

'Remember,' he said, 'I don't want anyone going anywhere on their own while we're here. I don't know about everyone else, but I got a very uneasy feeling standing on that pier a little earlier. Almost as if I could feel someone's sights lined up on me.'

'You're not the only one, sir,' said Lieutenant Dixon.

'Make sure you take the rifle and a Sten gun with you,' he said to the petty officer. 'Everyone else around here seems to carry heavy weaponry, so you won't stand out. Once the medical officer has got what he needs, could you take another close look at the pier and the boat, to see if we missed anything? It would be helpful to know how deep the water is there, and whether there is any chance of checking the floor of the lake by the jetty. We know the hat was dropped in the attack. It would be helpful to know if the captain or his attacker dropped anything else in the water.'

Lieutenant Dixon said, 'Sir, you may not know about it, but there's a naval base at Fort William. It's known as HMS *St Christopher* and they train the crews of motor torpedo boats and motor gun boats. I'd be surprised if they didn't have some divers on the establishment, if only for sorting out torpedoes that have gone astray during test firings or training. I can telephone them and see if we can get some divers up here, if you like? Petty Officer MacDonald and I paid them a visit a few months ago and found some big holes in their security. I think they'll like the idea of us owing them a favour next time we visit. Not, of course, that that will make any difference to our assessment.'

'Thanks, Michael, could you do that?' Bob looked at his watch. 'It's a bit late in the day now, but perhaps they could come tomorrow morning? I'm sure they wouldn't mind working on a Sunday as it is genuinely urgent. It will just make it a slightly bigger favour they think you owe them.'

When Lieutenant Dixon had gone to make the call, Bob turned his attention back to the petty officer. 'When you've finished at the pier, Andrew, could the two of you see if you can find anyone who saw Captain Bell heading up that way last night? Now we know where he went, it makes things a little easier. The military police at the gate out there must have seen something, and there have to be other people who were around at the time.'

Having set everyone else going, Bob went to find a phone he could use, ideally in a private office with a door that closed. Monique also set off in search of, she said, a way of discovering how things were progressing in Glasgow in her absence.

'Hello, Bob, I've been expecting your call.'

Bob thought that Commodore Cunningham sounded weary.

'Sir, if you really don't have any faith in me, why did you choose me for this job?'

'Rest assured that I do have faith in you, Bob. But please remember that I've got Major General Sir Peter Maitland breathing down my neck. With all the ructions in the military intelligence community just recently, largely thanks to you, I must be seen to be open and cooperative. That's true even when I think that MI5 are responding to our misfortune in an opportunistic and predatory way. Which I do, incidentally. You've worked with Vera Duval, Monique Dubois if you prefer, very successfully before. It seemed better to accept an offer of help that meant her joining the investigation than having something less acceptable imposed on us from on high. You are well aware that we are trying to get the various arms of military intelligence to work better together. Look on this as an opportunity to show how we put that into practice.'

'Do you really believe her presence will help, sir?'

'It doesn't matter what I believe, Bob, or what you believe for that matter. We just need to track down Captain Bell's killer. Is there any progress to report on that, by the way?'

Bob told his boss of the results of their first afternoon's work.

Lieutenant Dixon came back with the news that the Royal Navy in Fort William would be delighted to provide two divers the following morning. He had also, in passing, accepted an offer from Captain Sanderson to lay on some tea and biscuits for them. Bob realised that he had missed lunch entirely, though the late breakfast in Pitlochry had been good.

Monique returned from making her phone call. Bob got the impression she wasn't happy about what she'd heard.

'Right,' said Bob to Sergeant Potter. 'What we would like to do now is talk through how far you and Captain Bell got with the investigation into the first murder, the one that took place on Wednesday night. We want to make sure that there's no duplication as we move forward. It also seems to me possible that something Captain Bell said or did led the murderer to feel sufficiently threatened to kill him. I know that's an assumption right now, but the idea of there being two separate and unrelated murderers, or two completely unconnected motives, does seem very unlikely.'

'I've got my notebook here, sir,' said Sergeant Potter, holding it up. 'What do you want to know?'

'We can discuss the first victim in more detail shortly. Let's start with the actual murder. What do we know about it?' asked Bob.

'It seems they go in for competitive sports at Achnacarry, sir, though not as you might normally recognise them. There are a series of competitions that pit one troop against another. I'm not sure why, but the commandos appear to have adopted the cavalry convention of organising themselves into troops. On Wednesday night they held what they call the 'milling' competition. As I understand it, it's a bit like boxing, but more manic, with ten men from each troop going into the ring at one-minute intervals and each fighting for that minute.'

'It sounds like quite a spectator sport,' said Bob.

'Apparently it is, sir, and that's the point in a way. They've got what they call the "big hut". It's a sort of greatly enlarged Nissen hut. I think the technical term is a Romney hut. In summer they hold the event outside, but at this time of year the milling takes place in the big hut. There's a boxing ring in the centre, with rows of seats surrounding it, but for the most part it's standing room only, and everyone we spoke to commented on how crowded it was on Wednesday night. The victim's name was Private Hannes Lambrechts. A little before 8.30 p.m. the medical officer, who was supervising the contest in the ring, was called to one end of the hut where a man had collapsed. When the medical officer examined him, it became clear that he had been stabbed in the back. Several men who had been close to the victim at the time came forward when we made a request for them to do so. But none of them saw anything they regarded as suspicious, and none saw the actual attack. One problem may be that the place was so crowded it's been suggested that the victim might not have collapsed immediately, effectively being held up by the men around him, so giving his attacker time to distance himself without anyone noticing immediately.'

'Any sign of a murder weapon?'

'The cause of death was a single deep stab wound in the back that penetrated the heart. It was made by a narrow-bladed knife. The medical officer had no hesitation identifying the weapon that killed Lambrechts as a Fairbairn–Sykes fighting knife.'

'A what?'

'It was a new one on me too, sir. But I understand that it's the standard fighting knife issued to the commandos. Apparently, it was designed by the two men it's named after, who served as officers in the Shanghai police in China in the 1920s and 1930s. They came to Britain at the outbreak of war and served as instructors at the Special Training Centre opened by the War Office out at Lochailort, south west of here, in 1940. The unarmed and knife combat skills they taught there have influenced the training that takes place here now. And the knife they designed is now issued to all commandos.'

'Which means that everyone at Achnacarry has been issued with a knife that could have been the murder weapon?'

'Well, not really, sir. You see, the idea is that each new commando gets issued with his F-S knife, as they call them, at the parade at the end of his course. It's apparently quite a ceremony.'

'I'm confused,' said Bob. 'Does that mean that the men here don't have access to the type of knife that killed the victim?'

'All the training staff have passed the course, so have been issued with the knives. But the F-S knife is also widely used in training. I think it would be fair to say that pretty much everyone here could lay his hands on one if he wanted to, even if he had not been personally issued with one.'

'That doesn't narrow things down far, does it?' said Monique.

'No, ma'am. Captain Bell and I felt that wasn't likely to be a productive line of enquiry.'

'Did the medical officer say anything specific about the stab wounds inflicted on Captain Bell?' asked Bob. 'Could they have been caused by the same weapon?'

'It seems almost certain they were caused by the same type of knife, sir,' said Sergeant Potter. 'But while that gives a strong link between the two murders, it gets us no nearer to finding who the murderer is.'

'Fair enough,' said Bob. 'What can you tell me about the man who was killed on Wednesday, Private Hannes Lambrechts?'

'He was Belgian, sir,' said Sergeant Potter, 'and as with many men who came over from the continent in 1940, or have done so since, there's a sense that we only know as much as the individual has chosen to tell people about themselves. It's not really possible to do a background check on someone from a German-occupied country, or even know for certain that information such as their date of birth or even their name is correct.'

'No, I understand that,' said Bob, thinking of Sergeant Winograd. 'But what do we think we know?'

'As far as we can tell, sir, Private Lambrechts was nineteen-years-old. His home town was Nieuwpoort on the Belgian coast, not far from the French border. He came over to Britain in one of the last boats that got away from Dunkirk during the evacuation.'

'So he would only have been about seventeen at that time?'

'Apparently so, sir. He made the trip in a Belgian Army uniform he'd taken from a corpse and joined up with the Free Belgian Forces once he arrived in Britain. He told them at the time that he'd taken the uniform because he didn't believe that civilians would be allowed on the boats. After initial training, he joined the 1st Fusilier Battalion, a Belgian unit.'

'How did he find his way to Achnacarry?' asked Bob.

'Move forward in time to August of this year, sir, and the request went out for volunteers to join a Belgian troop of what is known as No. 10 (Inter-Allied) Commando. Private Lambrechts volunteered and was selected for training here at Achnacarry, like all other potential commandos. He arrived on Tuesday, but it seems that there had been an administrative error, because most of the rest of the thirty Belgians who were due to start training arrived at the end of a period of leave on Thursday. Until then, there were only three Belgians here at Achnacarry, or two once Private Lambrechts had been killed.'

'Who were the other two?'

'Sergeant Thomas Mertens and Private Jerome Wouters, sir. What I said about background checks applies to them, too, of course, but they both say that at the time Lambrechts was killed they were playing chess together in the tent they'd temporarily been allocated with him, and where they had spent a very leisurely day by Achnacarry standards, waiting for their comrades to join them.'

'Did you talk to them yourself?' asked Bob.

'Captain Bell and I saw them individually,' said Sergeant Potter. 'Their stories were completely consistent and very believable. And we couldn't come up with any reason why either might have wanted to hurt him.'

'It certainly seems to suggest they either did it together, or not at all,' said Bob. 'Alright, let's park them on one side for the moment. What else have we got?'

'When we were talking to Private Wouters, he said that Lambrechts was a fairly quiet man. He also said, however, that after being friendly and relaxed on Tuesday evening and most of Wednesday, Lambrechts had acted very strangely at the evening meal on Wednesday. Wouters asked him what was wrong. Lambrechts told him that he thought he'd seen someone he'd been trying to find for over two years, but he wasn't sure. He wouldn't say anything more when asked and took himself off somewhere. Neither Wouters or Mertens saw him again before he was killed.'

'Interesting that he said, "for over two years",' said Bob. 'That seems to take us back to Belgium in 1940.'

'That's what we thought,' said Sergeant Potter, 'though I suspect we then headed off at an unproductive tangent. I don't know how much you know about the commandos, sir, but they are organised into a series of discrete units, who tend to get mixed and matched according to skills and experience when it comes to operational deployment.

I mentioned No. 10 (Inter-Allied) Commando a few moments ago. This formed earlier this year and is a highly unusual unit. It is made up of a number of small troops, each coming from a different part of Europe. The three men we've been talking about had volunteered to become part of No. 4 Belgian Troop, for example. There is also a No. 1 French Troop which trained here a few months ago, as did No. 2 Dutch Troop. There is also a No. 5 Norwegian Troop, and a No. 6 Polish Troop is just forming. The idea is to have a pool of knowledge about these various European countries, and their languages, which can be drawn on by other command units during raids.'

Lieutenant Dixon said, 'If that's a complete list, then you missed out No. 3 Troop.'

'Well spotted, sir. That unit does exist, and it's knows as No 3 (X) Troop. With the "X" in brackets. Some of those who have volunteered to fight with that troop are being trained at Achnacarry as we speak. The thing that made us sit up a little and take notice was that the troop comprises men who are classified as enemy aliens, from countries such as Germany, Austria, Czechoslovakia and Hungary. On the face of it, these men appear to have more reason to dislike the Nazis than most of us, because they are all Jews, and for that reason their unit is sometimes called No. 3 (Jewish) Troop. It's official policy that men serving in the unit, and those who volunteer for it, can do so under assumed names, to protect families back home. Lambrechts, Wouters or Mertens were part of a 200-strong group of trainees of a number of different nationalities who had volunteered for 10 Commando and who were all due to arrive on Thursday.'

'But at least three of them arrived early,' said Bob.

'That's right, sir,' said Sergeant Potter. 'It seems the gremlins, as you might call them in the RAF, had a busy week. The three Belgians arrived prematurely on Tuesday. And then on Wednesday a group of ten Germans and Austrians arrived. There was no-one to meet them at Spean Bridge Station, so they phoned from there. Unusually, they were picked up and avoided the seven-mile march that marks the start of most training courses here. They got to Achnacarry in the afternoon and were assigned tents.

'And it was not long after their arrival that Lambrechts told the others he'd seen the man he was looking for?' asked Bob.

'That's right, sir, and I think that led us up a blind alley which wasted a lot of time yesterday. We spent quite a bit of effort trying to establish whether any of the group that arrived on Wednesday could be placed in Belgium in early 1940. I still can't give you a definitive answer to that question, but I'd already reached the view that we were wasting our time when Captain Bell said as much to me, shortly before he went out for his walk.'

'Why did you come to that conclusion?' asked Bob.

'I think that Captain Bell was unhappy that we'd gone off in pursuit of something that was just too obvious to be true, sir. As he put it, if Lambrechts had been looking for a German for over two years, the last place he'd try to find him would have been in Britain. And as Captain Bell pointed out, in the run-up to the Dunkirk evacuation there was no shortage of British troops in Belgium, all there to try to counter the German advance. I think he's right. I think that whoever Lambrechts had been looking for is

British, and it was just coincidence that Lambrechts saw him here at Achnacarry on Wednesday, on the day that the Germans and Austrians arrived.'

'Which implies that same person killed him that night, presumably because he also recognised Lambrechts?' said Bob.

'Yes, sir,' said Sergeant Potter.

'Unfortunately, like with the murder weapon, that moves us one step forwards and three steps backwards, and once again our list of suspects extends to almost all the trainees and staff who were at Achnacarry on Wednesday. All those who were in Belgium in 1940, anyway.'

'Am I understanding this correctly?' asked Monique. 'Are you saying that the two of you dismissed the possibility of the murder being linked to the presence here of the German and Austrian trainees?'

'Yes, ma'am. As I said, the captain wasn't happy we'd wasted so much effort on it.'

Monique looked meaningfully at Bob. He got the sense she was thinking pretty much exactly what he was thinking.

It was Lieutenant Dixon who broke the silence that followed. 'It would be possible, in theory at least, to look at the service record of everyone here to find out which of them were in Belgium at the relevant time, sir.'

'It would,' said Bob, 'but it's not going to be a trivial job. And I don't see anything in what we've been discussing that would lead the killer to feel nervous enough to want to kill Captain Bell. Perhaps before we embark on a major paper exercise we should try to find out if anyone at Private Lambrechts' home unit knows anything more about him? He must have had friends he confided in, or a sweetheart, or someone who can give us a lead on the person he was looking for, and why he was looking for him.'

Dixon looked at his watch. 'I'll get in touch with them tomorrow, sir. I don't think we'll find anyone who knows anything at this time on a Saturday evening.'

'No, you're right,' said Bob, 'but perhaps I should make the call. Meanwhile, I said I would see Lieutenant Colonel White, so I had better do so. Remember, we are promised a show tonight. I'm not sure what to expect of that, if I'm honest. Sergeant Potter, could you wait until Petty Officer MacDonald and Private Jenkins are back and then organise a meal at the NAAFI canteen for yourselves? Please remember what I said about staying together. It's doubly important at night. Michael, could you start drafting a report of what we've done and where we think we've got to? I'd like to document this while it's still fresh in our minds. I've already given Commodore Cunningham a brief verbal outline.'

'Yes, sir,' said Lieutenant Dixon.

At that moment there was a knock on the door and Petty Officer MacDonald poked his head round the door. 'May we come in, sir?'

'Yes, we're done here,' said Bob. 'Have you got anything for me?'

'Not much, I'm afraid, sir. The medical officer confirmed that what we found was blood, and he will know tomorrow if it is the same blood type as Captain Bell's. We found nothing more of interest on the pier or the boat. Oddly, when I dusted the boat's tiller, engine start button, fuel filler cap and throttle lever for fingerprints, I found none. It's as if the last person to use the boat deliberately wiped it clean to avoid leaving fingerprints. I tried a couple of other locations on the boat where I thought someone might have placed a hand or held a gunwale, but again came up with nothing.'

'That raises an obvious question, doesn't it?' said Bob.

'Yes, sir,' said MacDonald. 'Why would anyone bother unless they'd done something, such as killing Captain Bell, they didn't want to get caught for?'

'You may well be right, Andrew' said Bob. 'Did you find anyone who saw Captain Bell on his walk?'

'One of the military policemen at the end of the drive said he was on duty at the time. He thought he could remember a captain coming from the castle and walking off in the direction of the White Bridge, but he wasn't sure. And an old man fixing some slates on the roof of a building, a couple of hundred yards west of here, said he talked to someone who could well have been Captain Bell, at about the right time. The officer he described sounded like Captain Bell. He had come over to ask the man about the ivy-covered stack of masonry next to the track. It seems it's the remains of the old Achnacarry Castle, which was destroyed in 1746 by the army because the Camerons had supported the Jacobites during the 1745 rising. We walked past it earlier, sir, but I have to admit I only noticed it when the old man mentioned it.'

'But you found no-one who saw Captain Bell with anyone else, or talking to anyone, or doing anything out of the ordinary?'

'No, sir. In fact, other than those two people, we found no-one who could remember seeing Captain Bell at all. The old man told me he probably would not have noticed the captain if he hadn't come over to talk. As he pointed out, there are a lot of men in khaki at Achnacarry and even officers are hardly unusual or noteworthy.'

'No, I suppose that's true,' said Bob.

'Have you got a minute, Bob?' asked Monique. 'I made my telephone call earlier from an empty office just along the corridor earlier. Perhaps we can talk there?'

Monique closed the door and turned to face him. 'I'm almost at a loss to describe just how angry I am right now, Bob.'

Bob thought no description was really needed. Her face gave a pretty good indication of how she felt.

'Angry? With me?'

'Yes, with you. That guff you were spouting about German trainees being involved. It's turned out to be complete nonsense. If it wasn't for that, Matthew Sloan would never have had the bright idea of muscling in on your investigation and I'd still be doing what I'm meant to be doing in Glasgow. You can't imagine what an utter joy it is to be stuck out here, miles from nowhere, the only woman in a place with God-knows how many men who are being trained to kill for their country.'

'Aren't you forgetting something, Monique? I told you about the Germans while I was baring my soul to you about the new job. The next thing I know, you've repeated it to your boss and given him a great excuse to stick his oar in where it's not wanted. I was being open and honest with you because I trusted you. So much for trust! What else did you tell Matthew Sloan this morning? Did you tell him how you rated my performance in bed?'

'Don't be stupid, Bob.' Monique was clearly as aware as Bob himself that they had no idea who was in the neighbouring offices, and she was now almost hissing at him in an effort to vent her feelings without being overheard.

'I'm not being stupid. You might as well have done.' Bob was almost shouting in a whisper.

'For God's sake. I can't help it if that damn head injury of yours has given you some sort of inferiority complex. You also told me last night that you had some growing up to do. You were so right. Get over it. Start behaving in a way that befits your rank and your uniform.'

Monique turned back towards the office door as if to leave.

'Yes, that's right,' hissed Bob. 'Nine hundred men and you. Why don't you see how many you can work your way through while you're here?'

She turned and took two steps towards him. The slap came from Bob's left, so he didn't see it coming. He certainly felt it.

Monique stepped back with a look of fury on her face. In a much more controlled tone she said, 'I promised myself a long time ago that I'd never let any man say anything like that to me again. It's a bit rich anyway, coming from you. I didn't exactly see you fighting Lady Alice Gough off on that first night at Sarclet Castle.'

'And which of us was it who tried to get her to share a bed with us just a couple of nights later?'

'Jesus, Bob. Grow up.'

She turned and left. Bob noted that she hadn't slammed the door. He stood silently, wondering what had possessed him to say what he had. It was as if he'd been standing outside his body, watching himself trying to hurt her. She'd responded in kind, of course, but that wasn't really the point. He wondered where she'd gone, before deciding he didn't care.

CHAPTER TWELVE

'I'm sorry it's taken me so long, Colonel.' Bob looked around Lieutenant Colonel White's office. The maps, charts and blackboard helped conceal the drab walls.

White saw him looking. 'It's a fairly soulless place in which to spend most of your waking hours, isn't it, Group Captain?'

'Call me Bob, please, Colonel. When they offered me this job and a promotion to group captain I said I thought it sounded like an old man's rank. Now I am one, I'm beginning to think I was right.'

Lieutenant Colonel White laughed. 'You, an old man? How old are you Bob? I'm known to my friends as Edward, by the way.'

'I'm 30, Edward,' said Bob.

'Thanks for not asking in return, but I'll be 50 next year, and compared to you, I can lay claim to some real age,' said White.

'I see you served in the last war,' said Bob, pointing at the lieutenant colonel's medal ribbons.

'You might say that,' said White. 'I stayed in afterwards. Then I volunteered for the commandos in 1940 and somehow ended up here.'

'I had an introductory lunch with General Gordon and Brigadier Blackett in Edinburgh yesterday,' said Bob. 'They were highly complimentary about what you have achieved here.'

White laughed. 'I think they'd prefer I reported directly to them, on the grounds that Achnacarry is in Scotland. But it's much more complicated than that. I bet they complained about the ammunition we get through here.'

'They did mention it,' said Bob. 'Apparently you consume more than any other army unit in Scotland.'

'That's hardly a surprise, since no other army unit in Scotland is actually firing at anyone,' said White. 'Even the anti-aircraft and coastal defence units have relatively little to do these days.'

'To an outsider, the idea of loosing off live ammunition at trainees sounds like a recipe for disaster,' said Bob. 'How do you make it work in practice?'

'We've worked very hard to perfect the art of what some of my instructors call "firing to miss, but not by much". The aim is to give those training here a true sense of what it's like to be on the receiving end of live rounds buzzing over their heads, or explosives going off next to their boat or beneath them in the river when they're crossing the toggle bridge. It seems to work, as well. One of the instructors I had here in the early months of the centre was posted to No. 4 Commando in the summer. He took part in the raid on Dieppe, where they did an excellent job despite the problems the main Canadian force ran into. He visited us a month or so ago and told me that the beach landing at Dieppe had been an intense experience. The thing he remembered more than anything else had been advancing off the beach alongside a commando private who, in a brief lull in the firing had said, "Bloody hell, sir, this is nearly as bad as Achnacarry." When I heard that story I knew that we were doing the right thing here. The men who take part in the night assault landing you will see a little later will have an experience that builds their character. But more importantly they will have an experience that ensures that when it's their turn to land on the shores of France, or Norway, or Greece in the face of enemy fire, it won't be new to them. The training here will make sure they respond in the right way and that could well keep them alive.'

'Do you have many casualties in training?' said Bob.

'The demands we place on the men mean that we have more than our share of injuries, especially foot and leg injuries caused by the running and the speed marches, and broken bones in climbing accidents and on the Tarzan course, that sort of thing. We do everything we can to work as safely as possible but must always remember that we are training men for war. We have to balance the risks they run here against the reduction in risks they will see when actually pitted against a real enemy. We have had a small number of fatalities, including two men who drowned in the River Arkaig, but the number is smaller than the number of dummy graves out there on the drive. The aim is to make it feel dangerous and seem dangerous but do everything we reasonably can to avoid it actually being dangerous.'

White looked at his watch. 'Look, should we go across to the mess for dinner? Things kick off tonight at 9 p.m., and

I'd like us to be in position half an hour earlier. Madame Dubois is welcome to join us.'

'Thanks, Edward, I'll pass that on. I hope we'll see her at dinner.'

'I was rather surprised when she arrived earlier. Still, we managed to find a room for her. You hadn't mentioned you were expecting someone from the Security Service to be joining you.'

Bob paused. 'The honest answer is that I didn't know she was coming until she arrived. It seems my boss, and hers, felt it would be good for the two sections to work together. Do you mind if we collect my lieutenant en route to dinner, Edward? I've instructed my team not to go anywhere as individuals and I'd prefer him not to starve.'

Bob realised that Monique would have taken no notice of that and for the first time felt a little concern for her.

The officers' mess at Achnacarry was a comfortable place, housed in the castle itself. As he looked round Bob reflected that, perhaps thanks to Lieutenant Colonel White's approach, it was also a down-to-earth place.

It transpired that Monique and Michael had gone to the mess together, and Bob and the lieutenant colonel joined them.

The lieutenant colonel looked around the busy room. 'We always tell the men who come to train here that their officers are tested every bit as hard as they are. In keeping with that principle, the same food is on offer to the trainees and their officers, and to all the permanent staff here at Achnacarry. The officers on my staff can dine here rather than in the NAAFI canteen in the grounds, but otherwise they get the same treatment as the latest group of volunteers to have marched in from the train at Spean Bridge.'

Lieutenant Dixon attacked his food with enthusiasm. 'Sir, all the staff I've seen are wearing green berets. Is this something new? I thought commandos wore the headgear used in your various home regiments.'

'I'm glad you spotted that, Lieutenant,' said White. 'The decision has been made to issue green berets to all existing and newly trained commandos, as of this month, as it happens. There's a sense that as the men are all volunteers, they will always remain part of their home regiments, but the idea of the green beret is to give a sense of achievement and accomplishment, and a sense of belonging. The compromise is that commandos will continue to wear the cap badge of their home regiment on their green berets.'

'Your staff have a tartan backing to their cap badges, as have you, sir. Is that specific to Achnacarry?'

'Yes, it is, Lieutenant. Achnacarry Castle is the traditional home of Clan Cameron, and in recognition of that, everyone based here wears a patch of Cameron of Locheil tartan behind our cap badge.'

Bob looked around to check if they could be overheard by men on the neighbouring tables and decided they couldn't. 'Edward, I'll not bore you with the details, but it's looking like whoever killed Captain Bell last night also killed Private Lambrechts on Wednesday night. We're also considering whether the killer might have been someone Lambrechts met in Belgium, immediately before or during the Dunkirk evacuation. We know he's been looking for someone, but not who. How much information do you have here about the trainees and staff? Do you hold service records that would be sufficiently detailed to allow us to know if someone was serving in Belgium at that time?'

'Not for the trainees, I'm afraid,' said White. 'They are formally on the books of their home regiments, to whom we can return them any time we want if they don't come up to scratch. We only have the forms they filled in when they volunteered, plus the comments of their commanding officer and the officer who undertook the initial interview, in addition to notes on their performance here. On the other hand, we do know what their home regiments are, so you could get an idea of whether they might have been in Belgium at that time by knowing whether their regiments were. It wouldn't be a simple job, though. As far as the staff here are concerned, then yes, we do hold their service records, and you would be welcome to look at them if you wish, or at the trainees' application forms.'

'Thank you,' said Bob. 'Incidentally, you might wish to know that we have a team of navy divers coming up to Achnacarry tomorrow morning from Fort William. We've asked them to look at the bed of the loch around the pier, just beyond the White Bridge.'

'Yes,' said White. 'Captain Sanderson told me that you thought Captain Bell might have been killed there.'

'Do you use Loch Arkaig much, sir?' asked Lieutenant Dixon. 'It seemed a bit quieter than Loch Lochy, and I wondered what the boat up at the jetty was used for.'

'We use the land around and beyond the loch extensively for training exercises,' said the lieutenant colonel, 'and some of my staff have a nice sideline in stalking deer to supplement the cuisine at Achnacarry that they think I don't know about. But our amphibious and water-borne training concentrates almost exclusively on Loch Lochy. As for the boat you refer to, it's used as a runabout to support exercises and by the staff for fishing when time permits, and for transporting dead deer as well, I am sure. The road along the north shore of Loch Arkaig turns into a pretty rough track part of the way along and a boat is the best way to reach the western end.'

'Thanks, Edward, that's helpful,' said Bob. 'It's possible the killer was using that boat before Captain Bell was murdered.'

There was a pause as the four of them finished their meals.

Lieutenant Colonel White looked up. 'Bob, I don't suppose you've considered volunteering for the commandos yourself, have you?'

Bob laughed. 'After seeing some of what you put them through here, Edward, I don't think that's the life for me. Besides, I'm wearing the wrong colour uniform.'

'Not necessarily. We've already trained RAF commandos here at Achnacarry, and more will be coming.'

'Really?' said Bob. 'Now you come to mention it, I do recall seeing some sort of request for volunteers back in the summer. I commanded an operational training unit at the time, down in southern Scotland. What do they do?'

'The aim is to have mobile units that are able to accompany front line troops when they go ashore in Europe and fight if necessary. They are called servicing commandos, and their job when the time comes will be to make captured German airfields fit for use by allied aircraft, or operate temporary airstrips constructed by the army engineers. They have to have the fitness and the full range of skills of every other commando who trains here and be able to service and operate a wide range of allied aircraft types.'

'Yes, once we get back into Europe, I can see why they would be valuable,' said Bob.

White looked at his watch again. 'Time for us to move. The reception we are planning to give the men landing tonight will be very hot, but standing around and watching it can be numbingly cold. We can lend you some naval duffel coats if you wish, plus Wellington boots, thick socks and gloves. That should help keep the cold at bay. Do you want to join us, Madame Dubois?'

Monique smiled brightly at the lieutenant colonel. 'I'm very grateful to be asked, but I'm trying to keep closely in touch with some of my people in central Scotland, so fear I will be spending at least part of the evening on the telephone.'

Bob felt distinctly overdressed when he and Lieutenant Dixon climbed into a car with Lieutenant Colonel White outside the main entrance of Achnacarry Castle a short time later. But there was no denying that the duffel coat had the edge on his RAF raincoat when it came to keeping him warm.

The car took them a short distance down to the gates that gave access to the castle grounds from the road alongside Loch Lochy. Bob wasn't quite sure where they went then, but they seemed to drive for no more than a few hundred yards before they got out of the car.

White led the way. 'We've got an observation point on the bluff overlooking the bay from the south. Here we are.' Bob followed him into a heavily sandbagged roofless structure. He was aware of the vague shapes of other men moving on the bluff around them but surprised by how quiet they were.

White said, 'It's a full moon tonight, which is why we've selected it for the exercise. And it looks like the weather forecast for reasonably clear skies is coming good. What that means is that the men taking part in the landing have got enough light to prepare for the exercise, get into the boats, and then position themselves well out on the loch. It also means that those of us on land will be able to see what's going on. With live ammunition being used, it's important that the attacking force stays within certain agreed pathways, and for that reason members of my own staff accompany them. We've got clear rules in place to ensure that if any of the attacking boats stray into the fields of fire of the defenders' weapons, those weapons can cease fire before men are killed. It works much better, though, if my staff on the boats make sure that doesn't happen.'

Bob could dimly see groups of men boarding boats down on the shore below them, in almost complete silence, while others rowed out into the loch. It was the silence that was the most striking thing. Large numbers of men were deploying without any obvious need for spoken orders, and with very little clanking of weapons or scraping of boots. Despite all the activity in the bay below and around him, Bob could hear the breeze moving the branches of the trees a little to the south of the observation point.

'How many men are involved tonight, Edward?' asked Bob.

'Around 260, plus over a dozen of their officers and some

of my own staff", said the lieutenant colonel. 'This exercise tends to be regarded as the culmination of the Achnacarry course. We've got two groups of trainees, a Scots Guards detachment and a 24th Guards Brigade detachment, who are here on short courses of a fortnight or less. They leave on Monday, and tonight is their chance to take part in the night assault landing.'

'What boats do they use, sir?' asked Lieutenant Dixon.

Lieutenant Colonel White said, 'We have a range of craft we use for training, but tonight the men will be using collapsible assault boats. These boats offer no protection from enemy fire, unlike the landing craft we also have here which have thin armour, and they need to be rowed, but they are totally silent. We find they work best for the night assault exercise because they leave the occupants feeling totally unprotected and vulnerable. The aim of the exercise will be for the landing forces to come ashore, clear the beach, and then storm the high ground behind the road over there. At that point the heavy machine guns you will shortly see in action will change their role. Until then they play the part of defenders firing at, or rather just over, the attackers. But at that point they start simulating covering fire for the attackers, firing over their heads as they advance inland. The culmination of the exercise will be the demolition of a building we've erected for the purpose on the top of the hill. The attackers will then withdraw, get back into their boats, and paddle out into the loch, still under enemy fire.'

Bob again sensed men around them but had no idea of how many. It was still very quiet, with just the occasional splash from a misplaced oar as the boats moved out towards the centre of the loch.

'Any moment now,' said White. In the moonlight, Bob could see that the dark shapes of the fleet of boats on the loch had turned and were picking up speed as they moved back towards the shore. A whistle was blown somewhere near Bob, and all hell was unleashed. A volley of flares was fired into the air and what sounded and looked like three or four heavy machine guns opened fire from points along the shore. Bob could see tracer rounds passing over the heads of the men in the boats, forming a criss-cross pattern because of the widely separated locations of the guns. He was grateful to be viewing the spectacle from his vantage point rather than from one of the boats.

And then, close by, Bob heard the highly distinctive sound of mortars being fired. Some of these produced large flares that hung below parachutes above the invading fleet, while others were clearly firing live high explosive rounds – detonations could be heard from out on the loch, followed by columns of water being thrown high into the air around the oncoming boats. Bob realised why it was so important the boats followed their allocated paths to the shore. A live mortar round landing in one of the flimsy craft would have catastrophic consequences.

The attackers' boats seemed to Bob to be moving agonisingly slowly, and he could only imagine how it felt to those on the receiving end of the fire from the shore. Finally, however, they closed with the beach, at which point the intensity of opposing fire seemed to increase, and now Bob could see explosions amongst and between the incoming boats, as grenades were thrown by figures he could see down on the shore. Then the first boats grounded and men could be seen jumping out over their prows and running up the beach. Orders were being shouted to clear the beach, and for a while Bob lost sight of the attackers as they started to climb the high ground, off to his left. Then the machine guns opened fire again, this time firing up the hill over the heads of the attackers and towards the imaginary defenders beyond them.

Suddenly Bob's good eye was blinded by a huge flash on top of the hill, which was followed quickly by the physical concussion of the shock wave caused by the demolition of the building. Bob didn't think he'd ever heard a louder noise and wondered if they'd hear the explosion in Fort William, the better part of 20 miles away. Perhaps they were used to this sort of thing around here, he thought.

By the time Bob had recovered some of his lost night vision, the attackers could be seen clambering back into their boats, which they then paddled back out into the loch. Again, the mortars around the observation point came to life, and again the heavy machine guns kept up continuous fire above the heads of the men in the boats. Then a whistle was blown by someone nearby, perhaps by Lieutenant Colonel White himself, and more whistles were blown around the bay. Silence descended over Loch Lochy once more.

Bob wondered how long he had been holding his breath. Lieutenant Dixon, standing next to him said, 'Good God, sir, I've never seen or heard anything like that before.'

'That's the idea, Lieutenant,' said White. 'When those men out there on the loch are called upon to do that for real, they will have seen something very like it before, and many more of them will survive because of it.'

'Well, thank you for the invitation, Edward,' said Bob.

'Now I understand why your ammunition bill is so large. Do the neighbours ever complain?'

'We don't have many,' said the lieutenant colonel, 'and those we have seem happy to accept what we do as a price worth paying for freedom.'

CHAPTER THIRTEEN

After a good breakfast, Bob and his team met in their tiny office, so he could assign tasks. Monique was not present, though Michael said he'd spoken to her at breakfast. She apparently intended to spend the morning 'talking to people'. Bob was frustrated at what seemed her deliberate effort to undermine his authority with his team but decided there was nothing he could do about it. He'd spent a lot of time during the night thinking about their argument. It had been some years since he'd had to share accommodation with anyone he wasn't romantically involved with and for a young and fit man, Lieutenant Dixon did snore quite badly, and loudly.

'We will again split our resources,' said Bob. 'Sergeant Potter, I would be grateful if you could begin trying to narrow down the very large list of possible suspects by looking at the available paperwork. Private Jenkins will assist you. As I understand it, you ought to be able to lay your hands on reasonably complete service records for all personnel serving on the staff here at Achnacarry. For the trainees, I believe that all you will have available are their application forms, plus notes made by their commanding officers and interviewing officers.'

'How do you want us to approach the process, sir?' asked Potter.

Bob sat back in his chair. 'You might have to play it by ear a little. Ideally, I would like you to end up with two lists. One will have the names of all the men who we actually know served in Belgium, or France for that matter, in the period before Dunkirk, and the other will be the list of men we know did not serve in France or Belgium during that time.'

'It may not be as simple as that, sir,' said Lieutenant Dixon.

'No, you are right, Lieutenant. I think that in practice, Sergeant Potter, you could end up with as many as four lists. There will be a "definitely did" list, and a "definitely didn't" list as I've just outlined. Some of the "definitely didn't" list will be men who have only joined the armed forces since that time, while others will be men who were serving elsewhere at the time. The only men on the "definitely did" list will be men whose service records or application forms specifically place them there. I think that the third list will be a "may have been" list. We could do with laying our hands on a list of the units who were fighting in France and Belgium at the time, and yes, I know it is likely to be a long one. Men who we can't place on either of the other two lists, but who we know were serving in one of those units at the time need to go on the "may have been" list.'

'You talked of four lists, sir,' said Sergeant Potter. 'What's the fourth?'

'We should perhaps head that one "no bloody idea",' said Bob. 'There will inevitably be men, possibly a lot of men, who we don't have enough information about to place on any of the first three lists. Once you have done that first sift, and I have no feel for how long that will take, we can discuss what to do next, and whether there is any point approaching those men's home units to fill in gaps or help assign them to one list or another.'

'Will the staff here be expecting us, sir?' asked Sergeant Potter.

'Well, they don't seem to treat Sundays as a day of rest here,' said Bob, 'and I discussed our need to look at staff records with Lieutenant Colonel White last night. So yes, if they've not actually been told, they should be able to quickly confirm with the colonel that you can look at the records. Meanwhile, Lieutenant Dixon, could you and Petty Officer MacDonald meet the divers from Fort William and show them what we want them to do around the pier?'

'How big an area do you want them to search, sir?' asked the lieutenant.

'I think it might be best to tell them what we've found so far and ask for their advice on how widely they need to look. Finally, and in case you are wondering, I'm not planning on putting my feet up. I intend to track down the most senior officer I can get hold of in the 1st Belgian Fusilier Battalion and get him to find out all he can about Private Hannes Lambrechts.'

'I've got Private Lambrechts' application form here, sir,' said Sergeant Potter. 'We asked for it on Friday. You might find it helpful to know the name of the senior officer in his unit who recommended him.'

'Thank you, Gilbert,' said Bob. 'I doubt if I will get any answers immediately, but given we are investigating Private Lambrechts' murder, I would hope to get some worthwhile background today. Right, let's get moving. Lieutenant Dixon, when I've made my phone call, I'll come up to the pier to see how things are going there.'

'You did tell us not to go anywhere on our own, sir,' said Dixon.

'Yes, I did, but unless we are going to get embroiled in some sort of real life "fox, goose and bag of grain" puzzle, I don't see a simple way around that and to be on the safe side I will come up in one of the cars. It shouldn't take longer than a couple of minutes.' As Lieutenant Dixon started to say something else, Bob held up his hand. 'Don't worry, Lieutenant, I had a good session on Friday on the firing range at RAF Turnhouse with the pistol they've issued to me. It would short circuit things nicely if I had cause to use it in anger.'

Bob pulled the car off the track near the southern end of the White Bridge, behind the lorry he assumed had brought the navy divers up from Fort William. He walked to the stone pier, where Lieutenant Dixon and Petty Officer MacDonald were talking to three other men. Two were wearing heavy diving suits on which were hung assorted gas bottles and other pieces of equipment whose purpose Bob couldn't guess at.

'Hello, sir,' said Lieutenant Dixon. 'Can I introduce Petty Officer Johnson and Petty Officer Heal, who will be going down to see what they can find, and Able Seaman Pym, who is providing support. We've agreed that they

155

should take an initial look around the west side of the pier and under where the boat was moored to see what turns up. We can then consider the east side of the pier, and widening the search on the west side, if time permits. As you can see, we've pulled the boat around to the east side to help with the initial search.'

'Thank you for coming, gentlemen,' said Bob. 'How long can you dive for?'

'We're pleased to be able to help, sir,' said Petty Officer Johnson. 'It will be a pleasant change to be looking for something that isn't explosive. The rebreather units we use are good for a maximum of 90 minutes, and we've got spares in the lorry. I'm guessing, though, that 90 minutes ought to be long enough. We're going to go in at the shoreline on the west side of the pier. If we've not found anything by the time we get to the end of the pier, we'll surface and agree how to proceed from there. Are you happy with that, sir?'

'Yes, that sounds fine,' said Bob.

The two divers walked to the landward end of the pier and waded into the loch. The able seaman kept a close watch on proceedings from the pier itself.

'Did you get anywhere with the Belgians, sir?' asked Lieutenant Dixon.

'I hope so,' said Bob. 'It seems Private Lambrechts was never likely to be the life and soul of any party, but he was a good soldier and they recommended him very highly when he volunteered to join the commandos. The officer I spoke to, a Major Leclercq, knew nothing about Lambrechts having come to Britain to look for someone, but it seemed to me that he understood the importance of what I wanted to know. When I ended the call I was confident that if anyone back at Lambrechts' home unit knows anything of use to us, then Major Leclercq will find out and pass it on to me pretty quickly. Meanwhile, a first look at the service records and applications forms suggests that Sergeant Potter has got a huge job on, and I'm no longer convinced it's going to get us very far. I hope I can take a decision about that after I hear back from the Belgians.'

'Let's just hope we come up with something here,' said Lieutenant Dixon.

Bob watched as the able seaman leaned over the side of the pier. 'How do you know where they are?' he asked.

'You get occasional flashes of the torches they are carrying, sir, as visibility seems fairly good. Otherwise the rebreathers leave no signs on the surface. No bubbles or anything like that. The water isn't very deep immediately around the pier but according to the Ordnance Survey map it falls away steeply as soon as you get any distance from the pier. It goes down to over a hundred feet deep quite close to the shore on this southern side, and to over three hundred feet deep when you get out into the centre of the loch. The suits and rebreathers are designed for fairly shallow water, so they can't stray too far away from the pier.'

One of the divers surfaced about two thirds of the way along the pier, a little past the stone steps built into its side. He held something out of the water with one hand.

'Hello, he's got something,' said Lieutenant Dixon as the able seaman clambered down the stone steps. He came back up with a pair of very wet binoculars on a leather strap.

'May I?' said Bob, taking the binoculars, which he turned over in his hands. 'These are made by Carl Zeiss, and I'm guessing that the army doesn't normally stretch to issuing quite such good binoculars?'

'The Royal Navy certainly doesn't, sir,' said Dixon. 'We'd need to check with Sergeant Potter, but I imagine that those are just the sort of thing a keen ornithologist might own.'

'A keen ornithologist like Lieutenant Bell?' asked Bob. 'That was my thinking too.'

The two divers surfaced at the end of the pier, then swam round to climb the stone steps.

After they had climbed out and taken off their masks. Petty Officer Johnson said, 'Sir, I think we now need to decide whether to try round the other side of the pier, which would mean moving the boat back round to this side, or whether to have a second sweep on this side. From what Lieutenant Dixon had told us, I was half expecting to find a knife down there. But it would be easy to miss, and on our first sweep we didn't want to risk stirring up too much muck from the bottom. As you know exactly where the captain was killed, it might be worth spending a couple of minutes taking a closer look at the bottom of the loch next to that part of the pier.'

Lieutenant Dixon said, 'It was here, at the top of the steps, though most of the blood got washed away by rain on the first night, leaving just these traces. The problem is that the stern of the boat was at the bottom of the steps. If someone tossed the knife into the water after killing Captain Bell with it, and I'm not convinced they would have done as they'd already used the knife to kill once before, then I guess they'd have tossed it down there, beyond where the rear of the boat was positioned.'

'Well, it will only take a few minutes to check, sir, and I'd like to think we are doing a proper job. Then we can look round the other side.' Petty Officer Johnson looked at Bob for a decision.

'That sounds fine,' said Bob.

The two divers climbed back down the stone steps that led into the waters of the loch and disappeared beneath its surface.

Able Seaman Pym leaned over the side of the pier again. 'You can tell from the quality of the torchlight that they are feeling their way along the bottom, sir, just down there, and the visibility is decreasing because of muck being stirred up.'

This time there was no triumphant raising of an arm when the divers surfaced and no sign of a knife as they climbed back up onto the pier. When Petty Officer Johnson removed his face mask, Bob said, 'Never mind, it was worth a try.'

'It certainly was, sir,' said the petty officer, holding out his right hand. 'We may not have found a knife, but we did find this.' There, nestled in the palm of his gloved hand was a coin that looked to be about an inch in diameter.

'That's gold, isn't it?' said Bob.

'It looks very much like it,' said Johnson. 'When, in years to come, my grandchildren ask me what I did in the war, I can tell them I once found gold treasure. Even if it was just the one coin. And before you ask, sir, I'm pretty sure there are no more of them in the same area.'

Bob said, 'There's a woman's head on it, with some Latin text around the edge.'

'I think that may be a man, sir,' said Lieutenant Dixon.

'There's a definite Adam's apple there in the throat, even if the hair does look distinctly feminine.'

The petty officer moved his hand to turn the coin over. Bob said, 'The other side's got two oval shields under a crown. And there's a date, 1742.'

'Do you think it's related to your captain's murder?' asked Petty Officer Johnson.

'I'm sorry, petty officer, but I think it's too much of a coincidence that it should turn up where the captain was killed. I don't think you're going to be able to keep it.'

The petty officer grinned. 'I'd worked that out for myself, sir. But I'd love to know what its story is when you find out. You know, so I can tell the grandchildren when I have some.'

'I can promise you that,' said Bob. 'In the meantime, Petty Officer MacDonald, you seem to know about fingerprints. Is there any chance that there could be any on the coin?'

'Well we know it's been in the water for at least 36 hours, and then there's the contact with the loch bed and with Petty Officer Johnson's glove. I'd say the chances are slim, sir, but it's worth a try. The fingerprint kit is in the boot of the car.' He pulled an envelope out of an inner pocket, removed the letter from it, and held it open for Johnston to drop the coin into.

Petty Officer Johnson said, 'That's this side and the end of the pier done and I'm quite keen to look on the other side now, if that's alright with you, sir. You never know what we might find!'

Bob and Lieutenant Dixon helped the able seaman pull the boat around the end of the pier and moor it back where it had started.

The two divers entered the water again from the shore just to the east of the pier. This time the star find was a badly corroded cigarette lighter that looked as if it had been in the loch for some years. 'I bet you are going to say we can keep that, aren't you, sir?' said Petty Officer Johnson, grinning again.

Just then, Petty Officer MacDonald returned from the car. 'Sorry, sir. As I thought, there were no usable fingerprints on the coin. Do you want to hang on to it for the moment?'

He handed the coin over to Bob, who turned the beautiful object over in his fingers before carefully wrapping it in a handkerchief and putting into one of his breast pockets.

Lunch with Lieutenant Dixon passed without Bob really noticing the food. Monique joined them, part way through.

She sat next to Michael, and when she spoke, she addressed herself to him. 'I spent my morning tracking down and interviewing six of the group of German and Austrian trainees who initially attracted Captain Bell's attention. I just went for those I could find first. I was able to conduct reasonably thorough interviews with each and will produce a report as soon as I can.'

'Did you find anything of value?' asked Michael.

'No, though I suppose it is of value that we can say with reasonable confidence that none of them, nor, probably, those few I couldn't talk to, were involved in Private Lambrechts' murder.'

Bob started to say something, but Monique interrupted. 'Yes, I know that was fairly obvious already from the work Captain Bell and Sergeant Potter had done. But as the presence of the German contingent was what got me attached to this investigation, I felt I had to make the effort. It wouldn't look very good, would it, if I were to assure my department head that the Germans had nothing to do with it, then have to admit that I'd not actually bothered to talk to any of them myself. Remember, I was able to talk to them in their own language and I might have picked up signals that would have been missed by Captain Bell. As I've said, there were none.'

The rest of lunch passed in slightly uncomfortable silence, despite Michael's efforts to start a conversation about the odd mix of people at Achnacarry. Monique was still eating when Bob stood up, announcing he had to see Lieutenant Colonel White. He asked Michael and Monique to see how the sifting of the personnel records was going when they'd finished lunch.

'Come in, Bob,' said White,' and no, I don't live in this office. As you saw last night, I do get out occasionally. What can I do for you?'

'I thought you might like to look at something the navy divers found in Loch Arkaig, next to the pier this morning.' Bob reached across the lieutenant colonel's desk and placed the gold coin on the desk's leather inlay.

'My, that's rather pretty,' said White.

'It's dated 1742,' said Bob. 'I've no idea how it came to be where it was, but I get the feeling it's tied into Captain Bell's death somehow.'

White picked up the coin, turned it over, then replaced it on his desk. 'Can you wait there a moment, Bob?'

He got up and walked out of his office, returning a few minutes later, followed by Captain Sanderson. White turned to the captain and pointed at the coin on the desk. 'What do you make of that, Clive?'

Captain Sanderson picked up the coin, looked at both sides, then held it up so the light from the window reflected from its surface.

White said, 'I should tell you, Bob, that before the war Clive was a historian, and has enlivened a few otherwise dull evenings in the mess with his stories of Clan Cameron's role in the 1745 Jacobite rising.'

'Ah,' said Bob, 'the reason why the old Achnacarry Castle was destroyed?'

'That's right sir,' said Sanderson. 'Which makes the date of 1742 on this coin very significant.'

'Do you know what it is?' asked Bob.

'I think it will turn out to be what they call a "Louis d'or", one of a series of gold coins minted in France between the 1600s and the 1800s.'

'How would a two-hundred-year-old French gold coin find its way into Loch Arkaig?'

'Would you mind coming with me to see someone, Group Captain?' asked Sanderson. 'There's an old gentleman called Archibald Cameron who you might find helpful. He used to be the estate factor who looked after the day-to-day running of the estate here, on behalf of the Chief of Clan Cameron of Locheil, who owns the place. I think Archibald retired some time before the war, but he is an absolute mine of information on the history of the area, and especially about the Jacobite connections. He lives in an estate cottage in a hamlet called Clunes, on Loch Lochy, a couple of miles north east of here. I met him when I went to apologise after one of our volunteers passing through

Achnacarry thought it would be a fine idea to go hand grenade fishing in the bay up at Clunes. As it turned out the volunteer passed through Achnacarry rather more quickly than he anticipated and was returned to his unit the following day. Anyway, I think Archibald Cameron will be able to tell you all you need to know about this coin and its significance.'

Bob had intended to collect Lieutenant Dixon en route to the car, deciding it would make more sense for him to hear what Archibald Cameron had to say first hand, saving Bob the need to tell him afterwards. On hearing what was proposed, Monique opted to accompany them. Bob felt helpless to object. He was deeply anxious not to let the rift between him and Monique become visible to his team. He felt that both his professional and personal credibility depended on it. He'd hoped that after her pronouncement at lunch about the German trainees that she'd decide she could decently return to Glasgow, but she was showing no sign of doing so, and he was in no position to ask.

CHAPTER FOURTEEN

On the Ordnance Survey map, Clunes was no more than a tiny collection of black rectangles near the shore of Loch Lochy and close to the point where the road running up its western side turned sharply left to head for Loch Arkaig.

Lieutenant Dixon pulled the car off the road not far from a small but beautifully-kept cottage whose smoking chimney was the obvious source of an aroma of burning peat.

'It looks like he's in, anyway,' said Captain Sanderson.

Sanderson knocked on the door seconds before it was opened. 'Hello, Mr Cameron. I hope it's not inconvenient, but I've brought you some visitors. The two gentlemen are Group Captain Sutherland and Lieutenant Dixon, and the lady is Madame Dubois. They are all from the War Office.'

The man who had opened the door looked to Bob to be in his seventies. He wore a baggy green jumper over a check shirt. He also wore a kilt, of the same tartan used by the instructors at Achnacarry to back their cap badges. The man was slightly stooped with age, but his eyes seemed as sharp and as alive as any Bob could remember seeing.

Archibald Cameron laughed. 'It has the makings of a good joke, doesn't it? "A man from the army, a man from the navy and a man from the air force came calling." I'm afraid you don't fit into the joke, Madame Dubois.' He smiled. Come in, please. Can I offer you a cup of tea?'

'That's very kind of you, Mr Cameron,' said Bob.

'Please, just call me Archibald. Round here everyone answers to "Mr Cameron".' He showed them into a sitting room that occupied a large part of one end of the cottage. The three armchairs didn't match one another or the sofa, but everything was spotlessly clean. Pictures of Highlanders in historical settings adorned the walls, and a peat fire burned in the grate. A black cat lay curled up on the mat in front of the fire.

'Thank you, Archibald,' said Bob. 'I prefer to be known as Bob, and this is Michael, and as I imagine you already know, this is Clive. This is…'

'Please call me Monique.' She smiled brightly at Archibald.

The four visitors obeyed their host's instructions to sit down, the three men choosing chairs, while Monique took one end of the sofa. Archibald Cameron busied himself in the next room, which Bob presumed was the kitchen.

When the tea was poured, Archibald Cameron sat next to Monique and looked at each of them in turn. 'It is very pleasant to see you all, but I don't think you are here just to pass the time of day, are you?'

Bob said, 'No, you are right, Archibald. Something turned up this morning, and when I showed it to Clive he suggested we come and talk to you about it.' He pulled the handkerchief-wrapped coin out of his breast pocket and passed it over to the older man.

The three visitors watched as Archibald Cameron unwrapped the coin. When it lay in his hand he sat very still, looking down at it, for so long that Bob asked, 'Are you alright, Mr Cameron?'

'Where did you get this?' asked Archibald. Bob was shocked to see tears in the older man's eyes when he looked up.

'It was found by a navy diver near the old stone pier, a couple of hundred yards from the White Bridge, at this end of Loch Arkaig,' said Bob.

'Were there any more with it?' asked Archibald.

'No, and there's reason to believe that one might only have been there a couple of days. It might help you understand why I think that if I tell you what's been happening this week.'

'Please do,' said Archibald.

Bob continued. 'On Wednesday evening a trainee at the Commando Basic Training Centre was murdered. It's my team's job to investigate that sort of thing. Two of my men travelled up from Edinburgh on Thursday. Then, on Friday evening, one of them was also murdered. It seems very likely that his murder took place on that pier on the shore of Loch Arkaig. This morning navy divers looked at the lake bed around the pier and found that.' Bob indicated the coin in Archibald's hand. 'Clive tells me that you might be able to help me understand how the coin got there. Knowing that might just help me find out who has been killing people at Achnacarry.'

Archibald Cameron stood up, and surprised Bob by

spinning the coin in the air towards him. Bob had never been very good at ball games, but his problems with depth perception since losing the sight in his left eye made games of catch something he avoided at all costs. He was relieved that he managed to avoid dropping the coin.

'Very well then,' said Archibald, 'but we're going to need something stronger than tea.' He went out to the kitchen again, returning a few moments later with an unmarked bottle full of golden-brown liquid. 'I know it's a little early in the day, but what I have to tell you might take a little time, and when I've finished you'll understand why I want to share some of our local delicacy with you.'

'That looks rather interesting,' said Bob.

'How much do you all know about the 1745 Jacobite rising? I think you know all about it, Clive. What about you three?'

'A little from school,' said Bob

'Very little, I'm afraid,' said Lieutenant Dixon.

'Only what you are about to tell us,' said Monique, smiling.

Archibald held up the bottle of whisky. 'I'd be pleased if you could join me.' He poured the whisky into five glasses on the sideboard and passed four of them around. 'A toast, please, to the "King Over the Water".' Then he grinned impishly. 'Don't worry, Bob, I think the Jacobite claim to the thrones of England, Ireland and Scotland died out long ago, so it's probably no longer actually treasonable to take part in that toast.'

'Thank you, Archibald, I'm not sure how reassured I am by that.' Bob also grinned. 'If this is illicit whisky, it puts the output of a lot of legal distillers to shame.'

Archibald sat back on his sofa, took a sip of the whisky, and closed his eyes. 'Let's go back just under 200 years in time. On the 19th of August 1745 a small rowing boat landed at the north end of Loch Shiel. It was early in the afternoon. Prince Charles Edward Stuart, "Bonnie Prince Charlie" as he is often known, came ashore and met his escort of fifty MacDonalds before retiring to a nearby barn to await the response to letters he had sent to possible supporters all over the Highlands.

'Another 150 MacDonalds were quickly on the scene, but for some time it seemed that Bonnie Prince Charlie was going to have to challenge for his father's right to the thrones of England, Ireland and Scotland with just 200 men. Then the sound of pipes was heard approaching from the north. In marched around a thousand men of Clan Cameron coming from Achnacarry and Loch Arkaig. It is worth remembering that the west end of Loch Arkaig lies under nine miles north of the north end of Loch Shiel.

'By the end of the day, 300 more men had arrived. Judging that he had enough support to mount his rebellion, Charles Edward Stuart climbed a nearby hill and raised his standard. A brief ceremony, translated into Gaelic for the benefit of the Jacobite clansmen, followed, and the Prince then ordered that brandy be distributed.

'And so, the '45 was born. It was to end in bloody failure at Culloden on the 16th of April 1746, less than eight months later. In its aftermath the Highland way of life that had existed for hundreds of years was swept away by brutality, suppression and self-interest.

'But in the meantime, Charles had come very close indeed to taking the crowns he sought. His army reached

Derby on the 6th of December 1745, before retreating after a closely argued meeting in the upstairs room of a Derby pub. Meantime, the Hanoverian court was packing its belongings onto ships in the Thames. Had Charles advanced, George II would probably have fled, leaving Charles' father as James VIII of Scotland and III of England.

'Some say that if that had happened the English and French would have avoided a further 70 years of conflict; the English would not have had to raise taxes in the colonies to pay for the French wars; the Americans would not have had cause to fight a war for their independence; and the French revolution might not have happened. The world would be a very different place. Perhaps, who knows, we might not be fighting a war against Germany today.'

Captain Sanderson said, 'I've also heard it said that if the Jacobites had advanced from Derby they might have been cut to pieces by government troops four months earlier than they actually were, and at somewhere like Northampton rather than at Culloden.'

Archibald smiled across at him. 'Aye, I've heard that said too, Clive. Who can know for sure? But given Bonnie Prince Charlie's real interest lay in London, he spent more time than he intended or wanted in western Scotland. Before raising his standard at Glenfinnan, Charles Edward Stuart had initially landed on Eriskay in the Western Isles. He then landed on the mainland in Loch nan Uamh, near Lochailort, some miles west of Glenfinnan.

'The irony is that after Culloden he passed this way again, several times, while evading the government troops searching for him. It says much for the loyalty of his supporters that no-one collected the vast reward placed on his head. And on the 20th of September 1746 he left Scotland for the last time when he was picked up by a French frigate on the shores of Loch nan Uamh, close to where he had landed just over a year earlier and perhaps 20 miles in a straight line from the western end of Loch Arkaig.'

'Where does our gold coin come into the picture, Archibald?' asked Lieutenant Dixon.

'Have a little patience with an old man, Michael,' said Archibald. 'A successful military campaign needs a number of things. It needs men, and weapons, and food, but as much as any of them it needs money. Unless you can keep paying your men they will sooner or later desert you, and unless you can pay for food and weapons, you will sooner or later run out of both.

'If you were a Jacobite, then the real tragedy of the 1745 rising was that several opportunities that could have made all the difference were missed through bad decisions, bad planning, or simple bad luck. We can argue about what would have happened if they'd not turned back at Derby, but that's just one example. Another is the way the Jacobite army prepared for battle at Culloden, which virtually guaranteed it would lose.

'And then we come to the gold. A classic example of bad luck and bad timing concerns the arrival in Loch nan Uamh on the 10th of May 1746 of two French frigates. That was less than a month after the final Jacobite defeat at Culloden. The ships brought weapons, ammunition and medical supplies. They also brought gold pledged by the Spanish government to help pay for an uprising that had by then already failed.

'It was decided that this gold, which was in the form of 35,000 French Louis d'or, just like the one you showed me, should be brought ashore, and used to help Jacobites in Scotland. Records suggest that 800 coins were stolen as the gold was being landed by clansmen from Barrisdale in Knoydart, leaving 34,200. These were taken overland to Loch Arkaig, in, it is said, seven large wooden caskets.'

'What happened to the gold?' asked Bob.

'For reasons I'll come to in a moment, the Clan Cameron archives have a fairly detailed account of what happened to most of it.' Archibald waved a very dog-eared notebook he had brought back through from the kitchen with the whisky. 'I looked at the relevant documents some years ago and took notes.'

Archibald looked the notebook. '4,200 of the Louis d'or were distributed to men who had served in the Jacobite army, or to their families, to cover arrears of pay, while 3,000 were sent to Edinburgh to cover expenses of Jacobite sympathisers there. Another 3,000 were taken with him by Charles Edward Stuart when he eventually escaped to France.

'This is where things begin to get rather murky. The remaining 24,000 Louis d'or were left in the charge of Macpherson of Cluny, the head of Clan Macpherson, but apparently remained hidden at Loch Arkaig. This is also where it begins to get very personal. An ancestor of mine was a man called Archibald Cameron of Locheil. As it happens I was named after him. He was a doctor and a leading Jacobite. He was badly wounded at the Battle of Culloden, but despite that he later managed to help Charles Edward Stuart escape from Scotland and departed these shores with him.

'While he was in exile, Charles never had enough money, and his thoughts often turned to the gold believed to remain here. In 1749 he sent Archibald Cameron of Locheil back to Scotland to find out what had become of the gold. During his visit, my namesake spoke with several people, including Macpherson of Cluny.

'When he returned to the continent, to the Jacobite court in exile, Archibald Cameron wrote a very detailed account of what he thought had become of the gold for Charles Edward Stuart. A copy of this later found its way into the Clan Cameron archives, which is how I came to see it. Within his account he described the expenditure of another 12,981 Louis d'or, for arguably legitimate purposes, which left just over 11,000. Of this remaining 11,000, Macpherson of Cluny had personally taken possession of 5,000, and Archibald Cameron was able to take 300 back to the continent with him, leaving 5,700 Louis d'or still hidden at Loch Arkaig. The various uses to which the gold had been put by Macpherson of Cluny and others were the cause of a huge amount of friction amongst Jacobites in Scotland, and Charles Edward Stuart later accused Macpherson of Cluny of embezzlement.

'In 1753 Charles Edward Stuart again sent Archibald Cameron of Locheil to Scotland, this time to try to retrieve all the gold that remained, which they must have hoped meant the 5,700 Louis d'or they believed was hidden at Loch Arkaig, plus at least some of the 5,000 that Macpherson of Cluny had taken. It is believed that Archibald Cameron did locate the gold that was still hidden at Loch Arkaig, only then to have to conceal it again as government troops, who had been tipped off about his presence, closed in on him.'

'Where did he hide it?' asked Bob.

'No-one knows for sure,' said Archibald. 'According to one story, he hid it temporarily in the loose earth of a freshly-dug grave in an ancient graveyard surrounded by an oval stone wall on the shore of Loch Arkaig at Murlaggan, and later moved it again. That time, it is said, he hid it in the valley of the Callich Burn, or the "Allt na Caillich" as you'll find it written on your maps. This climbs up from the north side of the loch. Another story claims that the gold was hidden in Glen Mallie, which is a side glen that heads west for some distance from the southern side of Loch Arkaig. Yet another story would have us believe that part of the gold was hidden near Arisaig, on the coast to the west.'

'Didn't your ancestor pass the information on?' asked Bob.

'I'm sure the Hanoverian government tried to make him say where it was,' said Archibald. 'He was betrayed and arrested and taken in chains to London. On the 7th of June 1753 he became the very last Jacobite to be executed for his part in the 1745 rising, in a savagely brutal way. The location of the hidden gold went to the grave with him.'

'I'm sorry,' said Bob. 'I can understand why seeing that coin was an emotional experience.'

'If that coin was only put where you found it recently, then it seems likely that someone has found at least part of what remains of the gold,' said Archibald.

'I've been thinking much the same thing,' said Bob. 'I'm just having a little difficulty making sense of how and why that coin ended up by the pier and the sequence of events that must have preceded that happening.'

'Well, thankfully, that's your job and not mine, Bob,' said Archibald.

'Surely over the years people must have tried to find the gold?' asked Lieutenant Dixon.

'Of course,' said Archibald. 'Over the past two centuries many have looked for it. There was a story that some of it was found in an unspecified wood near Loch Arkaig in 1850 but I've never seen any evidence to support that. When I was a child my father told me that when he was a small boy his two older brothers had spent weeks one summer searching the valley of the Allt na Caillich whenever they had any spare time. There's a waterfall on the main river, quite high up, and it seems they thought that was a likely hiding place. But they never found anything. The thing I've never understood about the traditional story is that by 1753, my namesake was in his mid-forties and had suffered severe wounds to his ankles at Culloden which weren't properly treated until he reached France with Charles Edward Stuart many months later. Even carrying the surviving gold wouldn't have been easy. He must have had helpers, but only one is known, a man called Alexander MacMillan of Glenpeanmore. He came from Glen Pean, which extends west from the west end of Loch Arkaig, and I've never discovered what became of him.'

'Perhaps Alexander MacMillan rehid the gold when things quietened down?' suggested Bob.

'Who can say?' said Archibald. 'Perhaps he removed it and used it to fund a new life for himself and his family in the new world? Given how everyone else had helped themselves to the gold, it would be hard to blame him.'

'How much of a burden would the gold have been?'

asked Bob. 'I've no feel for how much 5,700 of these coins would weigh.'

'That's a good question,' said Archibald. 'I looked into exactly that while visiting Edinburgh once, years before the war, and again I took notes. One of those coins weighs close to 8.16 grammes. If you multiply that by 5,700, you get over about forty-six and a half kilogrammes, which is a little over one hundred pounds in weight.'

'A hundred pounds of gold? That sounds worth taking a few chances for,' said Bob.

'My figures may be a little out of date,' said Archibald, 'but last time I looked, the price of gold was about $34 US Dollars per ounce. At the fixed exchange rate of just over four US Dollars to the Pound Sterling, that makes 5,700 of those coins worth a little over £13,800. You also need to consider that the gold in the coins is only about 92% pure, making the total value £13,800, minus 8%, or nearly £12,700. Call it two pounds and five shillings per coin. That is simply their value in gold, of course. It takes no account of their historical importance.'

'That's not as much as I'd expected,' said Bob, 'but if you assume that before the war an average house cost under £600, it's more than enough to set someone up for life.'

'It might be enough to drive a man to murder,' said Archibald.

Bob said, 'You've mentioned the west end of Loch Arkaig a few times, Archibald. What's there now? The map shows a school. Is there a village there?'

'No,' said Archibald. 'The area was once well settled, but that all changed a century or more ago, when sheep were considered better tenants than people. Before the war there were a couple of occupied crofts up at Strathan, and the old school. But when the men left to go to war, their families couldn't continue to live out there, so they moved to places like here at Clunes or Spean Bridge.'

'Is there anything else of interest there?' asked Bob.

'There's an old government barracks from the Jacobite era,' said Archibald. 'It's called "Tigh nan Saighdearan", which translates as "The Soldiers' House". It could only ever have been tiny to start with, and there are only a couple of walls left now, standing on a high point next to the track from the head of the loch to Strathan. The main thing of interest about the west end of Loch Arkaig is the way it serves as a crossroads for routes leading off in a variety of directions.'

'Thanks, Archibald. There is one more thing you might be able to help me with,' said Bob.

'What's that?' asked Archibald.

'If you stand on the White Bridge, or on the pier for that matter, you don't really get much sense of the real length of Loch Arkaig because of the landscape. But the one thing that does stand out is a little island perhaps half a mile along the loch. What can you tell me about that?'

'You are thinking that the gold might be hidden on the island?' asked Archibald.

'I don't know, really,' said Bob. 'It's just that it's close to the pier where we found the coin and where Captain Bell was murdered. There may be a connection.'

'Well there's no denying that it is an island with an interesting history, even if we don't know much of that history. It's called Eilean Loch Airceig. The west end of the island is natural rock, but in prehistoric times my ancestors expanded the size of the island with stones, and built a crannog on it, a sort of defensive island dwelling. You can think of the crannog on Loch Arkaig as the earliest predecessor of the first Achnacarry Castle. Nothing much remains of the crannog apart from the expanded island. Sometime later, in the medieval period, my rather more recent ancestors built a chapel on the island. This was called St Columba's Chapel and its ruins can still be seen on the northern side of Eilean Loch Airceig. It is also possible to see a wall that surrounded a burial ground beside the chapel. This was the traditional burial ground of the Camerons of Locheil. There are records that show the chapel was still in use in the 1600s, but sometime later it became a ruin. I can see why someone might think of it as a possible hiding place for the Loch Arkaig gold, but the stories that exist all seem to point further west.'

'I'm tempted to go and have a look anyway,' said Bob, 'mainly to look for signs of recent activity. The island looks fairly heavily wooded from a distance.'

'It is,' said Archibald. 'I'd say it had returned to nature if it weren't for the fact that part of it was artificial to start with. If you are thinking of visiting, the best place to land is probably on the southern side. You might not have noticed it, but there's another even smaller island a short distance to the south west of Eilean Loch Airceig. It's called An t-Eilean Beag. Again, there's nothing to suggest any link with the stories of the gold. And, if you are thinking about a boat trip on Loch Arkaig, make sure you watch out for the water horse.'

'The what?' asked Bob.

'The water horse. We've all read a lot in the newspapers

over the past few years about a mysterious beast in Loch Ness. Not many people know of stories of similar creatures in other lochs. Only eight miles west of the west end of Loch Arkaig is the east end of Loch Morar. That loch is over a thousand feet deep in places, and since the end of the last century there have been sightings of an unexplained creature there. As for Loch Arkaig, there have been many sightings dating back to the last century of what is known as the water horse.'

'You're pulling my leg, aren't you?'

The old man's eyes twinkled. 'Perhaps just a little, Bob, but the stories have existed for a long time, and what is it they say about smoke and fire?'

Bob laughed. 'Anyway, I'm sorry to have taken up so much of your time, Archibald, and I'm extremely grateful for what you've been able to tell us.'

'I'm happy to help at any time,' said Archibald. 'And I want you to promise to let me know what happens. The legend of that gold has been part of the background to my life, and it feels so strange to have seen and touched part of it, even if only a very small part of it.'

As Lieutenant Dixon drove the short distance back to Achnacarry, Bob sat in the back of the car with Monique, trying to get his thoughts in order. 'Well, I'm not sure what I was expecting from our visit to Archibald, but it certainly wasn't that. Thank you, Clive, I'm very grateful.'

'Did you notice how that black cat never moved a muscle the entire time we were there?' asked Sanderson. 'It just lay in front of the fire, as if we didn't exist.'

'Do you think we should visit Eilean Loch Airceig, sir?' asked Dixon.

'I rather believe we should,' said Bob. 'Clive, do you mind if we borrow the boat that's up there, either later today or tomorrow morning?' He looked at his watch. 'Most likely tomorrow, if I'm honest.'

'I am sure Lieutenant Colonel White will have no objection to your borrowing the boat, sir' said Sanderson. 'Everyone else does, apparently.'

'That's an interesting thought,' said Bob. 'I don't know how many military police you have available to look after security here, but would it be possible to have them guard the pier? I'd like to make sure the killer no longer has access to the boat. We may not know who he is yet, but there's no harm trying to put him under a bit of pressure.'

'I think we can manage that, sir,' said Sanderson. He smiled. 'If this were a story by Agatha Christie, I'd be asking how you were so sure the killer is a "he". After all, according to Kipling, the female of the species is deadlier than the male. But in the circumstances, I think you'll turn out to be correct.'

'On the grounds that the only female within miles wasn't actually here at the time?' asked Monique, smiling.

'That's right, Madame Dubois.'

CHAPTER FIFTEEN

'Hello, Major Leclercq, it's Group Captain Sutherland here from Military Intelligence Section 11. I'm sorry I wasn't available when you telephoned back.'

'That's no problem, Group Captain. Are you any nearer to finding who killed Private Lambrechts?'

'I think we've made some progress today, Major. Have you been able to find out anything that might help get us any closer?'

'I think so, Group Captain. I talked to most of the men in Private Lambrechts' former platoon during the day. The picture I've been getting from everyone fits very closely with the picture I gave you myself, when we spoke this morning. Hannes Lambrechts was of course a very young man, no more than a boy, really. He was also a very private man, and quite shy. He was the sort of man who would stand at the back of a crowd rather than push to the front of it to make his voice heard. As I told you this morning, this did not get in the way of his being a very good soldier. Whenever I saw him in training there was something totally committed about him. He worked harder than those around him, even though many of the other men are older and stronger. That was why I recommended him so strongly when he applied for the commandos.'

'Did he have many friends?' asked Bob.

'No, not many. During his time with us he did get to know a few of the men, though, and I've been able to talk to them today. Given what you said, I asked each of them directly whether they had ever heard him talking about looking for someone. Two of those I spoke to had heard him mention it, when they were talking about home or family, but he'd never revealed any details.'

'How about a sweetheart?'

'I was just coming to that, Group Captain. As I said before, he was a quiet and shy young man. We are based in Tenby, in south Wales, and it would be fair to say that over the two years since the Free Belgian Forces arrived in Wales, several relationships have developed. There have even been some marriages between our men and Welsh girls. I didn't expect to get a positive reply, but I did ask those who knew Hannes Lambrechts about any girlfriends. I was surprised to find that he had formed a close friendship with a local girl who is training to be a primary school teacher, Anne Davies. She is two or three years older than Hannes, but it seems that since they first met a year ago, they have become close.'

'Did he ever say anything to her about why he was searching for someone?'

'Apparently not, Group Captain, but I think I found out what you want to know anyway. Earlier this afternoon I had the unpleasant duty of going to see Miss Anne Davies

182

to tell her that Hannes Lambrechts was dead. We were obviously told on Thursday by the people at Achnacarry, but as he had no next-of-kin listed, there was no-one for us to tell. It was therefore news to her.'

'How did she take it?' asked Bob.

'She was very composed at first, but I think she was deeply shocked. We sat in the kitchen with her mother while I asked her about Hannes. I asked her if he ever talked about his home or his family, and I also asked her if she had ever heard him talk about someone he was looking for. She thought there had been a tragedy of some sort in his family, though he never talked about it. And he had never said anything to her about looking for someone in Britain. After I had been there a little while, it seemed that the reality of what I had told her sank in, and she started crying and went upstairs to her room.'

'But you said you had found something out?' said Bob, wishing Major Leclercq would give him the summary account rather than the blow-by-blow details.

'Yes, I did. When Anne Davies went upstairs, her mother followed her, but asked me not to leave. A little later the mother came back downstairs to say that Anne was asleep. The mother's name is Mary Davies. She's a homely, charming, middle-aged Welsh woman. She told me two things. First, she told me that when he died Hannes Lambrechts was going to be a father but didn't yet know it. Then she told me about something that had happened one night earlier in the year. Apparently the 30th of May this year fell on a Saturday. So Mrs Davies told me, anyway. On that day, Anne Davies had been away visiting relatives in Swansea. Late that evening Hannes Lambrechts woke

Mary Davies up, banging on the front door of the house. I understand that her husband is serving with the merchant navy, so she was alone at the time. Hannes was drunk, something Mary Davies had never seen in him before, and was obviously upset, so she took him into the kitchen and made some tea.'

'What happened then?' asked Bob.

'Hannes broke down in tears, and told Mrs Davies that exactly two years previously, on the night of the 30th of May 1940, his mother had been shot dead in front of him in the bar she ran in the town of Nieuwpoort on the Belgian coast. According to him, a drunk British soldier had come into the bar and demanded that Hannes' mother give him bottles of wine. When she refused, he shot her with his rifle. He then turned the rifle on Hannes and shot him. Hannes tried to evade the shot, and it only grazed the side of his head, but knocked him backwards and he struck his head on some furniture. I think that may have saved his life. He came to the next day. His mother's body lay where she had fallen nearby and when Hannes went outside for help he found the town in total chaos as the allies tried desperately to hold the Germans back from Dunkirk, not far along the coast. Hannes concluded that he had to escape to Britain, partly to avoid the Germans, but mostly so he could look for the man who killed his mother.'

'Was he able to say anything about the man?' asked Bob.

'Ah, the important question,' said Leclercq. Bob wondered for a moment if the major was being sarcastic, before remembering that the conversation wasn't being held in Leclercq's first language. 'He described the man as wearing British army battledress, with a sleeveless leather jerkin over the top. He was of medium height and wearing nothing on his head. He had light-coloured close-cropped hair, probably blond, and he needed a shave. Even though there was only candlelight in the bar because of a power cut, the thing he remembered most was the man's piercing blue eyes as he pointed the rifle at Hannes and pulled the trigger. He also remembered that the man had a badly broken nose. Hannes saw no rank insignia, so thought the man was a private. He had no idea about the man's age. Mrs Davies told me that it was as if Hannes had been reliving the moment when he told her about it. She had asked him if the man had any regimental badges that might help identify him. Hannes told her that he hadn't seen any.'

'So we are looking for a blond British army soldier of average height and unknown age with blue eyes and a badly broken nose, who was serving as a private in Belgium on the night of the 30th of May 1940?' asked Bob.

'That's what Mrs Davies says, and she has more interest than most in helping find this man. Because of him her future grandchild will never know his or her father.'

'Did Hannes tell Mrs Davies anything else?' asked Bob.

'He told her that he'd taken the uniform of a Belgian soldier to enable him to get on one of the boats at Dunkirk, and that when he arrived in Britain he joined the Free Belgium Forces. For a while he had been consumed with the desire to find the man who had killed his mother, but since meeting Anne he had started to think about the future again rather than just the past.'

'I'm very grateful to you, Major. What you have told me will be a huge help.'

'As I was getting up to leave, Mary Davies told me that she had never told Anne about Hannes coming to the house that night, or about what had happened to his mother. But as I left the kitchen, I found that Anne had come downstairs and was standing in the hallway outside. She had overheard everything. I promised both Anne and her mother that I would let them know if you catch the man, Group Captain, so I am asking you in turn to promise me that you will let me know.'

'I will,' said Bob. As he put the telephone down, Bob realised that was the third promise he had made that day to let people know how his investigation went. He hoped he wouldn't let them down.

Bob had been alone in their small office when he made the call, and after he finished he went looking for his team. He found them in the centre's main administration office, further along the corridor, surrounded by piles of files and other paperwork. Monique was with them. It seemed that Achnacarry's own clerks had felt it better not to get in the way and were nowhere to be seen.

'Hello, sir,' said Lieutenant Dixon. 'How did it go?'

'I'll tell you in a moment, but first, how much progress have you been able to make here?'

'I think we've extracted pretty much all we can from the records, sir, and it's as you expected.' said Sergeant Potter. 'As far as the permanent staff are concerned we've got a clear division between those we can place on the continent in the period leading up to Dunkirk, and those who definitely were not. We've also got a smaller number of those who might have been, based on the units they were in at the time. The "might have been" list is causing us real problems, sir. The British Expeditionary Force amounted to several hundred thousand men, divided into three Army Corps. Each corps comprised a huge variety of individual units. It turns out that it's not enough to know whether a man was serving, say, with the Royal Norfolk Regiment in May 1940. We actually need to know which battalion of the regiment he was serving in.'

'Yes, I see it's a huge task,' said Bob. 'And what about the trainees?'

'The position there is even worse, sir,' said Sergeant Potter. 'We have a small list of those we can show were in France or Belgium at the time, thanks to comments they have made on their application forms, or which were made by their senior officers or their interviewing officers on the forms. We also have a rather larger list of those who only joined up after Dunkirk, so could not have been there. But the biggest lists are the "might-have-beens" and the fourth list, which you called the "no bloody idea" list.'

'Fair enough,' said Bob, 'thank you for working so hard on this. It may be that we can make the job easier by coming at an identification from the opposite end of the process. Incidentally, does anyone know if the medical officer has looked at the type of blood we found on the pier?'

'Yes, sir,' said Petty Officer MacDonald. 'It was apparently Type B blood, which was the same as Captain Bell's. And according to the medical officer only 10% of people in this country have that blood type. Which means that the chances are fairly high that the blood we found was Captain Bell's.'

'Thank you, Andrew,' said Bob. 'It's good to have that

confirmation, on top of the cap badge. Incidentally, do we know if the binoculars were Captain Bell's?'

'They were the same type, sir,' said Sergeant Potter. 'His parents gave them to him for his birthday a few years ago.'

'Thank you.' Bob paused and took a deep breath. 'Right, I spoke to Major Leclercq of the Free Belgian Forces in south Wales. He had been able to talk to Hannes Lambrechts' sweetheart and, more importantly, to her mother. Incidentally, it seems that Hannes was going to be a father but didn't know it at the time he died. The summary version of the story is this. On the night of the 30th of May 1940, a drunk British soldier entered the bar run by Hannes' mother in Nieuwpoort on the Belgian coast not far from Dunkirk and, when she refused to hand over the wine he was demanding, he shot her dead in front of Hannes. He then tried to kill Hannes and probably thought he had, but only rendered him unconscious.'

'What do we know about the British soldier, sir?' asked Lieutenant Dixon.

'He was of average height, fair hair, probably blond, had piercing blue eyes and a badly broken nose. Hannes had said he was wearing a British army battledress with a leather jerkin over it. He was bare-headed, so there was no cap badge to see, and Hannes saw no unit insignia. He also saw no rank insignia, so assumed the soldier was a private. Accent was apparently not mentioned.'

'Other than the nose, that is so vague as to be nearly useless,' said Monique.

'I accept that, but it's all we've got.'

'How do you think we ought to proceed?' asked Lieutenant Dixon.

'I think it's time to try to find our killer,' said Bob. He looked at his watch. 'I think we have time before it gets dark. I'm going to ask Lieutenant Colonel White to assemble every trainee and every member of staff on the parade ground out there, then take roll calls to ensure everyone is present. We will then ask the officers to take the names of every man who fits the description we've been given. I suppose a lot depends on what Hannes meant by a "badly broken nose", and whether the man had it treated when he got back to Britain. At worst, though, we should end up with a list we can then cross-check against the lists that you gentlemen have been producing today. I've also got in mind the possibility that we might put pressure on our killer and push him to reveal himself.'

Sergeant Potter said, 'Even if our man was a private in 1940, sir, he might have been commissioned since.'

'That's true, Sergeant, which is why we will be discreetly checking every officer present to see how many of them fit the description.'

'I obviously don't know the figures, sir,' said Lieutenant Dixon, 'but it seems to me that a fair proportion of the population might turn out to be blond and blue-eyed. As you say, the broken nose might or might not be a help, and I don't think we can attach any significant to the "piercing" eyes. The man had just killed and was about to try to kill again. His eyes were likely to be reflecting the stress of that.'

'Again, that's true,' said Bob. 'But let's give it a try anyway.'

Lieutenant Colonel White had taken more convincing and

for a while Bob thought the man was going to refuse to cooperate. In the end Bob won him round by reminding him that, since he was the senior officer present, the responsibility for what took place would be Bob's, and that he was more than happy to justify himself to Lieutenant General Gordon, to Commando Group H.Q. and to Combined Operations H.Q. if any questions were asked. It was marginally more subtle than issuing a direct order to the lieutenant colonel, and White appeared to appreciate being left room to back down relatively gracefully.

It had then taken longer than Bob was happy about to assemble the men. White's comment they were lucky that none of the trainees were on long runs or out in the mountains didn't really help. Men were forming in three ranks along the sides of the irregularly-shaped parade ground set amongst the Nissen huts and other buildings. Bob stood with Lieutenant Colonel White, Monique and Lieutenant Dixon at the north eastern corner of the parade ground. The daylight was fading, and Bob hoped they had the time to complete the process.

'What are we looking at, Edward?' asked Bob, as the roll calls began.

'Over here, to our right, are the men who came to Achnacarry on the 3rd of October as what we call our Number 3 Intake. They are volunteers from across the British Army and are here on our standard five-week course. When they finish the course, those who are successful will be posted as replacements to various commandos. 417 men arrived to start the course. We are now down to around 350, with the others having returned to their units. They are divided into two training commandos run by members of my staff.'

'And on the other side?' said Bob, gesturing towards the slightly smaller number of men lining the southern and south western sides of the parade ground.

'Those are the men who took part in last night's assault landing. They form the Scots Guards detachment and 24th Guards Brigade detachment, both taking part in short courses here. They are due to leave tomorrow. Between them they came with 288 men and sixteen officers, and a much higher percentage has stayed the course. And to complete the picture, the men at this near end of the parade ground are my staff. As we agreed, the 200 men and thirteen officers who are being trained to join 10 Commando are not present. Most arrived in Achnacarry on Thursday, after the first murder and your people have spoken at length to the twelve who were here on Wednesday night. They are, in any case, not British, and you tell me we are now looking for someone who is. The roll calls should be completed quite quickly, and the officers will then produce lists of the men who fit the description you provided.' White paused for a moment, surveying the scene developing before them in the evening gloom. 'You know, Bob, I doubt if there's ever been a larger identity parade in history.'

'Funny you should say that, Edward. I was just thinking about something I read while studying for my sergeant's exams in the City of Glasgow Police, back in 1937. One of the first identity parades we know about took place in the 1820s after soldiers of the 1st Regiment of Life Guards opened fire without orders on a mob in Oxford Street in London and killed two men. The entire regiment was lined up to see if witnesses could recognise the soldiers who fired the fatal shots.'

'Did it work?' asked Lieutenant Colonel White.

'It failed to lead to any prosecutions, if that's what you mean,' said Bob.

'Well let's hope that we do rather better,' said White. 'We don't have much daylight left. Hello, what's this?'

While the process continued amongst the main bodies of men lining the long sides of the parade ground, Captain Sanderson approached from the formation at the near end.

The captain came to a halt and saluted. 'Sir, Sergeant Mallory isn't present on parade. No-one knows where he is.'

Lieutenant Colonel White surprised Bob by swearing, loudly, before catching himself and apologising to Monique.

She smiled. 'I've heard worse, Colonel.'

The lieutenant colonel turned to Bob. 'He's someone I should have thought of as soon as you described the man you are looking for. He's one of my fieldcraft instructors. He teaches the arts of living off the land, camouflage, stalking and so on. The thing is, he fits the description of the man you are looking for quite well. Blond hair, blue eyes, medium height. I'm not sure I'd call his nose "badly broken", but it's certainly not the shape that nature originally intended.' White turned to the captain. 'Clive, can you mount a search of the camp for him? It's possible there might be a good reason for the sergeant not being present, but either way we urgently need to find him. Bob, I think you and I need to look at his service record.'

Lieutenant Dixon waved an arm to take in the parade ground. 'Sir, do you want to carry on with this process, or stop it?'

'Let's press on here,' said Bob. 'Can you collect the lists of possible matches from the officers and bring them back into the office? And remember to look at the officers themselves. With any luck we know who our man is now, but remember that many of these men are leaving tomorrow, and we are never going to get another chance to complete this process if Sergeant Mallory turns up with a twisted ankle somewhere.'

Sergeant Potter, Petty Officer MacDonald and Private Jenkins were still in the main administration office, poring over the lists they had generated.

'Gentlemen,' said Lieutenant Colonel White, 'I hope you haven't disordered our records so much we can't find someone. We need to see the service record for a member of my training staff, a Sergeant William Mallory.'

Sergeant Potter looked up. 'The name rings a bell, sir. He was one of the first I was able to identify as definitely having been in the British Expeditionary Force in France and Belgium. Hang on a minute.'

He walked over to a pile of papers on a desk and shuffled through it. 'Here we are, sir. We know he was at Dunkirk because he was mentioned in dispatches. He was a private at the time. Apparently, he saved the lives of three men in his platoon as the Germans closed in on the troops still on the beaches. He was serving with the 2nd Battalion of the Bedfordshire and Hertfordshire Regiment, which formed part of the 10th Infantry Brigade.'

'Thank you, Sergeant,' said the lieutenant colonel. 'I think that gives us a prime suspect, Bob, don't you? If you'll excuse me, I'll go and see what we are doing to find him before it gets completely dark. Just our luck to be looking for a man whose particular area of expertise is staying hidden.'

Bob looked around after Lieutenant Colonel White had left the room. 'I think that perhaps we should put this exercise on hold for the moment. Is it possible to put the documents back where they belong without losing track of where you are?'

'As I said earlier, sir, I'm not sure there's much else for us in the paperwork. We've got our lists, and any further refinement is going to have to be done with home units. We can return the paperwork to the state we found it in, though it will take some time.'

At that point Lieutenant Dixon came in with several pieces of paper. 'We've got fairly long lists of men who fit the "medium height, blue-eyed and blond" description, sir. The list of those who also have an obviously broken nose is rather shorter. It's just one man, a corporal in the Scots Guards, but he and his officer both assure me that his nose was fine until the boxing tournament, or whatever they call it, that took place here the night the first victim was murdered last week. I'm no expert, but there are probably a few others with older nose injuries that are not what you'd call "obvious".'

Bob took a deep breath. 'Look, let's call a halt. If Mallory is our man, then this exercise has been a success in flushing him out. If he's not, then the departure of two of the courses tomorrow will make life even more difficult, but at least we have our lists.'

'If the men on these courses are still suspects, sir, shouldn't we hold them back?' asked Lieutenant Dixon.

'Let's hope I don't have to make that decision,' said Bob.

Having sent three of his team to have a meal, Bob went with Monique and Lieutenant Dixon to find Lieutenant Colonel White and see how the search was progressing.

'Not well' would have been a fair summary.

Bob had found it difficult to know how to respond to Monique since their argument. It was difficult to see how their relationship, such as it had ever been, could possibly recover after the things they had both said.

Michael had privately asked him if everything was alright. Bob realised that it must have been obvious to everyone in the team that everything was far from alright, though he replied with some platitudes that probably gave the lieutenant an eloquent commentary on the true state of things.

Bob was simply finding it very hard to talk to Monique. Even in a work setting, in the company of others, he had to make a conscious effort not to exclude her, and he only did so to try to shield the rest of the team from the awkwardness he felt. She didn't want to be at Achnacarry, and he didn't want her there. He just wished she'd leave.

Bob knew that for her part, Monique had made an effort to help Michael and the rest of the team, and her contribution was appreciated. Bob couldn't question her professionalism. It was just that the dark vacuum that their relationship had become was in constant danger of sucking the life and enthusiasm out of everyone around.

It was a huge relief to Bob when, over a slightly strained dinner with Monique and Michael in the officers' mess, she said that she would have to catch the train to Glasgow from Spean Bridge the next morning. There were arrangements that needed putting in place that she couldn't leave to anyone else. After checking they couldn't be overheard, she talked to Michael enthusiastically about how the plan to fake the sabotage of the Hillington factory was progressing.

Bob was less happy to hear this was to be only a temporary reprieve. Matthew Sloan had agreed to her travelling to Glasgow in the morning but had instructed her to return to Achnacarry by the end of the day, again in a departmental car. He didn't want to release the leverage he had on MI11's investigation until it had reached a conclusion. Monique would only have a few hours at the far end, but, as she told Michael, that ought to be enough to achieve what she wanted.

CHAPTER SIXTEEN

Bob, Lieutenant Dixon and Petty Officer MacDonald arrived at the end of the White Bridge shortly after 8 a.m. the next morning, where they parked the staff car. The sun was not yet up, but the sky was becoming lighter and it looked like being a fine morning. The military police guard on the pier on Loch Arkaig had been strengthened overnight at Bob's suggestion, and their passes were checked before they were allowed onto the boat. Lieutenant Colonel White had also placed a guard on the near end of the White Bridge to check on any movements out of the training centre towards Loch Arkaig. Bob remembered what he had been told about the river being fordable and wondered how effective the guard would be.

Dixon and MacDonald busied themselves removing the tarpaulin covering the boat. Bob had asked Sergeant Potter to remain at Achnacarry to work with Private Jenkins to help restore the staff records to a usable condition.

'Do you think they'll find Mallory, sir?' asked Petty Officer MacDonald.

'Let's hope so,' said Bob. 'Lieutenant Colonel White is planning to intensify the search this morning and mount sweeps across the area. 'The thing is, Mallory apparently knows the area like the back of his hand and is said to be highly skilled at keeping himself hidden and living off the land.'

'Someone will see him sooner or later, sir,' said Lieutenant Dixon.

'More immediately, how sure are you that you can get this boat started, Andrew?'

'I checked the fuel when we found it on Saturday, sir, and as you can see I've laid on more.' The petty officer gestured towards a 5-gallon jerrycan standing on the pier. 'And they've yet to make a boat I can't operate.'

MacDonald was as good as his word and it was only a short time later that they found themselves approaching Eilean Loch Airceig from the south east.

'Can we go all the way around?' asked Bob. 'That way we can get a feel for the place and spot any signs of recent disturbance.'

Circumnavigating the island only took a couple of minutes. 'It's not what you'd call big, is it, sir?' said MacDonald.

Bob said, 'It looks to me to be roughly oblong in shape, measuring perhaps 35 yards from east to west, and perhaps 40 yards from north to south. I suppose if it's partly artificial, they'd not have wanted to have to make it any larger than necessary. Archibald Cameron suggested the best place to land was on the south side. Can you see anything?'

They landed on a stony beach. The island turned out to be as heavily overgrown as it had looked from the lake, but faint traces of an old path led north through the undergrowth. 'I'm guessing that leads to the chapel, sir.' said Lieutenant Dixon as they stood on the shore. 'What are we looking for? Caskets of gold coins?'

'That would be nice, wouldn't it?' said Bob, leading the way. 'To my mind we are looking for anything that doesn't fit, anything that indicates recent activity or disturbance.'

It didn't take long for the three men to conclude that no-one had visited the island recently.

'That's disappointing, sir,' said Lieutenant Dixon.

'Do you want to try the smaller island, sir?' said Petty Officer MacDonald, pointing to a piece of tree-covered ground that barely rose above the surface of the loch a short distance to the south west.

'While we are here, we should,' said Bob. 'Archibald Cameron said it was called An t-Eilean Beag. It looks only a few yards across.'

Petty Officer MacDonald was able to tie the boat to a tree on the second island.

'I can't see this taking very long,' said Bob.

'Was that the sort of thing you had in mind, sir?' The petty officer stood, pointing to a spot near the centre of the tiny island.

'What is it?' asked Bob.

'It looks like a piece of camouflage netting covering something,' said the Petty Officer.

'Careful,' said Bob. 'Remember the sort of man we are dealing with.'

'It looks safe enough,' said Andrew, holding back the camouflage netting. It had been covering three 5-gallon jerrycans, just like the one they had loaded on the boat at the pier. There was also a collection of tools lying on the ground next to them.

'What have we got there?' asked Bob.

'Just the sort of thing any self-respecting treasure hunter would need, sir. A pick-axe, a long crowbar I imagine you could use for levering rocks out of position, and two shovels.'

Bob looked down at the collection. 'I think this rather proves that wherever the Loch Arkaig gold is hidden, it's not on either of these islands. If I'd hidden the gold here, the very last thing I'd then do is leave all my equipment here, to draw attention to this end of the loch. And the amount of fuel suggests our murderer was planning, or had undertaken, one or more trips in the boat to the far end of the loch.'

'The lack of evidence of recent activity on the larger island supports that view, sir,' said Lieutenant Dixon. 'On the other hand, this island is a very handy place to leave your kit if you are busy digging somewhere further along the loch. There's a lot of stuff here for one person to move around at Achnacarry without drawing attention to themselves. I wonder if it was activity on this island that Captain Bell saw, and which caused him to walk to the pier? Despite the trees it's possible to see right across the island, and anyone hiding that lot would have looked suspicious to someone at the head of the loch with good binoculars.'

The lieutenant's reference to 'one person' brought to the fore a thought that had been nagging away at the back of Bob's mind. 'Hang on a minute. What does the fact there are two shovels here tell us?'

'I see what you mean, sir,' said the lieutenant. 'It would leave one man rather over-equipped. The presence of two shovels suggests we are dealing with two treasure hunters.'

'Exactly, Doctor Watson,' said Bob. 'Which probably means that Captain Bell was killed by two men, not one.'

The lieutenant said, 'Perhaps we need to let Lieutenant Colonel White know he's looking for two men and that one of them may still be going about his normal business at Achnacarry in the belief no-one knows about him?'

'My thoughts exactly,' said Bob. 'Hopefully the military police will still be at the pier to keep an eye on the boat. I'm beginning to think we need another trip, this time to the west end of the loch. We've got the fingerprint kit with us. Let's check this stuff, then head back to tell the lieutenant colonel the news.'

Bob was surprised that Petty Officer MacDonald was unable to find any useful fingerprints on the jerrycans or tools, which they loaded into the boat.

Bob and Lieutenant Dixon found Lieutenant Colonel White in his office with Captain Sanderson. It turned out that White already knew he was looking for two men.

'You can't imagine how unhappy I am about this, Bob,' he said. 'The second man is a Sergeant Patrick Quinlan. He's a firearms expert and teaches trainees in the use of our own and enemy weapons. He's also one of the best shots I've ever seen. We've checked his service record, and though he was in the army at the time of Dunkirk, he was stationed in Egypt during the first half of 1940. He volunteered for the commandos in the middle of that year, and his firearms skills were so outstanding he was immediately taken on as an instructor. That was long before commando training was centralised here at Achnacarry, and by the end of 1940 he had been appointed to the staff of the Special Training Centre at Lochailort.'

Bob remembered that Sergeant Potter had mentioned Lochailort when talking about the origins of the commando knife. 'Is that the War Office establishment to the west of here?' asked Bob.

'It was,' said White, 'but it was closed down and handed over to the Royal Navy as a training unit a couple of months back. The Special Training Centre at Lochailort was where the sort of specialised training we now use here was developed. Without what they did there, there would be no Commando Basic Training Centre here at Achnacarry. And neither would the Special Operations Executive training units housed in various locations near the coast have come into being. Many of the instructors at Inverailort House, which was the H.Q. of the Special Training Centre, helped the SOE set up their operation. This was, and still is, headquartered not far away at Arisaig House. Many of the Lochailort instructors also ended up on my staff here.'

'Hang on a moment, Edward. I've reached the conclusion there were two murderers based on the number of shovels we found. Why do *you* think there's a second man?'

'It was getting dark when we started to search Achnacarry last night. We found nothing and overnight I placed strict security on all routes into or out of the place. As you know, there aren't that many of them. In the early hours of this morning, Sergeant Quinlan drove a lorry out of Achnacarry, apparently to pick up ammunition in Fort William from a boat he said was docking there early this morning. He was well known to the men on duty and his story was plausible, so they let him through. They did report what had happened to the duty officer this morning, however, and he was able to establish that there was no delivery of ammunition scheduled. We therefore alerted units more widely across the area and the military police at the checkpoints into the Protected Area, which effectively cuts off everything this side of the Caledonian Canal.'

'Was the lorry searched?' asked Bob.

'Yes, it was, though perhaps not thoroughly. The guards were confident that Sergeant Quinlan was on his own, however. That doesn't really mean anything. Assuming he and Sergeant Mallory were in this together, it would have been no problem for Mallory to walk across country to meet Quinlan and the lorry on the road south of here.'

'Where did the lorry go when it left here?' asked Lieutenant Dixon.

'We were a bit surprised to have found no trace of it this morning,' said White. 'But a short time ago it turned up abandoned at a place called Banavie.' He walked over to a map on the wall. 'Look, gentlemen. We are here, and Banavie is here. You can travel between here and there without crossing any of the Protected Area checkpoints. Mallory and Quinlan must have assumed that the alarm would be raised quickly and decided to take no chances.'

Bob also looked at the map. 'I suppose the critical question is where they went after abandoning the lorry. These are locks marked nearby, on the canal. Would there have been guards to prevent anyone crossing the canal on foot over the lock gates?'

'I very much doubt it,' said White. 'And if they crossed

the canal on foot, then there are railway stations on the other side, on the branch line to Banavie itself and on the main line to Mallaig.'

'Or they could have been making for Fort William, sir,' said Lieutenant Dixon.

'Which would give them access to the railway line to Glasgow,' said Lieutenant Colonel White.

'What about escaping by sea?' asked Lieutenant Dixon.

Bob asked, 'Given your knowledge of this area, where would you go looking for a boat, Michael?'

'There are some obvious places, sir,' said Lieutenant Dixon. 'I'm sure there will be boats in the canal basin at the southern end of the canal, a very short distance from where the lorry was abandoned. My personal choice would be to steal something like a motor gun boat from HMS *St Christopher* in Fort William. That way I could be hopeful of outrunning any pursuit.'

'But you're a naval man,' said Bob. 'Could we expect two army sergeants to know their way around a boat well enough to steal something like that?'

'Remember these men's backgrounds, Bob,' said Lieutenant Colonel White. 'We deliver training on many different types of boats here at Achnacarry, and my staff are expected to build a broad range of expertise, and not just focus on their particular specialisms.'

'They've got a good few hours lead on us,' said Bob. 'Presumably, if they were going to steal a boat from one of the places you've just listed, we'd know about it by now?'

'Perhaps, sir, but we need to check. If you look further afield there are plenty of other places within reach.' Lieutenant Dixon moved his finger across the map.

'Lieutenant Colonel White referred to the new Royal Naval training base at Lochailort. I've yet to visit it, but I bet they have suitable boats for what I have in mind. There will also be a choice of vessels on offer at Arisaig and at Mallaig, which can be reached by road or by rail from where the lorry was abandoned. Remember, we are talking about very resourceful, not to mention dangerous men.'

Bob looked at the map. 'The longer you look, the more options they seem to have.'

'That's true,' said White. 'We've suspended the course for our No.3 Intake and divided the 350 men into patrols, each led by an officer or NCO from the staff here. Each patrol has been assigned an area or a location across a wide swathe of the western Highlands, looking for any traces of Mallory and Quinlan and making sure that if they are still in the area and travelling overland we will find them. It goes without saying that all of the patrols are fully armed.'

'One thing I haven't asked,' said Bob, 'is how we can be so sure that Sergeant Quinlan isn't simply visiting a girlfriend in Corpach or in Fort William. Do we have anything to definitely tie him to Sergeant Mallory?'

It was Captain Sanderson who replied. 'They don't share accommodation or anything like that. And we've spoken to the men that each does share with, who are also instructors here. It seems Mallory and Quinlan didn't exactly seek out one another's company when not on duty, though our records do show that they had worked together on some of the training courses. I can tell you that both were absent from the camp on Friday afternoon and evening, for reasons that seemed legitimate at the time. And I can also show you this, found folded into a pair of socks when we searched Quinlan's quarters a short time ago. It will look very familiar to you, Group Captain.'

The captain leaned over and placed a gold coin in Bob's hand. 'I'm sorry if you'd have preferred to check it for fingerprints, but it was handled by the officer undertaking the search before we thought of that.'

'That's not a problem,' said Bob, turning over in his hand a gold Louis d'or identical to the one he still carried in his breast pocket. Or, on closer inspection, not quite identical. 'This one is dated 1740,' he said. 'I wonder why he left it? I take it that Mallory's quarters have also been searched?'

'Yes, sir, and we found nothing of interest,' said Captain Sanderson.

Lieutenant Colonel White said, 'In light of this conversation, I think our highest priority has to be to warn everyone in the area who might have a boat that could be of interest to Mallory and Quinlan to be on their guard, and to have them check to ensure that no boat has already gone missing. Can you look after that, Clive?'

'Yes, sir,' said Captain Sanderson, 'I'll do that now.'

'The thing I can't work out is the gold,' said Bob. 'Let's assume that on Friday, Mallory and Quinlan returned to the pier with one or more gold coins each, perhaps just a single souvenir they would be able to hide away somewhere. They could never have hoped to keep large amounts of gold hidden around the camp. Let's assume they had at some time previously found some or all of the hidden gold, somewhere further west along Loch Arkaig, presumably by accident. Following the pattern of what happened in 1753, when Archibald Cameron's namesake and ancestor came looking for the gold, the safest thing might have been for them to move it to a new hiding place that only they knew about. They could then return to collect it at their leisure, perhaps in some years' time, once the war has ended and these mountains are a little quieter.'

'Those seem reasonable working assumptions,' said Lieutenant Dixon. 'It's not going to be a very relaxing time for either of them, though. Let's remember that between them they have murdered two men, as well as a woman in Belgium, so moral scruples won't worry either of them. And, assuming our theory is correct, they are the only people in the world who know where they have hidden the gold. There's a strong incentive for either of them to murder the other, both to double his personal share of the gold, and to remove any possibility of the other one coming back prematurely to steal the gold or telling anyone else where it is hidden.'

'Both will be watching their backs very carefully,' said Bob. 'I'd still love to know how one of the coins was lost, and the other abandoned.'

'I've no idea about the first, sir. But we don't know what went on between Mallory and Quinlan yesterday evening. Perhaps if Quinlan shared his accommodation with another man, he was unable to return to collect his belongings, including the coin in his socks, for fear of alerting his room-mate to what was going on.'

'You may well be right, Michael,' said Bob. 'I'm not sure how much we can usefully add to the hunt that's under way for Mallory and Quinlan. With your permission, Edward, I'd like to borrow that boat again, and this time head up to the far end of Loch Arkaig. Archibald Cameron mentioned a couple of locations where the gold might have been hidden in 1753, and at least one of them is meant to be very close to the loch. I suppose as much as anything, I'd like to get a feel for the landscape in the area.'

'I have no problem with that, Bob,' said the lieutenant colonel, 'but let us kit you out a little better for the mountains before you go. I hope you don't mind if we don't accompany you? I've already told you of the searches that are under way. We've got a busy day planned here in other ways too. We've got the final parade later for the Scots Guards and the 24th Guards Brigade detachments. I'll hand out their green berets and commando knives, and then they will march off to Spean Bridge railway station with accompanying pipes and drums provided by our in-house demonstration troop. I am of course putting special measures in place to ensure that Mallory and Quinlan are unable to use the event to make good their own escape. I appreciate they are probably far away by now, but we can't take any chances. Once the two guards detachments have gone, we will start work on reorganising the accommodation. This coming Thursday we are to be joined by 84 men in what will be our third police intake.'

'I didn't know you trained police here, too,' said Bob.

'Not as police,' said White. 'We've had two previous intakes from the police and they've proved highly successful as commandos. As they have no military background, they spend three months here, and then go out to add maturity and experience to the various commando units.'

CHAPTER SEVENTEEN

It was still a fine day, but nonetheless there was a cold wind from the west. Bob sat with Lieutenant Dixon in the middle of the boat while Petty Officer MacDonald took the helm. He was grateful that he'd accepted Lieutenant Colonel White's offer of suitable clothing and equipment.

The three of them were dressed in what the lieutenant colonel had called Denison smocks; the camouflaged water-resistant jackets the training centre staff wore when the weather was poor. They also wore heavy army boots and gaiters and had been issued with cap comforters, the headgear worn by all the trainees at the Commando Basic Training Centre as well as by many of the staff when out in the field. Their initial efforts to turn an oblong scarf into a hat had caused some amusement. Bob had realised that this was a joke that was played out whenever new trainees arrived. In the end it was Petty Officer MacDonald who worked out that the secret lay in turning one end of the scarf inside-out within the other end, then rolling up the sides of what was left.

Right now, the cap comforters were earning their keep, as were the khaki woollen glove/mittens which separated the index or trigger finger of each hand from the remaining fingers. Bob and Lieutenant Dixon carried the two Sten guns, while the rifle lay in the boat close to Petty Officer MacDonald. The three had also been issued with canvas packs and a variety of rations. This had seemed unnecessary to Bob, but he went along with it anyway.

Sergeant Potter and Private Jenkins had not seemed too distressed at missing out on the boat trip. Bob had asked them to liaise with Captain Sanderson as the hunt for Mallory and Quinlan progressed, and work with colleagues in MI11 in London to see if anything more could be found out about the two men.

Lieutenant Dixon pointed off to the left. 'That's the entrance to Glen Mallie, sir. That's the first place we get to that Archibald Cameron said was traditionally believed to be a possible hiding place for the gold.'

Bob had been looking at the map. 'I think we press on by, Lieutenant. That glen extends for quite a few miles west of here, and to my mind if someone had stumbled over the gold anywhere there, even in its entrance close to the loch, they'd have elected to move it by another means. The map shows a track all the way along the south shore of the loch from the east as far as here. A lorry would attract less attention than a boat. And if the gold had turned up further along the glen, then it would have been easier, and more discreet, to access it from the south, from Loch Eil. I also suspect that if the discovery of the hiding place had been this far east along the loch, then Mallory and Quinlan wouldn't have felt the need for three jerrycans of petrol.'

'That's true, sir,' said the lieutenant. 'Even assuming multiple runs, you'd only need that much fuel if you were travelling to and from the western end of the loch.'

Bob kept a lookout for signs of life along the sides of the glen. He thought he glimpsed deer several times, but only in the distance. As they headed west, Bob began to appreciate the full scale of the landscape, and the loch, for the first time. At last he saw what he had been looking out for. He tapped Lieutenant Dixon on the shoulder. 'You see the distinct narrowing of the loch ahead of us?'

'Yes, sir,' said Dixon. 'The Callich Burn, or Allt na Caillich, is on the north bank about half a mile before we reach that point. That must be it there.' He pointed up to where a river had carved a valley down through the hillside, all the way from the skyline to the edge of the loch.

'That's where Archibald Cameron said his uncles spent one summer looking for the gold, isn't it?' said Bob. 'You can see how it twists and turns, and parts of it are wooded. If you wanted to, you could bring a boat ashore almost anywhere along that side of the loch to allow you to explore the valley. It would be good to know if there's been any recent digging up there, but I don't think the three of us are going to find that out today.'

Lieutenant Dixon turned his attention to the west. 'The next place Archibald Cameron mentioned was Murlaggan, sir. He talked about his ancestor temporarily hiding the gold in an ancient graveyard surrounded by an oval stone wall on the shore of the loch. That was before he moved it to a more permanent home in the valley of the Callich Burn.'

Bob pointed to a derelict cottage next to a track some

way above the shore of the loch. 'I think that has to be Murlaggan. I don't see a graveyard, though.'

'There's a walled area next to the cottage, sir,' said Petty Officer MacDonald.

'It doesn't really qualify as "on the shore of the loch" though, does it?' said Bob.

'Well how about that then, sir?' said MacDonald. 'There's a broken-down wall running along the line of the shore here, but if you look at the base of that group of old trees over there, it's just about possible to imagine another ruined wall forming an oval.'

'I see what you mean,' said Bob. 'I'd rather thought we were looking for something a little better defined, perhaps with gravestones. I suppose it depends how ancient is meant by an "ancient graveyard".'

'We could put the boat in there, sir,' said MacDonald. 'There's a tiny inlet and we could tie up to that tree growing out of the rubble of the wall running along the shore.'

They did just that and while Petty Officer MacDonald was tying the boat to the tree, Bob and Lieutenant Dixon walked the fifty yards to the possible graveyard.

'You know, sir, I think Andrew's right,' said Lieutenant Dixon. 'If you look closely you can just about see an oval rim linking up the trees, as if an old stone wall collapsed here many centuries ago.' He walked closer. 'Yes, look, you can see some of the stones, covered in grass or moss. I think this has to be where the original Archibald Cameron hid the gold for a while, before moving it on.'

Bob looked up at the north side of the glen. 'I keep thinking about what Archibald said about his ancestor. About him getting on in years and having been injured.

The Callich Burn is a bit of a distance from here. It enters the loch well over a mile east of this point. That seems a long way to haul a significant weight of gold. If it were me, especially if I knew the redcoats were closing in, I'd have picked somewhere a little more readily to hand.'

'You mean like the cottage, sir?' asked Petty Officer MacDonald, who had joined them.

'We don't know if that existed in 1753,' said Bob, 'but yes, it's a possibility. But if you assume he moved the gold from here to a valley on the hillside, then wouldn't it make more sense to hide it in that valley immediately above us? It looks to be deeper and more heavily wooded than the Callich Burn, and simply looks a better bet all round.'

'That's shown on the map as the Allt Mhurlagain,' said Dixon. 'Are you suggesting that when the story got told, it simply got attached to the wrong valley?'

'Well, this was in an age before maps were commonly available, and certainly not detailed maps,' said Bob.

'I suppose it has to be possible, sir,' said Lieutenant Dixon. 'Do you want us to go up and take a look?'

'Again, no. Let's go to the west end of the loch before deciding whether any of this needs to be looked at in more detail.'

'Sir!' Petty Officer MacDonald was standing beyond the bottom of the oval, close to the edge of the loch. 'I think we can now agree that this used to be a graveyard.' As Bob and Dixon walked down to him, he pointed at the ground close to his feet.

Bob saw a bleached piece of bone, possibly the top of a thigh bone. 'It does look human rather than from a sheep, doesn't it?' he said.

MacDonald moved a rock aside to allow him to return the bone to the ground.

'Right,' said Bob. 'Back to the boat, and we'll continue the last couple of miles to the western end of the loch.'

Petty Officer MacDonald was untying the boat from the tree when he called out again. 'Sir, look at the wall, about fifty yards to the east of here. It looks to me as if it's been disturbed.'

Bob and Lieutenant Dixon climbed back out of the boat and walked in the direction MacDonald suggested. The petty officer was right. Some of the stones on the side of the ruined wall showed signs of having been moved recently. Several were scraped and moss had been torn in places.

'Let's take a closer look,' said Bob. 'Can you bring the pickaxe and crowbar?'

As a child, Bob had always wanted to be a pirate, and treasure hunting had always been a dream. He felt a surge of excitement now as Dixon and MacDonald hefted rocks that showed signs of disturbance out of the wall. 'Is there anything there?' he asked.

'Just a hole behind the stones, sir,' said Lieutenant Dixon. 'It doesn't take much imagination to think that something has been hidden here. But whatever it was has gone now.'

Bob looked into the gap now left in the wall. 'I wonder what they did with the interior stones that had to be removed to create the void?' Then he laughed. 'It wouldn't be much effort to have thrown them into the loch, leaving as little sign of disturbance as possible on the wall itself.'

'I think you're right, sir,' said MacDonald. 'This looks like it was carefully done.'

Bob said, 'Am I jumping to conclusions if I suggest that while the graveyard over there might have been used in 1753 as a temporary home for the Loch Arkaig gold, before it was hidden somewhere else, the reverse process might have happened rather more recently, with the gold being brought here from wherever it was found, and hidden temporarily before being moved to a more permanent hiding place?'

'That sounds plausible, sir,' said Lieutenant Dixon. 'Now we simply need to know where it was moved to from here.'

'Hopefully Mallory and Quinlan can tell us when we catch them,' said Bob. 'In the meantime, let's carry on to the western end of the loch.'

The pier at the west end of Loch Arkaig had seen much better days. The wooden structure looked in danger of collapse but was still usable with care. It had been built out on piles from a large rock on the loch's north shore, close to the point where the conjoined Rivers Dessarry and Pean flowed into the loch.

Bob realised that he was going to have to choose between leaving the boat unattended or leaving someone on their own to look after it. 'Andrew, can you stay here with the boat, while Lieutenant Dixon and I visit the old settlement of Strathan about a mile west of here? The landscape here is wide open, so no-one will be able to approach without you seeing them. You keep the rifle, and if there's any problem, fire off a shot and we'll come running. We'll leave the packs in the boat.'

'No problem, sir. But we should keep an eye on the weather. It looks to me as if there could be a storm coming in. The wind has certainly increased over the past hour or so. We also need to leave enough time to get back before dark, and progress will be slower if the loch gets choppy, even with the wind behind us.'

Bob hadn't considered the possibility that the fine weather of the morning and early afternoon might change, but as he followed the petty officer's gaze west, he could see an approaching edge of cloud, with darker cloud beyond it. And Andrew was certainly right about the increasing strength of the wind. 'We'll be as quick as we can,' he said.

Bob and Lieutenant Dixon took the track that led a little way up the hill to the north before contouring to the west.

'Good grief,' said Lieutenant Dixon, 'do commandos actually run in these boots? I'm not sure mine are even foot-shaped. Walking is quite a challenge.'

Bob had been wondering much the same thing but tried to concentrate on the surrounding landscape rather than on his feet.

'Is this part of the village, sir?' asked Dixon. They had walked about half a mile from the pier, and now stood looking at a stone gable end, immediately to the south of the track.

'I suspect this must be the remains of the old barracks that Archibald Cameron talked about,' said Bob. 'I forget the Gaelic name, but he translated it as "the house of the soldiers", which looks about right.'

'It certainly commanded superb views along the loch and to the west and south,' said Lieutenant Dixon.

From the barracks the track descended to a small cluster of stone structures. Bob looked around, 'I don't see anything that looks like a school, do you, Michael?'

'No, sir, just a couple of run-down cottages and a stone shed with a corrugated iron roof.'

Bob and the lieutenant looked in each of the buildings but could find little evidence of the lives of the people who had lived here until only a few years previously. Each cottage comprised just two main rooms, each with a fireplace in the end wall. The last occupants seemed to have abandoned much of their furniture when they left. The remaining building was empty of furniture, but by a process of elimination Bob decided that it must have once been the school, still marked on the map.

Bob stood with Lieutenant Dixon in the more easterly of the two cottages. 'Perhaps the people who lived here hoped they would be able to return after the war, sir,' said Dixon.

'It does look that way, Michael. Lieutenant Colonel White said that training exercises take place in the area west of Loch Arkaig. I'd imagine that these cottages and the school are used for shelter when trainees are in the area. It doesn't look as if anyone has been here very recently, though.'

'Were you expecting to find something useful, here, sir?'

Bob said, 'I'd half wondered whether Mallory and Quinlan might have decided to make our lives easier by hiding the gold here, but on reflection that's not a very sensible idea. They'd know the area is used by trainees and these buildings are the very last place you'd want to hide something valuable. Besides, where would you hide it?'

'Lift one of the paving stones forming the floor and dig a hole underneath, sir?'

'It's possible, but just seems too high risk. And what if the residents returned to live here before the two sergeants could return to retrieve the gold? No, I think we're wasting our time, Michael. The dust on the surfaces and floor would be disturbed if anyone had been here in the past week, and we think that Mallory and Quinlan were relocating the gold as recently as Friday. The same is true in the other cottage and in the school.'

They left the cottage, taking care to shut the door properly against the increasingly strong wind. Lieutenant Dixon looked over his shoulder as they started back along the track. 'Andrew was right about the weather, sir, it is beginning to look very threatening.'

Despite the need to get back to the boat, Bob wanted to look at the slight remains of the old barracks on the way back along the track.

'It really was very small,' said Lieutenant Dixon. 'I can't imagine that it was a popular posting among the redcoats of the day.'

Bob said, 'The ground to the south seems to drop away quite steeply to the river.' He walked beyond the traces of the building to the visible horizon, appreciating the way the views into the river valley below expanded as he did so.

Then he noticed something odd. He turned back towards the ruins of the barracks. 'Michael, come and look at this.'

They say you never hear the shot that gets you, and Bob certainly didn't. The bullet hit him on the left side of his chest. The impact threw him backwards and his limp body tumbled down the steep slope to the south.

The last of the light had drained away beyond the western horizon a quarter of an hour earlier and Bob was flying his Hawker Hurricane single seat fighter back towards

Croydon Airport, some 70 miles to the west. He was tired. It was his second flight of the day. He'd shot down a Messerschmitt Bf 109 fighter fifteen minutes after sunrise that morning, ten hours earlier. Today was Friday. He'd shot down another Bf 109 last Sunday, and another the day before that. On the Sunday before, he'd shot down two Bf 109s. And a little under two weeks before, on Monday the 7th of October 1940, Bob had shot down five Bf 109s in a single day.

Yes, he was tired. Bob worked hard to drum into his pilots the old maxim, that they should never fly straight and level for more than 30 seconds in a combat area. It was a rule that he applied instinctively himself. Especially, as now, when he was flying alone.

But somehow, he never saw the one that got him. There was a noise like nothing he'd ever heard before, and flashes as cannon shells impacted the structure of his Hurricane. Then there was a sharp pain in the side of his head and he could smell hot oil and coolant and his doomed aircraft began to spin vertically down towards the ground. Despite the huge gravitational forces created by the spin, Bob fought to open his aircraft's canopy. He couldn't see the ground in the dark, but he knew it was getting closer and closer.

His first sensation was of a deep, numbing cold. The second was of an icy trickle of water, flowing down the side of his neck as heavy rain fell on his face. Then he felt crashing waves of pain, first from his chest, and then from his left arm, until these were partly displaced by the pain from the back of his head. Slowly, he realised that the vivid recollection of being shot down was from far in the past, but he also realised he couldn't remember anything between then and now.

What terrified Bob more than the pain, and more than not knowing where he was or how he had got there, was the knowledge that he was blind. He could feel his eyes were open, but he couldn't see anything at all. He knew he'd lost the sight in his left eye as the result of a head injury when he'd been shot down. But his head had been injured again and now he couldn't see anything out of either eye.

The memory of what had happened began to return. Bob took a deep breath to stem the rising tide of panic and then fought back the agonising pain in his left arm to slowly raise it in front of his face. The sense of relief he felt was perhaps the most intense feeling he could ever remember. The luminous face of his watch told him it was 8.20 p.m. He wasn't blind. It was dark. Really dark.

Bob knew he must have been lying where he had fallen for well over four hours. He shivered and realised that he had to do something to fight off the cold. He didn't know much about hypothermia, but he did know that it had been cold earlier in the day and it would be much colder now. He mentally thanked Lieutenant Colonel White for insisting they were issued with warm and water-resistant jackets.

He was lying on his back on a steep slope. He worked out that the old barracks and the track to Strathan lay at the top of the slope and that reaching the shelter of one of the cottages at Strathan was probably his only chance of surviving the night. He rolled over onto his front, groaning as the Sten gun, apparently still strapped to him, shifted, banging against his left side.

As Bob crawled painfully upwards it seemed to take forever until the gradient decreased, allowing him to stand upright on what he assumed was the flat ground south of the old barracks. He wondered if Michael had also been shot and realised he could trip over the lieutenant's body without even seeing it. Then, above the background noise of the rain and fierce wind, he heard metal clinking against metal, coming from the direction of the track. He froze. Then he heard the sound again.

Bob had an agonising moment of indecision before realising that he only had one chance. As loudly as he could manage, he shouted, 'Help!' Then he shouted again.

Nothing happened for a moment, and then he was dazzled by the glare of a torch shone straight at him.

CHAPTER EIGHTEEN

'It's Group Captain Sutherland!' Bob could see figures moving towards him in the periphery of the torch beam. Suddenly he felt very tired.

'Sir, are you alright?' He recognised Captain Sanderson's voice.

'If I'm honest, I've been better, Captain,' Bob said. 'I think I need to get out of the cold.'

'We'll take you down to Strathan, sir, and assess the situation there. Can you walk?'

Bob found he could. Sanderson assigned a commando to take each of Bob's arms to steady him, but after a yelp of pain and another brief flash of the torch they settled on supporting his right arm only.

'You need to find Lieutenant Dixon and Petty Officer MacDonald,' said Bob.

'All in good time, sir, let's get you warm and dry first.'

It was downhill most of the way to the cottages. Bob remembered that it had only been a few minutes' walk when travelling uphill in the opposite direction, but it seemed to cost him a huge amount of effort now. By the time he reached the nearest cottage, the commandos had already lit fires in the hearths in both rooms. Bob was amazed that they had been able to find anything combustible within miles in this rain.

With candles also lit, the interior of the cottage came to life, as perhaps a dozen men in khaki organised their kit and Captain Sanderson tried to make Bob comfortable on an ancient sofa.

The door banged open. 'I was sure you were dead, sir!' Lieutenant Dixon came into the cottage, followed by Petty Officer MacDonald. The lieutenant turned to Captain Sanderson. 'Did he tell you he'd been shot, Captain?'

'I was just about to look at him,' said the captain. 'He was close to going under with the cold out there, so I thought it best to get him here, then work out what else was wrong.'

Dixon looked at Bob with concern. 'Sir, you were shot by Sergeant Quinlan. You were standing on the edge of the slope beyond the ruined barracks and the shot knocked you off your feet and down the slope. The sergeant shot you with a Lee-Enfield rifle, and said he'd hit you in the chest. He said you were dead, and given his reputation as an outstanding shot, I didn't think to question that.'

'Are you alright?' said Bob.

'A badly wounded pride, sir, but otherwise fine. Mallory and Quinlan took me prisoner and threatened to kill me if Andrew didn't surrender too. Andrew had heard the shot and was on his way to help. After that they stove in the bottom of the boat to sink it, brought us here and tied us up in the shed, or school, or whatever it is. We've been in there ever since. Come on, let's look at you, sir. There's a nasty bump and a cut on the back of your head. It's not bled much, but you can feel there's a swelling there. I suppose you picked that up falling down the slope.'

Sanderson turned to Dixon. 'You are quite sure that Mallory and Quinlan were here this afternoon, lieutenant?'

'Yes, definitely.'

'Did you get any idea of what they were doing here, and where they went when they left?'

'No. After they left Andrew and I trussed up in the other cottage we didn't see or hear anything more of them. Frankly, I'm not sure why they didn't kill us. Look, can't this wait? We need to check on the Group Captain.'

'Can you look after him for a short while?' asked Sanderson. 'I need to let Lieutenant Colonel White know what's happening. We've got a field radio with us, but it will be touch and go whether we're within voice range. I'm going to take the radio operator back up to the high ground where we found the group captain. That should give a better line of sight. Otherwise we're stuck with Morse code.'

A commando corporal who said he was a first-aider helped Lieutenant Dixon lift Bob's camouflage smock as a precursor to pulling it off over his head. Bob's loud groan caused a change of plan, and in the end the smock was cut from him.

'Your uniform jacket's not in much better shape, sir,' said the lieutenant. 'You're bleeding from an arm wound, and there's a hole in your jacket over your chest, but no bleeding there that I can see.'

It was Petty Officer MacDonald who asked, 'Where are you keeping those gold coins, sir?'

'They're in the right-hand breast pocket, of my uniform jacket,' said Bob.

'I don't think a pair of gold coins will have protected the group captain from a high velocity rifle bullet,' said Lieutenant Dixon. 'But this might have done.' He had unbuttoned Bob's jacket to reveal the shoulder holster underneath it. Now he took the Walther PPK out of the holster. The pistol looked as if it had been hit, hard, with a heavy hammer, on the flat side of the slide above the hand grip.

'You might want to keep this as a souvenir, sir. It seems to have saved your life. It's not going to be much use for anything else in this condition.'

As they cut his uniform jacket free, Bob remembered that it was less than a week old. At least he'd not had to pay for it, he thought. 'Michael, can you look after the gold coins?'

'Of course, sir,' said Lieutenant Dixon. 'It looks like the bullet hit the pistol then ricocheted off to one side, causing a flesh wound in your upper left arm. We'll get your shirt and vest off, then bandage that. It doesn't look too bad. Oh, wow! That's a bruise to be proud of.' He pointed at Bob's chest as the vest was cut off. 'You can almost see the shape of the pistol, set within a much larger area of bruising. I'd be surprised if you don't have some rib injuries under that, sir, but there's nothing obvious and on the whole I'm relieved by what we've found.'

The commando corporal made a good job of bandaging what turned out to be a shallow wound on Bob's upper left arm. He then looked at Bob's head. 'To be honest, sir, I'd be tempted not to dress that. I've cleaned the cut, and it's not deep. We'll find you a cap comforter to keep your head warm, and that should do. I could also bandage up your chest, but again there's probably not much point. The medical officer will want to look at your ribs, but whether or not any of them are broken, a bandage won't really help. The most important thing is to get you warm.'

Spare garments were quickly produced, though Bob had no idea where from, and within a few minutes he was dressed in several layers of dry clothing, not without considerable pain from his chest as he donned shirt, a denim battledress blouse, and another Denison smock. He wrapped the shoulder holster in its strap, and placed it, still containing the damaged pistol, in one of the smock's pockets.

Dixon turned to Captain Sanderson who had re-entered the room, dripping wet. 'It seems Group Captain Sutherland's pistol deflected the shot. Is there any way we can get him back to Achnacarry tonight?'

'Possibly later, Michael.' He turned to Bob. 'For the moment I think we'd be best keeping you warm and dry here, sir. You've probably guessed that Lieutenant Colonel White sent us out to look for you when it became clear you wouldn't be returning before dark. Our lorries were able to cope with the track along the north shore of the loch as far as a place called Murlaggan, where it turns into more of a pony track, and proved impassable in the dark. We walked from there. Trying to get you out immediately would mean exposing you to a two mile walk in horrible weather, and then a very unpleasant and bumpy drive in the dark.'

'What about Mallory and Quinlan?' said Bob. 'We need to start looking for them before they get too far. They've got what must be a four or five-hour lead on us by now.'

'Tonight's storm may work in our favour, sir,' said Sanderson. 'They are unlikely to get too far in this, and I doubt if anyone is putting out to sea tonight. I've got thirty men here, and another half dozen guarding the lorries at Murlaggan.

'Lieutenant Colonel White hopes to join us before midnight with perhaps 200 more men, and will then push patrols out in the various directions Mallory and Quinlan might have travelled in. He has instructed me to remain here until he arrives. He is hoping to bring some of the men in lorries along the north side of the loch to Murlaggan and is also moving some collapsible boats from Loch Lochy to Loch Arkaig to transport more men along the loch that way. The weather is forecast to stay very poor until tomorrow evening at least, and if Mallory and Quinlan were hoping to get away by sea, they are going to have real difficulties until then.'

'Hello, Bob, I gather you've had a close shave?' Lieutenant Colonel White came into the cottage at about half past midnight, shaking the rain off his jacket as he did so. The sound of the wind and rain had steadily risen in intensity over the previous few hours, and the forecasts of a wild night appeared to be coming good.

'That's right, Edward, but I'm feeling a little more human now. Quinlan took a shot at me and it bounced off the pistol in my shoulder holster.'

'I've always said that pistols are bloody useless, Bob. It seems I may have to change my opinion. Anyway, now I'm here, we need to get on and start looking for my two missing sergeants.'

He accepted a cup of tea from Captain Sanderson and spread out a map on the floor in front of the fire. Bob and Lieutenant Dixon also gathered round. 'The one-inch maps all come together in the middle of the area we are interested in so are no real use at all. This quarter-inch map lacks detail but gives a much better idea of what our options might be.'

Bob said, 'To my mind their best chance is still to leave by sea. It would be nice to be able to check, but earlier, just before I was shot, I saw an area of ground that had been dug up, just below the top of the slope beyond the old barracks. Some stones had been moved and there were two entrenching tools on the ground. My guess is that on Friday afternoon Mallory and Quinlan hid the gold there that they had already previously re-hidden near the old graveyard at Murlaggan. This time they chose what they thought was a safer spot by the barracks. There would be no reason for anyone to walk out beyond the barracks, and certainly not for them to start digging into the top of the slope.'

'It sounds as if we caught them in the middle of digging up the gold, sir,' said Lieutenant Dixon.

'That's my guess. They probably saw us approaching along the loch, or certainly along the track, and hid somewhere on the higher ground to the north. I guess they intended to let us return to the boat and sail away, just as they had let us walk past on the way to Strathan.'

'But you walked close enough to the edge to see what they had been doing,' said Dixon.

'Yes, and that forced their hand,' said Bob. 'Thinking back to our earlier discussion, maybe it was never their intention to hide the gold here long-term. Or perhaps that was the intention, and the murders changed their minds.'

Lieutenant Dixon took a pace back. 'Or it could simply be that once they had handled the gold once, sir, the idea of trusting one another for an indefinite period into the future was no longer so appealing. Either way, it looks as if taking the lorry to Banavie was meant to be a diversion, and they travelled back overland to the head of the loch.'

It was Lieutenant Colonel White who voiced the thought in everyone's heads. 'What really matters now is discovering which way they have gone and how they intend to escape.'

Captain Sanderson ran a finger over the map. 'There are three routes west from here, sir. Along Glen Dessarry to the head of Loch Nevis, along Glen Pean to the head of Loch Morar, and less directly, south to Glen Finnan, and then down Glen Shiel or west along the road or railway to Arisaig and Mallaig. The men we are looking for are experts in living off the land and concealing themselves in this sort of landscape. And both know the area extremely well. Sergeant Quinlan was previously based at the Special Training Centre at Lochailort and while there he could easily have helped setting up the training for the Special Operations Executive based at Arisaig House and in various places north of there. He probably knows the lie of the land in this part of the country better than anyone else alive.'

'On the other hand,' said Lieutenant Colonel White, 'we believe that the two men we are looking for are burdened down with an unknown but possibly significant weight of gold coins. And we know that they are unlikely to be able to make an escape by sea until this storm passes over, which isn't due to happen until tomorrow night, I mean tonight, at the earliest.

'After talking to Captain Sanderson on the radio earlier, I dispatched additional patrols to cover all the inland routes away from here. We can't overlook the possibility that, having decoyed us once, Mallory and Quinlan might try to do it again. By now we should have men blocking off every conceivable route out of the area.' The lieutenant colonel ran his finger in an arc from east to west across the map. 'We've also alerted all military units in the area, and all naval units. As soon as the weather eases enough for them to get safely to sea, the Royal Navy will be patrolling the coastline intensively from Ardnamurchan in the south to the Sound of Raasay in the north. Incidentally, Bob, I should have mentioned that your Sergeant Potter came to see me earlier. It seems that although he comes from Liverpool, Quinlan has family in southern Ireland, so that sounds like a possible line of escape.'

'What will you do with the men you have here?' asked Bob.

'They are currently sheltering in the other room of this cottage and in the other two buildings. But I'd like to win back some of the lead that Mallory and Quinlan have on us. There are 220 men here, and another ten guarding the boats. I will send strong patrols out immediately to take up positions at the east end of Loch Nevis and Loch Morar, here and here,' he pointed at the map, 'and to Loch Hourn further north. Then at first light we'll use the rest of the men to mount sweeps along Glen Dessarry and Glen Pean to see if they can pick up any traces of Mallory and Quinlan.'

'Do you have men who are able to track fugitives?' asked Bob.

'You've been watching too many Saturday morning westerns, Bob,' said White. 'And if we did have trackers, I'm sure that anything very subtle would be swept away in the weather out there tonight. But Mallory and Quinlan might have left some sign of their passing, perhaps by lighting a fire, and if they have we ought to be able to find traces of them in the morning.'

'Is there any way I can return to Achnacarry tonight, Edward?' asked Bob.

'That may be a good idea,' said White. 'I'd like to have the medical officer check you over. The least uncomfortable option, and the quickest, might be to take you in one of the boats currently down at the pier at this end of Loch Arkaig.'

The walk to the head of the loch wasn't a happy one for Bob, partly because of the storm, but also because of the intense pain he felt in his chest every time he breathed. Lieutenant Dixon and Petty Officer MacDonald walked with him and the company helped.

Bob paused to catch his breath where the track passed the gable end of the old barracks. He looked over at Lieutenant Dixon, who was huddled into his smock for protection from the weather.

'I know what you are going to say, sir,' shouted the lieutenant over the wind. 'I think it would be better if I went. Andrew can stay with you on the track.'

'Fair enough, Michael,' said Bob, 'but one of us needs to look.'

Lieutenant Dixon switched on a torch, and Bob watched as he made his way past the walls of the barracks and over to the place where Bob had been shot. The beam from the torch flickered around the landscape for a few minutes, and then Dixon made his way back to the track.

'I didn't imagine it, did I?' shouted Bob, as they began the downhill walk towards the loch.

'No sir, there's a hole there, with debris down the slope beyond. I'm not sure how much gold you'd be able to hide there, but it is a significant hole. There was no sign of the entrenching tools you saw. Maybe they plan to bury the gold somewhere else?'

'Don't even joke about that, Michael,' said Bob, groaning as he stumbled on a pebble and another wave of pain shot up his left side.

'I'm not sure I was joking, sir,' said Dixon, leaning in towards Bob's ear as he tried to make himself heard.

'We've not met, sir. I'm the medical officer here at Achnacarry, Captain Hugh Harrington. Lieutenant Colonel White radioed to say that you were returning and needed checking over. I don't get to treat many men who have survived being shot in the chest with a .303 rifle bullet at fairly short range.'

When they had returned to Achnacarry, Captain Harrington had been waiting for Bob, and showed him directly into what Bob assumed was a consulting room. Bob had stiffened up over the previous few hours, so getting undressed was no easier than it had been in the cottage at Strathan.

'What do you think, Captain?' asked Bob, after Harrington had spent some time looking at the back of his head, and then his arm, before finally feeling the side of his chest.

'I think you'll live,' said the captain. 'And I think you are one of the luckiest men I've ever met. The odds against the rifle shot hitting the pistol were very high, and you even got away lightly with the arm wound that followed. It's very superficial. The head will also heal without any problems, but I'd avoid driving or excessive exercise for the next couple of days. If you feel dizzy, sit down. As for the bruise on your chest, well, it will hurt like hell for a few days, but I'm pretty sure there are no broken ribs and no internal damage in there. As I said, you are very lucky.'

As Bob approached the task of getting dressed again, Captain Harrington said, 'The lieutenant colonel asked me to dig this out for you. He thought you might like one that will work if you need it to. We have all sorts of weapons here, our own and the enemy's, and finding this wasn't difficult.'

The captain held out a Walther PPK. It wasn't as pristine as the one Bob had originally been issued with in London, but beggars couldn't be choosers, he thought.

'I'm extremely grateful, thank you.'

Bob's shoulder holster was still in his jacket pocket, and he put the weapon the captain had given him in the other pocket. 'How long do you think the bruising will take to go down, captain?'

'It could be up to a week, sir. We get all sorts of injuries here, as you can imagine, but the only time I've ever seen anything quite like that, it took about a week to begin to fade.'

'How did that happen?' asked Bob.

'Have you ever heard of the Boys anti-tank rifle, sir?'

'Vaguely,' said Bob.

'It's a beast of a rifle that's used to attack tanks. The weapon itself is over five feet long and very heavy. It's not popular and not very effective, and we are promised a replacement next year. But the thing that really sets it apart is the powerful recoil. We had a trainee a few months ago who decided that the way to ease the impact was to pack his cap comforter inside the top of his tunic, between his shoulder and the stock of the weapon. It worked well, until the time he forgot he was wearing his regimental beret rather than his cap comforter. The result was a perfect impression of a Royal Tank Regiment cap badge imprinted into his shoulder. The surrounding bruising wasn't quite as bad as yours, but it was impressive. It's not a mistake he'll make again, I'm sure. Look, sir, are you going to take any notice if I suggest that you need some rest?'

'Yes, I am,' said Bob. 'I've asked my team to reconvene at 7 a.m., so we've all got time for a couple of hours of sleep.'

'How are you, Bob?'

Monique had been standing outside the doctor's office. Bob thought she looked as drained as he felt.

'Hello, Monique. If you want the truth, I've been far better, but thank you for asking.'

'Michael came to my room to tell me you were back and what had happened. I wanted to see how you were. I thought *I* was having a bad day. The storm made the roads very difficult on the return journey, and we ran out of daylight. Then the car's electrics decided they didn't like rain, and to top it off, the ferry south of Fort William wasn't working and we had to take a long detour. I got back to Achnacarry so late that Lieutenant Colonel White had already left, after they'd found you. I can't believe you got yourself shot!'

Captain Harrington emerged from his office and looked quizzically at them before bidding them goodnight and walking down the corridor.

'Since you're asking, yes,' said Bob, 'I was shot, by a rifle, at short range, in the chest. The shot hit my holstered pistol, which saved my life.'

'Surely that sort of thing only happens in the John Buchan novels you talked about.'

'I've got the Walther PPK-shaped bruise to prove it.'

'I've been waiting for news since I returned. I was relieved when Michael told me you were back.'

'Thank you, Monique. I appreciate it.' Bob found, to his surprise, that he was telling the truth.

'What happens now?'

'In what sense?'

'I hear that the killers are two instructors based here. I imagine that the job now is to find them?'

'Yes. Lieutenant Colonel White has men blocking all the routes out, and despite the storm he is trying to track the men from their last known position. I've not had a chance to work out how we can usefully add to what he's doing. I think we'll probably head west first thing in the morning to see if we can help, as it looks likely they are heading for the coast. That will give us a few hours of sleep.'

'My colleague, the man who drove me up, is staying overnight. Given how things have developed today, I think I'll get him to drive me back to Glasgow first thing in the morning. I'll simply tell Matthew Sloan that I've done all

I can here, and that I'm much more needed there. If he doesn't like it, well, to hell with him.'

'You'll have had a wasted journey tonight, then.'

'Not really. At least I've seen for myself that you're still alive. Sorry, I know I'm keeping you up, Bob. I just wanted to say that I wish that things had worked out differently.'

'What, you mean you wish the bullet hadn't hit my pistol?'

'No, that's…' She saw the look on his face and smiled. 'Sorry, my sense of humour seems to have been one of a number of victims of this. Self-control has been another. I'm sorry I slapped you, Bob. I'm sorry for the things I said, too.'

'You weren't the only one saying horrible things,' Monique. 'I'm sorry too. I was hurt, and I was just trying to hurt you. We were both right. I need to grow up.'

'Look, we've both had tiring days. I don't want to keep you up any longer. Are you going to be able to get back to your room alright?'

'Let's see one-another to the main building. I'll be able to get to my room without any problem. Michael's probably already fast asleep and snoring loudly by now.'

CHAPTER NINETEEN

To say that Bob ached next morning was an understatement. But he had been able to secure hot water for a shower and with a little help from Lieutenant Dixon, he had donned the second of the uniforms he'd been issued with in London the week before. He left the damaged Walther PPK in the room and placed its substitute in his shoulder holster, which appeared completely undamaged by its close encounter with a bullet. Lieutenant Dixon also returned the two gold coins to him.

Before going to bed, Bob had removed the ammunition from the magazine of the damaged Walther. Lieutenant Dixon, who had still been awake, pointed out that if there had been a round in the chamber, the gun could have fired when it was struck by the rifle bullet. Bob began to realise just how lucky he really was.

The weather had, if anything, worsened overnight, and the wind seemed to have stripped the last of the autumn leaves from the trees. It was still pouring down with rain, falling sideways rather than vertically. Bob was grateful for the replacement Denison smock he'd been given, and spent a moment hoping that a commando now out patrolling the mountains hadn't had to give it up for his benefit.

The team didn't fit any more comfortably into the tiny office now than they had when Bob had first arrived at Achnacarry, despite Monique's absence. Bob explained her late-night decision to return to Glasgow.

Lieutenant Dixon had obtained a copy of the Ordnance Survey quarter-inch scale map the lieutenant colonel had used at Strathan and Bob laid it out on the desk. He quickly briefed the team on the steps being taken to capture Mallory and Quinlan.

'What do you want us to do, sir?' asked Lieutenant Dixon.

'I've been trying to think how the world might seem to the fugitives,' said Bob. 'Lieutenant Colonel White is closing down most of the possible avenues of escape and the weather will, or should, at least, prevent Mallory and Quinlan getting out to sea until tonight. That means they are trapped until then. I think that the two places where we might be able to add some value to what the colonel is doing are at the two places where Quinlan worked in the area before.'

'You mean what's now the Royal Navy training base at Lochailort, and the Special Operations Executive training schools run from Arisaig House?' asked Lieutenant Dixon.

'That's right,' said Bob. 'Michael, I'd like you and Andrew to visit the navy at Inverailort House. Let's think of it as a variant of the normal security visits you make to naval establishments. I want to be sure they have taken the warning they should have received from Achnacarry very seriously, and that they have stepped up their security as a result. We need to close that off as a possible line of escape.'

'Very good, sir. We can set off immediately in one of the cars.'

'Meantime, I fear I got Major Miller out of bed in Edinburgh a short time ago. He is currently telephoning the duty officer in the Ministry of Economic Warfare, which is responsible in Whitehall for the Special Operations Executive, and another in the SOE itself. Before we left Strathan early this morning, Lieutenant Colonel White told me that the SOE at Arisaig House are very twitchy about anything they consider outside interference and I'd need to prepare the ground if I was going to visit. I think he was joking when he suggested that my getting shot twice in under twenty four hours was beyond the call of duty, but he was serious about their security. The commanding officer there is a man called Major Rupert Massingham. I hope that by the time Gilbert, Taffy and I arrive, the Major will have been instructed to welcome us.'

'Do you want us to come back here when we've finished at Lochailort, sir?' said Lieutenant Dixon.

'No, could you telephone Major Miller and let him know when you've finished? I'll do the same and hopefully we can use him to help coordinate what we are doing. Unless Mallory and Quinlan have been caught by then, I think that we should meet up later today in Mallaig. You know, we really could do with a more effective means of staying in touch with one another. Glasgow City Police have had radios in patrol cars since 1936, and last month I was able to use some of the new American hand-held "handie talkie" radios up in Caithness.' He turned to Sergeant Potter. 'Gilbert, will you look into that for me when we get back to Craigiehall?'

'Yes, sir.'

Bob sat in the back of the car, trying to wedge himself into the corner of the seat to brace against the twists and turns of the road. Sergeant Potter sat with Private Jenkins in the front. They'd packed their kit before leaving Achnacarry and his, what was left of it at least, was now in the boot of the car. Lieutenant Dixon and Petty Officer MacDonald had borrowed a pair of Thompson submachine guns from the armoury at the Commando Basic Training Centre, leaving Bob and Sergeant Potter with the Sten guns and Private Jenkins with the rifle.

Bob had hoped that the quality of the ride might improve once they emerged from the back road at Banavie onto what the map showed as the main road from Fort William to Mallaig. But in truth it made little difference. The twists and turns continued and the width of the road meant no-one had ever needed to worry about painting white lines down its middle.

The storm continued unabated and Private Jenkins was having a hard time battling against the gusty wind and dodging branches and other debris scuttling along the road towards them.

Bob wondered how Monique's journey back to Glasgow was going. If her car had developed an aversion to rain, then she could again be having problems. If so, she wouldn't be the only one. 'Is it my imagination, Taffy, or do the windscreen wipers slow down when the car goes faster?'

'Yes, sir, which isn't a help in this rain. I've not noticed it before, so it may be a fault. I'll look at it when we get there.'

Despite the pain, Bob dozed, and was awakened by Potter. 'Sir, we've arrived. I think this is where we find out if they know we are coming or not.'

The three soldiers guarding the gate to the drive were dressed in capes, under which Bob could see they had rifles at the ready. 'Either they are naturally cautious, or word has reached them that there are dangerous men on the loose,' he said.

'Would you mind stepping out of the car, sir?' said one of the gate guards. 'The two men in the front, too.'

Bob was taken into the small wooden guard hut where his pass was checked against a document. Through the window he could see the car being searched before Gilbert and Taffy were allowed back into it. The soldier picked up a phone. 'Sergeant, I've got a Group Captain Sutherland here. Yes, his pass looks legitimate. Very well.'

The phone was smartly replaced, and Bob's pass was handed back to him by the soldier, who then saluted. 'I'm sorry to have detained you, sir, but we're on high alert.'

'Not at all.' Bob realised he wasn't sure of the rank of the man he was addressing.

The car took them to what looked to be the rear of a very large house. The drive terminated in a courtyard surrounded on three sides by other buildings.

Another soldier with a cape and a rifle came over to the car and saluted as Bob got out. 'The major is waiting for you and the sergeant inside, sir. If your driver would accompany me, I will take him to the canteen for a cup of tea and some breakfast.'

'Hello, sir, and welcome to Arisaig House. I must say that you could have picked better weather for your visit.' Major Rupert Massingham was waiting in the impressive hallway beyond the door. He fitted the image of a career army officer to perfection. About the same height as Bob, he wore an immaculately tailored army uniform, complete with lovingly polished Sam Browne belt. He was obviously not old enough to have seen active service in the Great War, but nonetheless wore a ribbon showing he had been awarded the Military Cross. Bob had, with some difficulty, taken off his Denison smock in the back of the car, and now realised that the major was carrying out a similar assessment of Bob's own medal ribbons. Bob wasn't sure how a Distinguished Flying Cross and Bar, a Distinguished Service Order and the recently-added Commander of the Royal Victorian Order stacked up against a Military Cross, but he didn't feel he was a poor second. The two men smiled as they realised they'd both been playing the same game.

'Thank you, Major,' said Bob. 'Though for reasons we will doubtless discuss, I'm quite grateful for this dreadful weather. I take it that you've been told to expect me?'

'Yes, sir. Otherwise, with all due respect, you'd never have got past the gate from the road. Even an MI11 security pass has its limits, you know.' The major smiled to take the sting out of his words. 'I've not been told why your visit is so urgent, but I have been told to cooperate fully with you. I assume that your visit relates to the current security alert?'

'Yes, it does, Major.'

'You must have set off early this morning, sir. Have you had any breakfast?' asked Major Massingham. 'I can lay on a bacon sandwich for you both if you wish?'

'Thank you, that would be very kind,' said Bob. 'I'm not sure I've properly eaten since breakfast yesterday morning.'

'Come on through to my office.'

The major led the way into what Bob realised before the war would have been the study. Wood panelling lined the walls, and a large fire was heating up the room from a fireplace set opposite a window that appeared to offer an elevated view out over parkland. Like every other army officer Bob could ever remember meeting, the major had a large map covering much of one wall of his office. Massingham sat one side of an imposing desk, while Bob and Sergeant Potter sat on the other.

After the tea and bacon sandwiches had been served, Bob waved towards the map. 'Do you mind if I turn to business, Major?'

'Please do, sir,' said Massingham.

'I've come to add some flesh to the security warning you've been given and to pick your brains a little. Last Wednesday a Belgian trainee at Achnacarry was murdered, and on Friday, a member of my own team, who had been investigating that murder, was himself killed. I'll not go into the details, but we are satisfied that the murderers are two sergeants on the staff of the Commando Basic Training Centre at Achnacarry. The two men are currently on the run and were last seen yesterday afternoon at the west end of Loch Arkaig. They are armed and dangerous. One of the men is a fieldcraft instructor, and the other specialises in firearms training and is an outstanding shot. They are also utterly ruthless. One of them took a shot at me yesterday afternoon.'

'But he missed?' asked Major Massingham.

'No, he didn't, as it happens,' said Bob. He touched his chest, quite gingerly. 'My trusty Walther PPK saved my life in a way the man who taught me to use it could never have imagined.'

The major raised his eyebrows. 'It was your lucky day, wasn't it, Group Captain?' He got up and walked over to the map. Bob joined him.

Bob placed his finger on the map. 'The men were last seen here, late yesterday afternoon.'

'Do you know which way they were heading from there?' asked the major.

'We think they might be trying to steal a boat to get to Ireland, where one of the men has family. That suggests they are likely to be heading towards the coast from where they were last seen. The other thing you need to know is that the men appear to have uncovered a hoard of gold coins hidden near Loch Arkaig during the Jacobite era. If it wasn't for the fact they are likely to be burdened by the gold and, we hope, have been prevented from putting to sea by this storm, I suspect they would have been long gone by first thing this morning, and we'd be asking the navy to try to find them.'

The major looked at the map again. 'And you are talking to me because we have a number of properties on the ground in the direction they are likely to be heading?'

'Yes, Major. We also believe that at least one of the men knows your operation here quite well. Sergeant Patrick

Quinlan was on the staff of the Special Training Centre at Lochailort and it's been suggested to me he might also have helped set up some of the training you run in the area.'

'It's not a name that rings a bell, sir,' said Massingham. 'But I've only been here a few months. Hang on a minute. I'll check.' The major left the room, returning a few moments later with a captain in a battledress top and kilt. 'Come in, Ian. This is Group Captain Sutherland and Sergeant Potter, from Military Intelligence, Section 11. Gentlemen, this is Captain Ian Smith, my deputy here. Ian has been here considerably longer than me. Ian, do we know of a Sergeant Patrick Quinlan who used to be on the staff of Special Training Centre Lochailort?'

'Yes, sir. He helped establish firearms training here and at another of our schools not far from Mallaig. He's a wizard with guns and a spectacularly good shot.'

The major said, 'Well it seems that Sergeant Quinlan and a colleague have murdered two men and tried to murder the group captain here. It also seems possible that they will pass through, or that they have already passed through, the area of most interest to us.'

'Can I ask where your properties are, exactly?' said Bob.

He saw Captain Smith shake his head before Major Massingham spoke. 'It's alright, Ian, I think we can bend our normal rules in the circumstances. Can you run the group captain through the locations of the schools?'

The captain pointed at the map. 'Arisaig House, where we are, serves as the administrative centre and headquarters of what we call our "Group A Schools" and we undertake some of the training here. The schools themselves tend to be small units run semi-independently to ensure security. For the most part the people we train will soon afterwards be parachuting into occupied territory, and if current experience is anything to go by, a proportion of them inevitably then fall into enemy hands. That makes it important they don't know any more than is necessary about our operation here and about the other trainees,'

'Do you have anyone specifically responsible for security?' asked Bob.

'Yes, we do, Group Captain,' said Smith. 'Security is in the hands of 49 Field Security Section, which reports to the army's Scottish Command in Edinburgh. The men are on the payroll of the army's Intelligence Corps.'

Major Massingham said, 'The section has men stationed at all our schools and we forwarded the security warning to them immediately when we received it, last night.'

'Did they all acknowledge the warning?' asked Bob.

'Yes, sir,' said Captain Smith. 'We keep in touch through a network of field telephones which link to a secure switchboard in this house. A number of the schools are so remote they didn't have any connections to the outside world before the war.'

'Do you want to finish telling the group captain where they are, Ian?' said Massingham.

'Yes, of course, sir. The simplest way is to work through them geographically. On the coast, north of Arisaig but south of Morar, we have three properties, at Camusdarach, Garramor and Traigh House. A few miles further north, a little south of Mallaig, we have Glasnacardoch Lodge, which specialises as a weapons training centre. Then we have two properties on the Knoydart Peninsula, at

Glaschoille House and Inverie House.' He pointed to each of these in turn on the wall map.

'What about further inland?' asked Bob.

'I was just coming to that, Group Captain,' said Captain Smith. 'Overlooking the west end of Loch Morar we have Rhubana Lodge. We also have two very remote properties a little over halfway along Loch Morar, assuming you are travelling by boat from the west, which we usually are. Meoble Lodge is here, about a mile south of the loch, and only accessible by boat and then on foot. Meanwhile on the north shore of the loch we have Swordland Lodge, which is connected by a track a couple of miles in length to the tiny settlement of Tarbet.'

'What do you do there?' asked Bob.

'Most of the schools are general purpose,' said Smith. 'But just as Glasnacardoch Lodge specialises in weapons training, so Swordland Lodge specialises in boat training. Landing from boats, including submarines, boat and ship sabotage, or simple boat handling. The Royal Navy maintain and crew as necessary a small number of boats on Loch Morar for us, as well as some boats and a couple of yachts at Tarbet on Loch Nevis.'

'And it's likely that Sergeant Quinlan knows about Swordland Lodge?' asked Bob.

'Our security between the individual schools is very strong these days, sir,' said Captain Smith. 'But when the Group A Schools were being established I suspect things were a little less rigorous. So, although his specialism was firearms training, I'd have thought there was a reasonable chance that Sergeant Quinlan would know what goes on at Swordland Lodge, in general terms at least.'

Major Massingham said, 'It might help if you understand the scale of what we are doing here, Group Captain. We are very much at the other end of the spectrum to the Commando Basic Training Centre at Achnacarry. While they must put many hundreds of men at a time through training, we can accommodate, assuming every school is fully occupied, a total of around 70 students at any given time, across the whole group of schools. My training staff comes to a total of some 15 officers and 25 non-commissioned officers, spread across the nine schools and based here at Arisaig House.'

Bob tapped the map again. 'To me, it looks as if Swordland Lodge is only a dozen or so miles west of where we last saw Mallory and Quinlan, at the west end of Loch Arkaig, and from what you say, it's likely they will know that there are boats at Tarbet on Loch Nevis, a sea loch. They could have reached Tarbet by mid-evening yesterday, and if I were in their shoes I think that's the first place I'd want to visit in my efforts to escape. I suspect that if the whole area hadn't been stormbound, they'd have stolen a boat and sailed overnight, before the alarm was raised. But you say that you were able to talk to Swordland Lodge last night?'

'Yes, we did, Group Captain,' said Major Massingham. 'But I agree with your assessment. He turned to Captain Smith. 'I will telephone Swordland again, and this time tell them we believe it very likely that two armed and dangerous men are in their vicinity. I will also ask them to make sure the boats are properly guarded. Meanwhile, I think we also need to increase our security there. Ian, can you round up as many personnel as possible, especially anyone from 49 Field Security Section? Make sure they are armed and if the weather permits get them onto a boat at Morar. If it's possible to sail from Mallaig in this storm, then getting men directly round to Tarbet via Loch Nevis might also help. I'll coordinate things from here.'

Bob and Sergeant Potter waited, as asked, in the main hall of Arisaig House while Captain Smith rounded up men to accompany him to Swordland Lodge.

Then Major Massingham reappeared with a worried look on his face. 'We can't raise Swordland Lodge on the telephone. The line appears to be dead.'

'When did you last speak to them?' asked Bob.

'Last night,' said Massingham. 'We immediately passed on the warning we'd received from Achnacarry. The fact that we cannot reach them now is therefore doubly worrying.'

At that point Captain Smith came into the hall. 'I've got a dozen men together, sir. They should be bringing a lorry round in a few minutes.'

The major said, 'There's been a change of plan, Ian. I'd like you to hold the fort here, while I go to Swordland Lodge. We can't reach them by telephone and I'm worried.'

'Very well sir,' said Captain Smith, who looked disappointed. 'It could just be the weather, you know. It's not getting any better out there.'

'Possibly,' said Major Massingham, 'but I don't want to take any chances.'

Bob said, 'Lieutenant Colonel White was planning to move men to the eastern ends of Loch Morar and Loch Nevis in the early hours of this morning. I know he's in communication by radio with Achnacarry. It ought to be possible to get them to ask him to move his men the few miles west to Tarbet and Swordland Lodge. And perhaps to Meoble Lodge as well, just in case.'

'Yes, that's a good idea, sir.' The major turned to Captain Smith. 'Ian, can you get onto Achnacarry immediately, and ask them to forward a request to Lieutenant Colonel White that he does that as soon as possible?'

'There's another thing, Major,' said Bob. 'The lieutenant colonel also moved men round by road to Arisaig, Morar and Mallaig yesterday. It might be possible to get them to lend a hand.'

The major paused, in thought. 'A dozen men is probably about all we can move up the loch from Morar to Swordland Lodge by boat in one go. Sir, would you be happy to go up to Mallaig and see if the conditions permit some of the commandos to travel around by boat via Loch Nevis to Tarbet?'

Bob had been considering whether he should join the group sailing to Swordland Lodge but realised that the major's proposal was a better one. 'Yes, of course, Major. Just remember that if my experience is anything to go by, these men are likely to shoot first and ask questions later.'

The major grinned. 'I thought my days as an infantry platoon commander were long behind me, but I don't think you ever forget how to ride a bicycle.'

CHAPTER TWENTY

As Captain Smith had said, the weather wasn't getting any better. Matters weren't helped because Private Jenkins had been unable to resolve the problem with the windscreen wipers while at Arisaig House.

Despite that, they had no problem seeing the results of Lieutenant Colonel White's efforts to ensure that Mallory and Quinlan would have difficulty leaving the area. Private Jenkins stopped at the first checkpoint, manned by trainee commandos on the main road leading into Arisaig. More men could be seen on patrol in Arisaig itself, and there was another checkpoint on the north side of the village.

'Good grief, sir, look at that!' They were following the twists and turns of the extremely narrow main road as it mirrored the convoluted line of the coast north of Arisaig. The tide seemed to be in and large waves were crashing into the rocks and beaches forming the shore. Jenkins had braked hard to avoid a plume of spray that had completely engulfed the road, just ahead of them.

'I don't see anyone putting to sea in this,' said Sergeant Potter.

'I just hope that the major and his men are able to get to Swordland Lodge along the loch,' said Bob.

'They stand a better chance of getting there than we do of getting out of Mallaig, sir,' said the sergeant. 'Were you able to reach Major Miller?'

'Yes,' said Bob. 'Lieutenant Dixon hadn't been in touch but will be asked to join us in Mallaig when he does. I've said we should use the harbourmaster's office there as a point of coordination.'

'Is there one, sir?' asked the sergeant.

'I'm assuming there has to be,' said Bob. 'Hello, another checkpoint.' This one had been set up just before a level crossing on the way into the village of Morar. There was another on the road out of the village, and yet another on the road as it crested the hill to begin the final descent into Mallaig. Here Bob asked where he could find the patrol commander. It turned out he was looking for a Lieutenant Darlington, who had based himself at the police office in the village.

Visibility through the rain wasn't good, but from the hill behind Mallaig it was possible to catch glimpses of large waves crashing against a pier at the north end of the harbour and forcing plumes of spray high into the air.

'Is that a train on the pier?' asked Sergeant Potter.

'It certainly looks like a line of railway wagons,' said Bob. 'You'd have thought they'd have pulled them clear of the reach of the waves.'

As they drove through the storm down into Mallaig, Private Jenkins voiced the thought in Bob's mind. 'We aren't seeing this place at its best, are we? I don't see many postcard photographers coming out in this weather.'

There were glimpses of more substantial stone houses down by what Bob assumed was the railway line, to their left, and there was an imposing hotel on the right. But Bob had to admit that the storm gave Mallaig a rather dismal air. 'I imagine that the harbourmaster's office will be on the harbour, somewhere,' he said.

'Yes, sir,' said Private Jenkins. 'I'll stop and ask.' Jenkins braved the rain and wind to ask directions from a pair of heavily-armed trainee commandos.

'Any luck, Taffy?' asked Bob.

'It's near this end of the smaller pier, sir. The harbour is not what you'd call picturesque. There must be half a dozen smokehouses over beyond where those commandos were standing, with smoke coming from one of them.'

They pulled up outside a small white building with a dark blue door and window. The sign on the door declared it to be the harbourmaster's office.

Bob pulled his Denison smock on over his head, noticing that the pain in his side seemed to have eased slightly since the last time he'd performed that manoeuvre. 'I suggest the two of you stay in the car.'

Bob knocked on the door but realised that any reply from within would be lost to the wind. He pushed the door, which flew open.

'Hello, who might you be? Close the door, will you?' Bob was greeted by a rather grizzled man of about sixty who was dressed in an oilskin jacket topped off by a black peaked cap. He was sitting behind a counter that stretched across the middle of the small outer office. The air in the office was thick with pipe smoke.

'Hello, my name's Group Captain Sutherland. I'm with

the War Office in Edinburgh. I wonder if you can help. I'm trying to find a way of getting around to Tarbet on Loch Nevis by boat. I take it you are the harbourmaster.'

'Yes, John MacLean at your service. Sorry, Group Captain. You'll not find anyone prepared to sail anywhere for a while. This isn't the best protected of harbours, even since the railway pier was built at the turn of the century. The storm's blowing from the west and anything trying to leave now runs a high risk of being swept onto the shore north east of here.'

'Is there anywhere along the coast someone could sail from?'

'Not if they value their life, Group Captain. The storm's quite widespread. I don't think there's much moving off the west coast from Cape Wrath in the north to the Mull of Kintyre in the south.'

'Do you know what the weather is forecast to do?' asked Bob.

'The latest forecast is for this to keep up until well after dark this evening, and then for it to ease off gradually. I doubt if we'll have anyone sailing out of here until midnight at least.'

'What boats are in harbour?'

'There are several small naval vessels either based here or taking shelter from the storm. Then there are a couple of Clyde puffers, the coastal steamers that carry supplies to the islands and remote communities. We've also got three or four small boats which are attached to the commando training unit at Inverie House. They get all their supplies from here.'

Bob was on the verge of correcting the harbourmaster

about the nature of the activity at Inverie House before realising that 'commando training unit' probably made a good cover story for what they did.

'We've also got the pretty dismal remains of what was a thriving fishing fleet before the war.'

'What happened to the fleet?' asked Bob.

'At the beginning of the war it was decided that the larger and more modern fishing boats would be better employed supporting the war effort as minesweepers or fleet runabouts, and many of the skilled crews were taken into the navy. Fish landings here, and everywhere else, collapsed. Then, a little too late, the powers that be realised that people needed to eat, that fish and chips was important to the country's morale, and that a shortage of supply had caused fish prices to soar. Given the idea was to avoid rationing fish, that was a self-defeating way to help feed the nation. They tried to make amends by encouraging retired fishermen back onto the boats that remained, and landings have increased over the past year or so as a result, but they are nothing like they were before the war. Ten years ago, enough fish was landed to support up to fifteen kippering sheds. Now we are lucky if there are more than one or two working at any one time.'

'But you think that it might be possible for boats to get out to sea again late tonight?' asked Bob.

'Yes, and I suspect some of the fishing boats will sail as soon as they safely can, even though it's more difficult to spot mines at night. This storm means that no fish will have been landed anywhere in western Scotland for well over twenty four hours. There are going to be very good prices on offer for the first boats to get back here tomorrow with fish they can get onto a train bound for Glasgow.'

'Thank you, Mr MacLean, I'm very grateful,' said Bob. 'Could you tell me where I can find the police office? And if a naval lieutenant arrives, a Lieutenant Dixon, asking for me, could you direct him there as well?'

As Bob pulled the door closed against a gust of wind, he wondered how long it was since he had smoked his pipe. He realised he didn't even know where it was.

Mallaig's police office was a short distance from the more southerly and older of the two piers, near the start of a road that led around the southern and eastern sides of the broad harbour.

Bob had again left Potter and Jenkins in the car and introduced himself to the constable on duty. 'I'm trying to find Lieutenant Darlington, commanding a patrol sent here from the Commando Basic Training Centre at Achnacarry.'

A man in a Denison smock and army officer's peaked cap came through from a back room. 'I'm Anthony Darlington, sir. How can I help you?'

'I understand you are commanding the troops that Lieutenant Colonel White sent here yesterday?'

'For my sins I'm in charge of the men we've got here, at Morar and at Arisaig, sir. You've just caught me, in fact. I was about to set out to check they've not been washed away by the rain.'

'Well if it helps, I can tell you that your checkpoints are proving very effective between Arisaig and here, and I certainly didn't see any lack of commitment from your men on the way up.'

'Thank you, sir, but I'll go and look anyway. When

each section was dropped off I told them their performance would be assessed just as much as on an exercise at Achnacarry, and anyone caught shirking would be returned to their home unit immediately. Anyway, how can I help you?'

'Have you been told why we are doing this?' asked Bob.

The lieutenant nodded. 'Mallory reported to me, sir. I tend to view what's happened as a personal betrayal.' There was something in the lieutenant's eyes that left Bob feeling he would not be a good man to betray.

'Alright. Well, a little earlier the Special Operations Executive people at Arisaig House found they couldn't contact their training school at Swordland Lodge, on the north shore of Loch Morar and close to Tarbet, which is on the south shore of Loch Nevis. It is possible that Mallory and Quinlan are there, or that they have been there. I am hopeful that by now Lieutenant Colonel White will have been able to move his men west from the far ends of those lochs and the SOE commander at Arisaig House is on his way along Loch Morar to the lodge. I agreed to try to find a boat here that could take me round to Tarbet via Loch Nevis and was going to ask you for the loan of some men. But the harbourmaster tells me that nothing is likely to sail from Mallaig this side of midnight because of the storm.'

'So, you don't need anything from me at the moment, sir?' asked the lieutenant.

'No, I suspect we are going to have to play a waiting game,' said Bob.

'Do you have many men?' asked the lieutenant.

'Two at the moment, and I'm expecting two more in the near future.'

'If it helps, sir, I've taken over the large guest house you can see on the opposite side of the road from the police station, just up the hill there. I think in happier times they made a living from passengers who'd arrived by rail and were planning to catch steamers to the islands. The two sisters who own it seemed very pleased to open the place up on the promise that we'd pay for all twelve rooms for a minimum of two nights, and for any more nights if necessary, and for all food and drink we consume. We don't know how long it's going to take to catch Mallory and Quinlan and some of my men spent the night there last night. I'm planning to have others sleep there this afternoon, so they can be fresher tonight. You and your men are very welcome to make full use of the facilities if you wish. There's also a telephone there you can use if you need, though it connects via the public switchboard so isn't secure.'

'Clearly Lieutenant Colonel White picks his officers for their initiative,' said Bob. 'I'm very grateful.'

The wind could still be heard howling outside, but as Bob, Sergeant Potter and Private Jenkins followed a lady who introduced herself as one of the two Miss MacLeods into the lounge, it was like entering an oasis of tranquillity. They pulled armchairs around a table set in a large bay window and it immediately felt like they were returning to a totally different pre-war world. The storm still threw itself against the windows, but with a roaring fire in the fireplace, Bob felt oddly immune from the effects of the weather. As he looked around, he thought that a passing AA hotel inspector might take issue with the dust, but as the place had been closed for the duration until only the previous day, it was a remarkable find by Lieutenant Darlington.

The slightly other-worldly feel continued when Bob, Gilbert and Taffy were served a reasonable wartime approximation to afternoon tea. Bob wondered how Lieutenant Darlington had been able to ensure the MacLeod sisters could get in supplies of food at such short notice and in such a remote location, then decided it might be better not to know.

Half a dozen very wet commandos came in and were led through to a separate lounge. Bob thought it ironic that the British managed to maintain class distinctions even in wartime. Then the door banged open again.

'Bloody hell, sir, it's like I've walked into Bettys in Harrogate for afternoon tea. How did you find this place?'

Lieutenant Dixon and Petty Officer MacDonald were both soaked. After they'd placed their Denison smocks on a fireguard to dry, they joined Bob and the others for tea and sandwiches.

'How did it go at Lochailort?' asked Bob.

'It's an impressive operation, sir. Obviously, the hatches are battened down during the storm, but they didn't know we were coming and I'd say that security is excellent. They'd received the general security alert of course, but it was more than just that. I'm confident that if our fugitives make it to Lochailort, they'll find it very hard to get their hands on a suitable vessel to get to Ireland. How did it go with the SOE?'

'There we've got some cause for concern,' said Bob. 'They seem to have requisitioned every large house for miles in every direction, but one of them is a place called

Swordland Lodge, on the north shore of Loch Morar. Three things are particularly interesting about it. The first is that it's within easy reach of where you last saw Mallory and Quinlan. The second is that it is used for nautical training and has boats nearby on Loch Nevis, which is a sea loch. And the third is that Arisaig House lost telephone contact with Swordland Lodge sometime between last night and this morning. The major commanding the SOE at Arisaig House is trying to reach the place by boat along Loch Morar, and I hope that Lieutenant Colonel White will have sent men in from the other direction. I agreed to try to get to Tarbet by boat from Mallaig, but the harbourmaster tells me that nothing's going to be sailing from Mallaig until at least midnight, so for the moment we have to sit and wait.' Bob looked at his watch. 'Waiting was never my strong suit, I'm afraid. I'm going to find the telephone I was told we could use and see what I can find out.'

'Hello, is that Captain Smith? It's Group Captain Sutherland here, calling from Mallaig.'

'Hello, sir,' said Smith.

'I'm calling on a public line which could well be insecure. However, I need to know if you've heard anything from our friends who went for a boat ride earlier.'

'Yes, sir. I have talked to... to the gentleman you met earlier, sir. He reached his destination successfully. It seems that the people there didn't know that their telephone wasn't working, and when checks were made it was found that a slate that had blown off the roof had damaged the line where it entered the building. It proved easy to fix and they were able to let me know what was happening, using the telephone, before setting off to return here.'

'Was any trace found of the two men we want to find?'

'None at all, sir. There was no indication they'd been there, and the boats were all accounted for. However, shortly after my people arrived there, they were joined by the much larger group you told us about coming from the east. I don't know the details, but the larger group felt they had found traces of the two men heading west. The larger group were sweeping across the ground both sides of the loch we discussed, towards Morar and Mallaig, and will continue to look for traces of the two men as they do so.'

'Thank you, Captain,' said Bob. As he replaced the telephone he thought about the odd-sounding conversation he had just had and wondered whether security might not have been better served by a shorter and more natural-sounding discussion. Anyone who'd overheard what had just been said would have been intrigued, to say the least, and probably able to work out most of what was meant anyway. Oh well, he thought, that was part of what he became when he signed up to this world of shadows.

'So where does that leave us, sir?' asked Lieutenant Dixon. The five men were still sitting in the bay window of the guest house lounge. The storm outside showed no signs of abating, and the afternoon was looking increasingly dark and dismal. Bob reflected that it was one of those days that never really got light.

'I was convinced that we were going to find Mallory and Quinlan at Swordland Lodge, or more likely at Tarbet,' said Bob. 'If what the harbourmaster told me is correct, no-one is going to be sailing anywhere until midnight at the earliest. I think we might usefully spend the daylight we've got left checking whether there are any vessels that appear to be preparing to sail, and perhaps take a closer look at them. Reading between the lines of what I've just been told, it seems that some trace of the fugitives has been found heading this way, but that it was unclear whether they would then have travelled north or south of Loch Morar. Let's look at that quarter-inch scale map again.'

The teacups and plates were moved to one side to allow space for the map on the table.

'From what you've just said, sir, it seems that Lieutenant Colonel White's men found traces of Mallory and Quinlan in Glen Pean, which links the west end of Loch Arkaig with the east end of Loch Morar. Once there they could pass either north or south of the loch.'

'If they want a boat then Mallaig is the obvious place for them to head for, sir,' said Petty Officer MacDonald.

'That's true,' said Bob, 'and as we've discovered it also has places you can hole up to get out of the storm. But I don't want to overlook the possibility they were heading further south. I'd be grateful if Petty Officer MacDonald, Sergeant Potter and Private Jenkins could take a drive down to Morar and then to Arisaig itself. Ask about any moored boats, or any indications that anyone is preparing to sail tonight once the storm abates. Once you've done that, return here. You'd better take the car with windscreen wipers that work properly.'

'That leaves you and I to look round Mallaig, sir,' said Lieutenant Dixon.

'It does, Andrew, though I am counting on some expert help. John MacLean, the harbourmaster, was wearing some impressive oilskins earlier. It seems a shame not to let him put them to good use. I'll ask him to give us a conducted tour to make sure we don't overlook anything.'

CHAPTER TWENTY-ONE

John MacLean appeared to be genuinely pleased to have been asked to help. 'Sorry to drag you out into the storm, Mr MacLean,' said Bob,' but it would be very helpful to see whether any of the boats here are likely to be putting to sea before morning.'

'Certainly, Group Captain. I need to do my rounds anyway, to make sure that anyone owing harbour dues has paid them.'

The harbourmaster added a sou'wester hat to his ensemble and walked past Bob and Lieutenant Dixon to the door. 'Mind it doesn't bang in the wind, gentlemen.'

Bob turned to follow. He and the lieutenant had both left their uniform caps in the guest house, feeling that commando cap comforters were less likely to be blown into the harbour. Both also wore their Denison smocks, and each carried a submachine gun, Bob a Sten gun and Dixon a Thompson. Bob was beginning to understand why those at Achnacarry able to get their hands on garments officially intended for paratroops prized them so highly. Bob had overcome his feelings of guilt at having been given two smocks in twenty four hours and had every intention of hanging onto this one. It might not look quite right when going to lunch with Lieutenant General Gordon in Edinburgh Castle, but for a wild day like today it was perfect.

The harbour at Mallaig comprised an outer pier, which Bob remembered the harbourmaster had earlier called the Railway Pier, and an older pier located rather closer to the foot of the road into the village. MacLean led them out towards the Railway Pier, which had several vessels moored against its inner face.

Lieutenant Dixon shouted, 'Isn't it dangerous having rail wagons on the pier when the sea is up like this?'

'Not really,' replied MacLean. 'When the sea gets really high, the railway makes sure that there's nothing out on the pier, but the truth is that some of the sidings that are the alternative are close to the shore and fairly prone to a sea coming in from the west. Two or three of the fishing boats moored along the sheltered side of the Railway Pier are preparing to leave. The others have shown no sign of life, so I imagine they are not going to risk it despite the value of the catches they might get. Those that are going are Mallaig-based, so I consider them my regulars. There are also two Clyde Puffers moored together here, and two motor gun boats also moored side by side, as well as a navy minesweeper. I doubt if any of them will be going anywhere until tomorrow at the earliest.'

As they approached the landward end of the pier, a group of three commandos who had been sheltering in the lee of an inactive smokehouse walked quickly over and, with guns raised, asked to see their identification. Bob was pleased to see that Lieutenant Darlington's men appeared to be on the ball.

Walking along the pier, Bob found the pain in his chest was aggravated each time he braced himself against the force of the wind, blowing from behind his left shoulder. He tried to put it out of his mind, just as he had managed to do for much of the day. There were a couple of vans parked on the pier, and down on the boats he could see men in oilskins, busying themselves on boats that looked far too dilapidated and vulnerable to trust their lives to in any weather, still less in the aftermath of this storm.

On reaching the last of the moored boats and having been challenged by a naval guard standing beside the gangway leading to the minesweeper, they turned and walked back to the landward end of the pier. Now they were having to bend into the wind. Bob could see that the two motor gun boats were also guarded, though here it was by men on the boats themselves. The commandos were still sheltering, and this time they saluted. Bob and Lieutenant Dixon returned the salute.

'The landward end of the space between the two piers is usually home to smaller vessels,' said the harbourmaster, raising his voice to be heard. 'We can look, but at the moment the area is occupied by some of the very small fishing boats that operate from here, the sort of boats that would never put to sea until this storm had long gone, as well as the launches that service the base at Inverie.'

'It looks to me as if it might be very easy to steal one of these,' said Bob.

'Can we see your passes, please?' Bob turned to find two commandos standing behind them, guns raised.

He showed his pass and returned the salute of the commandos. 'Fair enough, perhaps it might not be so easy,' he said.

The smaller pier had four fishing boats moored to it, two deep, on its north western side. None showed any signs of life. On the far side of the pier was another Clyde puffer and what appeared to be a private yacht. 'What's that boat?' shouted Bob, pointing at it.

'She's the *Orca*, Group Captain. Rather a nice yacht commandeered by the Admiralty earlier in the war and normally based along Loch Nevis at Tarbet. There's another commando training unit there, though they never let anyone near.'

Bob felt his pulse rise. Was it possible that Mallory and Quinlan had stolen a boat at Tarbet after all, and sailed it to Mallaig? 'How long has she been here?' he asked John MacLean.

'She came in yesterday morning, Group Captain, I think she needs minor repairs to hull damage. You've probably seen we've got a slipway and two boatyards beyond the pier. I believe the intention is to haul her out there and effect the repairs.'

Bob felt a surge of disappointment. 'Is that everything?' he asked. 'There are no other boats in harbour that we've not seen?'

'No, I'm afraid that's it, Group Captain. As I told you earlier, the fishing fleet is a pale shadow of what it was before the war. Look, I'm getting wet, and cold. If there's anything else you want to know, can we discuss it over a cup of tea back in my office?'

*

It took perhaps five minutes for John MacLean to produce three steaming mugs of tea. These he placed on a desk in the back room of the harbourmaster's office. 'Group Captain Sutherland, I hope you don't mind me asking, but did we go on that little tour just now to help you find a boat that might take to you Tarbet?'

Bob wasn't sure what the harbourmaster meant for a moment, but then the penny dropped. 'No. I'm sorry, Mr MacLean, it would have been polite for me to have told you what we are looking for. There's no longer a need for me to go to Tarbet. I'm sorry. The reason Lieutenant Dixon and I are here today is that we are seeking two dangerous fugitives. These men were based at the Commando Basic Training Centre at Achnacarry but are believed to be travelling overland in this direction. We think their aim is to steal a boat and try to escape, possibly to southern Ireland, where one of them has family.'

'You say they are fugitives, Group Captain. What have they done?' asked the harbourmaster.

'They killed a nineteen-year-old Belgian commando trainee last Wednesday, a boy who never knew he was going to be a father. And on Friday they killed one of my officers, who had been investigating the first murder. And yesterday afternoon one of them shot me, though, as you can see, with less effect than he might have hoped for.'

The harbourmaster looked down at the mug of tea he held between his hands. 'Is that why there are so many soldiers about? It might have saved some time if you'd told me that to start with, Group Captain.'

'What do you mean, Mr MacLean?' asked Bob.

268

'Is Pat Quinlan one of the men you are looking for?'

'Yes, he is,' said Bob. 'Do you know where he is?'

'I think I might. Let me just explain the background. You may not have noticed but on the far side of the harbour, known locally as East Bay, there are a few new houses that have been built during the last ten years or so, plus three three-storey blocks of flats. I live with my wife Margaret on the upper floor of the first of the blocks you come to as you walk round East Bay. We've lived there since they were built and, as you can imagine, it's very convenient for my job.

'The first floor flat immediately below us is occupied by Alasdair Gunn, one of the longer-serving skippers fishing out of Mallaig. He's lived on his own since his wife died five years ago. His boat is the *Silver Darling*, an 80ft steam drifter built sometime not long after the turn of the century. The navy didn't want her because she's old and expensive to run. And they didn't want Alasdair Gunn because he's even older. To operate her fully, Alasdair needs a crew of twelve, including himself, a mate, a cook, and nine deckhands. Finding a large crew in wartime has been difficult, and affording the coal needed to get up steam has also been difficult. As a result, the *Silver Darling* doesn't put out to sea very often, though when Alasdair can raise a crew with any experience she can land some impressive catches.'

'Is she out there now?' asked Bob.

'Yes,' said the harbourmaster. 'She's the inner boat at the far end of the old pier. But you need to hear the rest of the story before deciding whether I'm right or not. At about this time last year Alasdair began putting to sea with only a partial crew on board for day trips or overnight trips. This is a small place, Group Captain, and I soon began to hear stories that he had met a sergeant in the pub here, a man who was helping set up the training at Glasnacardoch Lodge, beside the main road not far south of the village. The man was Pat Quinlan. He and Alasdair, and a couple of the old men who Alasdair had managed to rope into the enterprise, were sailing off to remote parts of Knoydart, Skye, Rum and elsewhere. The *Silver Darling* has a boat, stowed at the stern, and they were using this to put ashore and poach deer. Alasdair once told me that Quinlan was the best shot he'd ever seen, and only ever needed one round to kill his prey. Once they'd killed a deer they'd gralloch it, which means removing the innards to make it easier to transport, then bring it back to the *Silver Darling* on the boat. By early spring this year, they were going out every week or two, and could return with several deer each time. Pat Quinlan often stayed with Alasdair in his flat. By then everyone in the village apart from the policeman knew what was happening, but as everyone was enjoying the cheap venison, probably including the policeman, no-one had any interest in stopping it. They were even selling it to a butcher in Fort William when they had more than they could dispose of locally.'

'You make it sound like it did stop, though.'

'Yes. Pat Quinlan's permanent base was at Lochailort, which meant he could travel here easily by train, or Alasdair would collect him in his van. But then he was posted inland, and couldn't get to Mallaig so easily, or at all. Alasdair's been out fishing maybe three or four times over the summer, but other than that the *Silver Darling*'s been sitting at the pier, gently rotting away.'

'Do you think that Sergeant Quinlan might have renewed his old acquaintance with Alasdair Gunn?'

'I'm fairly sure he has. I'm a heavy sleeper. But my wife sometimes has problems sleeping at all. She has a habit of sitting with the light out and the curtains open, looking out towards the harbour. She told me this morning that she'd had an interesting night. At about 2 a.m. she says she heard an odd noise from below, like gravel hitting a window. When she came to the window and looked down she got a sense there was someone standing outside the front of the building. There would have been no lights, remember, and in the storm there wouldn't have been any moonlight.

'Despite the sound of the wind and the rain she heard Alasdair leave his flat and go down to the front door. She then saw a flicker of a torch, lighting up two men in army uniform, which must have been Alasdair checking who was calling. A little later she heard someone leave Alasdair's flat and got the sense they had gone out. After a while she heard an odd noise outside, and from the occasional flash of torchlight realised that it was Alasdair returning with a trolley he uses to move his fishing gear. It's a bit like the sort of thing railway porters use to move luggage and he keeps it in a shed near the harbour. Then there was more movement on the stairs, and my wife saw three men wearing oilskins using torches to put things on the trolley. She said she thought they'd then gone back towards the harbour.'

'So she didn't actually see where they went?' asked Bob.

'No, but she was awake enough to stay up and hear one man, who she thought was Alasdair, return about half an hour later and go into his flat. I'm wondering if the men you are looking for are on board the *Silver Darling*.'

'Was she one of the ones preparing to leave?' asked Lieutenant Dixon.

'No, it didn't look as if anyone was aboard when we were there just now, but they'd hardly advertise their presence in the circumstances,' said the harbourmaster.

'So, you think that Alasdair Gunn might be doing a favour for an old friend and helping him escape?' asked Bob.

John MacLean laughed. 'Alasdair Gunn has never done a favour for anyone as far as I can remember. If he's helping Quinlan now, it's because he thinks there's something in it for him.'

Bob had a pretty good idea of what Mallory and Quinlan might have offered in return for their escape. 'If they are on board, how long would it take to prepare to sail?'

'As long as it takes to find a few crew, get up steam and load provisions for the trip,' said the harbourmaster. 'A couple of hours at most.'

'Which means that they are unlikely to show any signs of life until much later tonight?'

'That's right,' said John MacLean.

'Hang on,' said Michael. 'Wouldn't the troops have been guarding the harbour at the time? They seemed very efficient today. Surely they'd have stopped three men wandering along with a trolley in the middle of the night?'

'You'd have thought so,' said Bob. 'But we know they've not been caught, so we have to assume they found a way of evading or fooling the patrols.'

As he looked along the length of the pier, Bob reflected that there were times, though only a very few times, when the blackout was a blessing rather than a curse. It was very dark now, the only illumination coming from the occasional flicker of torchlight over on the Railway Pier as the boats there continued their preparations to sail.

It was a few minutes before 9 p.m., and as far as Bob could tell through the windscreen of the civilian fish lorry, the storm was finally easing off. The rain was no longer hammering against the side of the lorry quite so hard, and the noise of the wind had eased noticeably in the last hour.

Lieutenant Darlington had assembled twenty commandos for the operation to board the *Silver Darling* and, hopefully, capture Mallory and Quinlan. Some were from his original patrol, but others he had selected from among the larger number of men who had arrived in Mallaig late that afternoon, on foot from the east. Commandos were also forming a discreet but very tight cordon around the harbour, while others were enjoying the hospitality of the MacLeod sisters' guest house after spending eighteen hours or more out in the storm.

John MacLean had been happy to draw diagrams of the layout of the *Silver Darling* on a borrowed blackboard in the guest house earlier. Bob had taken a discreet look at the vessel before it had got dark. As MacLean had said, she was 80ft long. There were two masts, one towards the front of the boat and one near the rear. There was a bridge, which looked like a broad telephone box, located a little more than halfway back along the length of the boat. This was accessed internally by a ladder up from the deckhouse, which was partly set down within the hull of the boat. A door at deck level at the rear of the deckhouse gave access to steps down into it. From here it was a few steps forward into the area used for crew accommodation and meals, with the galley and the head, or toilet, behind. The engine room was below the bridge and came complete with a tall funnel which projected upwards immediately behind the bridge. MacLean was sure they would find anyone who was on board in the crew accommodation area of the deckhouse, which he described as having bunks on both sides and a fixed table and benches in the middle.

Bob's discussion with Lieutenant Darlington and Lieutenant Dixon had arrived at a plan which would see ten of the men board the *Silver Darling* from the fishing boat moored beside it, further out from the pier. Three men would meanwhile be shining lights down onto the boat from the pier above, and half a dozen more, led by Lieutenant Darlington, would board the rear of the vessel by climbing from a small boat onto its stern, which was at the end of the pier furthest from the shore. As soon as the boat was secured, Bob and Lieutenant Dixon would climb down onto it from the pier.

The storm might have been easing, thought Bob, but it was still fierce enough to help mask any noise made by the men as they moved into position. At exactly 9 p.m. Lieutenant Darlington blew a whistle and the operation began, in complete silence apart from the hammer of boots on the wooden decking, which could be heard above the wind even from where Bob stood on the pier.

Bob saw Darlington and his men enter the door at the rear of the deckhouse, but then, where there should have been shouts to indicate that the fugitives had been captured, there was simply silence. The men still on the deck looked up at Bob, who led the lieutenant down ten feet or so of steel ladder set into the side of the pier.

There was still no noise from inside the deckhouse when Bob reached the door at its rear. He looked at Lieutenant Dixon in the glare of the light being shone down from above. Then he shrugged and dived into the doorway, holding his Sten gun, cocked and ready to fire, in front of him. The steps beyond the doorway were steeper than he had expected, and he landed heavily on the deck at the foot of them, stumbling forwards as he did so. Thankfully he'd kept his finger clear of the trigger or his Sten gun would have gone off accidentally. He heard Lieutenant Dixon land equally heavily behind him.

The crew accommodation was lit by a single fitting set into the cabin ceiling. It wasn't the brightest light Bob had ever seen, but it was sufficient for him to realise that he had dropped into what at first glimpse looked like a frozen tableau from a waxworks museum. Lieutenant Darlington was standing just ahead of him and to his right. The lieutenant's men were standing off to the left of the table. Bob could also see a man in one of the bunks, on the right-hand side of the cabin as he looked along it. But all attention was focused on a man wearing a black fisherman's jumper who stood at the far end of the cabin, near the ladder leading up to the bridge and the lower level doorway to the engine room. He held one arm in the air, and in that hand he held a hand grenade. From the dark hair and straight nose, Bob took this to be Patrick Quinlan.

'Welcome, gentlemen,' he said. 'As I've just been saying

to your friends, please keep very still. The pin is removed from this grenade, so if I drop it we all die.' Quinlan caught Bob's eye, then turned white, as if he'd seen a ghost. 'You! But you're dead!'

Quinlan's arm wavered and he took a step backwards. Lieutenant Darlington responded by taking a step forwards, raising his Thompson submachine gun as he did so.

Quinlan dropped the grenade and was instantly shot by, it seemed to Bob, at least three of the commandos in the cabin. As Quinlan collapsed backwards into the doorway leading to the engine room, Lieutenant Darlington took another step forward and kicked the hand grenade past him. 'Take cover!'

Bob instinctively ducked and turned away towards the rear of the vessel. In the confined space of the engine room the blast would have been catastrophic, but Quinlan's collapsing body seemed to shield those in the deckhouse from the worst of the effects. It was Lieutenant Dixon who shouted. 'Everyone out, she's sinking!'

Bob felt the *Silver Darling* lurch beneath him and having seen Lieutenant Darlington and one of his men pull Sergeant Mallory off the bunk, hurried back up the steps and out onto the rear deck.

By the time Bob was back on the pier, it was clear that the *Silver Darling* was indeed sinking. The ropes tying her to the pier were cut, and the fishing boat that had been moored next to her was moved around to nestle next to another vessel. Within five minutes nothing could be seen except for the two masts, the roof of the bridge and the top half of the funnel. The *Silver Darling* had obviously settled on the bottom of the harbour.

Bob was happy to see in the torchlight that Lieutenant Darlington still had Sergeant Mallory under close guard. The lieutenant looked at him. 'I'm not quite sure what happened there, sir.'

'Quinlan shot me yesterday. I think he was a little surprised to find I was still in the land of the living.'

'It's just as well you provided a distraction, sir. I wasn't certain how that was going to end.'

'Nor me, Lieutenant Darlington. Do you know if the police office has an interview room? I would very much like to have a chat with Sergeant Mallory while things are still fresh in his mind.'

Bob turned to find Lieutenant Dixon and Petty Officer MacDonald standing close by.

'Michael, I'd be grateful if you could join me in the interview with Sergeant Mallory and take notes. And Andrew, could you have another word with our friends at HMS *St Christopher* in Fort William, please? I think we have need of their divers again, both to recover Sergeant Quinlan's body and to retrieve the gold. If they could be here at first light tomorrow, I'd be very grateful. And could you find Sergeant Potter and ask him and Private Jenkins to go and pick up Alasdair Gunn, please? I'd like to talk to him later. Can we also ensure that the *Silver Darling* is kept under guard until we can get divers aboard?'

CHAPTER TWENTY-TWO

It turned out that the Mallaig police office stretched to a small and rather grimy interview room, as well as a cell in which they could hold Alasdair Gunn until Bob had finished with Sergeant Mallory.

'It's a bit of a mess, isn't it, Sergeant?' asked Bob, thinking that Mallory was also a bit of a mess. He hadn't shaved and his eyes, which looked anywhere but at Bob or Michael, were red-rimmed as if he'd been crying. His hands were clasped tightly together, almost below the edge of the table, but Bob could see that despite the sergeant's apparent efforts to still them, they were shaking violently.

'Yes, sir. Do you mind if I smoke, sir?'

Bob did mind, very much, but judged that he might get more out of Mallory if the man was able to settle his nerves a little. The shaking proved so bad that Lieutenant Dixon had to light a cigarette and pass it across the table. Even then, Mallory dropped it and took two attempts to pick it up. Bob decided that no-one would notice one more cigarette burn on an already badly scarred table.

Bob leaned forward. 'You're not going to feel any better until you've got everything off your chest, Sergeant. You know that, don't you?'

There was a long pause. Then Mallory drew deeply on his cigarette, exhaled, and finally looked up at Bob. 'Yes, sir. What do you want to know?'

'Let's start with the gold,' said Bob. 'It would be nice to keep things in something like chronological order, and I'm guessing that the gold came first. Am I right?'

'Yes, sir. It was at the end of last month, sir. We had over 600 US rangers training at Achnacarry. Towards the end of a course we often send the trainees off to fend for themselves for 36 hours. That's what happened then. They were divided into three groups and each went off into the mountains. One group was scheduled to make a night march from the north shore of Loch Arkaig and over the higher ground to the north. The planned route took them up a steep-sided and wooded valley above a place called Murlaggan. Sergeant Quinlan and I were tasked with simulating an ambush. We set up an explosive charge under the roots of a tree that had been hit by lightning, to bring down the trunk in front of them, and then we fired live ammunition above their heads. It worked well, Next day we went back to the site to ensure the explosives had all detonated, and under the stump of the tree we found some rotted old sacks. When we poked at one, it simply fell to pieces, revealing a load of gold coins.'

'What did you do?' asked Bob.

'We covered the place up with stones and dirt, but we both agreed that without the protection of the tree, any heavy rain could expose the gold again. We therefore found a reason to head out along the loch a few days later. We went back up to the valley, transferred the gold from the rotten sacks to two army issue canvas packs we'd brought along, which we thought should be enough to hold what we'd found, and hid those under part of an old stone wall close to the shore of the loch near Murlaggan. The packs were large enough, but the weight of the coins was enough to make us think we were going to break the webbing straps.'

Lieutenant Dixon asked, 'How many sacks did you find under the tree?'

'It was difficult to tell, sir, as they had rotted away. Perhaps six or eight small sacks, and the gold coins were just sitting inside them.'

Bob leaned forward. 'What was the plan at that point?'

'The idea was to hide the gold until after the war. We weren't sure how good the old wall would be as long-term storage, because the level of the loch does rise and fall a little depending on the weather. Sergeant Quinlan and I therefore talked about the possibility of finding a better hiding place. I was also very nervous. Sergeant Quinlan is, was, I should say, a bit of a nutcase.'

Mallory subsided into silence. He was still shaking, and the mention of Quinlan's name seemed to have made things worse.

'What do you mean?' asked Bob.

'Well, he was utterly ruthless, and as far as I could see completely without morals. So long as he and I were the only people who knew where the gold was hidden, I felt my life was in real danger. If he killed me, he'd end up with twice as much.'

'That's a little rich, coming from someone who killed a woman in a bar for a few bottles of wine and then tried to kill her son.'

Mallory's head slumped forward and Bob bit his tongue. He knew that hadn't been the right thing to say. If he'd caused Mallory to retreat into himself, then the moment might pass, and they'd never get the full story out of him.

Then Mallory lifted his head and looked at Bob again. 'Yes,' he said, very softly, 'I know.'

'Do you want to tell us about that?' asked Bob.

'When I saw that Belgian boy last Wednesday, it was like a complete bolt from the blue. I knew I recognised him from somewhere and it was obvious that he also recognised me. It was only a little later that I remembered what had happened in Belgium. You must believe me when I say that, until that moment, I had never had any recollection of going into that bar that night. It was as if it had never happened. But as I thought about the boy's face, it all suddenly came back to me. I remembered going into the bar, I remembered shooting the woman, and then I remembered shooting the boy. It was like waking up from a nightmare, only to find that the nightmare was real.'

'I'm guessing you then told Quinlan?' said Bob.

'Yes, I did, and the nightmare got worse. Sergeant Quinlan was insistent that the only way to avoid my being exposed as a m-m-murderer was to silence the Belgian boy.'

'You mean, to murder him as well?'

'Y-y-yes, sir. We saw him going into the big hut during the milling and I let him see me there. When he approached me, Patrick stabbed him in the back.'

'How did that affect your plans for the gold?'

'Patrick felt we had to move the gold to somewhere with better long-term security as quickly as possible, sir. I wasn't in a position to disagree. On the Friday afternoon we took the boat we'd used previously up to Murlaggan and removed the gold from the wall. To spread the weight, we took along two full sets of 1937 pattern webbing, with the large front ammunition pouches. We kept one coin each as souvenirs, but divided the rest of the gold between the two packs and the four pouches, and while it still weighed just as much, it was less difficult to carry. We then reburied it in what we agreed was a good spot, not far from the old ruined building up beyond the head of the loch, just far enough away to make sure no-one would ever go looking there. We simply lined the hole with a groundsheet, and placed the packs, webbing and pouches inside it. With rocks laid on top, there was no sign of anything having happened there. On the way back, we stopped at the small island near the Achnacarry end of the loch and hid the tools and spare fuel for the boat there. Then we returned to the pier.'

'And that was where you found Captain Bell?' asked Bob.

'Yes, sir. When we got back to the pier, there was an army captain I didn't know there. He helped us tie up and then asked what we had been doing on the island. He had a pair of binoculars and had obviously been watching us. Sergeant Quinlan said something as he climbed up the steps to the pier, I didn't catch what. Then he flipped his gold coin in the air towards the captain and as the captain reached out to catch it, Quinlan stabbed him in the stomach. As the captain bent forwards to hold himself, Quinlan stabbed him again, this time in the chest. The coin bounced off the officer and went into the loch. Quinlan pushed the captain's body into the loch and then we went back to the island, to make sure we had left no fingerprints on anything we'd hidden there. When we got back to the pier we did the same for the boat, collected the lorry we'd moved the tools up from the camp in, and that was that.'

'If Quinlan lost his gold coin attacking Captain Bell, how was it we found one hidden amongst his property after he had left the camp?'

'He made me give him mine, sir,' said Mallory. 'He said it was my fault that our plans were in a mess, so it was me that should do without the coin.'

Bob felt a profound sense of relief. The most important part of the interview was behind them and Mallory was talking more freely. Bob looked at Michael, who lit another cigarette for the sergeant.

'What happened on the Sunday?' Bob asked. 'At the parade?'

'We were all told we had to assemble on the parade ground, sir, and it was obvious that something was up. Then I saw Quinlan and he told me the parade was to look for me, sir, or at least for someone whose description that I matched, with a broken nose. We agreed I had to leave and that I'd cut across country. He would pick me up in a lorry beside the road later. That's what we did, though it was only early the next morning that he was able to get away. Then, after we got to Banavie, we argued about what to do, sir. We eventually agreed that we should try to get to Ireland, where Sergeant Quinlan had family. Quinlan said he knew a man in Mallaig with a fishing boat that had enough range and wouldn't attract attention. But he said that the only way we could pay the man was by digging up the gold coins and offering him some of them for the passage. If I'm honest, I thought it was better to get the gold, too. That way I wouldn't need to spend the next few years wondering when Patrick was going to try to kill me to double his share. We left the lorry at Banavie to throw anyone off the scent. Then we doubled back and took an overland route over the high ground south of Loch Arkaig. It's difficult country and we could only travel slowly because we were concerned about being seen by any of the patrols we expected to be looking for us by then.'

'Then what happened?'

'The only people we saw were you and the lieutenant, sir, and the petty officer. We spotted your boat some way off, so stopped digging and hid on the slope above the track near the ruined building. Quinlan was all for killing both of you immediately when you came along the track. I persuaded him that it was safer simply to let you pass by, in the hope you'd then return to the boat, none the wiser, and leave. That worked until you walked out beyond the ruin and it was obvious you'd seen where we were digging. At that point the gold was still in the ground. Quinlan shot you. I thought he'd killed you. I persuaded him not to kill the lieutenant and the petty officer, and we tied them up in the building.'

'And then you finished digging up the gold?'

'Yes, sir. And then we walked out to Mallaig. That was hard. As you know, the weather was appalling, and the gold was very heavy. Add in the roughness of the terrain and... This isn't what you want to hear about, is it, sir?'

'What route did you take?' asked Bob.

'Sergeant Quinlan knew the area well, sir. We came along Glen Pean to the end of Loch Morar, then skirted along its northern shore. We were careful not to be seen at Swordland Lodge, which Sergeant Quinlan said would be heavily guarded, and from there it was a case of following a track, and then a road. When we got to Mallaig we cut across country, behind the village, so we could avoid any patrols, and dropped down on the east side of the bay. Patrick threw gravel at the window of the flat of the man whose boat he wanted to use. Captain Gunn, Quinlan called him. After we agreed a price the captain went and fetched a luggage trolley from the harbour. He'd put sets of oilskins and rubber boots in this, which we changed into. He also told us that there were patrols out around the harbour and we'd be challenged getting to the boat. He thought the bad weather and the oilskins would be enough to put anyone off looking too closely, even in the middle of the night. Patrick said it would be alright, as he also had false identity documents which he'd had illicitly made while working with the SOE. I was worried because I guessed that the patrols would be formed from trainees at Achnacarry, who might know us by sight. As it turned out, we were challenged, but only Captain Gunn had to do any talking and the sou'westers helped hide our faces. We reached the boat without problem and we stayed there throughout the day. You know the rest, sir.'

'You moved the gold coins onto the *Silver Darling*?'

'Yes, sir, along with our weapons and other kit. It all fitted neatly in Captain Gunn's trolley, with a fishing net on top to avoid it being too obvious.'

'How much did you agree to pay Gunn to take you to Ireland?' asked Bob.

'A hundred gold coins in advance, and 200 more when we arrived. He argued with Quinlan about the price, but I think he knew he would do really well from it.'

'How many coins had you found in total?' asked Bob.

'We'd never had chance to count them exactly until today, sir. We simply divided them roughly by weight, first between the packs and subsequently between the packs and the pouches. It was obvious there were a good few thousand, though. We had nothing else to do on the *Silver Darling* today, so we properly counted the coins, and divided them between us, again, using the packs and pouches to spread the weight.'

'And how many were there?'

'Eight thousand, two hundred and eight, sir. That didn't include the hundred we had already given Captain Gunn before we left his flat, or the two we took initially as souvenirs.'

Bob did a quick calculation. 'That much gold must weigh something close to 150 pounds. Are you telling me that the two of you managed to carry it over rough country at night and in bad weather for 25 miles to Mallaig in under 10 hours, in addition to your weapons and other kit?'

'Remember, sir, that instructors at Achnacarry have to be able to do everything that we demand from the trainees. It was the toughest march I've ever had to do, though.'

'And it could be the last, as well,' said Bob.

'I know that, sir. And throughout the march I had the feeling that Patrick simply saw me as a means of helping transport his gold to Mallaig rather than a real partner. I knew I was going to have to watch him very closely on the trip to Ireland. I'd already decided to offer Captain Gunn more gold if he'd drop me, by myself, somewhere other than the place he'd agreed with Patrick.'

'Well that's a fairly full account,' said Bob. 'How do we know that what you've been telling me is the truth?'

'Why would I lie, sir? I've had to try to accept that I murdered a woman in Belgium and tried to murder her son. I'm nowhere near understanding how that happened. And now I'm an accessory to two murders and an attempted murder in Scotland, not to mention what happened with the hand grenade. I know that I'm going to hang for what I've done, whatever I say.' There was a long pause as the sergeant again made an obvious effort to control the shaking of his hands. 'I might as well face the noose with the little integrity I've still got intact.'

'They told me they'd pay me fifty gold coins in advance and a hundred more when we reached Ireland, Group Captain.' Alasdair Gunn seemed calm, almost matter-of-fact.

Bob sat back in his chair. 'Those coins may look very pretty, but the gold content of each is worth around two pounds and five shillings, Mr Gunn. Would you really have risked everything for that much money? Well let's see, shall we? We're searching your flat right now and believe me we will find anything you've hidden there.'

'Alright, it was a hundred gold coins in advance, and 200 on arrival in Ireland,' said Alasdair Gunn. 'They're not hard to find, I just left them in a dresser drawer in the bedroom.'

'Where were you going to take the two men?'

'Quinlan wanted me to take them to Galway, about halfway down the west coast of Ireland. I agreed to take them as far as Bundoran, on Donegal Bay, rather further north and less distance to sail. That would give them access to a railway station, and they could travel on from there. That's all I know.'

'Who were the crew?'

'I had in mind a couple of old friends who need work from time to time. I contacted them today, though I said nothing about the gold. I need to get hold of them to tell them not to bother. We were due to sail at first light tomorrow.'

'What happens now? Is your boat insured?'

Alasdair Gunn laughed. 'Hardly, Group Captain, and I have a feeling the military isn't going to look sympathetically on a claim that it was sunk by you. I don't know what happens now, to be honest, but I'm sure I'll get by.'

Bob had little doubt that that much, at least, was the truth, the whole truth and nothing but the truth. 'You are free to go, Mr Gunn, but stay away from your flat until we've finished our search. If anything turns up that doesn't square with what you've told me, I will be in touch.'

It began to get light at Mallaig a little before 8 a.m. next morning. The MacLeod sisters' guesthouse had been full to bursting overnight, but Bob had pulled rank to ensure he had use of a tiny single room. That ensured he had a break from Lieutenant Dixon's snoring.

Bob had asked Sergeant Potter and Private Jenkins to escort Sergeant Mallory back to Achnacarry, where he would be handed over to the military police for later transport south. They were then due to make their way back to Edinburgh.

The morning was chilly enough for Bob to be wearing his recently-acquired smock, but it was wonderful to see blue skies. The absence of the perpetual rain of the previous 36 hours and the oppressive wind was also very welcome.

The navy divers were waiting beside their lorry on the harbourside when Bob, Lieutenant Dixon and Petty Officer MacDonald arrived.

'Good morning, gentlemen,' said Bob. 'I'm grateful. It couldn't have been a very pleasant drive from Fort William in the dark.'

'I wouldn't miss this for the world, sir,' said Petty Officer Johnson. 'I understand we are treasure hunting again?'

'Yes, we are.' Bob indicated the sunken form of the *Silver Darling* below them, with a little more of its bridge roof clear of the water than there had been the previous night, thanks to a lower tide. 'I believe there are two army issue canvas packs and four ammunition pouches on board which between them contain about 150 pounds in weight of the gold coins you found at Loch Arkaig. I'm afraid there is also a body to be recovered. The gold coins are likely to be in the crew quarters in the deckhouse, accessed through the doorway at the rear of the vessel, which as you can see is currently totally submerged. The body is likely to be in the engine room, which is accessed from the front of the deckhouse. The gold was divided between two men who didn't trust each other. It is likely that it was stowed in two different places.'

'Bodies are more our stock in trade than treasure, sir.

How long has this one been in the water for?'

'Less than twelve hours,' said Bob. 'But I'm afraid he was rather close to a grenade detonation, so it may not be very pleasant.'

'Is that what sunk the boat?' asked Petty Officer Johnson.

'Yes,' said Bob. 'The grenade went off in the engine room, and the sergeant was in the doorway between the engine room and the crew quarters so took the full blast. The boat sank soon afterwards.'

Removing Sergeant Quinlan's badly damaged body was a grim job for the divers and the commandos who assisted on the harbourside. Petty Officer Johnson and Petty Officer Heal then began their search for the gold, with Able Seaman Pym watching over proceedings from the quayside, alongside Bob, Lieutenant Dixon and Lieutenant Darlington.

The two packs and one set of pouches proved easy enough to find and were hauled out and into the back of an army lorry. It took rather longer to find the remaining set of pouches, which were on the bridge of the *Silver Darling*.

The gold was then moved the very short distance to Mallaig police office, where the coins were counted by Bob and the two lieutenants with the police constable, and, once he had changed out of his diving suit, Petty Officer Johnson, as witnesses.

'It seems that whatever their other failings, Mallory and Quinlan could count,' said Bob. 'That's a total of 8,208 gold Louis d'or coins carrying various dates before 1746. We also have the one hundred coins found when we searched Alasdair Gunn's flat, making 8,308 in total. That's not a bad haul, given that I'd been expecting to find 5,700 at most.'

Lieutenant Dixon looked at Bob. 'Sir, what about...?' He saw the look on Bob's face and stopped.

'What happens to this now, sir?' said Lieutenant Darlington.

'Do you have somewhere secure where it can be kept under lock and key at Achnacarry?' asked Bob.

'I'm sure we can find somewhere, sir, in the armoury or the guardroom,' said the lieutenant.

'Could you do so, please?' said Bob. 'I have a feeling that this will end up belonging to the Crown, which is a little ironic as it was originally landed on these shores to try to overthrow the person then wearing the crown. But until it's been decided who should take possession of it, we need to make sure it's kept safe.'

'Yes, sir, I'm sure we can manage that, though I'm equally sure that Lieutenant Colonel White will want it moved away from Achnacarry as quickly as possible. I'll get an armed guard together now and oversee its return myself.'

The lieutenant was as good as his word and the gold coins, returned to the packs and pouches Mallory and Quinlan had used to carry them in, were taken back outside to begin their journey to Achnacarry.

The last three men in the interview room were Bob, Lieutenant Dixon, and Petty Officer Johnson. Bob turned to look at Petty Officer Johnson with his good eye. 'You'll be able to tell your grandchildren that you really did find a hidden treasure.'

'Yes, sir, I will. Now I just need some grandchildren to tell.'

'Give it time,' said Bob. 'Do you have children?'

'No, not yet, though my wife talks about it every time I'm on leave.'

'Well, perhaps the grandchildren might take rather longer,' said Bob. 'But when you do tell them about the gold, this might help convince them you aren't pulling their leg.'

Bob held out a gold coin. 'Go on, take it. It was only thanks to you that we found it.'

Petty Officer Johnson took the coin and held it up between his fingers. 'Is that the one we found off the pier, sir? Doesn't this belong to the Crown, like the others?'

'Yes, it is, and I suspect it probably does. But the Crown is going to get 8,308 of the coins, and I'm sure it won't miss that one.'

On the way back towards Edinburgh with Lieutenant Dixon and Petty Officer MacDonald, Bob made a courtesy call on Lieutenant Colonel White at Achnacarry. He wanted to thank the colonel for all his help, to let him know how impressed he had been by Lieutenant Darlington, and to discuss the safekeeping of the gold until it could be collected.

Bob also wanted use of a secure telephone. His first telephone call was to Major Leclercq, Hannes Lambrechts' commanding officer in South Wales. The major agreed to let Anne Davies and her mother Mary Davies know that, thanks to the description Mary had provided, Hannes' killers had been caught.

Bob also had a rather longer telephone conversation than he had been expecting to have with Flight Lieutenant George Buchan, who he found at his desk in the office at Craigiehall. Then he had a third conversation, this time with Monique Dubois, who was still in Glasgow, before talking again to Flight Lieutenant Buchan.

Lieutenant Dixon and Petty Officer MacDonald were waiting in the car when Bob went back outside. 'There's been a slight change of plan, gentlemen,' he said. 'You will travel back to Craigiehall by road as discussed earlier, but I want you to drop me off at Spean Bridge railway station to catch a train to Glasgow. It seems the rest of the world has not been standing idly by while we've been busy here.' Bob looked at his watch. 'We've got plenty of time, though, to do one final thing here.'

'Do you want to go to Clunes, sir?' asked Lieutenant Dixon.

'After the war is over, you'll be able to make your living as a mind reader, Michael,' said Bob.

CHAPTER TWENTY-THREE

'Hello, Group Captain. I wondered whose car had stopped outside my cottage.'

'Hello, Archibald. Can we come in? You remember Lieutenant Michael Dixon, I'm sure. And this is Petty Officer Andrew MacDonald.'

Archibald seated them in the lounge, as before. And as before, a black cat lay curled up in front of the fire.

'Does your cat ever move, Archibald?' asked the lieutenant.

'Judging from the mice and other creatures I find as presents most mornings, I think Satan enjoys a full and active night life. He seems to make up for it during the day, though. Now, gentlemen, is this another occasion for breaking out the whisky?'

'You might think so, Archibald,' said Bob, 'but I'm afraid we have a long way to travel today, so we'll have to decline.'

'That's a shame,' said the older man, with a smile. 'So, to what do I owe the pleasure of this visit?'

'I thought you might like to hear the final instalment of the tale of the Loch Arkaig gold,' said Bob.

'Very much,' said Archibald.

'Last time we were here we discussed the history of the gold and you told us about your ancestor, Archibald Cameron. I can now add an account of what has happened much more recently. One night late last month, two instructors from the Commando Basic Training Centre mounted a mock ambush on a group of trainees high on the north side of the glen above Murlaggan. As part of their ambush they planted explosives under a tree that had been struck by lightning, to bring it down. They subsequently discovered that their explosion had uncovered a large quantity of gold coins under the roots of the tree, placed there in sacks that had rotted away over the years.'

'Was this in the valley of the Allt na Caillich?' asked Archibald.

'Interestingly enough, no,' said Bob. 'It seems to have been in the valley of the Allt Mhurlagain, the next valley along to the west.'

'So, my uncles were looking in the wrong place that summer,' said Archibald.

'It certainly seems so,' said Bob. 'I wondered if perhaps, when the gold was hidden there in 1753, they'd simply misidentified the valley, in the absence of detailed maps.'

'My namesake Archibald Cameron knew the area too well to make that mistake,' said Archibald. 'When you and I last discussed this, Bob, you suggested that Alexander MacMillan of Glenpeanmore might have re-hidden the gold when things quietened down. That may be exactly what happened.'

Bob said, 'When I stood in the old graveyard at Murlaggan, what you told me about your ancestor's injuries and age came to mind. Looking up at the north side of the glen from there, it would certainly have been easier for him to have hidden the gold in the nearest side valley, rather than in the valley of the Allt na Caillich, which is much further away.'

'Aye, perhaps you are right, Bob. If the story was later told by someone other than my ancestor, then the wrong name could have become attached to the hiding place at that point. We are never going to know, are we?'

'That's true,' said Bob. 'Anyway, to return to more recent developments, the two Achnacarry instructors who uncovered the gold then hid it in an old wall beside the loch near the graveyard at Murlaggan. They later reburied it in what they thought was a more permanent location, not far from the old barracks near the head of the loch. When we started to close in on them they dug it up again and carried it to Mallaig. That's where we caught up with them. One of the men was killed there and the other is in custody for various murders and attempted murders, both recently at Achnacarry and in Belgium in 1940.'

'It's a long walk from Strathan to Mallaig carrying a weight of gold,' said Archibald Cameron.

'All the more so as it turned out that they'd found over 8,300 gold coins, not the 5,700 suggested in the records you'd seen. 8,310 to be exact.'

Archibald Cameron sat back on the sofa. 'Now that is fascinating. It suggests that Archibald Cameron of Locheil was able to take possession of more of the original gold, most likely from Macpherson of Cluny, before the redcoats caught up with him. What will become of the coins now?'

'That's still to be decided. Right now, they are securely under lock and key. I strongly suspect, however, that they will be claimed by the Crown.'

Archibald Cameron laughed. 'Now, that's ironic, he said.'

'That's what I thought,' said Bob. 'I did keep this for you, though.' Bob flicked the coin so it span in the air, just had Archibald had done the last time they had met.

Archibald was more adept than Bob had been, however, and had no difficulty catching it. He looked at it. 'This one is dated 1740.'

'Yes,' said Bob. 'That was one of two Louis d'or kept as souvenirs by the men who found the gold. It subsequently travelled to Achnacarry and has since been in my possession. The Crown will get the rest. It seemed to me only right that Archibald Cameron of Locheil's descendent should have one to remember him by.'

There were tears in the older man's eyes. Then he laughed. 'I wonder if that Jacobite toast we drank on your last visit had more of an effect on you than I realised at the time, Bob? I'm not supposed to have this, am I?'

'No,' said Bob, 'but then you aren't supposed to have the illicit whisky you kindly served on our last visit and I didn't see that stopping you. Besides, only the four of us here know, and none of us are about to tell anyone else, are we?'

Spean Bridge railway station was quiet as the afternoon train from Fort William to Glasgow arrived. He'd heard stories of frantic activity here as hundreds of men at a time arrived by train from Glasgow and then formed up to begin their march to Achnacarry. Today, though, it was almost possible to forget there was a war on. Bob had, with difficulty, packed the Denison smock into his overnight bag and was back in his RAF issue officer's raincoat. The train proved to be as quiet as the station and he had no difficulty getting a first-class compartment to himself.

Bob had heard that the railway line from Fort William to Glasgow was one of the most scenic in the world. He saw very little of it. He was awakened by the ticket inspector as the train pulled into a remarkably remote station, apparently surrounded by mountains and moorland. He had no idea where it was. The station name boards had been removed, in common with most across the railways of Britain, as a wartime measure to avoid assisting an invading enemy.

'Where are we?' asked Bob.

'This is Corrour Station, sir. You've a way to go before we get to Glasgow.'

'No, I suppose there's no chance of confusing the two, is there?' said Bob.

A little later Bob woke up again, this time as the train crossed a bridge over a road in a village, before coming to a halt at another unnamed station. From his map he thought this must be Crianlarich. As he settled back down into his seat he realised that he'd barely noticed the pain in his side at all that day. He thought this was a little surprising given the jar he'd had when he'd landed heavily at the bottom of the stairs in the crew compartment of the *Silver Darling* the previous night.

Monique Dubois had agreed to have Bob met at Glasgow's Queen Street Station. He'd asked how he would know the driver, only to have Monique point out that there weren't likely to be many group captains passing through the station at that time. The driver would find him.

'Group Captain Sutherland?' A man in a civilian overcoat and hat that had both seen better days approached him on the concourse. 'I'm supposed to tell you that the lady from Sarclet Castle is waiting for you, sir.'

'Madame Dubois?' replied Bob, as agreed, wondering if he'd ever get used to this cloak-and-dagger stuff.

The driver didn't introduce himself and led Bob over to a parking area, where he held open the rear door of a saloon car.

As they headed south west through a city Bob had once known very well indeed, he asked where they were heading.

'I'm sorry, sir, I've been told not to discuss that with you.' Bob saw little point in pushing for an answer and sat back to enjoy the show provided by a spectacular sunset. For the second time that day he reflected on how the weather made such a difference to the way Scotland looked and felt.

Bob's mental map suggested they were approaching the eastern side of Paisley when the car slowed down and turned off the road, through a pair of open gates. Ahead of them was a house, built from a yellowish stone, standing in its own grounds. The sign on the gatepost had proclaimed it as 'White Cart Lodge'. Bob looked round through the rear window to see a man closing the gates behind them.

*

'Hello, Bob,' said Monique, as he was shown into a comfortable sitting room. 'As I told you on the telephone you've returned just in time. The simulated sabotage of the Rolls-Royce factory at Hillington takes place later tonight.'

'Will Geoffrey Smith actually be taking part?' asked Bob.

'No, there's no need for that. He's got all the information he needs to be able to produce a watertight account of his actions for the Abwehr when he returns to Germany. He's in the room he shares with Arthur Thompson at the back of the house here. Arthur and another minder are taking him into Glasgow later, to allow him to indulge his passion for night clubs and, perhaps, for women.'

'Arthur Thompson's job isn't one I'd want myself,' said Bob.

'No, Geoffrey Smith is becoming increasingly hard work for all of us,' said Monique. 'His first response when he met me was to suggest that I'd been laid on, and I choose my words carefully, for his benefit.'

'He's not your type, then?' asked Bob, laughing. He saw the look on Monique's face and stopped laughing. He bit his tongue, wishing again he'd not tried quite so hard to hurt her when they'd argued.

'As you know, Bob, there was a time when I didn't really pick and choose, unless "bastards" qualifies as a type. I thought I was getting more discriminating in my old age, but I came back from Achnacarry unsure whether you were my new leaf or just more of the same.'

'I know there's no excuse, but when you showed up it was on the back of Commodore Cunningham raising

300

questions of his own about my fitness to be running the investigation. It may not have been what he intended, but it was how it felt. Having MI5 forcing its way in seemed like just another kick in the teeth. It felt even worse because the pretext was built on something I'd told you privately.'

'I know, Bob, and I am truly sorry about that. But it really didn't seem to matter at the time. As I told you, I had as little desire to be at Achnacarry as you had for me to be there.'

Bob sighed. 'Have you ever wished you could wind back time a little, and have a second run at something? I do wish I could unsay some of the things I said.'

'Yes, I have. For my part I regret what I said to you about your injury. It was nasty, and it was untrue. I admire the way you've overcome what happened and succeeded despite it.'

There was an awkward pause.

'Sorry,' said Bob, 'I think I changed the subject. You were saying how you'd managed to keep Geoffrey Smith occupied.'

'Yes, I was. Building up the detail of the cover story has taken a fair amount of time. On Monday he was out with Arthur Thompson visiting chemists and ironmongers in the Glasgow area, looking for the chemicals he would need to manufacture explosives. There was a difficult moment when it turned out that the Abwehr handler who had taught Geoffrey how to make his own explosives had told him that the weedkiller he needed, "kalium chloride" in German, translated as "calcium chloride" in English. We had a very puzzled shopkeeper wondering why Geoffrey wanted to use calcium chloride as a weedkiller. Geoffrey's natural charm avoided awkwardness turning into nastiness and another brush with the police. We've yet to decide whether the Abwehr's failure to tell him that the weedkiller he wanted was called potassium chloride in English was down to incompetence on their part; or was a trap to allow them to test the story he tells when he returns. Given I don't think they expect or particularly want to see him again, I think it was just incompetence.'

'I assume he's not actually manufacturing explosives?' asked Bob.

'Good God, no,' said Monique. 'Anyway, we decided to go one better. Arthur Thompson took him down yesterday to a large quarry at a place called Greenoakhill, on the south east side of Glasgow, to allow him to familiarise himself with the place. Geoffrey will tell the Abwehr that he stole a car, used it to steal a significant quantity of commercial explosives from the quarry, and used that to sabotage the factory. That was Geoffrey's idea. It seems he regularly stole explosives from quarries during his safe-cracking days. He's also been back to Hillington to work out a plausible route through the security, and to look at the inside of the building he is meant to be attacking, again so he has a convincing story to tell.'

'What happens tonight?' asked Bob.

'Not so fast, Group Captain. I know you did me a favour last Thursday...'

'You said when you asked me to do it that it was a "large" favour,' said Bob.

'Yes, I did. But when we spoke this morning you told me that you had something to offer in return for having a ringside seat tonight.'

'That's right, I do,' said Bob.

'What is it?'

'Don't you trust me?'

'Do you trust me?' asked Monique.

'With my life, yes,' said Bob. 'To play fair when there's credit to be earned for MI5? I don't know.'

'Come on, Bob. Apart from anything else, I'm curious.'

'Fair enough, Monique. Think of this as an official invitation from MI11 to MI5 to take part in an operation tomorrow to shut down a Soviet spy ring in Scotland. In my absence the operation's been approved by Commodore Cunningham and Major General Sir Peter Maitland and is seen as a means of re-establishing MI11 as an active force in the intelligence community.'

'Do my people in London know about it?'

'No, they don't, Monique. But as the head of the Security Service reports to Sir Peter, I can't imagine he will be able to complain. And you'll be able to tell them all about it, though I'd be grateful if you could refrain from doing so until afterwards.'

'I promise, Bob. What's the background?'

'I'm only partly up to speed myself,' said Bob, 'but I'll make sure we are both briefed before the operation takes place. In the meantime, however, have I earned myself that ringside seat we were talking about for tonight?'

'I think so.'

'Do you have a spare room here I can use after we're finished at Hillington?' asked Bob. 'I've got a plane picking us up at RAF Renfrew in the morning to take us to Turnhouse.'

'Yes, of course, Bob.'

*

Bob knew that many thousands of workers were employed at Hillington. In thinking through what was proposed, he had always thought that the biggest problem would be preventing any of the workers realising that something out of the ordinary was going on.

In the event, the ruse was carried off in a very matter of fact way. Bob and Monique were driven the short distance north from White Cart Lodge to the factory at Hillington and having entered the site were directed to a car park near the most north eastern of the major blocks making up the factory. It was a clear night, well-lit by a moon that was only four days past full.

In the car park they found something like a dozen army lorries and some twenty men. The team responsible for the deception was led by a Royal Engineers officer who introduced himself as Major Murray. Monique also introduced Bob to Bernard Peterssen, the head of security for Rolls-Royce at the Hillington factory.

A short time later a police car arrived, and Lieutenant Jack Callaghan walked over to join them. 'Hello, Bob, couldn't you keep away either?'

'You know me, Jack. I always want to see the loose ends tidied up.'

Major Murray's men clearly knew exactly what was expected of them.

'Do you mind me asking what we're looking at, Major?' said Bob.

'Not at all, sir.' The major pointed up, towards the roof of the factory. 'My men are currently spreading out a very large canvas cover over the north eastern corner of

304

this building, it will cover about a third of the roof area and have an irregular curve at its far edge. Things are complicated by the design of the roof. This is set in a series of ridges, which are angled and glazed to make the most of the sun's light. Thankfully, blackout regulations mean that the glazing was painted over early in the war to prevent the factory drawing attention to itself at night. Otherwise anyone inside the building would see what we were doing, if not tonight, then certainly in the morning. My men are spreading and tying down this canvas, while trying not to put a foot or anything else through the glazing.

'The canvas is painted to give the impression, when viewed from an aircraft passing over at height, that the building has been badly damaged and that you can see wrecked machinery inside. Once the canvas is secure we will winch up and fix in place some papier-mâché components that add an element of the third dimension to the illusion. The result might look a little odd to anyone passing low over the roof, but from any height at all, it will look convincing.'

'With RAF Renfrew just a short distance to the north and RAF Abbotsinch not much further to the west, isn't there a chance someone will see the roof from close range and realise what is going on?' asked Bob.

'The bigger danger is that someone will start spreading stories that the building has been damaged, which is something we want to avoid,' said the major. 'But that's a chance we'll have to take. The illusion will be in place for ten days, which we think is long enough to be sure the Luftwaffe can come and take photographs; and is just about long enough for us to have begun to repair it if it had been damaged. Then we'll pack everything up and return it to the film studios we are based at in Shepperton.'

'It's a bit of an anti-climax, really, isn't it?' said Lieutenant Callaghan, quietly, when the major had left.

Bob agreed with him but didn't say so.

It took no more than three hours for the major's men to finish their work and leave the site.

Before he left, Bob agreed to visit Jack Callaghan and his wife that coming weekend and fended off the suggestion that he might like to 'bring a friend'. Even in the moonlight, Bob could see a glint of humour in the lieutenant's eye that suggested he had drawn conclusions about Bob and Monique.

It didn't take long to drive back to White Cart Lodge.

As they entered, Monique turned to Bob. 'Do you fancy a brandy?'

'If you like,' said Bob. 'Do you want to sit in the lounge?'

'No, that wasn't what I had in mind, Bob. You wait there, and I'll grab a bottle and a couple of glasses and we can take them up to my room.'

As Monique disappeared, Bob was left wondering whether he had heard her correctly. When she returned a few moments later she held the bottle up for inspection. 'I know you prefer the women in your life to offer you Cognac, but I'm afraid this is all we've got.'

'Does this mean I'm not staying in a spare room?'

'Well, you can if you want to, Bob. I'll not hold it against you if that's what you want to do. I just wondered whether we should try to put Achnacarry behind us. I do like being with you. How would you feel about giving each other one

306

last chance? I'll put you back in my "not a bastard" pile, for the moment at least.'

Bob smiled. 'So long as you promise that dig about Cognac is the last time you'll ever tease me about Lady Alice Gough. I still feel bad about how upset she was to find you in my bed.'

'Alright, and for your part, no more harlot references, please. Not unless I'm acting the part for your benefit.'

'I promise,' said Bob. 'Brandy will be fine, by the way.'

Bob half-expected Monique's response as he turned towards her in the glow of the bedside light.

'Good God, Bob, I didn't think it would be that bad!' Monique was looking at the purple and black bruise that still covered a large part of the left side of his chest. 'And your arm!'

'Yes, to say that parts of me are tender is an understatement. I'm not joking when I ask you to be gentle with me.'

'I promise, Bob.'

CHAPTER TWENTY-FOUR

'Hello, Flight Sergeant. We've met before but I'm sorry, I don't know your name.' It was the same man who had flown him to Renfrew the previous Thursday.

'It's Flight Sergeant Clapperton, sir. Do you want to sit up front again?'

'If it's alright with you, Flight Sergeant, Madame Dubois will sit in the co-pilot's seat and I'll sit just behind. There's something we need to look at once we've taken off. Once we've done that we can leave you in peace and move back down the cabin.'

'Of course, sir.'

The aircraft took off into the gentle westerly wind under clear blue skies. Bob raised his voice over the sound of the engines. 'Could we fly straight ahead until we're at 5,000ft and then reverse course, Flight Sergeant? We want to look at the Rolls-Royce factory. And I'd be very grateful if you'd keep to yourself what you see and hear when we do that.'

'No problem, sir.'

The pilot did as he had been asked. Bob was amazed by the effect of the illusion of sabotage. Ignoring the pain in his chest he leaned over the back of Monique's seat, so he could get a clear view out of the front of the cockpit. 'You know, Monique, at 5,000ft, I was convinced that we'd see the illusion for what it is. But even from here it looks very convincing, even when you are actively looking for edges or things that don't fit.' It seemed to Bob as though he was looking down into the building, onto pieces of damaged machinery lying around inside it.

Bob realised that his lack of depth perception might make him particularly susceptible to the illusion. 'Flight Sergeant Clapperton, could you tell me what you see when you look at that building down there, the one nearest the northern corner of the factory?'

'It looks as if it's suffered bomb damage, sir. But there haven't been any air raids that I know of for quite some time.'

'Thank you, Flight Sergeant. That's what I was hoping you'd say. It is quite important that as few people as possible know about this.'

'Know about what, sir?' said the flight sergeant with a grin.

Bob and Monique moved back into the cabin of the aircraft. The noise levels didn't allow easy conversation, but Bob found he was intrigued by what was going to happen next to Geoffrey Smith.

Monique leaned towards him, so she could be heard more easily. 'Geoffrey radioed his handlers in the Abwehr on Tuesday to say he was planning to attack Hillington last night. He radioed them again in the early hours of this morning to say that the attack had taken place, and that he feared the British were closing in on him. He asked for information about how he could be extracted by submarine.'

'You said the Abwehr aren't good employers,' said Bob.

'I did,' said Monique. 'I can tell you now that when he contacts them again tonight, the Abwehr will tell Geoffrey that they are unable to arrange a submarine extraction and that he will have to make his own way to Lisbon. He will be able to travel overland from there to France and then to Germany. Geoffrey will tell them tonight that the pursuit is getting too hot for him to continue transmitting, and that he intends to bury the radio. He will then spend the next few days lying low in the safe house in Paisley. In the middle of next week he will find a berth on a British-registered ship that is due to sail from Greenock to Lisbon, where he will make contact.'

'Rather him than me,' said Bob.

'Amen to that,' said Monique. 'But if his story is convincing enough then perhaps the Abwehr will feel they can use him a second time.'

'What if his story doesn't convince them?' asked Bob.

'Then he'll be moved swiftly to a concentration camp and never be heard of again.'

'How does anyone live like that?' asked Bob. 'It does raise the question of why he's prepared to go back, and whose side he's really on.'

'I know, Bob, and that thought's cost me a few sleepless nights. But though I don't like the man, I do believe he's on our side.'

'I got the impression you had wider plans in place to help back up his story,' said Bob.

'Well, there is the hope that the Luftwaffe will send over a reconnaissance aircraft sometime during the next ten days, of course,' said Monique. 'And the RAF are aware at senior level of the need to let any single high altitude intruders through unmolested during that period. We've also arranged for the early edition of tomorrow's *Daily Express* to print a short piece about an investigation into the cause of an explosion in a factory near Glasgow. This will be the edition that makes it onto the mail plane bound for Lisbon tomorrow morning. Meanwhile, one of the Abwehr agents we've turned in the Midlands will radio his Abwehr handlers tomorrow night. He will tell them that an agent he has recruited, one of many fictitious agents he runs, has told him that shifts at the Rolls-Royce engine plant in Derby have been extended to allow Merlin engine production to be increased, to make up for a sudden shortfall from one of their other two factories. Hopefully the Abwehr will add two and two together and arrive at a very reasonable but totally incorrect answer of five.'

After the propellers had come to a standstill, Bob thanked Flight Sergeant Clapperton for the flight.

'That's alright, sir, you're very welcome,' said the pilot. 'I'm told I'm needed to fly you up to Perthshire shortly, so I'll get myself a cup of tea and then stay with the aircraft.'

This was news to Bob.

The aircraft door was opened by Sergeant Peter Bennett. 'Good to see you safe and well, sir. By the sound of it you've had an interesting few days.'

'Thank you, Peter, it's good to be back.' As Bob got out onto the tarmac he looked around. 'Where to now?'

'We've borrowed the operations room, over by the control tower, sir.' Sergeant Bennett pointed to the nearby building.

Bob followed Monique into a room with a row of windows looking out onto the airfield. A group of men were standing by a table on one side of the room, on which cups and saucers and plates of biscuits had been laid out. Several of the men were smoking. Much of the room was occupied by a meeting table clearly formed from several smaller folding tables.

Major Walter Miller strode over to greet Bob, ignoring Monique totally, and holding out a cup and saucer to him. 'Hello, sir. Do you want a cup of tea?'

'Hello, Major. Can I introduce Madame Monique Dubois, who is with the Security Service? Monique, this is my deputy, Major Walter Miller.'

'Good to meet you, Major,' said Monique. 'Thank you, I'd love a cup of tea.' She took the cup and saucer out of the major's hands and carefully sipped the tea, blew on it, then sipped again.

Major Miller took Bob to one side. 'Sir, you do know that MI5 are not meant to be involved in this operation, don't you?'

'Yes, I do,' said Bob. 'Flight Lieutenant Buchan told me when I spoke to him on the telephone yesterday. However, Madame Dubois happened to be in Glasgow and is an expert on the Soviets and on the People's Commissariat for Internal Affairs in Moscow, or the NKVD if you prefer. I therefore took the decision to ask her to participate.'

It was clear that Major Miller would have appealed the decision if there had been anyone more senior present, but equally clear that he didn't want others in the room to notice that he'd objected and been overruled. 'Do you want to chair the meeting, sir?'

'No, Major, it's your show. You sit at the end of the table, I'll sit here, next to you, and Madame Dubois can sit next to me.'

Bob hadn't seen so many of his people in the same room together before. Flight Lieutenant Buchan was standing to one side, clearly preparing to brief those present. Also sitting around the table were Sergeant Bennett, Lieutenant Dixon and Petty Officer MacDonald.

Major Miller leaned over to him. 'Sergeant Potter would be with us, sir, but he is on his way down to Southampton. It's Captain Bell's funeral tomorrow. His family live near there.'

'I'm pleased we will be represented,' said Bob.

Major Miller began the meeting. 'Most of you know one another. Sitting to my right is Group Captain Sutherland, who is deputy head of MI11 and our senior officer here in Edinburgh. To his right is Madame Monique Dubois, from MI5. Could I ask the gentlemen at the end to introduce themselves for the benefit of the group captain and Madame Dubois?'

A police officer in uniform spoke first. 'I'm Inspector Steven Robertson, sir. My role will be to set up a secure area around the property in Leith and make sure no-one gets in or out.'

The smart-suited civilian beside him spoke next. 'Hello, sir, I'm Lieutenant James Bruce. I'm in charge of Special Branch in Edinburgh City Police. Do you mind my asking if you are related to Superintendent Sutherland? I know he has a son in the RAF.'

'Yes, he's my father,' said Bob.

'I report to the superintendent, sir.'

Bob smiled. 'Please pass on my regards and tell him I promise to call in on him and Mum to say hello, just as soon as the world slows down a little.'

After the members of MI11 had introduced themselves, Major Miller turned to his left. 'Flight Lieutenant Buchan, could you fill in the background, please, and tell us what is planned for today?'

'Yes, of course, sir. Good morning, ladies and gentlemen. In the early hours of last Thursday morning, an RAF Police guard disturbed an intruder trying to gain entry to a de Havilland Mosquito aircraft parked at RAF Leuchars. The intruder fired at the guard, who returned fire and killed him. The intruder turned out to be a Sergeant Jacek Winograd, serving with the 4th Polish Parachute Battalion in Fife. He'd been stationed at the Polish Army camp in Tents Muir, just a short distance from RAF Leuchars. Sergeant Winograd had only recently joined his unit, having previously served in a Polish tank brigade stationed in the Scottish Borders.

'Amongst Sergeant Winograd's effects was a page that looked like it had been torn out of a school exercise book. It was, in effect, a crib-sheet on how to start up a de Havilland Mosquito. It seemed clear that the sergeant was intending to steal the Mosquito, but we had no idea why. The Polish Army in Britain is responsible for its own security, so we were very much in their hands when it came to looking into his background, which is never an easy thing to do when most of that background lies in a country now occupied by the Germans.

'It was only when Group Captain Sutherland suggested,

via a note he left me on Saturday morning, that we might want to look for Soviet connections that things started to move.'

'That was Madame Dubois' idea,' said Bob. 'How did the Polish security people respond?'

'Like they'd been poked with a very sharp stick, sir,' said Flight Lieutenant Buchan. 'I'm sure they weren't being obstructive before then but giving them a direction in which to look produced remarkable results. By the end of Saturday, I knew that Sergeant Winograd came from eastern Poland, an area that was occupied when the Soviets invaded the country on the 17th of September 1939, just a couple of weeks after the Germans invaded Poland from the west. Large numbers of Poles were killed by the Soviets during the invasion and during the occupation that followed, which only ended when Germany launched Operation Barbarossa and invaded the Soviet Union in June of last year. Many Poles were also deported to labour camps in the far east of the Soviet Union.'

'And now we are allies of both Poland and the Soviet Union.' said Lieutenant Dixon.

'Indeed,' said Bob. 'The Poles are hardly blessed with the best of neighbours, are they? Carry on, Flight Lieutenant.'

'Thank you, sir. I also spoke on Saturday to Wing Commander Gill at RAF Leuchars, who confirmed that a Mosquito, if fully fuelled as that one was, could have been flown to Soviet territory. He said that if he'd been planning it, he'd have taken a route over Sweden and the Baltic that avoided Axis-held territory as much as possible, perhaps finishing up somewhere securely in Soviet hands beyond besieged Leningrad. An even more northerly route to Murmansk would have been within the range of the aircraft and might have been preferable in terms of likely opposition. He made the point, though, that the Polish pilot was woefully ill-equipped to make the flight in terms of equipment and clothing. He didn't even have a map that went much beyond Fife. In his view the whole enterprise was doomed to failure.'

'Anyway, on Sunday morning Major Kaminski telephoned to say that their security people had unearthed material of real value. Apparently, Sergeant Winograd had trained as a pilot, and had proved very proficient. But he was present when a close friend's aircraft crashed at a training base and the friend was trapped and burned alive. Winograd ceased pilot training and requested a transfer to the army, which was granted.

'Just as significantly, amongst Sergeant Winograd's effects was a letter which the Polish security people think was written by his sister, Adrianna. It had no date and no return address. It said that she and the sergeant's mother were well, but that nothing had been heard from his father. It went on to say that she was in terrible danger, and that she had been told that her safety, and their mother's safety, depended on Jacek going to visit his uncle Cyryl in Leith, and doing exactly what he was told when he visited. His sister also told him to burn the letter when he had read it. Obviously he didn't. The Poles' interpretation of the letter was that Sergeant Winograd's mother and sister are prisoners of the Soviets and he was being blackmailed.'

'Do we know how the letter got to him?' asked Major Miller.

'No, sir. We do, however, know who Cyryl is. From

what I heard, Sergeant Winograd was a good soldier, but as a spy he was mediocre. Three weeks ago he took a week's leave from his unit. He told them that an elderly relative who was a refugee living in Scotland was ill. Men going on leave have to leave contact information. The sergeant said he could be contacted via a Cyryl Winograd and left a telephone number.'

'I'm guessing the telephone number was a giveaway?' said Bob.

'Correct, sir. The telephone number linked to an office near the docks in Leith run by a gentleman called Sergei Avdonin. It seems he is a shipping agent who finds cargoes suitable for Soviet vessels intending to take part in the Russian convoys. Our friends in Special Branch kindly set up watch on the office and arranged to listen in to telephone calls.'

'Has anything interesting turned up?' asked Bob.

It was Lieutenant Bruce who replied. 'We had the premises watched and telephone calls intercepted from late Sunday night, sir. Over the next two days, by the end of Tuesday, we identified several visitors who were probably legitimate, plus two men who visited separately and who we have been able to identify as members of the Polish Army in Scotland. They each stayed for about an hour. On Tuesday evening Sergei Avdonin received a telephone call from a man we have been able to identify as Colonel Irakli Kuznetsov. He commands a Soviet Air Force unit based at a place called RAF Errol, between Perth and Dundee. The call was about transport arrangements for personnel and was innocuous enough in itself, but the fact that the two men are in contact seemed interesting.'

'We have a Soviet Air Force unit based in Scotland?' asked Bob.

Flight Lieutenant Buchan took up the story again. 'We do, sir. They're just forming at the moment but are known as No. 305 Ferry Training Unit. It seems that earlier this month the Soviets placed an order for the delivery of 200 Armstrong Whitworth Albemarle aircraft. The idea is that Soviet aircrews will train at RAF Errol, and after the aircraft are delivered to them from the manufacturer, they will fly them direct to Russia.'

Bob asked, 'How did we convince the Soviets to go for the Albemarle? It's had a few problems, hasn't it?'

'I get the sense that it was what we could spare, sir,' said Flight Lieutenant Buchan. 'I think it's the same principle as supplying them with large numbers of Hawker Hurricane fighters when the story is that Stalin really wanted Spitfires. What's interesting is that this time around the rumours are that the Soviets only settled for the Albemarles after being told they couldn't have Mosquitoes.'

'Ah, now that is interesting,' said Bob.

'I talked to the RAF Police flight commander at RAF Errol, a Flying Officer Frost. The Soviets have only been flying occasionally, and for the last month, in a couple of Avro Ansons and in Miles Masters that they've borrowed from No. 9 Advanced Flying Unit, which also operates from Errol. They have now received the first two Albemarles and have begun training on them. Apparently, there's a story doing the rounds on the base that one of the first pilots trained by No. 305 Ferry Training Unit didn't speak Russian. It seems he was overheard receiving instruction in English. That would have been at about the time Sergeant Winograd was on leave.'

Bob leaned back in his chair, wincing as the bruising on his chest made its presence felt. 'So, the theory is that we have an NKVD operation in Leith that is recruiting members of the Polish Army in Scotland to spy for the Soviet Union? And that almost as an aside they fed one of their recruits who happened to be a pilot through to this Colonel Kuznetsov, so he could arrange for a Mosquito to be stolen and flown to the Soviet Union?'

'Yes, sir,' said Flight Lieutenant Buchan. 'He couldn't use one of his own pilots because a Soviet turning up at RAF Leuchars would have been viewed with much more suspicion than one of the long-term Polish neighbours.'

'Just a thought,' said Bob. 'Does the map that Winograd was carrying, the one that Wing Commander Gill said didn't go much beyond Fife, cover RAF Errol?'

'The airfield is on the north bank of the Firth of Tay, sir, so I'd think it possible. We can check if you like. If it does, then as you know, the actual airfield won't feature, even if it existed when the map was surveyed.'

'No, there's no need. There will be a copy on the premises here. We can take a look when the meeting finishes. Let's get back to the bigger picture. What are we proposing to do today?' asked Bob.

'The Poles are keen to have the Soviet operation in Leith closed down as quickly as possible, sir. They can't be seen to be having anything to do with the closure themselves. The idea is simply to arrest Sergei Avdonin and see what he can be persuaded to tell us in the time it takes the Soviet Embassy in London to come hammering on the door and claiming diplomatic immunity for him. Meanwhile, we will go through his office in Leith with a fine-toothed comb and see what comes up. With your agreement, sir, Major Miller will lead that part of the operation. We thought you might like to pay Colonel Kuznetsov a visit and suggest that for the remainder of his stay in Scotland he becomes a model citizen.'

'A lot more could be achieved if you let the Soviet operation run and monitored what was going on,' said Monique. 'If you close it down, it will simply restart in another form sometime in the future, and without us knowing about it.'

It was Major Miller who replied. 'You are of course right, Madame Dubois, and I made that point to the head of MI11, and I know he made the same point to the Director of Military Intelligence, Major General Sir Peter Maitland. However, the Polish Government in Exile is in a hugely difficult position because of this and apparently decided at the highest level to ask us to close things down immediately.'

'Fair enough,' said Bob. 'Let's go and let the Soviets know they've been rumbled.'

CHAPTER TWENTY-FIVE

Monique had opted to join Major Miller and Lieutenant Dixon's group for the raid on the office in Leith, pointing out that her knowledge of the NKVD and her fluency in Russian could be real assets. It was obvious to Bob that the major wanted to find a reason not to involve her but couldn't think of a convincing one.

The weather over eastern Scotland was as beautiful as it had been over Glasgow. Visibility from the Avro Anson as it flew north over Fife seemed endless, and there wasn't a cloud in sight.

Bob was sitting in the co-pilot's seat, next to Flight Sergeant Clapperton. 'I bet you didn't get weather this good when you were training in a Canadian winter.'

'No, sir. But then it's not often this good in Scotland either.'

Flight Lieutenant Buchan leaned over Bob's left shoulder. 'Sir, how do you want to play it when we arrive?'

'I think we should treat this as one of your normal inspections. You and Sergeant Bennett can look at RAF

Errol's security and I'll have a chat with Colonel Irakli Kuznetsov. You are sure he's there?'

'Yes, sir. As you know I telephoned Flying Officer Frost when the meeting ended. At that point the colonel was in his office in the hangar that has been allocated to No. 305 Ferry Training Unit.'

'Are there any sensitivities at Errol?' asked Bob. 'Is the station commander going to be upset if I just breeze in and get nasty with the commander of a unit based there?'

'The station commander is a Group Captain Robertson, sir. Flying Officer Frost tells me that the group captain gives you his full blessing but wants nothing to do with the operation personally. He apparently feels that's the best way to maintain good working relations between him and the colonel in the future.'

'That's understandable. And it suits me perfectly,' said Bob.

RAF Errol was a larger base than Bob expected. The Avro Anson approached from the south, crossing the River Tay before landing on one of the runways laid out in the classic 'A' pattern. Bob counted five large hangars on one side of the site, and there were a significant number of smaller blister hangars dotted around the perimeter of the airfield. They followed a Miles Master training aircraft in to land, and Bob could see several more in the circuit, with others on the ground dispersed around the airfield.

Flight Sergeant Clapperton was directed to park the Avro Anson on a concrete hardstanding close to one of the hangars. Nearby were two aircraft Bob recognised as the recently delivered Armstrong Whitworth Albemarles. Bob was struck by the large amount of glazing in the fuselage, especially in the nose, and the twin fins. The nosewheel undercarriage was also something of a novelty.

A flying officer held open the cabin door as Bob climbed out of the aircraft. 'Welcome to RAF Errol, sir.'

Bob returned the salute. 'Thank you. You are Flying Officer Frost, I presume?'

'Yes, sir. I've got a car waiting.'

'What we had in mind was taking the opportunity for Flight Lieutenant Buchan and Sergeant Bennett to look around. You've not been open for business long, have you?'

'No, sir. The first unit only took up residence in August.'

'Meanwhile, I want to have a private chat with Colonel Kuznetsov. As his aircraft are here, I assume his office isn't far away?'

'That's right, sir, it's one of the offices attached to the nearest hangar over there. Do you want me to send anyone with you?'

'No, thanks, Flying Officer. I'll keep it as informal as possible. Does No. 305 Ferry Training Unit have many staff at present?'

'No, sir, it seems to be the colonel, supported by a couple of non-commissioned officers for administration, plus a major and two junior officers who apparently do the flying training and assessment, and perhaps half a dozen trainees. I think they've got two aircraft up on training flights now, sir, so I'm not sure how many of the colonel's men will be present.'

Bob smiled at the NCO he met in the corridor. It was a bit of a surprise to find someone in full Soviet Air Force uniform, complete with boots and riding breeches, on an airfield not all that far from Perth. 'Hello. I'm looking for Colonel Kuznetsov's office.'

'I'm Kuznetsov. Who's looking for me?'

Bob hadn't heard the office door open behind him and turned around to find himself face to face with a man of rather above average height, again in Soviet Air Force uniform, though this time of a finer quality and with more medal ribbons. His most noticeable feature was a moustache that looked just like Josef Stalin's.

Bob held out his hand. 'Hello, Colonel, I'm Group Captain Sutherland. I'm attached to the War Office.'

The colonel shook Bob's hand. 'I'm told that in this country "being attached to the War Office" is usually a euphemism, Group Captain. Is it in your case?'

Bob smiled. 'Yes, it is, Colonel.'

The colonel sighed. 'At least they sent a proper pilot.' He waved towards the wings on Bob's chest. 'And you've seen action, too, judging from your medal ribbons.'

'Yes, Colonel, I was a squadron commander during the Battle of Britain.'

'You are a fighter pilot? How many German aircraft have you shot down?'

Bob decided this was no time for false modesty. 'Officially, Colonel, the number is twenty two. By my count it is twenty four.'

'It is an honour to welcome you here, Group Captain. I'm not a fighter pilot, so can't compete. Should we go through to my office? Can I offer you coffee?'

They sat either side of the colonel's utilitarian desk, two cups of coffee gently steaming between them.

'What can I do for you, Group Captain?' asked Colonel Kuznetsov.

'I'm here to talk about Sergeant Jacek Winograd.' said Bob.

The colonel looked confused, but only for a moment. 'Ah, so that was his name. I assume you are talking about the Polish pilot I knew only as "Peter"?'

'I might well be,' said Bob. 'If you didn't know this man's name, how did he get on and off the base? He must have had a security pass.'

'He only arrived once and left once, hidden in the back of a lorry. For three days we kept him here.'

'While he was here you refreshed his skills as a pilot?'

'Yes. He was quite good, if a little nervous at first.'

'And you also taught him the procedures for starting up and taking off in a de Havilland Mosquito?'

The colonel smiled. 'I think you already know the answer to that, Group Captain.'

'Where did you get your information from?'

'From a set of RAF issue pilot's notes for the aircraft. And before you ask, no, I don't know where they came from, and neither do I have them here anymore. I returned them to the air attaché in the Soviet embassy in London, who had initially provided them to me.'

'You do know that Sergeant Winograd fired at a guard when he was trying to steal that Mosquito at RAF Leuchars, don't you, Colonel? And that he was then killed?'

'Yes, Group Captain, I was told that the operation was a failure. Are you here to tell me to behave myself in future and not abuse my position as a guest in your country?'

'That's pretty much what it amounts to,' said Bob.

'We don't wish to disrupt the work you are doing here, Colonel, but please be assured that if you are again found behaving in a manner that compromises British interests, or the interests of our other allies, then you will be asked to leave.'

'That's another euphemism, isn't it, Group Captain?'

Bob couldn't help sharing the colonel's smile. 'Yes, it is, Colonel.'

'I understand your message, Group Captain. You understand, of course, that I will pass on to the Soviet embassy the news that you have visited, and let them know what you have said?'

'Yes, of course, Colonel,' said Bob.

'Good, well, let's put that behind us,' said the colonel. 'At the risk of changing the subject, how much do you know about the Armstrong Whitworth Albemarle?'

'Not much,' said Bob.

'Well, I've had the dubious pleasure of flying one of them three times in the past two days, and please believe me when I tell you that it is what I believe our mutual American allies would call "a crock of shit". I have no idea what possessed our beloved leaders to sign up to take on 200 of these aircraft, but I can very easily see why you British are pleased to be rid of them. Look, come outside with me.'

Bob followed the colonel out onto the tarmac, and they walked together over to the nearest of the two Albemarles.

'Look at it,' said the colonel. 'It was designed as a medium bomber, but production has been so badly delayed that it has yet to enter squadron service with the RAF, and during the two years or more since it first flew, you have had much better bombers come into service. We are also told it's suitable for troop transport and parachute drops, but if you look inside, the cabin is very cramped. And yet we want 200 of them. Words sometimes fail me.'

The two men walked around the parked aircraft. 'Have you flown the Mosquito, Group Captain?' asked Kuznetsov.

'Yes, I have,' said Bob.

'That's the aeroplane we should be taking delivery of. You can't really blame us for trying to get hold of one, can you?'

'It's my job to do exactly that,' said Bob.

'Of course, Group Captain. But if you ever feel like adding an Order of the Red Banner to your collection of medals, I know that Moscow would be very grateful indeed if they could get their hands on a Mosquito.'

'Thanks for the offer, Colonel, but I don't think I'd be very suited to life in the Soviet Union.'

Kuznetsov smiled. 'I understand, Group Captain, but it was worth a try. Hello, what's that?' The colonel pointed upwards.

Bob looked up. High in the clear blue sky, far above, a condensation trail could be seen making its way south west. Bob had a feeling he knew what was making it but saw no reason to let the colonel in on the secret. 'It might be a photo reconnaissance Mosquito returning from Norway,' he said.

'It would never still be at such a height, if it was returning home,' said Kuznetsov. 'I think that's a Luftwaffe aircraft, though it really is at extreme altitude. It looks to me as if it's heading towards Glasgow.'

EPILOGUE

Bob missed Monique on his return from RAF Errol. Lieutenant Dixon told him that after the operation in Leith was over, she had asked him to take her back to RAF Turnhouse. Once there she'd used Bob's influence to commandeer a flight to RAF Renfrew.

Bob smiled at the thought.

'She also asked me to pass on her best wishes, sir.'

'I knew she had to get back to Glasgow to tidy up after the Hillington operation,' said Bob. 'I just didn't realise that she meant today.'

Bob kicked himself. He'd thought he would have time to talk to Monique before she returned south. At least they'd agreed that morning that they should meet when he was next in London. He knew that this time he would telephone her. That was something to look forward to, he thought.

The following day, Friday, Bob flew in a borrowed Hawker Hurricane MkIIc single seat fighter from RAF Turnhouse to Eastleigh, near Southampton. He attended the low-key funeral service that Captain Bell's parents had arranged in the church in the eautiful Hampshire village where the captain had grown up; and his burial in the adjacent churchyard. Sergeant Potter spoke at the service and stayed on after the burial to attend the family gathering in the village pub, which seemed to Bob to be only right since he'd known and worked with the captain. Bob simply offered his condolences to the captain's parents, then got back in the naval staff car he'd borrowed, drove back to the naval air station at Eastleigh and flew back to Edinburgh.

The weather over the weekend and the start of the following week was miserable. Edinburgh had always tended to do 'windy' with remarkable enthusiasm, but it really specialised in 'dreich', a lovely Scots word that carried with it the essence of mist, drizzle and bone-chilling cold. The weekend was truly dreich, and even a trip on Saturday to stay the night with Jack and Flora Callaghan in Renfrew and drink Jack's whisky did little to brighten Bob's mood.

But Wednesday the 4th of November 1942 dawned bright and clear. Bob climbed aboard a Hurricane at RAF Turnhouse with a lot more enthusiasm than he had the previous Friday. When he'd taken the job with MI11, Bob had been aware that he would quickly become very familiar with the journey from Edinburgh to London and back. It was a simple fact of life. He worked in Edinburgh and his boss and his boss's boss both worked in London. After takeoff, Bob turned the aircraft's nose south east.

It would have been even better if he'd been able to arrange to see Monique in London, but the meeting he was attending had only been set up the previous evening. There was always the next time, he thought.

If the weather had still been poor, Bob would have had to concentrate more on choosing and following his route. When he had learned to fly, the better part of a decade earlier, it was the norm to navigate across country by following linear features on the ground. There were more sophisticated ways of doing things these days, but Bob worked by the maxim of 'if it's not broke, don't fix it'. The obvious linear feature linking Edinburgh and London was the London and North Eastern Railway line between the two.

But when the weather was this good, it was possible to have more fun.

Bob thoroughly enjoyed a very low-level trip roughly down the line of the A68 main road, a route he knew had Roman origins. He then picked up the railway near Darlington and followed it south at an altitude more suited to someone of his age and rank. As he flew, Bob made sure he kept to the right-hand side of the line of the tracks. That way, if he met another lazy navigator following the same line but heading in the opposite direction, the two would pass one another with a safe distance between them.

'Hello, Bob. You've had a busy first couple of weeks.' Bob had met Major General Sir Peter Maitland, the Director of Military Intelligence, when he had been offered the job, but this was the first time he'd been in Sir Peter's office, located in one of the more anonymous buildings along Whitehall. It was quite modest in scale and almost austere in décor.

It nonetheless came with a set of four large leather chairs set around a low table at one end of the room. Sir Peter waved towards the seats. 'Make yourself at home.'

There was a knock on the door and Bob's immediate boss, the head of Military Intelligence, Section 11, Commodore Maurice Cunningham, entered and walked over to join him and Sir Peter.

'How are you, Bob? I was worried to hear about the shooting.'

'I'm fine, sir,' said Bob. 'The bruising is fading fast and I don't need a bandage on my arm any longer.'

Tea was brought into the room and served. Then Sir Peter sat back in his chair. 'Bob, there are a few reasons why we asked you down here today. The first is to discuss what to do about a complaint that Major Miller has made about you.'

'Could I ask what the major has complained about?' asked Bob.

It was Commodore Cunningham who replied. 'He has touched on a number of matters, but his central complaint is that although last Thursday's operation was not intended to include anyone from the Security Service, you chose to invite Madame Dubois to take part.'

Bob laughed. 'Yes, I did, sir. She was in Scotland, has knowledge of the Soviet intelligence scene, and is a fluent Russian speaker. She was willing to take part and I felt she would be an asset. This may be a slightly iconoclastic view, sir, but I don't think that we will achieve good results in MI11 by playing petty politics or empire building in competition with MI5, MI6, Special Branch, the Intelligence Corps or anyone else for that matter. Besides, as I understand it, Madame Dubois saved Major Miller's life in Leith.'

Sir Peter Maitland coughed, perhaps to cover a laugh, Bob thought. 'Yes, that does make his complaint seem a touch ungrateful. Apparently, it didn't cross the major's mind that Sergei Avdonin might pull a gun, still less that he might take a shot at him.'

'How is Mr Avdonin?' asked Bob.

'As you know, he was flown to London that afternoon, and I am told he will make a full recovery,' said Sir Peter. 'I understand that Madame Dubois said she was only shooting to wound, and she succeeded. Avdonin did us a favour, really. If he'd come quietly we'd have had to release him within hours, but by opening fire at one of my officers he made it much more difficult for the Soviets to play the usual "diplomatic immunity" card.'

Commodore Cunningham said, 'The views you have just expressed are certainly iconoclastic, Bob. But you were asked to take up your post in MI11 partly because we thought you'd work against the entrenched interests that have done so much to fragment the military intelligence community in recent times.'

Sir Peter said, 'What that means in practice, Bob, is that we have formally considered Major Miller's complaint against you and dismissed it as unjustified.' He paused for a moment. 'How do you feel about him continuing as your deputy?'

'If you want my total honesty, sir, I've barely met the man, and certainly don't know him well enough to have formed a considered opinion about him.'

Sir Peter said, 'I sense there's a "but" coming?'

'Instinctively, sir, I simply don't trust him. I've got some good people at Craigiehall, but he just doesn't seem to fit in. He comes over as one of those people who do things a certain way because that's the way they've always done them. And I suspect that others aren't wholly confident of him. On my first day in Edinburgh I walked into an office to hear one of the senior non-commissioned officers referring to "Major Mother Hen". It was a small thing, but it really chimed with my own feelings.'

'Fair enough,' said Sir Peter. 'We will find another post, preferably somewhere far away from Edinburgh, for Major Miller. Have you any thoughts on who should replace him?'

'Both of my team leaders are good, sir, but of the two I'd recommend Lieutenant Dixon for the post.'

Commodore Cunningham said, 'We can action that immediately. That gives you two vacancies at team leader level.'

'Subject to your approval, sir, I'd like to replace Captain Bell with an officer I met in Mallaig, a Lieutenant Darlington. I was impressed by him. And his commanding officer at the Commando Basic Training Centre, though he would be sorry to lose him, recommends him highly. I sounded out Lieutenant Darlington yesterday, and I know he would be happy to accept the post and the promotion.'

'I'm happy with that,' said Commodore Cunningham. 'And I'll get a list of suggestions for a suitable naval officer to replace Lieutenant Dixon as team leader drawn up for you to look at.'

Sir Peter took the lead again. 'Some of the comments you made just now bring us to a related issue, Group Captain. You were of course right in suggesting that the way ahead is to avoid competition or conflict with other agencies and to work with them. As I said, it was our belief that you would have an open mind that was one of the factors in our offering you the appointment.

'Against that background I was rather disturbed to hear

that you had opposed having an MI5 officer attached to your investigation at Achnacarry. Do you have anything to say about that?'

'I can only say that it wasn't my finest moment, sir, and I've learned from it and will do better in future. I could say that I was shaken by the loss of Captain Bell, and that the MI5 move seemed to revolve around a piece of gossip about Germans in training that turned out to be irrelevant. It's perhaps an indication of how I was feeling that I didn't even respond well to Commodore Cunningham's offer to become personally involved, which I also apologise for. My true views are much more those I gave expression to in talking about the operation that Major Miller complained about.'

'Thank you for clearing that up,' said Sir Peter. 'I am pleased you have, because there's another staffing issue we need to talk about. I very much want to encourage a more open approach to working between different parts of my still very Byzantine empire. It has been suggested to me by the head of the Security Service that this could be facilitated by seconding someone to your unit from MI5. They'd work alongside your new deputy, Lieutenant Dixon, or Lieutenant Commander Dixon as he will now become, and their role would be to help you with the unit's investigative work, and to make sure that liaison with MI5 works smoothly.

'Before you say anything, I recognise that this may appear from your perspective to be a predatory or threatening suggestion. There is a history of distrust between the different military intelligence sections, often with very good reason. If you agree, the commodore and

I will give you our full support in ensuring that it doesn't turn into a backdoor takeover of MI11 by a much larger and far better resourced MI5.'

Bob looked back and forth between the two men. 'For it to work, I'd have to be able to have complete trust in whoever came over. Do you have anyone in mind, sir?'

'MI5 have suggested Madame Vera Duval,' said Sir Peter.

It took Bob a split second to recognise the name. 'Sorry for being slow on the uptake there, sir. I know her as Monique Dubois.' Bob paused for a moment, trying to work out how to phrase his next sentence. 'Sir, there's something you need to know about Vera Duval and I.'

Sir Peter Maitland smiled. 'You want me to know that you formed a relationship with her during that business in Caithness, and that despite your response to her involvement at Achnacarry, it's continued more recently? Please, Bob, I know that jokes are made about "military intelligence", but I would not have been doing my job properly if that were news to me. It's the fact that neither of you have made any effort to conceal what's been going on between you that suggests to me that it won't be a problem.'

'Has the idea been put to Monique, or rather, Vera?'

'Yes, it has,' said Sir Peter. 'I believe she's amenable to the idea of working with your team in Edinburgh if you are amenable to the idea of working with her.'

'That's settled, then,' said Bob, deliberately committing himself before he had time for second thoughts.

'Excellent,' said Commodore Cunningham. 'There's one more thing I'd like to cover, Bob. How did your discussion with Colonel Irakli Kuznetsov go? One of the things touched on by Major Miller in his complaint was what he referred to as your tendency to jump into an aeroplane at the slightest provocation and forget that you are an intelligence officer rather than a pilot.'

Bob grinned. 'There was perhaps an element of truth in that when I flew from Leuchars in a Mosquito with the officer commanding 540 Squadron, sir. Though I would say in my defence that it did help me get inside the mind of the man who had tried to steal one of the aircraft. On the other hand, my flight from RAF Errol with Colonel Kuznetsov in one of his Albemarles had motives I think you'll find much more acceptable.'

Bob took a sip of his tea before continuing. 'Just before we saw what I correctly suspected at the time was a Luftwaffe aircraft en route to photograph the Rolls-Royce factory at Hillington, Kuznetsov had, apparently jokingly, told me that I'd be awarded the Order of the Red Banner if I defected to the Soviets with a Mosquito. It seemed to me that it might be some sort of gambit on his part. I took that flight with him to cement a friendship and by the time we landed we were on "Bob" and "Irakli" terms.

'It was during the flight, and beyond the hearing of any of his men, that Kuznetsov confirmed what I've put in my report. The plan was for Sergeant Winograd to fly the Mosquito from Leuchars to RAF Errol, only a dozen or so miles away. There the Soviets would check that it was fully fuelled up, something they couldn't otherwise guarantee. It would have been first thing in the morning and the idea was to get that done very quickly, before anyone on the base had a chance to interfere. Winograd would be replaced by two highly experienced and fully kitted-out Soviet aircrew who were posing as trainees with the unit, and they would fly the aircraft to Murmansk. Winograd would then be smuggled off the base and taken back to his unit, with no-one any the wiser.'

'That does help tie up the loose ends nicely,' said Commodore Cunningham.

'The flight had another outcome, sir. It turned out that Kuznetsov had indeed mentioned defection as a gambit. When I floated the idea of his passing any useful information that came his way to me on a personal basis, in exchange for a promise of a new identity and UK residence when he needed it at some point in the future, he jumped at it. He was very much on the periphery of the operation being run by Sergei Avdonin, but if it is restarted in another guise, then having Colonel Kuznetsov on board could help keep us ahead of the game.'

'Your report just arrived this morning, Bob, and I've only had a chance for a quick first read,' said Commodore Cunningham. 'I didn't notice you mentioning that part of your discussion with him.'

'No, sir, it seemed best not to put that in writing.'

Sir Peter laughed. 'I can see you'll go far in this game, Bob.'

AUTHOR'S NOTE

This publication is a work of fiction and should be read as such. Except as noted below, all characters are fictional and any resemblances to real people, either living or dead, are purely coincidental.

Likewise, the events that are described in this publication are the products of the author's imagination.

Let's start with the characters. Some of those who appear between the pages of this publication occupy posts that existed at the time, but nonetheless they are all fictional. This is significant because the military units mentioned were usually doing what I describe them as doing at the time the action takes place. Minor characters are also entirely invented. Some characters could be associated with real people because of their roles, such as the harbourmaster at Mallaig and the officers commanding the Commando Basic Training Centre, the SOE at Arisaig House, the Army's Scottish Command, RAF Leuchars, 540 Squadron, and No. 305 Ferry Training Unit. Again, the characters who play those roles in this publication are not based on their real-life counterparts and are fictional.

Group Captain Robert Sutherland is also an invented character, though he has a career in the Royal Air Force that will be recognised by anyone familiar with the life and achievements of Squadron Leader Archibald McKellar, DSO, DFC and Bar. Bob Sutherland's family background and pre-war employment were very different to Archibald McKellar's, but the two share an eminent list of achievements during the Battle of Britain. Squadron Leader McKellar was tragically killed when he was shot down on the 1st of November 1940, whereas the fictional Group Captain Sutherland was only wounded when he was shot down on the same day, allowing him to play a leading role in this publication and its predecessor.

And Madame Monique Dubois or Madame Vera Duval? She is a fictional alias for a real woman. The real Vera Ericksen, or Vera Schalburg, or take your pick from any number of other aliases, had a story that was both complex and very dark. She disappeared during the war after the two German spies she landed with at Port Gordon on the Moray Firth were tried and executed by the British. To hear her full story, you will need to read my first novel, *Eyes Turned Skywards*.

Geoffrey Smith, or Stan Harrison, is a fictional character whose story is largely based on the pre-war and wartime exploits of a man called Eddie Chapman. While the fictional Stan Harrison parachuted into Scotland to sabotage the Rolls-Royce engine factor at Hillington, the real Eddie Chapman parachuted into England to sabotage the de Havilland factory at Hatfield, where Mosquito aircraft were made. The details of the deception and illusion described in this publication closely parallel real events: they are simply moved several hundred miles north.

Military Intelligence, Section 11, or MI11, was a real organisation which had a responsibility for military security. Its organisation and other aspects of its operations described in this publication are entirely fictional.

The Commando Basic Training Centre was located at Achnacarry Castle from early 1942, and this story draws as closely as possible on the training that took place there. Achnacarry Castle returned to its role as the ancestral home of Clan Cameron after the war (despite an accidental fire that took place in 1943) and remains a private residence. It is possible to stay in nearby steadings let out by the estate. The Clan Cameron Museum, also nearby, has information about the commandos at Achnacarry and publishes a 'Commando Trail' leaflet for anyone wanting to know more about what took place at Achnacarry and visit some of the locations. The commandos in Lochaber are also remembered in exhibitions at the Spean Bridge Hotel in Spean Bridge and at the West Highland Museum in Fort William. They are most poignantly commemorated at the Commando Memorial, a 5.2m high statue of three commandos standing on a plinth that was erected beside the road from Spean Bridge to Achnacarry in 1952.

The organisation of the Special Operations Executive training schools run from Arisaig House was much as described here. At the time of writing Arisaig House operates as a country house hotel, while the other properties used by the SOE in the area returned to roles as private homes after the war.

Craigiehall was taken over by the army during the war,

and later became the main army headquarters in Scotland. It remains an army base at the time of writing. Edinburgh Castle continues to have a military role but has also become one of Scotland's most popular visitor attractions.

The Rolls-Royce factory at Hillington was established just before the war as a 'shadow factory' to produce Merlin engines. Parts of it remain standing and its scale is astounding: though much of it has been cleared or modified since the war. White Cart Lodge is fictional.

RAF Renfrew existed. Its main runway now lies under the line of the M8 motorway immediately to the south of Renfrew itself (and immediately to the north of the remains of the Rolls-Royce factory at Hillington). Nearby RAF Abbotsinch became Glasgow Airport after the war. RAF Turnhouse has since become Edinburgh Airport. Many of its domestic buildings still stood as recently as 2007, according to online photographs. Most have since been demolished. RAF Leuchars, after nearly a century of service to the RAF, was transferred to the army in 2015. 540 Squadron operated from Leuchars in October 1942, as described in this publication. The Polish Army did have a camp in Tents Muir, as the 1945 one-inch Ordnance Survey map calls the area that has since universally become known as Tentsmuir. Slight traces of the camp can still be found in the forest, if you look in the right places.

The Royal Naval Air Station at Machrihanish later became RAF Machrihanish, and though the military have now departed, it still operates commercial flights.

RAF Errol was a real place and continues to have some aviation connections while also serving as an industrial estate. No. 305 Ferry Training Unit actually existed, and was established at RAF Errol for the rather inexplicable purposes described in this story.

The North British Hotel in Edinburgh became the Balmoral Hotel some decades ago. Its clock continues to be set three minutes fast.

The legend of Jacobite gold at Loch Arkaig is much as told in this publication. The Archibald Cameron who appears in this book is fictional. However, his ancestor, Archibald Cameron of Locheil, was a real historical figure and his efforts to retrieve the Jacobite gold were also real. The detailed account he produced for Charles Edward Stuart of what became of the gold survives in the Clan Cameron archives, and is as described in this book.

The story I have woven around the gold is entirely fictional and the treasure, if it still exists, has never been found. I should apologise to my grandson Alistair for adding our names to the long list of those who over the centuries have failed to find the gold when we visited Loch Arkaig at the time this story was beginning to take form and substance. I at least came away with some compelling locations.

The price of $34 per ounce quoted for gold in 1942 may seem very low, but accurately reflects the situation at the time. The treasure would be worth considerably more today, with the price of gold (in February 2019) standing at over $1300 per ounce and an exchange rate of around $1.3 to £1 instead of the $4.03 to £1 that was fixed from 1940 to the end of the war and beyond.

To conclude, in my view it is the duty of a fiction writer to create a world that feels right to his or her readers. When the world in question is one that is as far removed in so many ways, some predictable and others not, as 1942 is from today, then it is inevitable that false assumptions will be made, and facts will be misunderstood. If you find factual errors within this publication I apologise and can only hope that they have not got in the way of your enjoyment of the story.

I would like to express my thanks to Astie Cameron for background information about the weir on the River Arkaig at Achnacarry. The responsibility for the way the information he provided has been used is mine alone.

Remember, as I said at the start of this note, that this publication is a work of fiction.